A PITCH FOR LOVE

Michael Zielinski

BookLocker

ISBN: 978-1-60910-666-9

Published by BookLocker.com, Inc., St. Petersburg, Florida.

Printed on acid-free paper.

BookLocker.com, Inc.
2018

First Edition

Dedication

To my beautiful wife Janice and our wonderful family for their love and support.

Chapter One

Matt Meredith sat at his desk, staring at his PC screen. The words on his screen stared back at him. He didn't like what he saw. There was no way of knowing, of course, what those words -- his words -- thought of him. But had they been words of the female gender, they would have thought quite well of him. Thoughts spiced with hot sauce.

Matt Meredith was a catch for any woman. The star columnist for the *Braxton Bugle*, a medium-sized Pennsylvania newspaper in a city 70 miles west of Philadelphia, Meredith was as appealing as his prose. A writer who could turn a phrase with a delicious blend of passion, sensitivity, imagery and humor, he could turn heads just by walking into a room. He was 35 years old and his handsome face could pass for 25. He had flowing blond locks and, at 6-2 and an athletic, long-legged 180 pounds, he was broad at the shoulders and narrow at the waist. Although he was a chiseled block of manhood, perhaps his best physical attribute was his smile, which was brighter than fireworks in a catacomb. And with his charismatic personality and playful nature, he gave his smile more frequent workouts than he did his sculpted pecs and biceps.

However, Matt Meredith wasn't smiling at the moment. He was trying to finish this particular column with a poignant flourish, and the words, which usually gushed from his fertile mind and facile fingertips, suddenly had dried up. He wrote four columns a week on anything and everything and was so prolific he always had six columns in the can just in case the muse suddenly left him. He never wanted to miss a deadline and he never had. And when the muse did leave him, as it did all writers, it never left for long. All he had to do was narrow his focus, squeeze out all distractions, and words popped from his brain to the screen. But on this particular day, he was having trouble focusing. After all, this was a big day in his life. He was coaching his first Little League practice, and he found his mind wandering from his column on a woman's valiant fight with breast cancer to what baseball fundamentals he should expose his 10- to 12-year-olds to on the first day.

Matt loved kids and related to them, considering that he, in many ways, had never grown up himself. A former star pitcher and quarterback at Braxton High School and Temple University, he figured coaching Little League would be a perfect way for him to have some fun and teach kids how to play ball. And since he was a bachelor and had no children of his own, he thought it would fill a void in his life.

Not that it was a gaping void, mind you. Matt's life was way too full to have time for deep voids. As the star columnist for the *Bugle*, he was quite the man about town. He attended all sorts of functions and dinners. Plus, he also hosted his own weekly cable talk show. It spotlighted local issues and personalities and Comcast telecasted it throughout the Braxton and Miller County area. Work, however, wasn't the only thing that kept Matt busy. He played plenty of basketball and golf, jogged daily and lifted weights every other day. Matt had a hyperactive social life. He frequently was seen in area restaurants and bars with a variety of attractive and charming women. He had had several serious relationships over the years but never had made the right connection. He didn't know why. The women he dated usually were upscale professionals who mixed intelligence and charm with their good looks. Now that he was 35, Matt was subtly hoping that he would meet that certain someone who would ignite the cockles of his heart. In the meantime, he was going with the flow of having fun and basking in his virility. And coaching Little League figured to be fun, if the parents weren't too psycho on him. Because as Matt and everybody who had ever played organized youth sports knew, some parents totally lose perspective when it comes to their children and athletics. Matt secretly was hoping that all his players were orphans.

But for now, Matt decided to get his game face on. And getting his game face on meant finishing his column and filing it so he could clear the decks in his mind and move onto baseball practice. Like a true journalist, Matt craved closure when it came to assignments. Deadlines defined his psyche. So, he gave himself a quick pep talk: Lose the baseball mindset for now and close the show on his column. Through sheer will, he re-channeled his thoughts on the breast cancer survivor and successfully generated the verbiage that he knew would pluck the heartstrings of his readers. That burst of creative energy had refreshed his spirits. Indeed, Matt often thought that -- next to sex -- creative writing was the most satisfying element of his life. And God knows, there were times when he felt that writing a particularly good column was even better than sex. He smiled as sent his column to his editor. It was time to play ball.

It was a beautiful late spring afternoon, just perfect for baseball. As Matt drove up to the field where his team, the Sorbonne Township Cubs, would practice, he noticed that several kids and their parents already were on the scene. When he exited his car and walked to his small trunk to retrieve some baseball bats and balls he had somehow found room for in there, he could feel the eyes of the kids and their parents checking him out. Being a Little League coach can make one a marked man. His players (and their parents) don't want their dreams of major league stardom hijacked at the start by some dolt of a coach. They look upon Little League as the first depot on a long glory ride to the big leagues, and they don't want their first coach to be blind to their astonishing abilities. After all, nobody wants their hopes derailed before the engine even leaves the station. After that first practice, Matt thought it highly unlikely that any of his young charges would likely wind up in the Baseball Hall of Fame. But he had a lot of fun working with 18 boys ranging in age from 10 to 12. He put the boys through infield fielding drills to see if they could catch a ground ball without risking their teeth. He hit fly balls to them in the outfield to see if they could catch a pop fly without risking life, limb and cranium. And he pitched batting practice to them to see if, by sheer coincidence, they could put a bat on a ball every now and then. Generally, he was encouraged. And the workout had infused him with an adrenaline rush of youthful vitality.

However, there was a moment when Matt didn't feel as bouncy and breezy as a young calf during the practice. Mikey Lane had a ground ball take a bad hop and hit him in the chin, drawing blood.

"Are you all right, son?" Matt yelped as he sprinted to the boy at third base.

Mikey was trying to hold back his tears, but he didn't succeed.

"I'll be OK, Coach," the boy sniffled, dabbing at the blood on his chin.

"You'll be fine, a tough guy like you," Matt said, encouragingly.

"He'll be fine, Coach," cooed his mother, who had appeared suddenly at Matt's shoulder as if she were an apparition.

Natalie Lane did dab some of her son's blood with a Kleenex, but she seemed to be focusing on Matt, not Mikey. Matt certainly focused on Natalie once he got a glimpse of her because she definitely was worth the sacrifice of making eye contact. A saucy, sexy divorcee in her early 30s, Natalie Lane had lots of brown curls and enough curves to make for a breathtaking road course. She was flashy and she was brassy. She wasn't exactly Matt's type, but any man with a pulse certainly would give her a good, hard look. She, meanwhile, was giving Matt a good, hard look. Considering the context of their meeting, with her son kneeling in front of them, bleeding from the chin, Matt thought her smoky look was a bit inappropriate and uncomfortable. Plus, he knew the other parents were watching them and probably wondering why they weren't tending to her son.

"Come on, Mikey, let Mom clean you up," Matt quickly interjected. "If you're OK, you can field another ground ball. Nothing like getting back on the horse right away."

The analogy escaped young Mikey, who stood and allowed his mother to wipe away some more blood. While Natalie was looking to see if her son needed stitches, she couldn't resist picking up on Matt's analogy.

"You'll be good as new, Mikey," she purred. "No stitches needed. And there's nothing like getting right back in the saddle. Right, coach?"

She shot Matt a provocative glance. Natalie certainly had swung for the fences in letting her son's coach know that she was hoping to reach home with him.

As Natalie and her son walked off the field, a flustered Matt decided to get back to the business of baseball. He had heard that Little League parents could be a problem, but he hadn't anticipated having a Little League mother like Natalie Lane to deal with. But thoughts of her vanished as he started pitching another round of batting practice. He wanted to vary his drills during practice because boys at that age have notoriously short attention spans. And this time, some of the kids were stinging the ball during batting practice.

Especially Timmy Baxter. He already had impressed Matt with his athleticism, reflexes, range, speed and hand-eye coordination while catching grounders and fly balls. Plus, the kid had good size and a strong, accurate arm. He was born to play shortstop, Matt noted. And now Timmy Baxter was crushing line drives. He had excellent bat control, a fluid swing and power. When that first practice ended, Matt knew he had made the right decision to coach this team.

Especially when he got a glimpse of Timmy Baxter's mother and saw that she wasn't wearing a wedding ring. Matt thought she was the most wholesome-looking/sexiest-looking woman -- an enticing blend of vice and virtue with her killer body and sweet face -- he had ever seen. He found her to be utterly striking and captivating, juicer than a summer peach, an ideal lady to bed and wed.

"Damn, getting involved with one of my players' mothers probably isn't too smart," Matt said to himself. "But look at her. Look at the smile, that face, that body. I've got to get to know her."

Chapter Two

Robbyn Baxter was having a bad day. And it started before she even woke up. A young widow, who had closed her mind and heart to even the possibility of another relationship, dreamt she found a new love. A dream that left her conflicted, horny and totally freaked out when she awoke.

Still disturbed and distracted by her dream, her normally agreeable disposition was now being severely tested by Chad, a cranky and temperamental designer she worked with at Missonis Advertising.

Chad was a repressed homosexual trapped in a marriage with an overbearing woman who somehow bore him a daughter and then proceeded to drain his bank account on a seemingly daily basis. His chronic unhappiness made him particularly irritable. And Robbyn's pleasant demeanor at times rubbed him as raw as the wind swirling around Braxton's landmark fire tower high above the city on Mount Park.

"Too damn many words in this copy," Chad spouted, with a pout. "Robbyn, how many times do we go through this? Keep your copy tight. Excess verbiage clashes with my visual concepts."

Chad was overstating the case. Robbyn knew perfectly well that a copywriter shouldn't be verbose. And she really wasn't. But to Chad, any print ad with more than three words had two words too many. But Robbyn was less confrontational than the other two copywriters in the office. Therefore, she bore the brunt of his attitude.

Still, on rare occasions, Robbyn flexed some of the steel in her spine. When pressed, she could be ballsy.

"I don't want to hear it," she fired back at Chad. "There aren't too many words. This ad needs some explanation. I'm not cutting the copy. Make it work!"

Chad threw a short, hissy fit and angrily retreated. Robbyn didn't care. She knew that he would get over it. And she had grown weary of trying not to provoke him.

Life experiences had put some sour moments into her sweet temperament. The sweet and sour combined to give her an inner strength she wouldn't have thought possible before "it" happened.

The "it" in Robbyn's life was the car accident that claimed the life of her husband four years earlier. Her husband's car hit a piece of black ice while driving to work early one morning. He lost control of the car and spun off the East Shore bypass. His car crashed into a tree, killing him instantly. The accident left Robbyn, a petite but buxom, beautiful brunette with brown doe eyes, a widow at 30 years of age. And it left her with two adorable boys, Timmy, then 8 years old, and Billy, then 6. Bob Baxter's death had devastated Robbyn. They had an ideal marriage, one spiked with ample amounts of playfulness, romance and passion. The best part of their relationship was that they were the best of friends. Bob had a marvelous sense of humor and loved to make Robbyn laugh. Robbyn, in turn, had a playful side that Bob adored. Having children only enhanced their relationship. They loved being parents. They doted on their boys without spoiling them -- a tricky balancing act few parents achieve.

After her husband's death, Robbyn was nearly frozen in bitterness. She would have been almost paralyzed with grief had she not borne the heavy responsibility of being a single parent. Gradually, her bitterness thawed, but the massive void in heart still gave her chest pains occasionally. There were times deep in the night when she found it difficult to sleep, to close her eyes without tears trickling from them. And when she did close her eyes, images of Bob would flicker on the backs of her eyelids. In her waking hours, she found plenty of emotional support and comfort in her boys. She tried to be both a mother and a father to her sons, and having been a high school athlete herself, she found it fun and bonding to "jock it up" with them. Every now and then, she had a fleeting thought about what it might be like to remarry and provide her sons with a role model. But such thoughts were transient and focused merely on the beneficial aspects such a relationship would have on her boys.

As for herself, she was not ready to have a relationship with any man. She dearly loved her husband and didn't think anyone could ever replace him. In fact, she never gave it much thought, as if even thinking about it would be an act of betrayal to her late husband's memory. Her striking looks and infectious smile had made her the target of numerous male advances in the last four years, but her total lack of interest had quickly snuffed any chance of a future alliance.

Robbyn hadn't worked after she had the boys ... until she became a widow. She had worked as an advertising copywriter before her first child but had no need to work thereafter. Her husband had been a sporting goods buyer for Benton's, a department store chain based in Braxton, and she had no economic incentive to work. After his death, even though he had provided reasonably well for his family, she found it necessary to work. Except for her hectic schedule as a single parent, she enjoyed working. She loved being creative, turning a phrase just a certain way to capture the message she was trying to convey in an ad. She specialized in copy that was creative as well as poignant.

When she got immersed in writing ads, the rest of the world didn't exist. Her workdays often were a blur of creative energy, leaving her energized, not drained, when the business day ended and the domestic night began.

She was determined to be there for her boys, so she always made sure she was there to ferry them to practice and to their social events. She made it a point to spend quality time with them each evening. They had entertaining, delightful dinners talking about sports, school, nonsense, even their dad.

"Do you think Dad watches us from heaven?" young Billy had asked one night.

"Of course, he does," replied Robbyn, smiling gently.

Timmy, quickly putting his fork down on the table even though it still had a piece of roast beef dangling from it, jumped right into the conversation.

"That's good, when I'm being good," he said. "But I don't want him seeing me when I'm bad."

"Well, just don't misbehave then," said Robbyn, punctuating her words with a chuckle.

"Like that's gonna happen," responded Timmy.

"You're a good kid, Mr. Macho," said Robbyn.

"He's mean to me!" chirped Billy.

"That's because you're a nerd!" snapped Timmy.

"See, I told you he was bad," counter-punched Billy.

"OK, boys, time for homework," interrupted Robbyn, once again playing the role of referee.

"Stupid homework," complained Timmy. "If it hadn't rained tonight, we'd be at baseball practice."

"You really love baseball, don't you?" asked Robbyn.

"Especially this year," Timmy said, excitedly. "Coach Matt is cool. He's so nice and he's fun, too. He told us he pitched for Temple University and had a tryout with the Phillies. Did you know that, Mom?"

"No, I didn't," said Robbyn. "That's nice. But I do know that he writes a column for the *Braxton Bugle*. He's a pretty good writer."

"He writes about sports?" Timmy asked.

"No, he writes about other things," said Robbyn.

"Boring things," said Billy, laughing.

"Well, he's not boring," Timmy said. "He's fun. And he knows baseball. He told me I'm gonna be the shortstop and maybe pitch a little."

"That's great," said Robbyn.

The kids then were off, grudgingly, to do their homework. Robbyn, while cleaning up the dishes, wondered why Timmy seemed so enthusiastic about his coach. He rarely got that excited about a coach. It made her happy that he was looking up to a male figure. But as for any thoughts she may have had about Matt, well, she had none that involved any hint of romance. She had noticed that he was handsome, and he had the shredded musculature that was eye candy to women, but they were merely casual, detached observations. Men, as such, even after the dream that had made her temporarily horny, were not even on her radar screen. The only men she cared about were her boys. And her late husband. To Robbyn, Bob Baxter still was her husband, late or not. To her, the phrase "until death do us part" held no meaning. In her heart, Bob Baxter was very much alive -- a vibrant presence she had internalized seemingly forever. And to Robbyn, there were only two categories of men --spouse and non-spouse.

Chapter Three

It had been quite a day for Matt on this particular Wednesday. His column that morning in the *Braxton Bugle* had been a major hit with his readers, judging by the amount of favorable emails and voicemails he had received. He obviously had struck a nerve. His column spoofed Braxton mayor Jimbo Cummings, a retired carpenter who someone had gotten elected and then proceeded to seemingly turn everything he touched into splinters. Jimbo was a likeable old coot, but extremely impulsive and in over his head. Plus, he took advice from nobody. Consequently, his administration was chaotic. His feuds with City Council bordered on the juvenile. Mayor Jimbo made for perfect column material for a talented pundit like Matt, but Cummings wasn't doing anything for a city riddled by drugs, crime and poverty. At least the mayor was a good sport. The old fool agreed to be a guest on Matt's cable television show that night even after having read Matt's morning column.

Mayor Jimbo, a portly bear of a man who was three inches taller than Matt at 6-5, sat rumpled in his director's chair on the set of Matt's TV show. He was in good humor despite Matt's column that morning.

"Matt, what really upset me about your column was you wrote I had been a lousy carpenter, too," Cummings said, jocularly. "Well, that's just not true, Matthew. Yep, I may not have been perfect. May have a cut a few pieces of lumber a tad crooked. But I know only one carpenter who was perfect, and they crucified him. Like that carpenter, I've made a career change, trying to help my fellow man. And now my enemies are trying to crucify me."

"I'm not trying to crucify you, Jimbo," Matt said, cracking a smile.

"The hell you aren't," barked the mayor. "You're a regular Pontius Pilate. But you're not tough enough to hammer nails into my hands and feet and hang me on a cross. Not a soft ladies' man like you!"

Mayor Jimbo Cummings had a smile on his face so huge it might have been bigger than one of his crumbling Braxton Parking Authority garages. Matt's column had alleged that the mayor's petty politics were ruining the management of the downtown parking garage complex.

The mayor's jab may have flustered another man. But not Matt. He was smooth, glib and sure of himself. So, he adroitly counter-punched.

"Your Honor, I wouldn't want to be a hard man because hard men are hard-headed," Matt said calmly. "And I'm not even dating anyone at the moment because I've been too busy checking into your mistakes. The least you could do would be to set me up with one of your cute secretaries."

Perhaps the mayor and Matt could start their own comedy team. After all, the days of Abbott and Costello, Martin and Lewis, Gleason and Carney, Rowan and Martin, and the Smothers Brothers were long gone.

"Yeah, right," bellowed Jimbo. "Wouldn't you just love that! Get one of my honeys in the sack and grill 'em for the dirt on me. Pillow talk sinks ships!"

Matt, chuckling with just the right pitch and volume, corrected the mayor: "Loose lips sink ships, your honor, not pillow talk. Unless, of course, you were chummier with your fellow sailors than we thought. Are you giving me and our viewers an exclusive about your days in the Navy?"

The mayor screamed an obscene response, which got on the air. The budget on Matt's cable show didn't include having a seven-second delay.

The mayor then jumped out of his chair and stomped off the set. But not before he tripped over his chair and almost stumbled to the floor.

"I could point out that the mayor evidently is even clumsier than his politics," Matt said to his viewing audience. "But that would be a cheap shot, now wouldn't it?"

After the show, Matt's director, Ellen Stephens, told him that the closing sequence with the mayor had been the best two minutes of live television in the history of Miller County. And the town had had a long list of live cable talk shows for over 40 years.

Robbyn, at Timmy's insistence, had watched Matt's TV show that night with her two boys. Of course, the boys had no interest in city politics. Actually, neither did Robbyn. But Timmy wanted to see his TV star/coach on the air. The boys and Robbyn had been, for the most part, bored with the show. But she did notice that Matt did have a certain on-air charisma. And when they watched his closing confrontation with the mayor, the boys howled with laughter, although some of the sexual references went over their heads. Robbyn thought it was funny as well and was very impressed with how Matt handled the buffoon who was mayor. But for some strange reason, she found it somewhat disconcerting that the mayor had called Matt a ladies' man. If that was true, she wondered whether Matt Meredith was a proper role model for Timmy and Billy. After all, she didn't want her boys looking up to some notorious womanizer. Still, at the same time, she could tell why many women would find Matt's looks and charm to be electrifying attractive.

Chapter Four

The Sorbonne Township Cubs were involved in quite a ballgame with the Madison Township Orioles, who had a 10-9 lead in the bottom of the sixth inning. But the home-team Cubs had the bases loaded with two outs. And at the plate was Timmy Baxter.

"God, why aren't you more nervous?" asked Cindy Loeper, nudging Robbyn in the ribs. "If I were you right now, I might pee my pants."

"I've got a better bladder," laughed Robbyn, who despite her calm exterior was frothing with anxiety.

Cindy Loeper was Robbyn's best friend. Cindy's son, Derek, was the Cubs' second baseman, forming the team's double-play combination with Timmy, their star shortstop. Cindy and Robbyn had little in common, except for their friendship and being mothers of boys the same age. Cindy, whose husband was an orthopedic surgeon, didn't have to work. She was plump, blonde and rock-band loud. And outspoken. Speaking of speaking, Cindy seldom didn't. There is an old line about someone talking so much that they'd give a dead man a tin ear. Cindy Loeper could give a whole cemetery-worth of departed souls tin ears.

"Come on, Timmy! Come on, Timmy!" screamed Cindy as Robbyn's son approached home plate. "You can do it, baby! Take this kid downtown!"

Robbyn winced as Cindy screamed into her ear but said nothing. She was too busy praying for Timmy to hit the ball. She knew how important this moment was to Timmy, how her boy would be mortified if he let the team -- and Coach Matt -- down.

Of course, Timmy hadn't needed much divine intervention in the Cubs' opener so far. He had hit a pair of three-run homers. He also had made several spectacular catches and throws at shortstop. Last year he hadn't made consistent contact at the plate. But Matt had worked with Timmy to take the loop out of his swing, and thus far the results had been dramatic.

Now the game was on the line. Matt called a timeout to give his star hitter some advice and a few moments to calm his nerves.

"Timmy, just wait for your pitch," Matt said calmly. "This kid doesn't want to walk you. He's probably going to give you something good to hit. Don't try to kill the ball. Just make contact. Can't hit a home run every time. Or can you?"

With that, Matt laughed to further relax Timmy. As Matt walked back to the bench, Cindy Loeper, despite the tension of the moment, couldn't resist playing matchmaker.

"Coach Matt is quite the hunk," Cindy said to Robbyn. "You know all the boys think he's so cool. And I hear he's single. Why don't you start talking to the guy? Make a pitch for him before that damn Natalie Lane sinks her claws into him!"

"Don't be silly," Robbyn said quietly. "Like I have time for a relationship. I hear he's a womanizer. He's right up Natalie's alley. She can have him."

"I think Matt is a class act," Cindy replied. "Maybe he does go out with a lot of women. But what the hell! Look at him! Maybe he's ready to settle down. At least you won't have to worry that he hasn't had a chance to sow his wild oats."

Cindy still was laughing as Timmy stepped into a fat fastball and hit a grand slam to deep center. Three home runs, all of them towering shots, and 10 runs batted in were quite an astounding start to the season. As soon as Timmy touched home plate on his grand slam, he was mobbed by his jubilant teammates and by Matt. The smile on Timmy's face rivaled a bright sun for radiance.

"Thanks for all the help, Coach," Timmy yelled in the midst of the din, his face glistening with accomplishment.

"Thank YOU," Matt said, laughing. "You made me look like a genius in the first game I ever coached. You keep hitting like this, and the Phillies will be calling you. Plus, you played a great game at shortstop." In the stands, Cindy Loeper gave Robbyn such a bear hug of glee that Robbyn thought her ribs would shatter right into her lungs.

Cindy shouted "Oh, my God!" so many times it seemed she was undergoing a religious experience.

"I just wish his father was here to see this," Robbyn said, suddenly sniffling.

Even Cindy realized that this was a bittersweet moment for Robbyn and stopped celebrating for a moment.

"Robbyn, I truly believe that Bob is up in heaven, looking down and seeing all of this," she said sweetly. "I'm sure he's as proud and happy as if he were here."

"But he's not," Robbyn said quietly.

Her feeling of loss didn't have time to linger. Billy, who had been off playing with friends behind the stands, leaped into her arms, almost knocking her over.

"Timmy won the game, Mom! Timmy won the game, Mom!" he yelped.

"Wasn't it wonderful?" an excited Robbyn asked. She certainly wasn't expecting an answer.

But an answer is what she received. Not from Billy, but from Matt. With Timmy in tow behind him, Matt climbed quickly into the stands to congratulate Robbyn. He didn't even realize he was going to do it until he did it. He instinctively thought it was a great opportunity to say hello to the one parent on the team who had yet to say hello to him, the one mother whom he found to be quite attractive and appealing.

"I just wanted to say that your son had a marvelous game, Mrs. Baxter," Matt said, excitement punctuating every word. "And it couldn't have happened to a nicer kid. You should feel so proud of him!"

"I'm happy for him and all the boys," Robbyn said softly, barely making eye contact with Matt. "Timmy enjoys playing baseball."

Her voice was flat. Her body as stiff as a mannequin.

Matt sensed from Robbyn's muted response that she felt uncomfortable with him. He wondered if one of his columns had angered or irritated her. He had no other rationale for why she would feel that way. He walked away to give the kids a few words of congratulations and inspiration. As he was packing away the bats, balls and gear, his elation over the game was tinged with regret that he hadn't gotten a warm reception from Robbyn. He knew plenty of attractive women but found her to be an enchanting blend of sexy wholesomeness.

As he was packing up the last of the equipment, Natalie Lane excitedly ran up to Matt, her ample breasts jiggling in a top tighter than a clam with lockjaw.

She playfully smacked him on the butt and exclaimed: "Great game, Coach! We ought to celebrate with a drink later tonight. I'm free if you are."

Matt, bummed by Robbyn's inattentiveness, certainly but fleetingly found Natalie's overt attention to be tempting. But there was no way that he was going to get involved with somebody like her. Yeah, the sex probably would be sensational. But Matt had had sensational sex before. There was just something about Natalie's aggressive behavior that signaled bad news for him ahead. He wasn't about to board a ship that was bound for turbulent waters.

"I'm sorry," Matt smiled as a lie formed on his lips.

"I already have plans tonight."

"Maybe some other time," Natalie said, fetchingly. Her ensuing wink was about as subtle as a fastball to the ribs.

Matt didn't want to be rude, so he smiled again and said, "Maybe we can have a team picnic for all the parents and the players."

"That would be nice," Natalie said, disappointment dropping her voice an octave. "But I was hoping that you and I could, uh, get to know one another more intimately."

Matt quickly lightened the mood with a joke.

"Fraternizing with team mothers violates Rule 101 of the Little League coaching manual," Matt said, laughing.

He decided to throw Natalie a compliment to be diplomatic. So, he added: "Especially when the mother is as attractive as you."

Natalie, re-energized by the flattery but not wanting to be even more pushy, simply smiled and said seductively, "Rules were made to be broken."

She then strutted away, all her curves moving in the right direction. Matt looked at her wistfully but knew he had been right to parry her advances. As he did so, Cindy and Robbyn were walking to their cars. Cindy had noticed that Matt and Natalie had been talking. Robbyn, who had been excitedly talking to Timmy, hadn't noticed.

"I'm telling you, Robbyn," Cindy scolded, "you had better make your move on him. Natalie is going to beat you to first base!"

"What's this about first base?" Timmy asked, innocently.

"Stick to shortstop," Robbyn tried to say lightly while her eyes shot sharp daggers at Cindy.

Robbyn was upset because she thought Cindy's comments were inappropriate in front of Timmy. But more deeply, she was disturbed because she felt a faint pang of attraction toward Matt. Which left her feeling as if she had committed adultery.

Chapter Five

Robbyn was standing next to her husband's tombstone at Miller County Memorial Gardens. It was raining, definitely not an ideal day to visit a cemetery. Robbyn didn't care. She made it a habit to visit Bob's gravesite at least once a month. She would speak to the tombstone as if he still were alive, sitting there on the tombstone and listening to her every word.

Bob Baxter had been a marvelous listener, a quality that Robbyn hadn't found in any other man she had dated. Not that she had dated all that much, but she had had at least three serious relationships before she met Bob in their senior year at Penn State. It would be trite to say that it had been love at first sight for both of them, but there had been an instant, mutual attraction. In addition to the physical chemistry, their relationship had been based on a deep friendship. It was her best friend that Robbyn missed most of all. And when the burdens of being a working single mother weighed heavily on her, she found it helpful to vent to the spirit of her husband, friend and lover. But she also used these cemetery visits to communicate the everyday details of her and the boys' life to Bob, to somehow keep him a part of the family fabric. She had tried to bring to make the boys part of this dynamic, but she found bringing them to the cemetery to be a mistake. They were too young to understand what she was trying to do. They thought it silly to talk to what they called "the ghost of their father" -- a phrase that Robbyn found disconcerting. Timmy preferred to remember his father as the vibrant person he was, not as some ghost. Meanwhile, Billy, only 6 when his dad died, didn't remember him as well as Timmy did and consequently missed him less. That bothered Robbyn, who went out of her way to bring Bob into their dinner conversations. She never wanted them to forget their father. She never would because his memory was ingrained in her. They had been true soulmates, and as Robbyn often said to herself, souls are eternal.

"You should've seen Timmy hit the ball," Robbyn said to Bob's tombstone. "You would have been so proud. He was hammering home runs like Jose Canseco."

Jose Canseco had been quite a slugger and had been Bob Baxter's favorite ballplayer before steroids ruined Canseco's reputation and career.

Robbyn paused and patted Bob's tombstone.

"Timmy also made some great plays at shortstop," Robbyn continued. "He's a real chip off the old block, I would say. Timmy is so excited about this season. And he loves his coach. Says he's a great guy who's given him some great hitting and fielding tips. His name is Matt Meredith. You probably remember him. I know you didn't read the paper much, but he's a columnist for the *Braxton Bugle*. Cindy thinks he's a real catch and has been insisting that I get to know him. Like I'm interested. I know you sometimes said that if something ever happened to you that you wanted me to remarry -- for my sake as well as the kids. And I know it's been four years, but to me, it would be like cheating on you. You're my husband. You're the one I love. I know we'll be together someday forever in heaven. So, I don't need another man in my life. I have you. You're the man in my life. The boys think I'm cool enough to be both their dad and mom when the situation calls for it. And since they play sports, their male role models can be their coaches and the professional athletes they root for. Timmy thinks Mike Trout is the best ballplayer in history but Billy worships Bryce Harper. And I keep telling them what a jock you were. Trust me, Bob. I'll make sure that you'll always be an important part of our boys' lives."

Chapter Six

Matt had just finished a column on why some Miller County women thought the area was full of losers when it came to eligible bachelors. Matt knew this column would elicit a tremendous response because it was a sequel to a column he had written the previous week on why some men thought Miller hardly was a fertile area if you were in your 30s and shopping for a mate. That column had Matt's phone ringing off the hook. He received 43 voicemail messages in addition to the 117 emails -- both personal records for column response. Actually, many of the voicemails and emails agreed with the guys in Matt's column: That Miller was crawling with a bunch of ladies who were losers. Of course, many of the responders were women who claimed the men hardly were the pick of the litter either. Matt had struck a nerve with the first column, and he knew he would hit another gusher with this one.

To research both columns, Matt had spent a couple of Wednesday nights in the Goodtime Lounge at the Shamrock Braxton Hotel. It was the place to be in Miller if you were 30 and above and unattached -- or married and on the prowl. It sort of was a cliché barroom scene with folks looking for love -- or simply sex -- amidst the clink of glasses and ice, the forced, awkward small talk, the swirling cigarette smoke (yes, smoking was allowed) and the smoky glances that had nothing to do with the cigarettes.

As Matt observed the scene, he felt sad for these people. As he chatted with them, he realized many of them were poor souls who had been wounded by love and were carrying enough excess emotional baggage to fill up the cargo area on the old show The Love Boat. Matt wrote the two columns with a sense of humor, but he also shaped them with a sense of sensitivity. These people were hurting, and he wanted his readers to relate to their pain.

Of course, it was inevitable that a few women on each of Matt's "research" nights came onto him. Even when he told him he was a newspaper columnist researching a story, they didn't seem to care. Matt could have scored several times each night, but the pickup scene wasn't his style. He had to admit that certain elements of the female scenery were pleasing to the eye. Yet he never had been a hound, and he wasn't about to start now. He simply had too much depth of character to wallow in the shallowness of mindless and loveless conquests. He prided himself on being a man who thought with his mind and his heart, not with his dick.

The plight of his column subjects, many of who were divorced, gave Matt greater insight into the void people must feel when a relationship ends. However, divorce, as tragic and bitter as it can be, isn't as traumatic as becoming widowed. Divorce usually comes when at least one spouse and sometimes both have fallen out of love. When a person is widowed and was involved in a loving, fulfilling marriage, it's a heartbreak that is devastating. Especially when it happens relatively young in life. Matt couldn't help thinking of what Robbyn must have gone through -- must still be going through. He hadn't realized that she was a widow until Timmy had told him during baseball practice the previous day that his father had been killed in a car accident. Matt had merely assumed Robbyn was divorced. He felt truly sorry for her and her boys when he heard that Bob Baxter had been dead for four years. Matt thought that must be why Robbyn had been so aloof with him. He figured that she perhaps wasn't yet comfortable going out with other men. But he also thought that maybe she already had a boyfriend or simply didn't find him attractive.

During practice, Matt innocently had asked Timmy if his dad had ever worked on Timmy's hitting fundamentals.

Timmy casually replied that he hadn't done so in four years because he had been killed in a car crash. Matt had wanted to tell Billy how profoundly he felt for his loss.

But Matt simply had said, "I'm sorry to hear that, Timmy."

Matt had been surprised at Timmy's casual response.

"That's all right," Timmy had said. "I'm used to it by now."

Timmy had proceeded to work on his stance and Matt had dropped the subject.

When Matt was perched at the Shamrock bar in the midst of singles Wednesday, he felt sympathy for the Baxters. And somehow, he felt drawn even more so to Robbyn. Matt suddenly was hit by a fireball of an admission that left him pulpy with shock. The flash of insight that Robbyn might be everything he had ever wanted in a wife nearly shocked his eyebrows off. He rationalized that perhaps this out-of-the-blue revelation was rooted in his admiration for the wonderful job she had done as a single mother. It was not as if Matt was looking for a ready-made family, but he had grown quite fond of Timmy and he thought Billy was a neat kid, too. Plus, he and Robbyn were young enough to have a child of their own.

When that last thought pinballed through his mind and scattered brain neurons everywhere, his eyeballs almost went TILT as blurted out: "Talk about putting the cart before the horse!"

"What?" asked the bald, portly guy sitting next to Matt.

"Oh, nothing," Matt said, embarrassed.

"How much have you had to drink?" asked the bald, portly guy. "Talking to yourself in a bar jammed with people."

The place was pulsating with flashing lights and throbbing music, not ideal conditions to elicit good quotes. But Matt somehow managed. He was just about to leave on his second "research" night when he spotted Natalie Lane across the crowded bar. He could tell right away that she seemed a bit tipsy. She was wearing a low-cut dress that exposed more of her cleavage than was tasteful. He immediately decided to leave before she spotted him. But as he rose from his barstool, she spotted him and began waving at him frantically. He knew that she knew he had made eye contact. He was stuck. To simply leave would have been rude, and it would have made things awkward at the next practice. But he was determined to just say hello and get the hell out of there. He knew there was something about Natalie Lane that could be bad news. And he only liked bad news when it made for good copy. And he wasn't writing his autobiography.

Natalie had been chatting with a man with a ponytail who seemed about 10 years younger than she was. But when she glimpsed Matt, she quickly but clumsily navigated through the crowded bar area to be at Matt's side.

"Fancy meeting you here, slugger," she laughed. "I knew you were a player on and off the field."

Matt was startled a moment later when Natalie's hand rubbed across his crotch. At first, he thought it might have been an accident. But the devilish look in her eye convinced him that it definitely had not been an accident. Natalie then got so close to his cheek that he could smell the Scotch on her breath.

"Buy me a drink, darling! You won't have to worry about getting to first base," she said, laughing wickedly. "You'll be sliding home. That is, if you want to."

She then smiled seductively and ran an index finger down his left cheek.

Matt never blushed, never lost his cool. As a journalist, he could handle extreme pressure for sure.

He knew how to move stylishly out of a corner, like an experienced prizefighter who knew out to spin out of trouble on the ropes.

"You're about the sexiest thing I've ever laid eyes on," Matt said, putting a hand on her heavily perfumed neck. "And I'd love to have a drink with you. But not tonight. I'm just leaving, unfortunately. You see, I brought a date and she had too much to drink. She's in the ladies' room, probably throwing up. I promised her I'd come get her and take her home once I settled the tab. After all, a gentleman takes care of his date."

"Damn it, can I get a rain check?" Natalie said, continuing the baseball analogy.

"I said you were sexy as sin," Matt said, delicately avoiding a direct answer.

He then caressed her cheek and spun away from danger.

He quickly walked away as Natalie proudly said, "Damn right I am!"

Matt hated to lie, but he knew he needed to concoct some excuse without making Natalie angry. And he certainly didn't want to get intimate with her. Although he had to admit to himself as he drove home that Natalie Lane probably was a grand slam in the sack.

Chapter Seven

It had been a productive day for Robbyn at Missonis Advertising. She had cranked out copy for a few "quickie" ads, met with two clients on upcoming ad campaigns, and finally had gotten around to doing some research on an upcoming major project -- developing image ads for the Braxton Emergency Shelter during its capital campaign. The Emergency Shelter was seeking to raise $2.5 million to renovate and expand its building in one of the poorer sections of the city. Capital campaigns raise most of their funds from corporate donors, leaning on local CEOs who are community-minded. The Emergency Shelter also wanted to reach out to the community itself. Its mission was twofold: Tap the purse strings of individual citizens and pluck their heartstrings as well. The Shelter wanted to raise public awareness about its programs. Too many people thought all the Shelter did was give the homeless a place to sleep over night and a bowl of soup. In reality, the Shelter had a number of educational and support programs designed to get people back on their feet. Robbyn's job was to produce a series of poignant newspaper ads that spotlighted various Shelter programs in a compelling way. It was work that Robbyn loved. She was quite adept at crafting copy that evoked a certain mood. She knew how to turn a phrase a certain way and how to create a poignant headline that, in tandem with a commanding visual element, jumped off the page or tablet or phone at readers.

Robbyn had been given a packet of information on the Shelter. As she was leafing through the material on this particular afternoon, she came across a clipping of a column Matt had written on the Shelter. The column was about a young Latino mother whose husband had died in an industrial accident. She was left with three young girls, no formal education, no insurance, no job skills and no job. One desperate night she and her girls wound up at the Shelter. It proved to be a prudent decision by the mother. With the help of some educational programs, some well-placed contacts and a lot of encouragement, the widow got a job at a local food market and a place to live in subsidized housing. In addition, the Shelter provided her with free childcare at its daycare center until she became more financially solvent. Somehow the mother even found the time to take some courses at Braxton Area Community College. It made for great column material. And Robbyn, who knew good writing when she read it, was deeply impressed with how well Matt had written this woman's story. She thought he had hit just the right tone. He had used some stirring verbiage to embroider the drama of the woman's situation. But he hadn't overwritten the column, freighting it with too much imagery and drama. In fact, his sentence structure had been relatively spare. In so doing, his words had an impact that had resonated deeply in Robbyn as she read it.

But Matt's writing ability wasn't what impressed Robbyn the most. It was quite vivid to her that a man who could write such an eloquent column with such sensitivity must have a compassionate heart.

The one attribute that Robbyn, even though she herself could be pre-judgmental at times, valued above all others was compassion.

For a brief moment, she found herself attracted to him. Attracted to him not just as a writer and a compassionate person, but also attracted to him as a man.

That moment of attraction was short-lived. She would not allow it to linger because of two key things: Her sense of loyalty to her late husband and her distinct impression of Matt as a womanizer. These two elements formed the prism of perspective through which Robbyn saw Matt. In fact, as she looked at the photo of the attractive Latino woman and her girls that accompanied Matt's column, Robbyn wondered if Matt had hit on the poor woman.

"Maybe that's why he was so compassionate," Robbyn said cynically to herself.

"What did you say?" asked Chad, who had just approached Robbyn's desk to discuss some ad concepts with her.

Snapped back to reality, Robbyn blurted out: "Nothing. Nothing. Just talking to myself."

"Well, whatever nothing is," said Chad, smiling, "it sure made you blush."

"Don't be silly," Robbyn said, way too defensively. "I think it's hot in here."

"Yeah, right," Chad said, laughing. "Everybody has been complaining all day about how the air conditioning in this place is cranked up too high. And you're hot. Aren't you a bit young to be having heat flashes?"

"Don't be a wise guy," Robbyn said, regaining her composure. "Let's get back to work."

"You work too much," Chad said. "You need to lighten up. Have some fun. Go out. No wonder you wind up alone, talking to yourself."

"There's a difference between being alone and being lonely," Robbyn pointed out.

Robbyn had regained her sense of psychological balance and deleted all thoughts of any possible attraction to Matt from her mind. To make sure they didn't return, she made sure there was no vacuum for them to fill. So, she did what she always did when she didn't want to think about something: She buried herself in work. But before she did so, she couldn't resist lightening the moment with Chad.

"You could cure my alleged loneliness if you married me," she cracked, punctuating her words with a naughty smile.

"You're not my type," Chad retorted, joining in the banter.

"I know, I have boobs and no penis," Robbyn said, getting more sexually graphic than normal.

Her candor elicited some hearty laughs from Chad, who made no pretense about being gay, even if he was married.

"Yeah, but you do have a cute butt. Don't bend over near me," he joked. "I could suddenly undergo a quick change in orientation, since I am bisexual occasionally."

"You're too much," Robbyn said, smiling.

"And you're not yourself, I'd say," Chad replied.

That evening, Matt's undefeated baseball team was going for its fourth straight victory. Timmy Baxter was having a stellar season, at the plate and in the field. Part of his success could be attributed to Matt's tweaking of Timmy's technique. But most of Timmy's accomplishments were rooted in his exceptional hand-eye coordination and his unbridled enthusiasm for the game. Of course, his enthusiasm for baseball was spiked by Matt's enthusiasm. They fed off each other's energy.

Matt didn't require the players to be at the field until 6 for the 7 p.m. game. But Timmy insisted to Robbyn that she drop him off at 5:30. He wanted to get a little extra work in on his fielding since he had allowed a groundball to scoot between his legs for an error in the previous game.

"You certainly are gung-ho," Robbyn said to Timmy in the car as they drove to the field. "But I wish we would have had time to eat something more filling than a quick bowl of soup and crackers. It's hard to find time for a good dinner when you want to get to baseball at 5:30. And a good dinner helps give you home run power."

"I'll buy a hot dog from the snack bar before the game," Timmy said. "Babe Ruth used to eat hot dogs during games."

"Suddenly comparing yourself to Babe Ruth, huh?" Robbyn observed, laughing. "He might have been the best slugger of all time."

"Mike Trout will be the greatest slugger ever," Timmy pitched in. "Those old guys never lifted weights."

"But they ate hot dogs," Robbyn said, giggling.

As Robbyn drove up to the baseball field to drop off Timmy, she noticed that Matt already was there, working on the field.

Coaches at the youth level have other duties in addition to coaching. Mundane chores like toting around equipment, raking the infield dirt to make it smooth, lining the batter's box and the foul lines, and making sure the pitcher's mound isn't a no-man's land for broken ankles.

Robbyn did a double take when she saw Matt raking the infield. He had his shirt off, and she could see that he worked out. He was trim, but muscular, with excellent definition. Shredded was the contemporary word. She couldn't help but stare at him for a moment until a signal in her brain reminded her once again she was a widow. So, feeling guilty, she looked away and drove off.

But she couldn't drive away from the lingering feeling that, under different circumstances, Matt Meredith would be a man who drew her attention. To distract herself, she turned on the car radio. WBAM, 670 AM on your dial, was airing a commercial that encouraged people to subscribe to the *Braxton Bugle* so they could read award-winning columnist Matt Meredith.

"What is this? Some kind of conspiracy!" Robbyn yelped as she emphatically turned off the radio. "Matt Meredith is everywhere in this damn town!"

When Robbyn and Billy returned to the ball field for Timmy's game, Matt had his shirt back on. But Robbyn, still disturbed by her unwanted emotions, made a point of avoiding eye contact with him. Of course, that's easier said than done when you're watching a ballgame and the coach is flashing signals from the third base coaching box, warming up the pitcher between innings and slapping high-fives with his players. He gave Timmy a couple high-fives after he hit two more home runs -- one for each of the hot dogs he had eaten before the game.

After the game a conflicted Robbyn was determined to go nowhere near Matt. She just wanted Timmy to come up to the bleachers so they could get out of there. She hated dealing with her muddled state of mind over Matt Meredith.

So, she was determined to just make a quick exit. Hopefully out of sight, out of mind. Well, unless she opted to stare at the ground while Matt talked to her, it wasn't happening. Matt, who was looking for an excuse to talk to her anyway, didn't have to manufacture one.

Before the game, Matt had received a call from the league commissioner, informing him that his team's representative on the league's traveling all-star team was Timmy Baxter. But in order to be officially selected, Robbyn would have to agree to the travel commitments -- several weekend tournaments in August in such places as Cape May, New Jersey; Wilmington, Delaware; and Altoona, Pennsylvania.

So, Matt decided to take advantage of the situation. Even before picking up the team equipment, Matt made a beeline for Robbyn, with Timmy in tow. Robbyn couldn't help but notice their approach, even though she was trying to avoid eye contact. So, she suddenly struck up a conversation about nothing with Cindy Loeper, hoping Matt wouldn't want to intrude. But Matt didn't have to intrude.

Once Cindy saw him bounding toward them, she became as giddy as a young girl as she yelled out: "Great game, Coach! And way to go, Timmy."

"It was a nice win," Matt said, smiling. "Timmy here and all the boys had good games."

Then turning to face Robbyn, who was looking down, he said emphatically: "Mrs. Baxter, you should be proud of your son here. He's having a great season."

"He's having fun," Robbyn said softly, looking more at Timmy than at Matt. "He likes baseball."

You could hear the nervousness in her voice. Matt found her reaction strange. He thought either she disliked him very much, or she felt some sort of uncomfortable tension in his presence. He wasn't sure. He had discovered over the years that some people did have preconceived notions about him, either from something he had written or said on television. He wanted to think that her aloofness was spawned by some weird sexual tension, but he somehow felt she simply didn't like him. He had intended to be glib and charming, but her obvious discomfort changed his mind.

"Timmy has been selected to the league's traveling tournament team," he said in a monotone to Robbyn. "It does involve some travel and expense on your part. Here's the schedule and an informational packet."

Since Robbyn had averted her eyes in the direction of Timmy, who was standing about two feet to Matt's left, she hadn't noticed Matt handing her an envelope containing the tournament team information. For a moment, she stood there unresponsive as Matt stood there with his arm extended, envelope in hand.

When Robbyn finally realized what was going on, she quickly and awkwardly tried to grab the envelope from Matt. In her haste, she knocked the envelope from Matt's grasp. It plummeted through the bleachers and onto the weeds beneath them.

"Oh, I'm so sorry," Robbyn said, flustered but finally looking Matt in the eye. "I, I ...."

Matt looked into her eyes and it took his breath away. He had been with a number of beautiful women in his life. Robbyn was beautiful. But there was something special in her limpid eyes that Matt found to be utterly enchanting. He always had been attracted to a woman's eyes, even more than her face, legs or breasts. When he would tell people that, they would tell him that he was putting them on. But he never was. Granted, a woman had to have more than just pretty eyes to grab Matt's attention. But eyes were his focal point. As he looked at Robbyn, he felt a quiet sadness tug at his heart. This was a woman he somehow felt he could settle down with. It had just been an intuitive feeling. He always was so comfortable with women, but Robbyn's demeanor made him feel like he just wanted to get the hell out of there. It was a mutual feeling. Robbyn swore that if she didn't get away from him in a hurry, she surely was going to die from embarrassment.

Timmy, however, did manage to lighten the mood. When he saw his mother knock the envelope to the ground, he laughed and said: "The error is on Mom. You need more practice. Maybe Coach Matt could come over for dinner some night and give you some fielding tips."

The spines of both Robbyn and Matt shuddered when they heard his offer. Not so Cindy. She leaped at the opportunity.

"Sounds like a great idea, Timmy!" Cindy exclaimed. "You guys could discuss the tournament team logistics over dinner."

Robbyn visibly blanched. Matt couldn't help but notice. Nevertheless, he suddenly had regained some backbone in his spine. He decided to make a pitch for love.

"Better yet, why don't I take you and the boys out to dinner, Mrs. Baxter?" he said, so tentatively that the pitch was more of a tepid change-up than a roaring fastball.

"How about we all go to a Braxton Bulls game and we can eat there?" Timmy chimed in.

Robbyn thought she was going to faint at any second. But before she did, she swore she would strangle Cindy and Timmy. However, first she had to think up a quick excuse. Finding none, she blurted out the blunt truth.

"There's no need to discuss the tournament team," Robbyn said. "Timmy won't be playing on it. I'm a widow and between work and home, I can't afford to spend entire weekends out of town."

"That's not fair!" yelled a visibly angry Timmy.

"At least think about it," Matt said quickly, knowing how much the opportunity meant to Timmy.

Matt also couldn't help but notice that Robbyn had avoided responding to his dinner invitation.

Then Matt had a brainstorm.

"If you don't have the time, Mrs. Baxter, I'll gladly take Timmy to the tournament games," he offered. "I'll even pick up all the expenses."

"I said I was a widow, not a pauper," snapped Robbyn, now so frazzled that her frustration and confusion bubbled into anger.

As quickly as her anger erupted, it dissipated, leaving Robbyn standing in a puddle of remorse and embarrassment.

With tears glistening in her eyes, she softly added: "I'll discuss the matter with Timmy later."

Then turning to Timmy, she said sternly: "Please pick the envelope up from under the bleachers. We have to get home. You have a science project to finish."

She then abruptly walked down the bleachers, putting Matt behind her.

Cindy felt as awkward as Robbyn and Matt did.

"Sorry, Coach," Cindy said to Matt. "Robbyn's been through a rough few years. It's been hard on her, not having a father for her boys. You understand, don't you?"

Matt didn't understand why Robbyn had behaved so strangely. But he did understand that Robbyn had opted not to swing at his pitch. As far as Matt was concerned, Mrs. Baxter never would have the chance to evolve into Mrs. Meredith. And he beat himself up mentally for even thinking that Robbyn Baxter might have been the one for him.

"What the hell was I thinking?" he asked himself angrily as he loaded up the last of the equipment into his car.

Matt vowed to himself that he never again would think of Robbyn Baxter in any context beyond being Timmy's mother.

Robbyn, meanwhile, drove home in the midst of tears and jeers. The tears were coming from her and Timmy. The jeers were coming strictly from Timmy.

"I can't believe you won't let me play on the tournament team," he screamed.

"Lower your voice," Robbyn said sharply.

Internally, she felt awful for Timmy that she had not immediately approved of his participation on the traveling tournament team. She really had no logical rationale for her behavior, other than feeling very awkward around Matt Meredith. And now she had permitted her conflicted feelings toward him to ruin a dream for Timmy. He had spoken often about his hopes for making the team, and now she had dashed them simply because ... well, because she was a mess around his coach. It was as simple -- and complicated -- as that. She was terribly angry with herself. And utterly embarrassed and ashamed. She knew she had come across like an idiot. But her primary emotion right now was remorse for depriving Timmy of something he so richly deserved. She decided she had been selfish. She was going to allow Timmy to participate on the travel team, even if the tournament travel was inconvenient and expensive. She just hoped and prayed that Matt wouldn't be one of the tournament team coaches. But considering that his team was in first place, she assumed he would be. It was an assumption that made her feel lime-green with nausea. She never wanted to be anywhere near Matt Meredith again. She felt like such a jerk. She found some strange solace in realizing that he probably would avoid her as much she would him. So, she bit her quivering lip and said as she drove into their driveway.

"Timmy, I'm so sorry," she said, reaching into the back seat to tousle his hair. "I was being selfish. You know how busy I am around the house on weekends. And you know money is tight sometimes. But this is important to you and to Billy and me. Right, Billy?"

Billy, who had been reading a comic book and really not paying much attention, distractedly asked, "What did you say, Mom?"

"She said I could play on the tournament team, dummy," Timmy yelled, reaching over to hug his mother. "Thanks a million, Mom. And if you can't make one of the tournaments, Coach Matt can always take me."

"That won't be necessary," Robbyn said. "We don't need him there. I'll be there. And so will Billy."

"And so will Coach," Timmy said. "He's the traveling team's head coach."

Robbyn's heart sank. It was going to be a long, awkward summer. She couldn't explain to Timmy that a very significant part of her had feelings for his coach that she hadn't felt for anyone except for his father. And she couldn't tell Timmy that an equally significant part of her prevented her from acting upon those feelings for Matt because of her feelings for her late husband.

She was a mess. The whole situation was a mess. But she could find no resolution. She missed her husband desperately. But now she realized she missed being in a relationship as well. She hadn't realized that until Matt Meredith had popped up in their lives.

Chapter Eight

Matt loved the diversity of subject material that a general columnist encountered. He appreciated the free rein of column topics that his editors afforded him. He could write about anything, local or non-local. He wrote about everything and anything. And he did so with as much thoroughness as he could muster. He never wanted to be superficial, even though 17-inch columns hardly lent themselves to great depth. Nevertheless, he always did his homework. And with such a wide range of topics, he probably did as much as research as a college student.

Of course, some columns were more fun to research and write than others were. Such was the case on this particular day. Indeed, it was an unusual day for Matt as well as the City of Braxton. A major Hollywood film focusing on inner-city drug trafficking was beginning a couple months of location shooting in Braxton. The film folks had come to the right town. Braxton's drug trafficking was out of control. Dealers, many of them gang-bangers, had found that medium-sized cities like Braxton didn't have the resources -- enough cops and money -- that major cities like New York and Philadelphia enjoyed. Braxton was a fertile drug town for another demographic reason. Mushroom plants in the city's outskirts were the magnet for seasonal Latino workers for decades. Over the years many of them settled permanently in Braxton. And many of their relatives and neighbors joined them. Braxton now had the nation's largest concentration of Latinos in an urban locale. Because of cultural, social, economic, educational and language complications, many of the young Latinos had limited opportunities. So, they gravitated to the instant appeal of drug dealing. A lot of dealers from New York and Philly had migrated to Braxton as well. Constant turf wars were the result, and drive-by shootings were common in town. Indeed, many residents of Miller County's suburbs were afraid to come into the city at night. A new downtown civic center had made some inroads in attracting people to town after dark. But the civic center was on the main thoroughfare at Seventh and Park streets, a relatively safe haven. Go several blocks in any direction, however, and you were entering a dangerous world of drugs, despair and bullets. Inept politicians and an apathetic and/or beleaguered city populace added to the explosion in drug-related activity and crime. A once prosperous and safe city had morphed into the badlands in many areas.

The working title of the movie was "Drug Town" – a name that had everybody in Miller County in an uproar. Business leaders said the movie title would smear Braxton's image, already tainted by its crime rate, and further retard economic development and urban revival. Politicians were blustering in righteous indignation as well. Matt had mined the controversy for several hard-hitting columns. And now he had booked an exclusive: The female lead in the film, Tiffany Underhill, had not only agreed to be interviewed for his *Braxton Bugle* column, but also had agreed to appear on his cable television show.

Tiffany Underhill was not yet a star. But she seemed destined to become one. She was built like a supermodel -— a curvy 125 pounds amply distributed over her leggy 6-1 frame. She had abundant mounds of luxurious red hair framing a sexy, pouting face. She had received a good deal of acclaim for her last film. In "Broken" she had a supporting role in which she had several steamy scenes playing the mistress of the President of the United States. That role had landed her the lead -- her first -- in "Drug Town."

The entertainment editor of the *Braxton Bugle* wasn't thrilled that Matt had scooped up Tiffany Underhill for his Miller and Beyond column. But the managing editor knew that Matt's column would draw more readers and had sided with him. Besides, Matt was a much more talented and creative writer than anybody on the Entertainment staff and the city editor, a crusty, journalistic throwback of an editor named Charlie Kunkel, knew when you had a hot horse, you rode it. Of course, when Kunkel wasn't at the office, he usually could be found at the racetrack. And Kunkel knew that if anybody on his staff could establish a rapport with a bombshell like Tiffany Underhill, it would be Matt. Kunkel meant that in a constructive, non-sexist way. Meredith was a master at listening to people, and he did in a subtle, charming and ultimately seductive way. People -- men and women -- felt comfortable talking to Matt. And Charlie Kunkel knew that Matt had an air of sophistication about him that enabled him to relate as well to celebrities and luminaries as he did to the common folk of Braxton. In his own world of Braxton, Matt Meredith was a star. And now he was about to meet the star power of one Tiffany Underhill.

Frankly, it was an assignment that would have had most red-blooded male journalists drooling. Granted, Matt was looking forward to meeting her. But truthfully, he was as excited about the journalistic benefits of the interview as he was meeting a beautiful actress in her physical prime at 26. Matt had long passed being stuck in the adolescent phase of sexual development -- a stage that many grown men never grew out of. Part of it was because Matt's good looks, charisma and confidence combined to give him enough self-esteem to never be intimidated or awed by anyone. And part of it was that Matt had dealt with so many different people from all sorts of backgrounds over the years that he thought all people were just that -- people. Having said all that, Matt still was a guy with hormones. And he was not totally oblivious to the charms of a lovely young lady.

Matt took a deep breath when he first saw Tiffany Underhill up close and personal. She was every bit as beautiful -- even more so -- in person than she appeared on the screen and in the promotional material the studio PR assistant had given him. Matt assumed she probably had an enormous ego and enough attitude to cower any man. Matt was standing on the corner of Front and Elm streets, where Underhill and the cast were shooting on location. The intersection of Front and Elm was one of the most dangerous areas in town, a locale riddled with drug-related violence.

"This place must be the safest place in town today with all these people and cameras," a city cop joked with Matt. "No drug dealer in his right mind would get anywhere near this place right now."

"Perhaps we should have movies filmed in Braxton every day," Matt said, laughing. "That's one crime-fighting plan the mayor never thought of."

"The mayor never thinks of anything outside of what he's having for dinner that night," the cop cracked.

"Don't be nasty," Matt said, smiling.

It was a smile he kept wearing as he watched Tiffany film her scene. Tiffany was playing the role of a Manhattan socialite whose younger brother had fallen into drug use and was murdered by a dealer in Braxton. Tiffany's character had decided to track down her brother's killer herself after Braxton police were unable to solve the crime. Actually, her character was being assisted in her search by the star middle linebacker for the New York Giants, a charismatic football star with plenty of street smarts. Playing this leading role was Bronk Cassidy, an actor who specialized in action roles. He excelled in grimacing as he flexed his biceps. In the scene, Matt was watching, Tiffany's and Bronk's characters were grilling a couple of low-level dealers on the street corner. One of the dealers pulled out a gun, which Bronk's football player stud kicked away from him. Bronk's character then drilled the guy with a crunching left hook. Tiffany jammed a spiked high heel into the shin of the other dealer, doubling him over in pain.

After the director yelled "cut" and the cast started to scatter for the day, Bronk Cassidy asked Tiffany if she wanted a bite to eat.

"I can't," she replied. "I'm having dinner with a local newspaper columnist."

"Well, I'm sure that will suck," Bronk said, cockily. "Blow him off. How many movie tickets will that small-town hick be able to sell?"

"That's not the point," Tiffany said. "We can't just talk to the reporters in L.A. and New York."

"Screw them, too," Bronk yelped. "I just like photographers from *People* magazine. All right, well I'm going to go work out. Call me when you're done with the schmuck reporter."

"OK," Tiffany said, fixing her hair. "I'm sure the interview won't last long."

"Are you kidding?" cracked Bronk. "You love talking about yourself and you know it."

A public relations assistant approached Tiffany and pointed Matt out to her.

Tiffany matter-of-factly glanced over at Matt and sighed to her assistant: "For a small-town newspaper hack, he doesn't look all THAT boring."

Laughing, she pranced right up to Matt.

"So where are you taking me to dinner, handsome?" she said, teasingly.

"Wherever your public relations person made reservations," Matt said. "He hasn't told me yet."

"Carl," Tiffany said, turning to the PR guy. "Cancel those reservations. And you're not going on this interview. I want this reporter to show me the real Braxton. I've done some homework on this town. I want to eat at the Nut Bar, just him and I. Speaking of him, what's your name?"

She turned and stared into Matt's eyes. She expected him to blush and become flustered. She was pleasantly surprised when he did neither.

Instead, Matt smiled casually and stared back confidently.

"Matt Meredith," he said quietly. "I know it doesn't sound as glamorous as Tiffany Underhill. Braxton isn't Hollywood."

"Your byline would look silly if it read Tiffany Underhill under your column picture," Tiffany said. "Readers would think you underwent a sex-change operation."

She laughed at her joke, pecked him on the cheek, and announced: "I'm famished. We'll take your car to dinner. You can give me a lift back to the Homewood Suites when we're done. You up for that, Matt?"

Again, she hoped to elicit an embarrassed response from him. Again, she was pleasantly surprised to discover that Matt's composure never left him.

"I've taken women home after dinner a time or two in my life," Matt said, somewhat provocatively.

"Indeed, I'm sure you have, handsome," Tiffany cracked, her giggles as abundant as her curls.

So, it was off to the Nut Bar, which was a downtown Braxton institution. Located across the street from the *Braxton Bugle* in the heart of downtown in the 300 block of

Park Street, the restaurant featured upscale dining with a homey ambience. Actually, homey may not be the apt description. Because nobody sober tosses peanut shells on the floor at home. But the Nut Bar encouraged the practice. And since all patrons were treated to an endless supply of peanuts, the shells were quite abundant by week's end. And the floor was swept only at week's end. Indeed, there was one Monday morning when the weekend cleanup man was discovered dead from an apparent heart attack. His body and his broom were found in a large pile of peanut shells. The story became part of restaurant folklore.

The Nut Bar had been the keynote watering hole over the years for newspaper reporters and editors; politicians; community leaders; cops and civilians, including several political science professors who enjoyed talking local politics. But over the years as the old-school newspaper types and politicians died off, the Nut Bar had become more noted for its fine dining than its hard drinking. Matt, for instance, had been known to routinely stop in for a drink or two after work. But now he mostly frequented it for lunch or an occasional dinner. Of course, some politicians still drank there. And when Matt and Tiffany walked into the Nut Bar, seated at the bar, along with his regular entourage of City Hall flunkies, was his honor, Jimbo Cummings, mayor of Braxton. When Jimbo saw Matt walk in with the stunning Tiffany Underhill, a smile wider than his ample waist erupted across his face. And it was difficult to smile that broadly while drinking from his glass of beer. But Jimbo managed.

"Well, well, Matt," Jimbo bellowed for all to hear.

"If it isn't that womanizing newspaper reporter!"

Matt didn't even blink.

"This is business, not pleasure," Matt replied quickly, smiling with a twinkle in his eye. "I'm always working. I presume your associates and your honor are meeting here to discuss the city's severe fiscal crisis."

You could have walked across the words in Matt's last comment because they were layered stiff with sarcasm.

"All work and no play, Matt my boy," huffed Mayor Jimbo, scoping out Tiffany.

"You've obviously noticed Tiffany," Matt said. "Tiffany Underhill, meet the mayor of Braxton."

"Please to meet you, your honor," Tiffany purred.

"Charmed," Jimbo spouted exuberantly, turning redder than a candy apple.

"Maybe you shouldn't be," Matt interjected. "Tiffany is starring in 'Drug Town' -- the movie that will let the whole world know what a drug problem we have here in Braxton. The city you are the esteemed mayor of."

"No need to be nasty," Jimbo said, looking at Tiffany. "I'm sure the movie will show some of our fair city's good points as well. Do you think I could have a cameo in the film, Tiffany? If I can call you that?"

"Why sure, sir," Tiffany said dreamily. "I don't make casting decisions. But please stop by our Front and Elm location tomorrow and I'll introduce you to our director."

Ol' Jimbo had instantly become a Tiffany Underhill fan for life.

"Thank you so much, young lady," he gushed. "I'll certainly do that. I won't hold it against you that you're hanging out with Matt Meredith here."

"We're having dinner because I'm writing a column about Tiffany's role in the film and what it means for Braxton," Matt said.

"Don't be silly," Tiffany cooed, messing with the mayor's mind. "Matt and I are here on a date. I love guys who can turn a phrase. Now come on, Matthew. It's not nice to keep a lady waiting."

With that, she grabbed Matt's hand and sauntered past the boys at the bar.

"See you tomorrow, honey," she said softly to Jimbo Cummings.

Poor ol' Jimbo would have gotten an erection if hadn't had so much to drink.

Once seated at their table, Tiffany stopped playing the tease. She was delightful, witty, intelligent, charming -- the perfect dinner companion. She made small talk with Matt, but also thoughtfully answered his questions with good quotes. She did more than echo sound bites. Matt knew he was getting quite a column out of a remarkable person who had plenty of substance to match plenty of style.

"I know some people in Braxton think the movie will give the town an unfair black eye," she said between delicate bites of her flounder. "But I believe the script is sympathetic to the overwhelming problem that city officials confront here. And it does have an upbeat ending in which good triumphs over evil -- at least temporarily. So at least Braxton isn't characterized totally as a city of despair."

She then smiled, picked up a spent peanut shell, and playfully tossed it at Matt's shoulder.

"To brighten up the script, we should film a scene here at the Nut Bar," she said, semi-seriously. "This place is charming. Fine dining and old-time ambience found amidst peanut shells."

"I'm glad you like it," Matt said, refilling their wine glasses.

"So, tell me about yourself," Tiffany suddenly said, giving him a penetrating look.

"Who's doing the interview here?" Matt asked. "You're the column subject, not me."

"OK, but only if you promise to tell me about you after I tell you about me," Tiffany said, daintily wiping her chin with a napkin.

"You got a deal," Matt said. "All right, we've talked in depth about your career and this movie. But we haven't touched upon your personal life."

"There's not much to tell, really," Tiffany said.

"Yeah, right," he said, laughing.

"I'm serious," Tiffany said, running a finger through her hair. "People are always cynical, but I pour a lot of energy into my career. I've always wanted to be a major actress. I've spent several years taking all sorts of acting lessons, working with voice coaches and fitness trainers. In the early days, I did all that while working nights as a waitress. My road to fame and fortune in Hollywood is littered with clichés. My career is my life. Because of my career, I don't have much time for anybody but me. I really have no personal life, except for my parents and family back in Iowa."

"You're from Iowa and your first name is Tiffany?"

Matt playfully tossed a peanut shell back at her shoulder. "What's your real name? Martha or Mary Sue?"

"Funny," Tiffany laughed. "That's something else people find hard to believe about me. It's my given name. My mother does amateur theater work back home in Ames. She was hoping I'd grow up to be an actress. I guess she had a grand vision of having my name on a theater marquee someday. Tiffany, she thought, sounded glamorous. Actually, I hate my name. It sounds so superficial."

"I'm getting the impression that you're hardly superficial," Matt said.

"I'm not, and I thank you for noticing that," she said. "But most people don't. Actually, I've let my hair down around you. When I'm dealing with the public, I feel I have to conform to their expectations. People look at me as this hot chick who is sort of sassy. So, I play that role. But there are times when I hate myself for it."

"Conflicted movie star?" Matt asked.

"Not that dramatic," Tiffany said. "I'm not spending my hard-earned dollars on some dandy Hollywood shrink."

Matt cleared his throat and popped the question that had been caught in his throat, along with the peanuts and the chicken Caesar salad: "I noticed on your bio that you're single? Do, uh, you have a boyfriend?"

Tiffany laughed very loudly.

"That's the first awkward moment you've had with me," she said, turning serious. "A lot of guys are a mess around me. I intimidate them even when I'm not trying to do so. You're different. You're so self-assured. Except when you asked that silly question. Why? Are you interested in me?"

"Of course I am," Matt said, laughing. "Do you think I am a eunuch or something?"

"I'm not touching that line," Tiffany said, smiling.

Matt was not smiling. He took one of Tiffany hands and held it tightly.

"I never mix business with pleasure and I'm not one of those heavy-handed guys who hit on women," he said earnestly. "But I must tell you that I find you to be utterly fascinating and interesting. I don't have to tell you that you're beautiful. But you are much more than that. You are great fun, a wonderful conversationalist, and you listen to me when I talk. Plus, you seem so down to earth, not some sophisticated star with an attitude bigger than her wardrobe."

Matt gulped *Did I just say all of that?* to himself.

"Well, I'm flattered," Tiffany said, smiling softly.

"Truly I am. I've had a number of men in my life, but nothing really serious. I've haven't had the time to focus on a serious relationship. Or maybe I just haven't met the guy who made me want to be more serious. Since I'm being so candid, and I have no idea why I am unless it's the wine or the fact that you can make people open up to you, there have been times lately when I have found myself thinking that it might be time to find Mr. Right. So, do you think you're Mr. Right?"

This time Tiffany clutched Matt's hand.

Matt didn't blink.

"I'm hardly Mr. Right, but I think I'd like to find out if you could be Mrs. Right for me," he said with conviction.

Tiffany stared at him for several long moments in silence.

"You just might," she said. "But what's your story?"

"Same as yours," Matt said, bluntly. "On a much smaller stage here in Braxton and beyond, I've had the opportunity to date a lot of women. Some were semi-serious, most were casual. I don't think I'm superficial, but I have had trouble connecting with the right lady. People think I'm lying, but I don't think I ever have really been head-over-heels in love. I'm embarrassed to tell you that."

"Don't be," Tiffany said, her eyes welling up. "I never have either."

Over coffee, Matt and Tiffany began telling each other what they had missed in each other's lives all these years -- giving each other a quick overview of personal highlights and lowlights, families and friends, triumphs and frustrations. One cup of coffee lingered into a second and then a third.

"I don't what this night to end," Matt said, his eyes glistening as he looked into Tiffany's eyes. "Would you like to come back to my place?"

"I thought you would never ask," she laughed. "I was ready after the first cup of coffee. It's not polite to keep a lady waiting."

They should have left after the first cup of coffee. Because just after Matt settled the bill, they rose from the table only to find Bronk Cassidy heading right for them. A tipsy Bronk Cassidy, who tripped over his feet amid the peanut shells and smacked into their table.

"Going so soon?" Bronk asked, regaining his footing and slightly slurring his words. "Why don't you two have a seat again and have a drink with me?"

"We were just leaving," Tiffany said, blatantly annoyed at the timing of Bronk Cassidy's arrival. "Do you want us to drop you off at the Homewood Suites?"

"Well, maybe we should leave," Bronk said thickly. "You and I have some homework to do anyway. So, we'll let the newspaper guy leave and you and I can catch a cab to the hotel. I want to rehearse some of our scenes that are going to be shot tomorrow."

"You can rehearse by yourself," Tiffany said sharply. "Matt and I will get you to your suite safely, and that's it. We have a date."

Matt looked at Bronk, smiling like a kid who had just discovered a stash of his favorite candy. Bronk blinked back at Matt, trying to focus.

"I can't believe you're hooking up with this small-town writer," Bronk said. "You're my leading lady. All my leading ladies hook up with me. After all, I'm Bronk Cassidy!"

Bronk essentially was telling the truth. He had a well-deserved reputation as a ladies' man and indeed had bedded most of his leading ladies. Of course, once the filming wrapped, so did the relationship. He had been unsuccessfully hitting on Tiffany, and he wasn't used to striking out.

"That's precisely why I'll never sleep with you," Tiffany said, started to giggle, "because you're Bronk Cassidy. I won't be just another one of your conquests."

"I'm insulted," Bronk said, laughing and then sitting down at their table. "Come on, sit down for one drink and we'll go."

"No," Tiffany said. "Two questions: How did you know we were here? And how did you get so drunk so quickly?"

"Well, I was at this downtown dive, drinking shots and beer with some local yokels," he said. "I asked them if there were any restaurants near the newspaper plant. I figured this cheap bastard couldn't afford to take you to an upscale restaurant."

"I can't," laughed Matt. "But enough about me. We're out of here. Are you coming with us or not?"

"I bought so many rounds at the last bar, I don't have enough cash for a cab," Bronk said sadly. "So I'm coming with you. You guys can have a drink with me at my place."

"Yeah, right," Tiffany said sarcastically.

So the three of them piled into Matt's car. Tiffany sat up front with Matt. Bronk sat in the small back seat, complaining about sitting on a bag of baseballs.

"You still play ball, old man?" Bronk asked.

"I coach it," Matt said. "One of the local Little League teams."

"Man, what a schmuck," Bronk laughed.

"I think that's great," Tiffany said. "I'd love to see one of your games."

"Well, you'll have to catch a game," Matt said, "but you probably would be bored."

"I wouldn't be bored watching you," Tiffany said sweetly.

"I'm gonna be sick," Bronk said, alarm sounding in his voice.

Tiffany and Matt thought Bronk meant figuratively.

Unfortunately, Bronk meant literally.

He proceeded to projectile vomit. Since he was sitting behind Tiffany, he managed to spray puke all over her hair and shoulders. Her startled scream of horror was so piercing that poor Matt almost drove off the bypass and into a bridge abutment.

"Damn you, Bronk Cassidy. This is gross!" gagged Tiffany.

The odor of Bronk's vomit was so pungent that it nauseated Tiffany, who suddenly vomited into her own lap. She began crying hysterically.

Matt pulled off onto the shoulder of the bypass to comfort Tiffany. He put his arm around her even though it meant coating his sleeve with Bronk's vomit.

"This is terrible, terrible," Matt said, who also was thinking that his poor car likely would smell of puke forever. "We'll get you home and help you get cleaned up."

"No, no, no," Tiffany sobbed. "I don't want anybody seeing me like this. Just please drop me off at my suite and let me shower for about 20 hours. I hope you understand. I need to be alone."

"The proverbial raincheck, I mean puke check!" Bronk cracked, feeling better now that he had tossed his cookies.

"I hate you," Tiffany yelled back at Bronk.

"Screw you," Bronk barked back.

A moment later Bronk was wiping blood from his lips, lips that already were caked with vomit. The blood came courtesy of a wicked right cross by Matt.

"Who said movie stars leave glamorous lives," Matt said, trying to lighten the mood.

Bronk was too stunned and drunk to fight back. He said nothing and sat still in the stinking car. Matt pulled up to the

Homewood Suites and let Bronk out. He immediately stomped away to his suite. Matt escorted Tiffany to her suite.

"I wish this evening had ended differently," Matt said, hoping perhaps to change Tiffany's mind.

"I think you're someone special and I think we might have something special," Tiffany said, her eyes glistening with tears, tears produced by conflicting emotions. "I don't want to remember our first night as the same night this disgusting thing happened."

"You're right," Matt said, kissing her messy forehead. "And trust me, our first time will be very special."

"I knew you'd understand," she said, smiling.

"Now go wash that puke off," Matt said, trying to cheer her up. "You're lucky I don't write for one of those tabloids. I could ruin your career."

He laughed. To his relief, she did, too.

Matt wasn't laughing when he got home and began cleaning up his car. It was gagging work. The next day he hung a half-dozen air fresheners in his car. He also christened his car the Pukemobile.

Chapter Nine

Matt was pleasantly surprised the next evening at baseball practice when Timmy told him that his mother had had a change of heart. She had given Timmy permission to join the traveling tournament team.

"And she said she would come to every tournament," Timmy said, excitement underlining every syllable. "She said that you're off the hook. You won't have to baby-sit me at any of the tournaments."

"Well, that's great your mom changed her mind," Matt said. "It will be great for you to have her there."

Matt had been hoping that Robbyn would opt not to go on some tournament trips. He felt her presence would be awkward. But after just having met Tiffany the previous day, Timmy's announcement concerning the tournament team elicited no thoughts -- positive or negative -- about Robbyn in Matt. He was merely happy for Timmy's sake that he could play tournament ball. As for Robbyn, she had been totally eclipsed in his mind by the sumptuous Tiffany Underhill. In fact, this was the first practice all season that Matt planned on cutting short. His team was an undefeated powerhouse, he rationalized, and didn't need another lengthy practice. But the real reason was he had a date with Tiffany after practice and he couldn't wait to see her. He still was frustrated by the way their first date had ended prematurely, brought to an abrupt, disgusting halt by a cascade of vomit. Matt tried to put a sense of humor on it in his mind's eye, thinking it would have made for a funny column, but no humor could ease the sting of a lost opportunity. Matt sensed that he had missed out on a spectacular climax.

Tiffany did joke about the situation with Matt when they had spoken on the phone that morning. But Matt couldn't bring himself to, partly out of respect for her and partly because he wanted to impress her with his empathy for her plight. It was genuine empathy: He wouldn't have wished that on his worst enemy, let alone on a beautiful young woman he had just met and had lusty designs on bedding.

He was taking her to an out-of-way restaurant called Tailgaters in rural Bentwood, a place that Bronk Cassidy couldn't find even if he had a GPS stapled to his large forehead. Matt was taking no chances of having his plans interrupted. He was taking Tiffany to dinner and then to his place. He couldn't wait to explore the lush physical resources of Tiffany Underhill. But he had more than lust in mind. He truly had connected with the actress over dinner at the Nut Bar and was looking forward to spending some quiet moments with her in an intimate setting. Of course, he was hoping that some spectacular fireworks preceded those tender, quiet moments. There was something about Tiffany Underhill that made him think that she was a real keeper. Still, he had concerns that a movie star ultimately would find a newspaper columnist in Braxton to be too small of a fish. The thought that she would lose interest in him once they put a wrap on the location shoot in Braxton had crossed his mind more than a few times all day. Still, she had seemed genuine and sincere the previous night. His cynical journalistic mind harbored some doubts about the long-term scope of Tiffany's commitment to him. But he wasn't thinking with his mind as baseball practice wrapped up 30 minutes early. He was thinking with his heart, not to mention another organ farther south. He didn't even care when some of the kids complained that they still wanted to practice. And a couple of them said their parents hadn't yet arrived to pick them up.

"Well, just play catch among yourselves," Matt said, somewhat abruptly. "Or work on your cutoff throws from the outfield. You need work on them. I have an important work assignment I must get to."

Lying was out of character for him and he wasn't happy with himself that he was deceiving the very kids he had grown to truly cherish. But he wasn't *that* unhappy with himself.

Just as he was packing away the last of the baseball equipment into his car, Matt's cell phone rang. Thinking it might be Tiffany, he quickly answered it. It wasn't Tiffany. It was Cindy Loeper. A sick-sounding Cindy Loeper.

"Coach Matt," Cindy essentially groaned into the phone, "I've got a problem. I was supposed to pick up the boys, Timmy Baxter and my son Derek, after practice. But I think I'm suffering from food poisoning. I'm a mess. I can't stop throwing up."

Matt grimaced. Suddenly an epidemic of vomit seemed to be complicating his love life.

"Anyway, my husband is out of town and Robbyn is at a meeting at the Emergency Shelter," Cindy continued. "I, uh, was wondering if you could drop off the boys at the Emergency Shelter. I'd have you drop them off here, but my neighbor is running me over to the emergency room at Braxton Hospital. And Robbyn never gives the boys a key, so you can't drop them at the Baxters. Billy Baxter is staying with a friend. I really appreciate this. Robbyn can have the boys play in the daycare center at the Emergency Shelter until her meeting is over."

"Well, I've gotta ...," Matt stammered, frantically glancing at his watch.

Before Matt could finish his sentence, he heard Cindy quickly say "Thanks" and hang up.

"Man, I'm screwed," Matt said to himself.

He and Tiffany had dinner reservations at Tailgaters in 45 minutes. And he still had to go home, shower and change; pick up Tiffany at her hotel suite in Providence, which was about 10 minutes from his home in Sorbonne Township; and then get to Tailgaters, which was a good 20-25 minutes from the Homewood Suites. Now with a detour to the Emergency Shelter, there was no way he would make it in time unless he drove 120 miles per hour and took a 15-second shower.

"Timmy Baxter and Derek Loeper," he yelled out. "You guys are leaving with me. Now! I gotta run. I've got a meeting I can't miss."

"We were gonna work on our double-play combination for a few minutes," Derek complained.

"Not tonight, son!" Matt said with gusto.

"Well, all right," said Timmy, ever the good soldier.

Matt did some quick calculating about directions and time management as he pulled out of the parking lot. He figured it would be quicker if he took the boys home with him while he showered and changed; picked up Tiffany and then dropped the kids off at the Shelter and proceeded to Bentwood. Direction-wise, it was the logical way to go. But he felt funny having the boys meet Tiffany, especially Timmy. He didn't know why, but he didn't want Timmy knowing about Tiffany because he didn't want Robbyn to know. Of course, he ran the risk of running into Robbyn at the Shelter, running into her with Tiffany and the boys. But he was planning on just dropping them off at the door. Still, he wrestled with his conscience: Was that the right way to proceed? He needed another voice to soothe his conscience. As he drove to his house, he called Tiffany and explained the situation. Tiffany was perfectly understanding and couldn't have been nicer about the situation.

"We can skip the restaurant and get takeout with the boys," Tiffany said. "It would be fun having pizza and soda with them, then you can drop them off at the one boy's home. No need to interrupt his mother during her meeting.

And after you drop the boys off, we finally can be alone. I can't wait to be alone with you."

Matt certainly didn't want to have pizza with the boys and Tiffany at his house. He wanted a more intimate meal with Tiffany in a more romantic setting. But he admired her response. It reinforced to him that this wasn't some self-centered, superficial, selfish actress.

"I can't wait either," Matt said to Tiffany, purposely being generic because the boys were in the back seat. Of course, they weren't even paying attention to him, but he was a bit paranoid. "Pizza at my place it is. We'll swing by and pick you up. Then you can entertain the boys at my house while I shower and change."

"Do you mind if I just wear jeans and a T-shirt? I'm sick of dressing up," Tiffany said.

"You look great in anything," Matt said, softly. "Besides, pizza is casual dining."

As Matt and the boys pulled into the parking lot at the Homewood Suites, Tiffany already was standing outside, waiting for them.

"Your girlfriend is, uh, is gorgeous," stammered Derek Loeper, his young hormones stirring.

"Yeah, check her out," Timmy agreed. "Coach Matt, how did you meet her?"

"On the job," Matt said, laughing. "I'm writing a column about her. She is an actress. They're shooting a movie in town."

"Cool," Derek said excitedly. "A movie star!"

"It's not every kid who gets to eat pizza with a movie star," Matt said, again laughing.

"Wait until I tell Mom," Timmy blurted out. "She won't believe it."

For some reason, Matt felt himself wince at Timmy's words. But he had no time to reflect upon his reaction. Tiffany, filling out a pair of jeans and a designer T-shirt in such a lovely manner as to arouse the fantasies of males ages 10-100, had just slid beside him in the front seat.

"Hi, boys!" she said in a disarming, friendly voice that melted their hearts and put them at ease in two simply delicious words.

"This is Miss Underhill," Matt said to the boys.

Tiffany slapped him on the shoulder.

"Knock off the stuffy protocol," Tiffany laughed. "Miss Underhill sounds like I'm one of their teachers." She turned around and shook hands with both boys -- boys with eyes looking like fried eggs -- and said: "Call me Tiffany. And what are your names?"

After both boys simply uttered their names in bewildered fashion, Tiffany asked: "And what kind of pizza do you guys like? I like it with pepperoni."

"I love pepperoni!" Derek said.

You got the impression that Tiffany could have said she loved pizza with chocolate-covered roaches and Derek would have given it an exuberant endorsement.

"So do I," said Timmy, quickly falling in lockstep.

"Well, I'll complete the grand slam," Matt said, winking. "Speaking of baseball, Tiffany, these guys are my shortstop and second baseman. They're good ballplayers and good kids."

"Well, I'm so impressed," Tiffany said. "I have to confess that football is my favorite sport. I used to be a cheerleader in high school. But I like baseball. My first boyfriend was our school's star pitcher."

"Lucky guy!" Derek squealed, then suddenly blushed when he realized that his voice was an octave or two higher than normal.

"So he made a pitch for you, a pitch for love, eh?" Matt said, giggling through every word.

"Funny guy," Tiffany said, slapping him again.

"Well, we're here," Matt said, pulling into his driveway.

Matt lived in the Laurel Park section of Sorbonne Township, a sprawling residential/commercial suburb west of Braxton. It was a beautiful four-bedroom colonial, with a large family room and a large deck that made for great parties inside and out. He also had eye-popping landscaping that was the envy of his neighbors.

"Your home and your shrubbery are gorgeous," Tiffany said, surveying the place as she got out of the car. "Are you sure you're not married? I can't believe a single man about town like you doesn't live in a townhouse. Where do you find the time to take care of this place?"

"Actually, I don't get around town as much as you think," he said, ushering them all into his home. "I get up early every morning, work out, and then putter around my yard and my house. I love decorating and landscaping. It relaxes me. And it gives me a creative satisfaction that's different from creative writing."

"This is beautiful," Tiffany said as she checked out the living room, family room, dining room and kitchen. "Your colors and designs are simply lush. I am so impressed."

More so than the boys, who only seemed enamored with Matt's 60-inch TV screen in his family room.

"Can we watch TV until the pizza comes?" Derek yelled into the dining room, where Matt and Tiffany were examining his glassware collection in the hutch.

"Absolutely," Matt said, bounding into the family room. "Let me turn it on. The Phillies are playing the Braves tonight."

Tiffany followed along, looking out the family room's French doors, which opened onto the largest wooden deck she had ever seen.

"You could throw a Hollywood bash on that deck," Tiffany said, laughing. "And you have a pool, too!"

"A pool," yelped Timmy. "Cool. Can we use it?"

"We don't have swim trunks," Derek said somberly.

"You can use the pool next time," Matt said. "I'm going to have a team party here after the season. I'm inviting all the boys and their parents."

"That's so nice of you," Tiffany said, impressed that a bachelor like Matt could be so domestic and so into kids.

She was finding out that there was a lot to like about Matt Meredith besides his good looks, his charm and his sense of humor.

A lot more.

"Well, I'm going up to shower and change," Matt said. "It won't be long. It better not be. I called for the pizza with pepperoni. It should be here in 15 minutes or so. Help yourself to some soda. There's Coke and root beer in the fridge."

With that, he sprinted upstairs.

Tiffany served the boys some soda and the three of them sat in the family room while the Phillies played the Braves.

"My mom probably won't come to the team party," Timmy said, sadly, looking at Tiffany. "I don't think she likes Coach Matt."

"Why is that?" Tiffany said, her curiosity getting the best of her.

"I'm not sure," Timmy said. "I don't think she likes men ever since my dad died."

"Oh, I'm so sorry," Tiffany said, patting Timmy on the shoulder. "I'm sure you had a great dad."

Before Timmy could answer, Derek blurted out: "My mom thinks Coach Matt is a dreamboat. That's what she calls him, 'Coach Dreamboat.' Isn't that silly? I heard her telling Timmy's mom that he's a real catch. But to me, he's just our baseball coach." "Really?" Timmy asked, his mood suddenly brightening.

But then his mood ramped down a notch. "But now Coach has a girlfriend."

He looked at Tiffany with sad, hound-dog eyes.

"Well, I'm not really his girlfriend, just a friend he just met," Tiffany said. "You really like Matt, don't you, Timmy?"

"He's the best coach I ever had," Timmy said. "And he's a cool guy. He's not like other coaches."

"All the guys think he's great," Derek said. "But since we're undefeated, nobody is bitching."

He almost bit his lip.

"Uh, I'm sorry," he said, recovering. "I mean complaining."

Tiffany laughed again. The boys resumed watching the game while she sat in silence for a few moments, thinking that if Matt made a pitch for her, she surely would make the catch. But she did have some fleeting thoughts of how she could reconcile a relationship with a columnist in Braxton with her busy, global lifestyle. Surely, there would be severe logistical challenges to sustaining a relationship, she thought. But at this particular point in time, logic wasn't part of the equation. She wanted to have a fun pizza party with the boys, drop them off, and spend some serious time alone with a man who in a brief slice of time had cast a spell of enchantment over her heart.

Her quiet, warm thoughts came to an abrupt halt when Derek spilled his Coke on Matt's white rug. Almost simultaneously, the doorbell rang: It was the pizza delivery man.

"Derek, quickly look for some napkins in the kitchen and sop up the soda," Tiffany said calmly. "I'll get the door. It must be the pizza."

Frazzled, Derek scampered away in search for napkins. Tiffany headed for the front door. Before she could answer it, Matt, wearing stylish shorts, sandals and a golf shirt, bounded down the steps and yelled: "I got it. This pizza is on me."

"OK, you're the last of the big spenders," Tiffany said. "You get the pizza. Derek spilled some soda on your rug. I'll help him clean it up."

"There's a sponge on the kitchen sink," Matt said, calmly -- once again impressing Tiffany. She was all too familiar with how minor domestic disturbances used to send her father into a rage. "Just wet it and try to sponge it up before it stains the carpet. Now I know why I never had kids. They're house-wreckers." Matt's grin was wide and inviting. Tiffany would have kissed him right then if Matt hadn't just opened the door to the pizza delivery man.

Tiffany and Derek cleaned up the soda before it left a lasting residue. And the four of them had a delightful pizza party on the deck, talking baseball, school and generalities. Matt was totally impressed with how great Tiffany was with the boys. And vice versa. Tiffany imagined that Matt would be the most wonderful father.

"Look at the time," Matt said, looking at his watch. "It's almost 8. Timmy, you had better call your mom. See if she's home yet and we'll drop you off. Derek, we'll take you there as well, just in case your mom isn't home from the hospital yet or not feeling all that well."

Robbyn was quite upset when Timmy called her.

"I'm out of my mind with fear," she yelled into the phone. "I had no idea where you guys were. I was scared sick. Thank God you're all right. Why didn't you leave a message on my phone? Mrs. Loeper isn't home. You guys were supposed to be there!"

"I know, Mom," Timmy said, trying to calm her. "But Mrs. Loeper got sick and asked Coach Matt to watch us. He didn't want to disturb you at your meeting. We had fun. We had pizza and soda with Coach and his girlfriend. You should see her! She's a movie star! Real pretty. And nice. She seemed surprised when I told her that I didn't think you liked Coach Matt. Please, when he has his party, you'll come, won't you?"

Robbyn was beside herself. Still a nervous wreck about not knowing where Timmy and Derek or Cindy were, she was profoundly embarrassed about what Timmy must have said to Matt's girlfriend. *What girlfriend?* Why did the thought of him having a girlfriend bother her so? And a movie star? He must be a skirt-chaser! How many guys from Braxton have a movie star for a girlfriend? And what party was Timmy talking about? A million questions and thoughts pinballed through her mind in a matter of microseconds.

"What party?" Robbyn asked, not knowing what else to say.

"The team party," Timmy said. "All the guys will be here. And their parents. Coach has a big pool."

Robbyn was reeling. She knew she had to talk to Matt and thank him and ask him for directions to his home so she could pick up the boys. She knew she had to compose herself but was afraid she couldn't. What in the hell was there about Matt Meredith that made her feel like such a fool in his presence. And now she wasn't even with him and she felt like an idiot. She felt like a tongue-tied junior high girl.

Somehow, she found the strength to calm down, at least a little bit.

"Coach, my mom wants to talk to you," Timmy yelled to Matt.

Robbyn Baxter was the last person that Matt wanted to talk to at that point. Timmy had quickly told him that his mom was upset over not knowing where he and Derek were. Compounding matters, Robbyn always gave Matt uncomfortable vibes. Vibes that were made worse by Tiffany's presence in his house. Strange, he thought to himself. What *is* it about this woman? But he just wanted to appease her, to get the kids back to her, and be alone with Tiffany. He refused to admit to himself that he still harbored some feelings of attraction for Robbyn, even with the spectacular Tiffany Underhill in his life.

"Hello, Mrs. Baxter," Matt said, trying to sound calm himself. "Let me apologize. I should have had Timmy leave you a voicemail. You must have been terribly worried when you got home. Cindy Loeper thinks she got food poisoning and asked me to take the boys to the Emergency Shelter meeting you were attending. But I didn't want to bother you."

There was silence on the line for a few awkward moments of agony for both Matt and Robbyn.

Finally, Robbyn, her voice quavering slightly, said softly and simply, with an air of detachment that Matt found quite surprising considering the content of her words:

"I'm the one who needs to apologize. You have been wonderful to Timmy as a coach. But you've been much more than that to him. You've been like a second father to him. Frankly, I've had mixed emotions about that. On the one hand, I've been thrilled that you're in his life. I've tried to be a mother and a father to him, but that's really not possible. On the other hand, I, uh, sort of have resented having you in his, in our, lives. I still miss my husband dearly, and, uh, I guess, well, I think of him as irreplaceable. I wanted *him* to be there for the boys as they grew up. So even though you've been marvelous, part of me feels as if you have been an intrusion."

She paused for what seemed like an eternity.

"I know you must think I'm crazy and I can't expect you to understand. Because I don't understand. I can't even understand why I'm telling you this. Especially on the phone. I guess because I don't have the courage to tell you this in person. But I will. Please don't think I'm crazy. But there is something about you, even though I don't really know you, that makes me feel goofy inside. My emotions are a mess when I'm -- oh, God -- near you. I haven't felt this way about anyone in years. Since I was first dating my husband. You see ... I consider myself married to my late husband for eternity. But it is so tempting ... oh, I can't finish it!"

Of course, she stopped at the very worst time for Matt, who couldn't believe but yet somehow could believe what he was hearing. He had had some psychic connection with Robbyn himself and somehow sensed they might be destined for each other. Now he found himself sitting on a chair in his living room, with Timmy and Tiffany walking into the room, wondering what was taking him so long and why he was sitting on the phone without talking.

"Is everything all right?" Tiffany asked, concerned.

Matt hated to lie to her, feeling that he was betraying her in favor of Robbyn.

"Oh, yes," he said, trying to act casual. "She was just called away for a couple moments. Something on the stove apparently was boiling over."

"Why don't we just take the boys to her house now that she's home?" Tiffany asked.

"Well, because she insists that she pick up the boys here; she doesn't want to further inconvenience us. I told her it was no bother. I told her we had a great time. But she insisted I give her directions to our house."

Robbyn, of course, could hear everything Matt had said because he purposely hadn't covered the phone.

"Thank you for lying for me," Robbyn said softly, hoping that nobody but Matt could hear her. "We need to talk soon. But please. I'm so shaken, I can't drive. So pretend you're convincing me to let you drop off the boys."

Matt acted so well, one would have thought he had taken lessons from Tiffany's acting coach. Neither Timmy nor Tiffany had any inkling about what a strange, awkward conversation Robbyn had just had with Matt.

"You drop the boys off and I'll stick around here and tidy up a bit," Tiffany said, winking.

"You got a date," Matt said, perking up.

But he thought his voice sounded a tad hollow. If it did, Tiffany hadn't noticed. She cheerfully hugged the boys goodbye and gave Matt a playful hug, too, before they drove away.

Fortunately for Matt, the boys were bantering with each other in the back seat and paying him no mind as he drove them to Robbyn's house. Because Matt was distracted and a little perplexed by what he had just heard from Robbyn. He had sensed that Robbyn had found him enticing. And he had been so attracted to her. But then he thought she was weird. Now, he realized she wasn't; she was just a conflicted widow. Perfectly understandable. And her words "you've been like a second father to him" rang in his head. But now Tiffany had entered his life, and she seemed spectacular in every regard. Plus, she seemed not to carry any emotional baggage, unlike the heavy burden weighing on Robbyn.

When Matt arrived at Robbyn's house, she was standing in the driveway waiting for them. As Matt pulled up, he could see that she was wearing a sheepish grin.

The boys piled out of the car and zipped into the house while Timmy shouted an enthusiastic "Hi, Mom!" that was punctuated by a wave to his mother, Robbyn walked up to the driver's side of Matt's car and semi-leaned into the open window.

She reached out and put a hand on Matt's left shoulder. He could see the emotion etched on her face. He felt drawn to her, but not in a full-blown romantic way. Tiffany Underhill had cooled his jets as far as Robbyn was concerned. Still, he couldn't deny that he was flattered by Robbyn's apparent interest in him. But he had essentially moved on in his heart and mind and had no intention of establishing a relationship with Robbyn. Nevertheless, he was intrigued by what Robbyn found so tempting about him.

"You must think me such a fool," Robbyn said, forcing a hollow laugh. "Forgive me. I'm not really nuts."

Matt let out a genuine laugh, which Robbyn echoed.

"Actually, I understand," Matt said. "No need to apologize. I think you're a special person to have done such a wonderful job with your two boys."

"I get tired of being just a mother," Robbyn said, gripping his shoulder. "I hate myself for thinking that way at times. I hate myself because even though I miss my husband dearly, there are, uh, times, when I admit to needing a relationship again, to be involved with someone. And I surprised myself by realizing that someone might be you. Do you have time for a cup of coffee?"

She leaned over and kissed him ever so gently, so ever so tenderly on the forehead.

Matt felt light-headed, not from passion but from sheer shock.

"I," he said, pausing to think. "I would love to. But I have somebody expecting me. Maybe some other time."

"Is your girlfriend waiting for you?" Robbyn asked, resting a hand on his shoulder.

"Actually, I don't have a girlfriend," Matt said. "But I have just started seeing someone who could be my girlfriend."

Robbyn smiled and said: "Who said timing is everything? Well, I'll guess I have to be content with being the eternal widow. I was content with that until you showed up. But I'll tell you this: I believe in destiny. There is something about you. And something, I believe, about you and me. Maybe we're just destined to be friends. Maybe more, maybe much more. But I do know that I, and my boys, need to be at least your friend."

A tear trickled down her left cheek. Matt welled up, put her hands in his, and said: "Robbyn, you caught my eye from the first time I saw you. But you seemed so distant, even hostile. Now, I've met someone else, someone whom I really like. And unlike some of the rumors about me, I only get involved with one woman at a time."

Robbyn, to even her utter shock, let alone Matt's, leaned over again and kissed Matt hungrily on the lips. Without inserting her tongue in his mouth, it was a first kiss so fabulous that they both could feel the air around them suddenly grow still and sweet.

She then stepped back from the car and a stunned Matt could see the strong sensuality boiling inside her through the windows of her gorgeous eyes.

Matt was dizzy with confusing thoughts. In the midst of his fog, he saw Robbyn run back through the fog to her driveway and semi-shout: "Thanks for letting Timmy play shortstop. You've made his dream come true. Next time maybe you'll make my dream come true, too."

Robbyn said one more thing that would stick with him as if the words had come attached with adhesive to his soul: "When it comes to the next time, let that woman be me," she said provocatively. "I promise you that it will be the last time you'll ever need to change women."

Matt couldn't believe his ears. He wasn't sure if she had even said it. He literally pinched himself to see if he was dreaming. The whole thing seemed so surreal. Actually, downright unreal. He began driving home, driving back to Tiffany. He began to rationalize the whole interlude with Robbyn. "Her maternal instincts simply made her feel grateful," he said aloud.

He tried to put her out of his mind and focus on the upcoming evening with Tiffany. It was a focus that wasn't too difficult to regain. Tiffany had that effect on him. But his focus wasn't 100 percent on her. Down deep he knew there would be times when he would go to bed that images of Robbyn Baxter would be playing on the back of his eyelids. But for now, he had no time to reflect on Robbyn's bizarre behavior toward him. For now, as he pulled into his driveway, he had the luscious Tiffany Underhill playing on the front of his eyelids.

When Matt walked into his living room, Tiffany was watching television. She arose, skipped over to him, and playfully poked him in the ribs.

"What was that for?" he asked, wondering what was up.

"I saw a commercial on the local news promoting your column on me that's running in the *Braxton Bugle* on Sunday," she said, a teasing lilt to her voice. "How about a sneak preview? If it's flattering, perhaps I could be persuaded to be quite friendly to the author of that column tonight."

Matt flashed her a mischievous grin.

"You know I never show any of my column subjects an advance look at my columns," Matt said. But then he smiled and added with a laugh: "But I think I could be persuaded in your case. After all, my journalistic ethics are no match for your enticing charms."

"I appreciate that," Tiffany said. "But I was just teasing you, testing you to see what your answer would be. I never, ever read about myself. It's boring. Although I must say that I am curious what you might write about me. Perhaps I shouldn't give you any X-rated material before your column on me runs."

"That's not physically possible," Matt said, grabbing her close. "I couldn't possibly wait until Sunday to do this."

He kissed her tenderly, gradually increasing the fervor. Sometimes first kisses can be awkward. Not this one: Matt and Tiffany had a kissing compatibility that romance novels were made for. Their inner embers were ignited by the flames of sexual abandon. Their foreplay was epic in scope as they cascaded together in a torrent of kissing, fondling, rubbing and sucking that had their souls bursting through their skin. Even iron has a melting point, but Matt wasn't quite ready to forge ahead.He didn't penetrate her right then and there on the living room carpet. Instead, he paused for a few special moments that were ripe with lustful expectancy and gazed into her eyes.

"I have never wanted anyone so badly in my life," he said, his voice husky. "I've been waiting for someone like you my whole life. And I'll be damn if the first time that we make love is going to be on the floor. It's a privilege to be here with you, sharing our bodies. If I'm going to bed you, damn it, it's gonna be in bed!"

His voice dramatically rose in volume during his last few words. And as he said them, he lifted her up and began carrying her upstairs to his room.

"You're so gallant," Tiffany said, smiling dreamily. "Nice touch. But hurry up. I appreciate the romance mixed in with the passion. You know how to treat a girl."

"God, you're beautiful and sexy," Matt said, softly.

"Shut up and get me to your bed," Tiffany said, erupting in laughter. "I can't wait for you to screw my brains out."

Matt laughed, too.

"If I had said that, you'd think I was a pig," he said.

"Maybe not," she laughed. She then saw all the laundry on Matt's bed.

"Maybe you are a pig," she laughed.

"It's not DIRTY laundry," he said, dropping her into the pile of clothes.

She playfully tossed some of his boxer shorts at him while Matt pushed the rest of the clothes onto the floor.

"So much for my Prince Charming," she giggled.

She didn't giggle long. Passion supplanted humor and they commenced on their mutual journey to sublime sexual satisfaction.

When their urges had been spent, they cuddled for seemingly an eternity, whispering and touching body parts as well as hearts.

“I think I could be persuaded to fall in love with you,” Tiffany said sweetly, stroking Matt’s hair.

She then dramatically shifted gears, her playful side bubbling up deliciously.

“Of course, even if I didn’t love you, I’d let you fuck me,” she said. “And I never say fuck. But then, I’ve never been fucked like this.”

“I meet the girl of my dreams and she has a bad case of potty mouth," Matt fired back, laughing.

Meanwhile, Robbyn Baxter literally had potty mouth. Her head was in her bathroom toilet. Overcome by nausea and emotion, her stomach wouldn’t stop churning until she vomited. But she was more than just sick to her stomach. She was heartsick. On the one hand, she had the sickening feeling that she had somehow committed psychological adultery to the memory of her husband by blatantly professing her feelings to Matt. On the other hand, she felt sick because she sensed that her timing had betrayed her. Matt had found another, she had found out to her horror, and she feared that she had squandered her opportunity to establish a relationship with him. She feared that she had waited too long to spill her guts to him.

It was hard to tell who had moaned more that night -- Robbyn or Tiffany.

Chapter Ten

Tiffany and Matt were inseparable when she wasn't on the set and when he wasn't writing a column or coaching baseball. They found they loved each other's company immensely -- whether it was talking, making love, laughing, playing tennis and golf, going out to dinner and just plain hanging out.

Of course, sometimes they got to combine pleasure with work. Tiffany had just loved Matt's column about her, finding it flattering but also insightful in analyzing her film career and the possible ramifications of "Drug Town" on the Braxton and Miller County community. So, she was very happy to appear with Matt as his only guest on his cable television show.

"Now, don't act too gushy towards me and ask me softball questions," Tiffany teased him as they drove over to the television studios.

"How about some penetrating questions about your sex life?" Matt teased. "Like do you prefer being on top or bottom?"

"Stop that," Tiffany yelped, playfully smacking Matt's shoulder.

"Do you want me to have an accident," Matt said. "It would look somewhat suspicious if we both walked onto the set with cuts and bruises."

"We'll just say on the air that we just had a kinky, rough sexual encounter," Tiffany joked.

"Very funny," Matt said, exuding the satisfied look of someone whom had just had a very fulfilling lovemaking session. Which he and Tiffany had just enjoyed.

"I hope we don't have a post-coital glow on camera," Tiffany said, giggling. "Oh, well. The makeup will hide it."

Matt laughed.

"What makeup?" Matt said, grinning. "They don't have makeup."

"I must be the only actress in the world who would go on camera without studio makeup," Tiffany said. "The things I do for you."

"You know I'd do anything in the world for you," Matt said, his tone turning serious as he pulled into a parking spot at the studio.

"Good," Tiffany said. "Take me out to dinner after the show. And tell me that you love me."

"I love you," Matt said. "You know I do. I love you so much that I'm afraid that somehow I'm going to lose you. That this is too good to be true, too good to last. Even too good to be real. I feel like pinching myself. This seems like a fantasy to me ... being in love with a beautiful lady who is such a beautiful woman on the inside."

"That's absolutely beautiful," Tiffany said, tearing up. "And I feel absolutely the same way about you. You're a dream come true. You're gorgeous, so talented, so much fun, and so self-assured. You're not intimidated at all by what I look like or who I am. And that's important, because I'm NOT what I do for a living or what I look like. I'm just me -- and you connect with that me."

"Ditto," Matt said softly, leaning over to kiss her. "Now dab your eyes. It's time for the Matt Meredith Show. And tonight, we have a very special guest."

The show was a lively 30 minutes. Matt asked a lot of questions about the movie's impact on Braxton and Tiffany gave serious answers. But there also were frequent light-hearted moments when Matt contrasted the glamor of Hollywood with the grit of Braxton.

Their banter and their dialogue were entertaining and provocative. They had a chemistry that was apparent to the viewing audience.

Robbyn Baxter was part of that viewing audience. She watched the show with rapt attention. She could tell by just how Matt and Tiffany looked at one other that they were in love. Robbyn had come to grips with the fact that she had spilled her guts to Matt about her attraction toward him. And she was beginning to come to grips with the fact that her husband had passed on and it was time to move on with her life -- for her sake and for the sake of her children. She was even comfortable with the thought of being friendly and acting like nothing had happened when she next bumped into Matt at the next baseball game. Until now, she had avoided seeing him as she sorted things out in the cluttered corners of her mind. But now she knew she just had to be herself in front of him. She still held out hope that she could still have him for her very own someday. But that hope was flickering as she watched Matt and Tiffany on screen. Her only hope, she thought as they rolled the show's closing credits, was that Matt was just a fling for Tiffany and when she went back to Tinseltown, Matt would wind up with a real Braxton girl like herself.

Indeed, Robbyn was quite friendly and relaxed when she spoke to Matt after the next game, a game in which Timmy pitched a two-hit shutout and hit a pair of homers.

Robbyn never mentioned her "true confession" that night in her driveway, and neither did Matt. He was cordial as well, and he couldn't help but notice that Robbyn was wearing a cute jumper instead of her usual game attire of baggy shorts and a plain blouse. Their topic of conversation centered on Timmy's first tournament weekend.

"Do you have directions to Fort Dix, New Jersey and the hotel information?" Robbyn asked, smiling.

"Yes, I do," Matt said. He ruffled through some papers in his briefcase. Ruffling through his mind, however, were remembrances of what Robbyn had said to him that night. He had to admit he found her very attractive. And he was intrigued by her sudden friendliness. He absolutely knew what his reaction toward her would have been if he hadn't met Tiffany in the interim. He was flattered by Robbyn's feelings, flattery that was enhanced because he thought so much of Timmy and Billy. And he no longer considered her to be a head case. He realized now that Robbyn was just being someone who loved her husband so much that she couldn't even let go after his death.

"Here's all the information," Matt said, handing Robbyn a packet with details on the league traveling team weekend. "We're having a team dinner at the motel at 7 p.m. Friday. Our first game is 10 a.m. Saturday."

"I'm bringing Billy along with me," she said. "Can he eat with the team and the parents on Friday night?"

"Of course," Matt replied. He paused for a moment and really didn't know if there was any motivation behind his ensuing comment other than a coach extending a friendly invitation to a team mother.

"In fact, you guys can sit me with me at dinner," Matt said.

"That would be nice," Robbyn said, "because I don't think I know many parents who have boys on the traveling team."

"You'll get to know them," Matt said, cheerfully. "In the meantime, you can hang out with me."

He smiled.

"It should be fun," she said.

Matt then was interrupted by one of the other team mothers who had a complaint about her son's perceived lack of playing time. While he was delicately handling that, he noticed that Robbyn drifted away. But before she was totally out of sight, he caught her glancing back at him. He felt a twinge in his heart. And immediately and quietly cursed himself for feeling that way. He felt as if he had betrayed Tiffany. He had never been unfaithful to any woman he was in a relationship with. And since he found Tiffany so utterly spectacular, he absolutely had no intention of ever betraying her. But he had to admit that there was something special about Robbyn. So, he vowed right then and there that he strictly would be a coach in his relationship with Robbyn.

Meanwhile, Robbyn was quiet as she drove Timmy and Billy home after the game. She, too, had just made a vow to herself: A vow that she would not make a play for Matt. She wasn't that type of girl. Instead, she would just be friendly and just be Timmy's mother. If Matt eventually broke up with the actress, then she would be more aggressive. If he didn't, well, she would be content being with her boys. Although she finally and wrenchingly had come to grips with the fact that she didn't have to remain a widow forever, she wasn't going to rush into a relationship for the sake of being in a relationship. The only reason she had even thought about any of this was because she had found Matt to be someone she envisioned would be a perfect fit for her and her boys. If there was no Matt, there would be no other man in her life.

It was as simple as that.

She dropped the boys off at home and decided to go to the grocery store. The boys were big eaters and she always was running out of something. She hated food shopping and tried to zip through the process as quickly as possible. She knew what she wanted, and she spent little time browsing. She would fly up and down the aisles, grabbing her preordained items and tossing them into her cart. Considering that she always was in a perpetual fight against the clock in trying to balance her professional and domestic duties, this was an approach that was effective in making up for lost time. But suddenly, time stood still for Robbyn as, in her haste, her shopping cart collided with the shopping cart of one Tiffany Underhill.

Of course, Tiffany didn't know who Robbyn was. But Robbyn obviously knew who Tiffany was. And Robbyn was taken by how beautiful and slim Tiffany was up close and personal. And Tiffany appeared to be wearing little, if any makeup. And she simply was wearing a pair of form-fitting jeans and a tight *Braxton Bugle* T-shirt that accentuated her bust.

"Oh, uh, I'm so, uh, sorry," Robbyn stammered, mortified. She found herself intimidated, and her embarrassment over the colliding carts didn't help her lack of composure.

"No big deal," Tiffany said calmly, trying to put the frazzled Robbyn at ease. "These shopping carts should come equipped with bumpers."

"Aren't you the actress who's filming a movie here in Braxton?" Robbyn said almost too loudly.

"I am," Tiffany said, adding with a laugh: "But don't tell everybody. I don't like any fuss."

"I'm sorry," Robbyn said. "I, I guess I didn't expect someone like you to food shop."

"Well, even actresses have to eat," Tiffany laughed. "Of course, not too much. The camera puts 10 pounds on you."

"I guess I imagined you would have somebody food shop for you," Robbyn replied.

"Some stars with attitudes do that. Or stars who get mobbed in public," Tiffany said. "But a lot of times people don't recognize me. So I do go out in public. And I can't stand having people wait on me. I like to do things for myself."

Robbyn could tell that Tiffany was an actress who wasn't tripping over her own ego. There was something about her that was instantly likeable. But there was something in Robbyn's heart that didn't want her to like Tiffany, especially when she heard her say: "I'm just picking up a few things because I'm cooking dinner for my boyfriend tonight. And I'm not a very good cook. I hope I don't poison him."

Robbyn was hoping that Tiffany was such a lousy cook that Matt would leave her. But Robbyn certainly didn't want Matt poisoned. For a moment, Robbyn thought it would be fitting justice if Tiffany got food poisoning from her own cooking. Robbyn immediately hated herself for thinking that. She normally wasn't that catty.

"You won't believe this, but I know your boyfriend," Robbyn said, recovering her composure and enjoying being able to say that.

"How?" asked a shocked Tiffany.

She and Matt hadn't told anyone about their relationship, although they hadn't tried to hide it either. They had been in several different restaurants in the area.

"My boy plays for Matt's baseball team," Robbyn said cheerfully. "In fact, he was at Matt's house one night when you were there. My son told me he had met a beautiful actress who had helped clean up the Coke his friend spilled on Matt's carpet."

"Is your son Timmy, the star shortstop?" Tiffany asked, feeling less stunned.

"Yes," Robbyn said, proudly.

"He's a wonderful boy," Tiffany said. "You must be so proud. Matt adores him. He said not only is Timmy a great ballplayer, but more importantly, he's a great kid. He said if he ever has a son, he wants him to be a clone of Timmy's."

"Well, that's certainly flattering," Robbyn said, beaming.

"I can't wait to see the team play," Tiffany said, brightly. "I have this weekend off, so Matt is taking me along to the tournament games in New Jersey."

Robbyn's heart sank to at least her knees, knees that suddenly felt shaky.

"Timmy, uh, is on that team," Robbyn said quietly.

Tiffany noticed the abrupt change in Robbyn's demeanor, but simply said: "Well, I'll see you then. It should be fun."

Robbyn, who thought she had no designs of interfering in Matt's relationship with Tiffany, found herself profoundly disappointed that Tiffany would be at the tournament games.

She somehow felt that Tiffany was invading her turf, her world. And her chance to be out of town for a weekend with Matt.

As for Tiffany, she thought Robbyn to be a bit odd, but didn't dwell on her. She was anxious to cook a good meal for Matt.

As Tiffany and Matt were finishing their dinner that night, Matt said for -- the fifth time -- what a feast it had been. Tiffany sensed that Matt was being too generous in his praise of her culinary skills and was trying to placate her.

"You're just sucking up to me because you want to mess around after dinner, aren't you?" she asked, a devilish look in her eye. "After all, how good can sausage, lima beans and home fries be?"

"No, not me," Matt said, smilingly. "And just to prove my sincerity, let me clean up the dishes."

"We'll do it together," Tiffany replied, rising to clear the table.

As they rinsed the dishes and put them in Matt's dishwasher, Matt started talking about that weekend's tournament games and how anxious he was to see how well his team performed.

"By the way, I ran into Timmy's mother at the food store," Tiffany said casually. "She was quite friendly, but then seemed withdrawn when I mentioned that I was going along with you to the tournament. What's up with that?"

She then smiled and added: "There's nothing going on between you two, is there?"

Matt didn't want to lie to Tiffany. But he didn't really want to tell her the complete truth either. Still, if pressed, he decided that he would be candid. He didn't want to jeopardize anything with Tiffany, but he had always prided himself with being straight with people, especially with those he was involved with.

"I noticed that she has been, uh, somewhat awkward in my presence," Matt said. "It was somewhat uncomfortable, to say the least. But she's been better. To be honest, I think she was attracted to me, but had some personal issues complicating her emotions. She's been a widow for a few years, and evidently hasn't come to grips with seeking a new relationship."

"How do you know all that, Dr. Freud?" Tiffany asked, obviously curious.

Matt paused to clear his throat.

"Because she eventually told me," he said. "She did so when she apologized for her strained behavior. I told her I had a girlfriend and she seemed fine with it."

"Are you attracted to her?" Tiffany asked.

"She's cute, and to be totally honest, I was attracted to her," Matt said calmly. "But I sensed she was a little weird. I didn't know at the time she was wrestling with the memory of her late husband. But then I met you and suddenly Mrs. Baxter wasn't that attractive to me."

Matt laughed, but he knew deep down that there was some shading to his definition of attractiveness. Yes, Robbyn wasn't quite as attractive to him as she had been before he met Tiffany. Still, he was very attracted to her -- and if Tiffany somehow suddenly morphed into a Hollywood goddess and split permanently for the trappings of Tinseltown, Matt could see himself in a relationship with Robbyn. But that thought was not something he obviously cared to share with Tiffany. Besides, if Tiffany remained as sweet and loving and available once her filming in Braxton wrapped up, he saw no reason to even casually entertain the thought of a relationship with Robbyn.

"Are you sure?" Tiffany said, feeling more secure. For a few moments, she had felt a tad insecure in their relationship, a feeling essentially foreign to her. When you looked like her, hanging onto a man seldom was a problem. Her problem had been meeting a man that she wanted to hang around for a while. She thought she had met that man in Matt. And when she found out that Robbyn was interested in Matt, it made her a bit jealous, another emotion that hadn't been part of her nature. She took that as a sign that she truly loved Matt, and she felt comfortable and secure with his answer.

"Damn right I am," Matt said, grabbing her with gusto despite still have a plate in his left hand. He then gave her a kiss powerful enough to suck her soul into his. Any thoughts of Robbyn Baxter that were residing in both their minds were sucked away with the intensity of their kiss.

But what that kiss couldn't suck away was the reality that as sweet and loving and grounded as Tiffany could be, she remained a woman with a strong self-focus ... a good person, who nevertheless, always wound up being all about herself. It was a trait that had been amply stitched in her throughout her life, a trait that she was in denial about and a trait that had derailed most of her prior relationships.

Chapter Eleven

As Matt and Tiffany pulled into the parking lot of their hotel in Fort Dix, Matt noticed a paneled truck with signage that read "Hello Hollywood!" on both sides and immediately he turned to Tiffany.

"Word must have gotten out that you were coming here. Because I'm sure as hell they didn't come here to see me or the tournament kids," he said, somewhat irritated.

"I had to tell the production people on the set where I would be just in case something came up," Tiffany said, somewhat defensively. "I bet somebody in the studio PR department tipped off 'Hello Hollywood!' in the hope they could generate some publicity for the movie."

"Yeah, big-time Hollywood actress suddenly becomes die-hard Little League fan while screwing one of the tournament coaches," Matt said, not hiding the sarcasm.

"Don't blame me," Tiffany said. "I didn't cause this. Listen, you are part of the media. Reporters always are fishing for a story."

"I'm not part of that tabloid junk," Matt interrupted, while parking the car as far away from the TV truck as possible.

"I wasn't suggesting that you are," Tiffany said, not losing her cool. "It's just, well, if you're going to be part of my life … well, there's some things you're going to have accept as part of my life. Listen, I'll give them a quick interview at one of the tourney games, plug your team and the movie. And that's it. End of intrusion."

"And what will you say about me?" Matt asked, his tone softening.

"That we're just good friends, silly," Tiffany said, laughing. "That's what we celebrities always say. Of course,

I'll tell them you're the sexiest Little League coach in America."

"Big deal! Have you seen some of these coaches?" Matt said, becoming playful again.

His mood became less playful as the TV crew -- a video guy with hair almost to his waist, a sound guy with a waist larger than some Third World countries, and a reporter with more hair, teeth and makeup found in most Third World countries -- exited the truck and approached them.

The reporter, Holly Huckabee, was positively gushing during the introductions.

"This will be so great," she said to Tiffany. "The leading actress in 'Drug Town' becomes so enamored with the city that she even follows its Little League team on the road. Cute. Of course, I think you've followed the Little League coach as well. I take it this is Matt Meredith?" she asked, cocking an eye at Matt, who was holding two suitcases and a grimace in place.

"Nice to meet you," Matt said politely, out of deference to Tiffany.

He was uncomfortable being on the other end of the media spectrum. His world was asking the questions, not answering them.

"How about some questions here and tomorrow at the game?" Holly asked.

"That's fine," Tiffany said pleasantly. "Fire away."

"Some questions here are fine," Matt interrupted. "But I don't want the cameras to be a distraction at the game tomorrow. These are kids and this tournament is important to them. Your cameras are going to mess with their focus."

"I promise we won't be intrusive," Holly said sweetly. "Just some quick shots of the game, a quick shot of you coaching and some shots of Tiffany cheering you guys on."

"It'll be fun, Matt," Tiffany said, straightening her hair. "OK, Holly. Ask me something."

Matt was a bit perturbed at Tiffany for being so cooperative with the TV lady. He realized that publicity was important to an actress, but he did sense that Tiffany was a tad too eager to embrace it.

"So, we've heard of soccer moms, so are you a baseball girlfriend?" Holly asked.

"Cute," Tiffany said, flashing plenty of teeth herself to counteract the dental display of Holly Huckabee. "Just say that I've found Braxton to be a small town with plenty of wonderful small-town elements. And Little League baseball is important there. So, I'm here to lend my support to the Sorbonne Township team here in the Fort Dix Invitational."

"Well, I'm sure there's more than one Little League baseball team in Braxton. Why this team?" Holly probed, trying to elicit a gossipy, romantic response.

"Well," Tiffany cooed, flashing her eyelashes at Matt in a comic, overly dramatic fashion. "I'm friends with one of the coaches. And, Holly, as you know, we're just friends. And be careful what you say about us because Matt's a great newspaper columnist."

"Matt Meredith, baseball coach and esteemed columnist for the *Braxton Bugle*, right, Matt?" Holly asked, flirting with him. Even though a bee was buzzing near her face, she didn't stop smiling.

Matt smiled a megawatt smile to continue the plenty-of-teeth theme.

"Tiffany is just hanging out with me, hoping to get her name in the *Braxton Bugle*," he said, playfully. "So, if you give her and 'Drug Town' a good plug on 'Hello Hollywood!' it could merit a headline in the *Braxton Bugle*."

"Would you say Tiffany is your favorite column topic?" Holly asked.

"Tiffany was a marvelous column topic, but my favorite topic is the one I'm working on next," Matt said.

"Very diplomatic there," Holly answered. "What do you have to say to that, Tiffany?"

"I'd loved being profiled by Matt in the *Braxton Bugle*, but I always adore it when I'm featured on 'Hello Hollywood!' But I'd have to say Matt's more my type than you, Holly."

Holly laughed. The video guy laughed hard enough to send his ample hair into shimmers. The audio guy laughed hard enough to send his ample stomach into quivers. The interview obviously was over.

"Bet you that last line doesn't make the show," Matt laughed, picking up the suitcases. "See you tomorrow. And again, don't distract the kids too much with your cameras."

"Promise," Holly said before walking over to Tiffany and whispering in her ear: "This guy's adorable. Are there any other men like him in Braxton?"

"I don't know," Tiffany said. "Once I saw him, I stopped looking."

As Tiffany and Matt walked into their room, Matt asked Tiffany what the TV reporter had whispered to her.

"She thinks you're adorable, and so do I."

They made love before dinner, another session of passion that was a delicious mix of raw passion and tender romance. The lovemaking, however, put a tight crimp into their schedule. They barely had enough time to get showered and dressed and meet the team for dinner in the hotel restaurant.

Actually, they didn't have enough time. They were late for the team dinner. When they walked in the hotel restaurant, they noticed that the players were sitting with their parents at various tables. Cindy and Derek Loeper were sitting with Robbyn, Timmy and Billy Baxter. Robbyn Baxter had reserved a seat for Matt at their table of six. She knew there would be no room for Tiffany if she showed up, but Robbyn didn't care. She knew Matt wouldn't sit with them without Tiffany, and Robbyn didn't want any parts of having Matt and Tiffany sitting as a couple at her table. Robbyn knew her feelings were juvenile and catty, but she couldn't help herself. She just wasn't experienced anymore at cultivating a relationship, especially when the object of her affections already had a girlfriend. Robbyn hated herself for acting this way, but there sat one empty, solitary chair at the table.

Matt looked for the Baxters when he walked into the restaurant. Although he saw open chairs at several other tables, he didn't notice that the Baxter table was short a chair for both Tiffany and him. So, when he saw Timmy Baxter wave at him, he, with Tiffany in tow, made a beeline for their table. Only upon reaching the table did he and Tiffany notice there weren't enough seats for both of them.

Just as Matt was going to excuse themselves and search for another table, a star-struck Cindy Loeper promptly dispatched Derek to sit with third baseman Jimmy Lynch and his family at an adjoining table.

"Derek, go sit with Jimmy so we have room for Coach Matt and his friend," Cindy said, almost gushing with excitement.

Robbyn tried to look stoic.

"Ah, Mom, do I have to?" asked Derek, copping an attitude.

"Yes, you do," Cindy barked back. "Just be grateful you were named to the tournament team after Ben Wilson broke his arm."

"No, that's all right, we can sit elsewhere," Matt protested, casting a glance at Robbyn, who seemed to be overly occupied playing with her salad fork.

"Nonsense," Cindy said, motioning for Tiffany to sit next to her in the chair that Derek had just reluctantly vacated.

A startled Tiffany looked to Matt for direction. Matt nodded for Tiffany to sit down beside Cindy. Matt then sat in the seat next to Robbyn, who was sitting next to Cindy. To say that Matt felt awkward would be a gross understatement. But he felt no less awkward than Robbyn. Tiffany, meanwhile, had no time to feel awkward. Cindy wouldn't let Tiffany up for air. She rattled off, with breathless excitement, a series of softball questions and syrupy compliments to Tiffany.

While Cindy was acting like an energetic fan and Tiffany was polite enough to play the role of a gracious and polite celebrity, Matt had Robbyn all to himself in terms of conversation because Timmy and Billy were busy arguing over whether the Boston Red Sox or the New York Yankees were going to win the American League East title.

"Any trouble with the directions?" Matt, opting for small talk, asked Robbyn.

Robbyn decided that instead of being petulant and childish in the presence of Matt and Tiffany, she was going to simply be herself and not allow her feelings for Matt to make her come across as a fool in front of him and the others at the table.

"They were just fine," she said, flashing Matt a broad smile and leaning close to him. "By the way, Timmy is so excited about tomorrow. He can't wait to play the game. Of course, he's thrilled that Derek's on the team as well."

Then Robbyn laughed and looked over at Cindy and Tiffany.

"I think Cindy is thrilled, too, because now she has met a real, live movie star," Robbyn said loud enough to interrupt Cindy's benign interrogation of Tiffany.

Robbyn then enthusiastically reached over to shake Tiffany's hand.

"So how did the dinner go the night I bumped into you at the food store?" Robbyn asked. Then Robbyn turned her gaze to Matt and added: "Or maybe I should ask Matt that. He looks healthy enough to me, so I assume he didn't suffer food poisoning."

Matt and Tiffany both laughed. Cindy didn't, very perturbed that Robbyn had interrupted her animated chat with Tiffany.

"Well, I'm lucky if I can boil water," Tiffany said, obviously exaggerating, "so I'm grateful that I didn't poison Matt. He obviously is a trusting man to allow me to cook for him."

"I offered to take her out to eat," Matt said, smiling, "but we poor newspapermen can't afford expensive dinners that cater to the stars."

Robbyn and Tiffany both laughed, and Cindy seized the moment when she noticed a slight lull in the conversation.

"You sure don't act like a star, Tiffany," she said, buttering her up with more gusto than she exhibited when buttering her roll.

"We're just regular people, except we have to put up with grouchy directors and probing media people," Tiffany said, grinning at Matt.

"Have you ever dated a member of the media before?" Robbyn asked. "I know Sharon Stone married a newspaper editor in San Francisco, but isn't rare for an actress to be involved with a reporter?"

"Well, this is the first time for me," Tiffany said, sweetly. "But Matt is such a rare guy, it doesn't seem rare at all. It just surprises me that in such a small town like Braxton that no lady has yet to tie him down."

"Yes, he certainly has been the dashing man about town," Robbyn said almost too fervently. "So, tell us Matt, is Tiffany the lady who will tie you down?"

As she said it, she gave Matt a look hot enough to melt the butter on his roll. It was a look withering enough to get Matt's attention. It was a look that amply conveyed a striking message to him that there was more to Robbyn Baxter than being a confused, grieving widow and single mother. It was a look that demonstrated that passion once had flowed abundantly through her veins.

Matt blatantly blushed, which got everybody's attention at the table except Timmy and Billy, who were arguing over whether Barry Bonds was the greatest ballplayer of all time. Tiffany and Robbyn zeroed in on Matt's red face, waiting for a reply. Both had a vested interest in Matt's response, although Tiffany didn't realize the depth of Robbyn's interest. Cindy was staring at Matt simply because she was a gossip queen. She had been pitching Matt to Robbyn, but now that she had met Tiffany, she wanted Tiffany to catch Matt, not Robbyn. It wasn't anything against Robbyn, but Cindy was enamored with meeting a movie star. And, besides, she no longer thought Robbyn had any shot at landing Matt now that he was involved with Tiffany.

Matt regained his composure after a few moments of awkward silence and said: "The better question is whether I'm the man who will tie Tiffany down?"

Before anybody else at the table could say anything, an assistant coach with the tournament team walked up to the table and engaged Matt in a conversation about tomorrow's starting lineup. Matt tried to listen with his full attention, but his mind was preoccupied beating himself up for dodging Robbyn's question. He didn't know why he simply didn't say "yes" to her question. Actually, he did know. For some deep, underlying reason in his psyche, he couldn't bring himself to say it to Robbyn. For her part, Tiffany read nothing sinister in Matt's reply. She thought he simply didn't want to state his feelings in front of Robbyn and Cindy. And she took comfort in the fact that he had blushed. She felt it reflected how deeply he felt about her.

Robbyn took Matt's blushing and non-response as hopeful signs that he wasn't totally committed to Tiffany. Their dinner finished with strictly small talk and with everyone but Matt feeling content. Matt was quieter than usual as minor pangs of a Tiffany-Robbyn dilemma gnawed on the fringes of his mind. Why he felt this way, even in a small way, he had no idea. It confounded him. He found Tiffany to be absolutely ravishing, wonderful, delightful, funny, sensitive and fun to be with. He wasn't awed by her celebrity. He found Robbyn to be beautiful and a wonderful mother but thought she had too much baggage being a widow. Still, there was something about her ... something that seemed more tangible, wholesome and real than Tiffany.

And something in his subconscious thought was telling him that Tiffany might be nothing more than just a brief fling and a Hollywood fantasy, a lady who would disappear when the credits started rolling on "Drug Town" on its premiere night.

Matt really didn't get to talk privately with Robbyn that night. After dinner, he gave Timmy and Derek a quick pep talk -- telling them how thrilled he was to be a part of the tournament team with them and how they richly deserved to be a part of it. But as he was leaving the table and saying goodbye to Cindy and Robbyn, he found himself kissing Robbyn on the cheek. The kiss shocked him as much as it did her. But he wasn't flustered enough to prevent some quick action on his part. He immediately kissed Cindy on the cheek as well. Again, Tiffany read nothing into those kisses. Neither did Cindy. But Robbyn and Matt did.

After dinner, Tiffany and Matt had an enjoyable evening. They had a couple of drinks at the hotel bar with the other coaches and their wives. The other coaches and their wives gushed all over Tiffany and even Matt by association. Matt did get an indication of what it must feel like to be Mr. Tiffany Underhill. It didn't bother him immensely, but he found it to be somewhat superficial and somehow contrived. And he did feel they suddenly treated him a little differently because of whom he was dating.

But all reservations he had about the reality of Tiffany's affection for him disappeared an hour later back in their room as her loving performance in bed was worthy of an Academy Award. An Academy Award rated XXX. Matt felt so content and sublime in her arms. Until he closed his eyes and saw Robbyn on the back of his eyelids.

Chapter Twelve

The next morning was bright and sunny. A perfect day for tournament baseball. Matt was up at 7 for breakfast and then a coaches' meeting. He, the other coaches and the players were on the field by 8:45 for their game at 10. Matt hitched a ride from the hotel to the field 20 minutes away because Tiffany opted to sleep in a bit and then had to shampoo her hair.

Game time arrived, and Matt noticed that Tiffany wasn't there yet. He was concerned that she might have gotten lost coming from the hotel. As she admitted to Matt, she was directionally impaired. And the GPS in his car was broken. Matt figured she couldn't be hopelessly lost because it was just a matter of three turns. But when the game started, Matt's thoughts lost track of Tiffany. Coaching strategy and encouraging the boys were his focus.

But he did think of Robbyn when Timmy hit a two-run homer in the first inning to stake the Sorbonne Township League All-Stars to an early lead. After Matt gave Timmy a high-five after he had rounded the bases, Matt noticed Robbyn and Cindy jumping up and down in the bleachers and shouting encouragement. Matt noticed how cute Robbyn looked in her tight blouse and short shorts. He didn't remember her dressing that hot at previous games. But the thought was fleeting. Matt had to resume coaching from third base and flashing signals to the next hitter.

Tiffany didn't arrive until the third inning, with Sorbonne Township clinging to a 2-1 lead. Tiffany, however, didn't arrive in Matt's car. She had misplaced the directions to the ballfield. In a panic, she had bumped into Holly Huckabee and her TV crew in the hotel parking lot. She opted to bum a ride with them.

When the TV panel truck bearing "Hello Hollywood!" in garish letters drove right past the parking lot and parked right next to the bleachers, everybody in the stands and all the players stopped and stared. And all of them saw Tiffany exit the van along with Holly Huckabee, the video guy with all the hair and the sound guy with all the stomach.

Holly was wearing a halter top that amply revealed her impressive cleavage. Tiffany was wearing a brightly colored sundress and an artsy hat. She looked dressed for a polo match, not a Little League game. The video guy was wearing a mechanic's uniform that seemed stained with crankcase oil. The sound guy was wearing billowy shorts and a tank top that didn't come close to covering the enormous expanse of his stomach. To say that the quartet was a major distraction would be a gross understatement. Matt was embarrassed and angry. He had told the TV crew that he didn't want them to be a distraction. And now they had pulled up their truck practically next to the field during the game and had shown up wearing silly clothing. Compounding matters, Tiffany had arrived with them! And Matt thought she looked too, well, Hollywoodish in her dress and hat. Her eyes sought him out and gave him an exaggerated wave. She seemed surprised that Matt didn't smile when he gave her a weak wave in return. She figured he was just preoccupied with the game.

Matt's anger worsened when an assistant coach, a gruff guy named Jack Martin who owned a small trucking company, growled at Matt: "What the hell is with your girlfriend and those TV assholes? This isn't about them. This is about the kids."

"I'm sorry," Matt said. "I couldn't agree more. I'm pissed at them, especially Tiffany. But screw them for now."

Matt then waved to the home plate ump and yelled, "Play ball!"

"I thought that was my job," said the umpire, who reverted back to gazing at Holly and Tiffany. His eyeballs Ping-Ponged back and forth between the two as if he were watching a tennis match.

The game resumed, but it was obvious the fans and the players were paying attention to the TV crew as it zeroed in on Tiffany cheering in the bleachers and on Matt coaching at third base. The only thing that placated the parents was the allure of the camera and the enticement that their sons could appear in footage on national television.

Robbyn Baxter wasn't amused or enticed by the prospect of having Timmy appear on the "Hello Hollywood!" program.

"Look at Tiffany," Robbyn said to Cindy, "playing the role of instant Little League fan. The way she's cheering, you'd think she had two sons on the team."

"Nobody with two sons ever had a supermodel figure like that," Cindy said, taking the last bite of her doughnut.

"Stop that! She's not that hot," Robbyn said, annoyed.

"My, my, aren't we catty?" Cindy chirped.

"Yes, we are!" Robbyn said aggressively.

Sorbonne Township was playing a team from Egg Harbor, N.J., and the Egg Harbor pitcher had quite a fastball.

In fact, Timmy Baxter was the only Cub who had gotten a hit off the kid. Actually, Timmy had two hits, a double to go with his home run. Now Timmy was batting in the fifth with Sorbonne Township trailing 3-2. A walk and an error had put runners on first and second. It was prime time for Timmy to come through at the plate. Otherwise, it looked quite apparent that Sorbonne Township would fall into the losers' bracket in the double-elimination tournament. And tournament losers' brackets eat up pitching with more gusto than kids eat pizza, meaning an opening loss likely meant that Sorbonne Township had no realistic shot at winning the tournament title. So, Timmy felt a lot of pressure as he swung through two pitches to fall behind 0 and 2 in the count. Matt called timeout and walked up to Timmy, who stepped out of the batter's box for some last-minute advice.

"Just relax, Timmy," Matt said. "Just meet the ball. This kid throws smoke. Choke up on the bat a bit. Forget about the scoreboard. Just concentrate on seeing the ball and driving it."

"OK, Coach," Timmy said confidently. "I'll be fine."

Matt patted Timmy on the back and strode back to the third base coaching box. The TV video and audio guys approached him with their camera and microphone. They were so close they practically were in the coaching box with Matt.

"Will you guys get the hell off the field!" Matt snapped at them. "We've got a ballgame to win. Right now, I don't want 'Hello Hollywood!' in my face. Go shoot Tiffany's hat in the stands." The sarcasm in his voice was crisper than a line drive.

"Mellow out, dude," said the camera guy. "We're not in the way."

"You're messing up our kids' concentration, so get back to the bleachers."

"OK, OK," said the camera guy, as he and the sound guy began walking away.

Matt turned his attention to the batter's box. Timmy fouled off a fastball, barely keeping his at-bat alive. Barely keeping his team alive.

"Just put the bat on the ball, Timmy," Matt yelled, clapping his hands.

In the stands, Robbyn was wringing her hands.

"I hate this pressure," Robbyn said to Cindy. "It's such a helpless feeling sitting here in the stands."

Then she yelled loudly to Timmy, "You can do it, honey!"

With Matt intently watching Timmy and the Egg Harbor pitcher, he didn't notice that the TV sound and video guy had ventured down the third base line closer to home plate. Just as Timmy was about to swing at another fastball, the corner of his eye caught sight of the camera and sound equipment. Momentarily distracted, he failed to pick up the ball -- a fastball that was boring it on him. He then swung awkwardly at the ball, his body turned more to his left than it normally was because he had involuntarily yanked his shoulder in the direction of the TV crew. The pitch was high and inside. It missed Timmy's protective earflap on his batting helmet because Timmy's face was turned square to the pitching mound. The fastball crashed into Timmy's nose and mouth, momentarily knocking him out. Blood gushed from his broken nose and split lips as he lay in a pool of blood at home plate. Fortunately, the ball didn't knock out Timmy's front teeth.

Matt screamed "No!" loud enough to be heard back in Braxton as he sprinted toward the fallen Timmy, who was being attended to by the concerned home plate umpire.

"He's unconscious," the umpire said calmly to Matt, who knelt beside him and joined him in hovering over Timmy.

Robbyn's cries and screams reverberated throughout the hushed bleachers as she ran, with Cindy and Billy trailing behind her, towards Timmy.

Coaches and players from both teams huddled around Timmy as Robbyn, Cindy and Billy arrived at home plate. Robbyn was hysterical, babbling "Oh my God!" constantly.

She knelt next to Matt, and even in her hysteria, was touched to see that Matt had tears in his eyes as he held Timmy's hand. Then Robbyn saw Timmy's face and emitted a blood-curdling scream. There was blood all over Timmy's face, even though Matt and the umpire had tried to wipe some of it off. And Timmy's broken nose was swelling alarmingly, dramatically distorting his features.

"Oh, baby," Robbyn cried, leaning over Timmy, kissing his forehead gently. "Please wake up! Oh, God. I think he's in a coma."

She cried uncontrollably, leaning on Matt as they both hovered over Timmy.

"Did anybody call 9-1-1 for an ambulance?" Matt yelled to the throng gathered around them.

A cloud of alarm hung over all of them.

"Already taken care of," said one of the tournament officials. "The ambulance should be here momentarily."

Standing behind the group closer to the backstop fence was Tiffany, a look of horror in her eyes. She wanted to go up and embrace Timmy and Matt but didn't want to intrude. Holly and her TV crew stood next to Tiffany. They didn't dare shoot any footage of the fallen Little League batter.

"The poor boy," a stunned Holly did say to her crew.

"Come on, big guy," Matt said softly to Timmy.

A moment later, Timmy's eyes opened, although the facial swelling made his opened eyes look more like slits.

Timmy seemed stunned to see so many people hovering over him.

"Give him some air, everybody," Matt said, taking charge.

"Yes, please," Robbyn added.

"Sorry, Coach," Timmy said softly. "I'm OK. I think. He put a hand to his bloody lips. My face really hurts. I shouldn't have let that pitch him me."

"That's OK, son," Matt said, comforting him.

"Oh, God, thank you," Robbyn repeated about a dozen times in 30 seconds as she kissed Timmy's forehead and dabbed gently at his bloodied face.

"Ouch, that hurts Mom," Timmy said sharply. "Don't touch it!"

The Egg Harbor pitcher came up to Timmy. He, too, had tears in his eyes.

"Sorry, man," he said, leaning over Timmy. "The pitch got away from me a bit. It was a little high and tight."

"It's not your fault," Timmy said. "Actually, I lost track of the ball for a moment because I saw the TV camera and it messed up my focus."

"What?" asked Matt. His compassion for Timmy was now mixing with anger towards the TV crew from "Hello Hollywood!" and indirectly towards Tiffany for being, well, for being a celebrity. "Did you say the TV people distracted you?"

"I know, it was stupid," Timmy said. "I have a bad headache."

The siren of the approaching ambulance could now be heard.

"You'll be OK, honey," Robbyn said quietly through her sobs. "I'm sure the doctors will give you some painkillers and check to see if you have a concussion."

Matt looked around, searching for Tiffany and the TV crew. He saw them standing near the backstop.

"I'll be right back," Matt said to Timmy.

Matt then arose and angrily jogged toward Tiffany and the TV people.

"Are you happy now?" he yelled loud enough to make his point without making a scene. "I told you guys to get the hell off the field and not screw with the kids' concentration. Timmy said he took his eye off the pitch because he saw your camera in his face."

Matt jabbed a finger in the camera guy's chest so hard that his long hair vibrated.

"Sorry, dude," the guy said. "Is the kid gonna be all right?"

"His nose probably is broken, his lips are a bloody mess and he probably has a concussion," Matt fired back with malice.

"I apologize," Holly said. "We were just trying to get some footage for a heartwarming feature on Tiffany, you and baseball."

Matt, for the first time, looked at Tiffany. She was ash white and awash in guilt.

"Matt, I'm so sorry," she said, misting up. "I should have told them not to shoot any game footage. I didn't think it would harm anybody, let alone, God forbid, Timmy. I had no idea something like this would happen. I just thought it would be good publicity for the movie and me."

"And *me*!" Matt yelled. "And *me*! Just because you're a star, you're not always the center of the damn universe."

"I don't deserve that," Tiffany said, her voice hardening. "I'm not like that and you know it! I came up here to be supportive of you and your team. I feel awful, terrible about what happened. It was just an unfortunate, terrible accident."

She began crying.

Matt was going to say something to her, but the ambulance had arrived by then and he zipped back to Timmy.

"They want to resume the game with the bases loaded since Timmy was hit by a pitch," one of the Sorbonne Township assistant coaches told Matt.

"That's fine, Timmy would want them to keep playing and try to get a win," Matt said. "But I'm going to the hospital with Timmy."

He then turned to Robbyn, took her hands in his, and said, almost pleading: "My car is back at the hotel. Can I go with you guys in the ambulance to the hospital?"

"Oh, yes, please," Robbyn said, touched by Matt's compassion towards Timmy.

Her immense appreciation was all over her face.

The ambulance personnel didn't want Matt to go in the ambulance with Timmy because Matt wasn't a relative but capitulated when Robbyn insisted.

"I'll come over to the hospital in Robbyn's car as soon as the game is over and give you guys an update," Cindy said to Matt and Robbyn. "Can you give me your car keys, Robbyn?"

"You're a good friend," Robbyn said, still shaken by her son's beaning.

The ambulance took off with Timmy, Robbyn, Billy and Matt. It was a quiet 15-minute ride to the hospital, although Billy kept exhorting his older brother to "suck it up."

"You're be fine, pal," Matt assured Timmy at one point.

"I know I will," Timmy said. "I just want to play ball again. And if my face is messed up, well, I wasn't going to be a movie star anyway. Those people are weird, aren't they, Mom?"

Robbyn looked at Matt, not sure how to answer Timmy. She was sensitive toward Matt's feelings for Tiffany. Her sense of concern for his feelings at a time like this affected Matt deeply.

For the first time it what seemed like an eternity, Matt smiled and said: "Go ahead, Robbyn. Tell Timmy that movie stars are weird."

"They're weird," Robbyn said emphatically while smiling at Matt.

"Besides, your face will heal up nicely," Matt said to Timmy. "When I was playing second base in a Little League game, the shortstop was trying to complete a double play. His throw caught me flush in the face. Fortunately, I didn't suffer any eye damage. But my nose was broken, and my face swelled so badly that I looked like an alien for a week or so. It was so bad that kids I didn't even know that well in my neighborhood were coming over to my house just to check my face out. I should have charged admission."

Timmy, Billy and Robbyn laughed.

"And you look much better than I remember myself looking," Matt said. "You're going to be fine."

"I just wonder how the team is making out," Timmy said.

"I'm sure they're getting their butts kicked without you," Billy said. "That pitcher on the other team is awesome."

Actually, Billy's prediction proved to be correct. Although his nerves were somewhat rattled by the beaning, the Egg Harbor pitcher dispatched Sorbonne Township without a run the remainder of the game, ushering them into the losers' bracket. By that point, the fight had gone out of the Sorbonne Township team. The players and coaches couldn't wait to get the game over with and find out how Timmy was doing.

After the game, several coaches and players came over to the hospital to find out that Timmy had been admitted overnight for observation. The doctor in the emergency room said that Timmy's nose was broken and that he had suffered a mild concussion. His lips were lacerated, with the upper lip receiving six sutures and the bottom lip four sutures. Fortunately, all his teeth were intact.

"You're going to be fine, son," the doctor told Timmy. "You'll be playing ball again soon. Once the swelling in your face goes down, you'll be ready for the movies."

His reference to the movies prompted Robbyn to flash a semi-smile at Matt, who just shook his head.

"Can I play ball tomorrow?" Timmy asked the doctor. "We're in the Fort Dix Invitational."

"Tomorrow's a little soon," the doctor said gently. "Next week is more like it. You have a mild concussion."

"Ah, that sucks!" Timmy yelped.

"Timmy! Watch your language," Robbyn said, embarrassed.

"That's quite all right," said the doctor, laughing. "It does suck. I used to play ball myself. Nobody likes to miss a game because of an injury. But a concussion, Timmy, is nothing to mess with. You only get one brain. You can't put a cast on it like you can a broken ankle. So, take care of yourself. I'm sure you'll be released from the hospital tomorrow and can go root for your buddies."

By the time Timmy was admitted to a semi-private room, some of his teammates and coaches were on hand to give him comfort. The whole team would have come, but the coaches didn't want to turn Timmy's room into a circus. Timmy was disappointed that the team had lost, but after a few minutes he was laughing at some of the good-natured ribbing he was getting from his teammates about his swollen and distorted facial features.

Cindy and Derek Loeper were both at the hospital. Cindy offered to drive Matt and Billy back to the hotel, since Robbyn was going to stay the night with Timmy.

"Do I have to share a bed with Billy?" Derek complained to Cindy. "Timmy told me that Billy farts in his sleep."

"That's gross for you to say that," Cindy said sharply to Derek. "I'm sure it isn't true."

"Yes, it is," Billy said, proudly. "I can leave some real bombs."

"Well, not tonight, OK?" Cindy said, smiling at Matt.

"Thanks for all your concern for Timmy," Robbyn said to Matt, delicately shifting the subject. "Your tenderness and care exceeded that of a coach. You're a wonderful man. Thanks for being Timmy's friend as well as a coach. He thinks of you almost like, well ... like a father."

Robbyn's eyes were misting as she gave Matt a quick kiss on the cheek.

"He's a special kid," Matt said. "I'm glad I got a chance to get to know him so well."

"So am I," Robbyn said.

As Cindy drove Derek, Billy and Matt back to the hotel, she grilled Matt on whether the TV camera had led to Timmy getting hit by the pitch.

"Timmy said the camera distracted him for a second," Matt said, obviously perturbed. "And I believe him. I warned those guys to get out of the way. I knew it was a mistake to have them at the game. But they showed up to film Tiffany and me, and I let it go. I didn't want to upset Tiffany. But it was selfish on my part. And I blamed her after the game for contributing to Timmy getting hurt. That wasn't fair of me. She had no idea. I would have called her cell phone from the hospital to apologize to her, but I left my cell in my car."

"You can use my cell phone," Cindy cheerfully volunteered, hoping to overhear Matt's apology to Tiffany.

"Thank you but no," Matt said. "We'll be back at the hotel in a few minutes. It can wait."

When Matt got back to his hotel room, he was shocked to find out that Tiffany had left. She left him a note, explaining that she knew he blamed her for the injury to Timmy and that she felt terribly responsible.

"I would just be a distraction to the team and a reminder to the team that I helped cause the injury to Timmy," she wrote further. "Under the circumstances, I couldn't spend the remainder of the weekend with you. I pray Timmy recovers and the team rebounds with a win tomorrow. Holly and her TV crew are taking me to New York, where I'm going to stay with a friend tonight. Call me tomorrow and let me know how Timmy is. By the way, Holly and the guys feel awful about what happened. And if it makes you feel any better, I'm heartsick about Timmy. And heartsick that you think I'm some superficial celebrity hound. I thought you knew me better than that. I guess I was wrong. And I guess I was wrong thinking that your world could mesh with my world."

Matt noticed that she simply signed the note "Tiffany" -- not the usual "Love, Tiff" signature she had used in other notes she had left for him.

Matt's stomach was in knots. The emotion of the day had his insides churning like a clothes dryer on full cycle. He was relieved that Timmy wasn't hurt worse, but sad that he had to be injured at all and knocked out of the tournament. And he was upset that he had upset Tiffany. He knew it really hadn't been her fault, and that he obviously had a predisposed bias towards her celebrity that he hadn't fully shared with himself until his angry emotions bubbled to the surface. Nevertheless, he was stunned by her departure, and longed for her to be with him in his hotel room. Further complicating his inner turmoil, he, at the same time, felt closer to Robbyn than he ever had. Timmy's injury had been the catalyst for an acute sense of family that he shared with Robbyn and her sons. He felt it and he sensed that Robbyn felt it. She did -- and then some. As Robbyn sat in Timmy's hospital room watching him watch a Phillies game on television, she couldn't help feeling that today's tragic pitch could have been a pitch that would change her life and that of her sons. When she fell asleep upright in a chair, she did so with a sense of contentment she hadn't experienced since before her husband had been killed.

Before he fell asleep that night, Matt finally -- after having an internal debate for several hours -- called Tiffany's cell number. She didn't answer. His message simply said that Timmy was essentially fine and had experienced a mild concussion, a broken nose and lacerated lips. And he added that he was sorry that she had left, but he understood why. He made no apology for rebuking her by the baseball backstop screen. But he did ask her to call him back that night if she got the message.

Tiffany got the message that night. Got it while she was sobbing softly in her friend's spare bedroom. She was crushed. She truly had fallen in love with Matt but couldn't forget the intensity of his anger. More than that, she couldn't forget, nor forgive, his knee-jerk reaction that she was just some publicity-crazed Hollywood bimbo who only cared about herself. Before she fell asleep that night, Tiffany still had a shred of hope that her relationship with Matt could be restored to its once vibrant state. But it was only a shred -- a shred soaked with tears.

Chapter Thirteen

The following morning Sorbonne Township was crushed 16-1 by a team from Newark, Delaware and eliminated from the Fort Dix Invitational. The Sorbonne Township team exhibited little vitality in the one-sided game, an obvious psychological fallout from Timmy's beaning the previous day.

Matt's sagging spirits, however, were buoyed when he drove over to the hospital after the game and learned that Timmy was going to be released shortly.

"My head hurts a little, but I'll be OK," Timmy said to Matt as Robbyn packed up his things. "It's a shame the team lost. I wanted to root them on this afternoon."

"Your lips look like you fought the heavyweight champ," Matt said, trying to lighten the mood. "I guess you won't be kissing your girlfriend tonight."

"I don't really like girls that much," Timmy said, his face scrunching into a grimace. "They talk about silly things I don't care about."

Matt and Robbyn exchanged amused glances.

"You'll change your mind when you get older," Matt said, "but for now, I'm sure you have more fun playing ball than hanging out at the mall with giggling girls."

"Hey, I giggle!" Robbyn said, playfully. "Besides, girls do more than giggle. Girls today play as much ball as the boys. You have to get more PC and current, Mr. Meredith. And I thought newspaper reporters dealt in current events."

"Just like there's always truth in advertising," Matt fired back with a laugh.

"Of course, there is," she responded, feigning shock that he would cast doubt on the veracity of ads.

It was obvious to both of them that they were subtly flirting with each other, a flirtation that ceased when a grumpy nurse entered Timmy's room and told Robbyn that her son was free to go.

"That's great," Timmy yelled, eliciting a frown from the nurse.

"You would think a nurse in pediatrics would have more charm," Matt said to Robbyn as they walked down the hall.

"Well, not all ladies are charming," Robbyn said, looking up into Matt's eyes.

Matt was seized by a strong temptation right then and there to kiss Robbyn's inviting lips.

"Well, some are," Matt said, giving her a stare that she gladly accepted.

He was finding Robbyn to be quite intoxicating, especially since her inner strength was bundled in such an intriguing physical package.

"Thanks for being there for Timmy yesterday and today," Robbyn said. "Actually, thanks for being there for him all summer."

"My pleasure," Matt said. "I've enjoyed hanging out with your son. Actually, both your boys."

Then he was struck with an idea.

"There's no tournament next weekend," Matt said, "and I know the Phillies are home against the Mets. Why don't the four of us take in the game? My treat."

"We'd loved to," Robbyn said quickly.

"All right!" Timmy said. "That'll be cool."

On the drive home to Braxton, part of Matt wondered why he had asked Robbyn out with the boys in tow and why she had accepted so energetically. But he was thrilled that he had. Even though part of him still had strong feelings -- especially sexual feelings -- toward Tiffany, he was beginning to realize that a relationship with Robbyn ultimately would feel more right; that a relationship with Tiffany was destined to always have distracting entanglements by the nature of who she was.

While Matt was heading home, his cell phone rang.

"Miss me last night?" Tiffany asked.

"Of course," Matt said. Part of him was lying, part wasn't. "You didn't have to leave."

"Well, I knew you should be with the team and with Timmy, not me. And I knew you were upset with me. You know, I feel terribly guilty about what happened. How's Timmy?"

"He's going to be fine," Matt answered, his voice flat. "He was released from the hospital today. He has a mild concussion and some bruised lips. Are you still in New York?"

"Yes, I am," Tiffany said. "I'm spending the rest of the weekend here with a girlfriend. The studio is sending a limo to pick me up Sunday night because we have an early location shoot in Braxton on Monday morning."

"So, what's the deal with us? Is one quick flash of anger while under stress enough to drive you away?" Matt asked.

"I hate being perceived as a self-centered celebrity," Tiffany said, "and you damn well know that. But you obviously thought Timmy got hurt because you think I'm a publicity hound who only cares about myself and my career. I thought you were a guy who definitely knew me, who didn't get hung up on my celebrity. I guess I was wrong."

Matt didn't answer.

"Wasn't I?" Tiffany semi-yelled into the phone.

"I don't know," Matt said, quietly. "But I wonder if you don't realize that you're more hung up on celebrity than you think."

"That's not true at all," she snapped, hurt by the suggestion. "If you feel that way about me, I'm not sure I can keep seeing you."

"That's an overreaction on your part," Matt said. "The question is: Will you still want to see me, no matter what my feelings may be, after you're done filming in Braxton?"

"That's a cheap shot," Tiffany said. "You know I will -- if your head's in the right place."

"I think you and I need to have a serious discussion, and not on the phone," Matt said. "Why not come back to Braxton tonight and we'll go out to dinner?"

"No, we both need time to cool off, to put yesterday behind us and move on. I didn't throw that pitch, and I didn't tell those TV guys to approach home plate. So, don't lay all this on me." Tiffany was getting worked up, and paused before deciding to throw a figurative fastball high and inside at Matt.

"Besides, I wonder if all your concern over Timmy Baxter isn't somehow related to Robbyn Baxter," she said, with icicles in her voice. "I'm not blind. I know that Robbyn Baxter wants you. And I think part of you finds her to be more comfortable than me because I'm an actress and she's just another woman in Braxton. I think she's weird because she's so hung up over her dead husband."

Matt was so livid he almost rammed the truck in front of him.

The phone line was frozen with silence for what seemed an eternity.

"Enjoy your weekend in New York," Matt said, a newspaper columnist at a sudden loss for words.

Actually, he had plenty of things he wanted to say to her, but he didn't want to say them while he was so angry.

"I'll call you Monday," he added, almost as an afterthought.

"Don't bother!" Tiffany snapped as she began crying. "Call your little Braxton housewife and mommy. You guys can play house together!"

The phone line went dead, so Matt couldn't hear Tiffany crying hysterically. And Tiffany couldn't hear Matt yell, "Hollywood bitch!"

The remainder of the drive home was a blur to Matt. All he could think about was how a baseball weekend he had looked so forward to had suddenly blown up in his face: Timmy had gotten hurt, Tiffany had left him, perhaps for good, and now he was going out with Robbyn and her kids. And while he was excited about the possibilities with Robbyn, he felt hurt and lost over Tiffany. Part of him thought that she would be absolutely perfect for him if she weren't a film star. But being a film star was as much a part of her being as being a mother and a widow was to Robbyn. It was all part of who they were.

When he got home that night, he did something he never did: He sat home alone and got drunk. He knew you couldn't drown your sorrows, but damn it, he was going to try.

When Robbyn got home that night and after she had tucked in the boys, she sat on her patio in quiet solitude. And prayed that Matt would be the man who could restore a semblance of normalcy to her life -- to be part of a couple again and to have a partner in raising the boys. She finally had come to terms with the fact that to accept another man in her life did not mean erasing the existence of Bob Baxter. She knew now that Matt would be perfect for her boys, and he seemed to be someone she could love as much as she did Bob. And she had come to realize that Bob Baxter and Matt Meredith could have been the best of friends.

When Tiffany went to bed that night at her girlfriend's Manhattan apartment, she couldn't fall asleep. She had fallen hard for Matt Meredith and thought that he was cool and astute enough to handle the extraneous trappings of her film career. Now she felt crushed, convinced that he would never be comfortable with her career and ultimately would never be comfortable with her. Her self-esteem also had taken a hit because she knew Matt was attracted to someone she perceived to be a wacky widow with two kids.

"Some movie star I am," she said sarcastically to herself. "I lose my leading man to *her*."

As Tiffany tossed and turned, so did her mind. One moment she was never going to see Matt again. Another moment she was going to lay all her charms on him, fight for him and not lose him to Robbyn Baxter or anybody else. Her troubled mind was so focused on herself that it left little time to think of poor Timmy Baxter.

Chapter Fourteen

The following Monday morning Robbyn was at the Emergency Shelter, overseeing a photo shoot for image ads promoting the Shelter's capital campaign. Robbyn and her camera were spotlighting some of the Shelter's staffers and facilities for the series of ads that would run in the *Braxton Bugle* as well in some brochures. Also appearing in some of the ads and the brochures would be the chairman of the capital campaign, Millie Paxton. Millie was a vibrant lady in her late 60s whose late husband had been a Braxton industrialist. Millie had dedicated her life to community causes and charities. She served on all sorts of local boards and committees, most of them for non-profits. She brought her time and her treasure to these organizations and was well respected in the Miller community.

Except for one lapse in judgment. She was the long-time girlfriend of Braxton mayor Jimbo Cummings. How the petite and refined Millie Paxton had put up with a bulbous lout like Jimbo Cummings for all those years had mystified several prominent Miller Countians.

The mayor was on hand for the shoot. He liked to hang onto Millie's apron strings. And while the photographer was taking a series of shots of Millie, the jocular Jimbo was busy semi-hitting on Robbyn in a joking but hardly PC manner.

"With those cute legs, I can't believe you're not remarried," Jimbo said to Robbyn. "You have to be dating somebody."

"Actually, I'm not," Robbyn said politely, in deference to Jimbo's office.

"Isn't a pretty lady like you lonely?" Jimbo pressed on.

"Lonely? With two boys to take care of and a busy job? There's no time to be lonely," Robbyn said, trying to keep the conversation light.

"Millie, we have to set up Robbyn here with your nephew Ralph," Jimbo bellowed to his lady friend, who was a good 30 feet away. "She's too busy to date, she tells me."

Millie gave Jimbo an indulgent smile, then frowned and replied in a voice loud enough to be heard from 30 feet but in a tone that was ladylike and hardly a yell:

"Now, Jimbo, mind your manners. I'm sure Robbyn doesn't need you or me to act as a dating service. Do you, Robbyn?"

"Absolutely not," Robbyn said, smiling and putting her tongue inside her cheek. "I'm actually dating six guys."

The photo shoot wrapped up without Jimbo marrying Robbyn off -- or pinching her.

"Thank you for all your creative input for this campaign," Millie said to Robbyn before departing with the mayor. "Your image ads will pluck enough heartstrings to enhance our purse strings."

Two days later, Matt, who had not yet had contact with Tiffany, was sitting at his desk in the newsroom when his managing editor, Ned March, approached him.

"A source I won't name tipped me onto something interesting last night," said March, a pleasant but hard-boiled news junkie in his early 60s. "He thinks the mayor is somehow skimming funds from some of the fund-raising causes his girlfriend Millie Paxton is involved with. My friend's take on it is that Millie is totally unaware of what Jimbo is doing. Evidently, Millie gives Jimbo access to everything, and he's been pocketing money."

"Why would he do that?" Matt asked. "Millie gives him all the money he needs to supplement his lousy salary as mayor. And don't capital campaigns and non-profit fund-raisers have pretty tight fiscal controls?"

"My source says Jimbo has a girlfriend on the side, and he spends a few bucks on her," Ned said. "Enough bucks that he can't spend without Millie knowing about it. So evidently Jimbo has been skimming funds to party with his other girlfriend."

"The Emergency Shelter capital campaign is under way, isn't it?" Matt asked Ned.

"Bingo!" Ned said, "And according to my source, they are a little loose with their fiscal controls, especially when it comes to Millie. They trust her so much that evidently Jimbo is taking a huge advantage of them. It could be to the tune of 50 grand. Or even more."

"How about I check into this baby?" Matt asked, his journalistic juices flowing.

"I know you're a columnist, but that doesn't mean you can't do this, too," Ned said. "But I must tell you this: My source swore me to secrecy that I wouldn't tell you his name. In fact, he will provide no details. His only contribution is the story tip. He said he is in no position to piss off Jimbo."

"All I would have to do is find out all the firms who do business with either Millie or the city and cross-reference it with your short list of friends," Matt said to Ned, only half-joking.

"Don't go there, Meredith!" said the managing editor.

He wasn't joking.

Matt sat back and smiled. This could be one great scoop, he thought. Then his smile turned upside down. He suddenly remembered that Robbyn was spearheading the advertising for the Emergency Shelter capital campaign. Her image advertising would be toast if a major scandal stained the capital campaign. If that were to be the case, Matt felt genuinely sad for Robbyn. She would have to put her ad campaign in overdrive to overcome the terrible fallout. And it would be a wicked fallout in a small town if the mayor was involved. But Matt knew he couldn't worry about that aspect. He had a job to do, and so did Robbyn. Both of them were adults, he reasoned, and getting positioned on opposite sides of a professional endeavor should not cause a rift in any budding personal relationship. For a moment, Matt wondered why there always seemed to be complications when it came to women. Tiffany was an actress, and that was a potential problem for him. Robbyn was an ad writer and PR person, and that was a potential problem for him and her. He smiled to himself and thought he should forget about both of them and just go out with that sexy waitress at the Burger Ranch, a burger and breakfast joint attached to the hip of the *Braxton Bugle* building. Matt frequently stopped in the Burger Ranch for morning coffee, and that waitress always seemed to go out of her way to talk to him and wait on him. Her mistake was talking to Matt. From her halting attempts at conversation, he guessed her IQ barely was in triple figures. But, he mused, the math sure added up when it came to her physical gifts. Nancee -- he didn't even know her last name -- had a killer body that hadn't been disfigured by all those cheeseburgers with mushrooms she ate at the Burger Ranch. But a girl's physical attributes were never enough for Matt. He liked women who stimulated him on every level. Women like Robbyn and Tiffany.

If the triangle in which he found himself wasn't conflicting and tormenting enough, now he had this major assignment to jump into -- one that potentially could jeopardize his relationship with Robbyn. Meanwhile, he wasn't sure what he wanted to say to Tiffany the next time they talked. They hadn't talked since she returned from New

York, taking turns playing phone tag. He wondered if it was intentional on her part. But then he put all thoughts of women aside and plunged into making some phone calls. Matt Meredith was first and foremost a journalist, and now the hunt was on. He had an uncanny ability to compartmentalize, a great asset when his professional and personal lives intersected at a rough crossroads.

Tiffany intentionally had been ignoring Matt's calls. She still hadn't decided whether to fight for him or dump him. She expected him to do more than call her. She expected him to show up at her suite or on the set and beg her for forgiveness. She still couldn't fathom why he had thought so little of her, had thought she was so superficial, even if he had been angry and scared because Timmy had been hit by a pitch.

But she couldn't deny that she missed him. Missed his humor, missed his smile, missed his touch. And missed making love to him. Tiffany hadn't had that many lovers. But she had been blessed with a few who had been rather accomplished. Nevertheless, she had never experienced the joy of sex to the degree she had with Matt. She strongly felt that the pleasure they derived from each other transcended the physical prowess on each of their parts. She strongly felt they had a physical and psychological harmony that was spectacular. She had been half-tempted to show up at the newspaper one afternoon to see Matt. But her stubborn pride would never let her do that. Tiffany didn't think of herself as having a big ego. But she definitely knew that she had a monumental reservoir or two of pride, an attribute that had given her the drive to become the actress she was today.

While Tiffany was being held hostage by her pride and inner focus, Matt was being held hostage by his job. He poured himself into digging up whatever he could find about the financial aspects of the Emergency Shelter. A beneficial aspect to being a practicing journalist in a medium-sized city like Braxton was that a good reporter knew most of the key players. And Matt was as well connected as anybody in town. He was respected in the community and didn't have the reputation of being a sensationalist. His strong credibility opened doors -- not to mention mouths -- for him. It also didn't hurt that he knew the executive director of the Emergency Shelter as well as five board members of the non-profit agency.

After several days of calls and meetings, it became clear to Matt that the Shelter's financial books were in order. But its capital campaign funds were a different matter. The accountant in charge of the funds wasn't aware of a $250,000 shortage until he, the executive director, Matt and an accountant friend of Matt reviewed them.

"All the fiscal controls are in place," Ted Mount, the respected capital campaign accountant, told Matt. "There are only two people who have access to the funds and can make withdrawals from the account at the bank -- the executive director and the chairman of the campaign. Even the chairs of our administration and stewardship committees don't have that access."

The executive director was Bob Tolliver, a man Matt knew well and trusted.

"I swear I never touched the funds," Tolliver said. "You know me, Matt. I would never skim any funds. But I can't believe Millie Paxton would either. Why would she? She doesn't need the money. Maybe it's just an accounting error."

"You were there when we inspected the books, you know that's not possible," Matt said.

"I guess there's no way in hell that you can ignore this?" Bob Tolliver asked Matt. "You know what bad publicity like this could do to our campaign."

"You know I can't do that," Matt said. "I'll pretend you didn't ask that."

"I'm going to talk to Millie," Bob said. "I'll get to the bottom of this."

"So, will I," Matt said, who opted not to reveal his suspicions about the mayor to Bob. He trusted Bob but working as an investigative reporter was like playing poker: You didn't want to show your cards prematurely. "Since this is late Friday afternoon, I'm going to call her first thing Monday morning."

"I'm going to talk to her tonight," Bob said. "And I'm going to confront her with this discrepancy."

"That's fine," Matt said. "Maybe she'll have an explanation for you. But whatever her answer, I'm going to ask her the same question you will. Encourage her to talk to me. If she has no comment, all our readers will assume she's guilty."

"I know, I know," said an agitated Bob, running a hand through his thinning hair.

Matt felt genuinely sorry for Bob Tolliver, a good guy caught up in a no-win situation. He and the Shelter did wonderful work. But if you are going to solicit funds from the public and from corporations, it's not good to have somebody dipping into the cookie jar.

The next day Matt's focus returned to Robbyn and the boys as the four of them drove to Philadelphia to watch the Phillies play the Mets. By now the swelling had subsided in Timmy's face, his lacerated lips were healing nicely and he was experiencing no post-concussion effects.

"The doctor said I can start playing ball again on Monday," Timmy said excitedly just a moment after Matt pulled out of the Baxter driveway.

"That's fantastic," Matt said. "I'm sure you can't wait."

"I can wait," Robbyn said. "I want you to be careful when you're in that batter's box. You can't afford to get hit by another pitch."

"You can't think like that, Mom," Timmy said, annoyance in his voice. "Otherwise I'll get gun-shy and step in the bucket on every pitch."

"He's right, Robbyn," Matt said. "He just needs to go up to the plate just like before and hit his pitch. If he's afraid, he'll flinch and bail and do everything but hit the ball. He'll be fine if he's just himself."

"I guess so," Robbyn said. "I guess I sound like a mother, not a coach. It's just that, well, it was so scary and all. Seeing him lying on the ground, then winding up in the hospital. I'll never forget that."

Matt smiled and said softly to her, who was in the front seat with him. "I can't blame you. It's only natural. But he'll be fine if he doesn't develop a complex about it."

"OK, slugger," Robbyn said, laughing to lift her spirits about the prospects of Timmy facing live pitching again, "go get 'em."

The four of them had a fun ride to the Phillies game. They didn't hit a ton of traffic on the dreaded Schuylkill Expressway, which was notorious for gridlock and a rash of accidents. And the conversation was delightful as the boys, Robbyn and Matt talked about everything -- the Sorbonne Township Cubs, the tournament team, the Phillies, favorite foods, favorite movies, favorite videos and toys. Eventually the boys began playing with video games on an iPad in the back seat. Robbyn then started filling Matt in on her awareness campaign for the Emergency Shelter capital campaign. When she brought up the subject, it was all Matt could do to refrain from wincing.

"We have a winning cause and people respond to that," Robbyn said, confidently. "People give to people. If our ads strike the right note, we'll create a contagious, enthusiastic campaign atmosphere. The campaign will get the heavy hitters from the corporate sector. But I believe our PR and advertising campaign will mine the private sector fairly well. And that area is what could put the capital campaign over the top."

"I think you have a good thing to work with -- just a matter of putting a human face on the cause," Matt said. "Some compelling photos and text."

He was sorely tempted to tell her about the capital campaign funding issue he was looking into, but he didn't think the timing was right. He didn't want to ruin the day. However, he realized that if he didn't tell her now, it would be quite awkward to tell her later. He decided to tell her now, hoping that the ballgame and the general fun of the day would mute any resentment on her part. After all, he reasoned, he simply was doing his job. But before he could say something Robbyn suddenly started talking about her late husband. She had resolved before the trip that she needed to share some of her life with Bob with Matt.

"You remind me a lot of my late husband," Robbyn said. "He was wonderful with the boys, loved interacting with them. I've noticed a lot of that in you as well. And Bob had a great sense of humor. He loved to make me laugh, to make everybody laugh. I don't know you that well yet. But from reading your columns, I can tell you have a great sense of humor, too. Being with Bob could be a riot. But he had a sensitive side as well. He was a great listener. I saw how sensitive you could be. You were wonderful when Timmy got hurt. And I know you must be a great listener because you couldn't draw out your column subjects as well as you do if you weren't.

"And I know this isn't the time or the place," she said in a lower tone as she slightly jerked her head back to indicate the presence of her boys in the back seat, "but you seem to have all the qualities I like in a man, in a relationship."

She paused for a moment and looked hard into Matt's eyes. Matt, of course, was driving on the Schuylkill Expressway. He didn't want to have his eyes on the road at this moment. He wanted to lock onto that penetrating gaze of Robbyn's for a long time. But unless he wanted the four of them to wind up as so much road kill on the Surekill, as Philadelphians called the Expressway, he had to avert his eyes back to the tractor-trailer he was gaining on in the passing lane.

As he did so, Robbyn put a hand on his right forearm, a touching move that sent a jolt of electricity to Matt's heart.

"But I want you to know one thing: I'm not looking for another Bob. There will be only one Bob in my heart. But I realize now that life must go on. And I do realize that if Bob hadn't gotten killed, you and I wouldn't be having this conversation. But he did. And now I've gotten over the notion that I have to be a widow for life. Not that I'm looking to get married right away or anything. But I sense you and I could be special together. And just so you know, you're hardly a clone of Bob's. In a lot of ways, you're a lot different."

She laughed.

"For instance, you're better-looking and you have a body to die for," she whispered.

Her candor shocked her almost as much as it did Matt.

He turned to her with a smile so warm that it singed her heart.

"I think you need to get a new prescription for contacts," said Matt, who always felt a tad uncomfortable when his good looks and physique drew a compliment.

"I've got 20-20 vision," Robbyn said, gleefully.

The four of them had a marvelous time during the Phillies game and on the ride back to Braxton. And Matt and Robbyn managed to have plenty of time to chat among themselves. They spoke of many things, profound as well as trivial. And found they had much in common. Robbyn laughed or giggled frequently, finding Matt to be charming and humorous. Matt found Robbyn to be delightful. They had such engaging conversations for the remainder of the trip that Matt didn't even think to broach the delicate subject of the problem with the Shelter's capital campaign funds.

It was late when Matt got the Baxters home and Matt didn't want to press the issue of intimacy, not with the boys there.

"Do you want to come in for a beer or so?" Robbyn asked him as the boys, who had fallen asleep on the ride home, grouchily said good night to him and walked up the driveway.

"I would absolutely love to have a beer with you, especially after the boys fall asleep," Matt said to Robbyn as he caressed her cheek with the palm of his hand. His touch sent chills through her. "But I think being alone with you would be so much better under more special circumstances."

As the boys scrambled into the garage, Matt touched Robbyn's hair and then gently took her hands in his. "This was one of the greatest days of my life," he said. "It was a privilege to spend it with you and the boys. I was attracted to you from the first moment I saw you. And now that I've gotten to know you, I know you're as beautiful inside as you are outside. I'd love to take you out to dinner next week, just the two of us."

"I think that can be arranged, Mr. Meredith," Robbyn practically cooed. What she once had found so frightening was now so mesmerizing.

She suddenly locked her lips on his as they exchanged a supernova of a kiss, one seemingly complete with galactic explosions of white light that consume everything else.

It was a kiss that left both of them with eyes as glazed as a Krispy Kreme.

When they finally parted lips, they stood there staring at each other in silence, frozen in the moment.

No further words were needed.

Matt slept very well that night, more soundly than he had in a week. Normally a good sleeper, he had been restless the past week as the dynamics of Tiffany and Robbyn, Timmy's injury, and the pressures of the Emergency Shelter investigative research toyed with his mind. So, it was like waking up from the dead when he heard a pounding on his front door, in conjunction with a hyperactive finger on his doorbell, the next morning at 8. Matt, roused by the noise, blinked at his alarm clock and realized it wasn't the culprit. It was the doorbell, in concert with what sounded like bongo drums on his front door.

"It's 8 o'clock on a freaking Sunday morning," Matt yelled as he threw on a pair of shorts and a T-shirt. "Who the hell could this be?"

He stomped downstairs, his hair a mess and his unshaven face wearing an annoyed grimace. He hardly was the picture of hospitality as he answered the front door. The grimace on his face quickly shifted into an expression of shock when his still-sleepy eyes focused on the person who had been punching the doorbell and pounding on the door.

"Sorry for the all the racket, but man, you're a sound sleeper," said Tiffany, looking wide awake and gorgeous in her flowered sundress.

"What's wrong?" Matt asked, confused.

"Nothing's wrong, silly," Tiffany said, giggling. "I just woke up early because I couldn't sleep. I haven't been sleeping well. I've missed you. Obviously, our separation hasn't affected your sleeping habits."

She playfully rolled her eyes.

"Actually, it has," Matt said, sheepishly. "I've had trouble falling asleep at night. That's why when I finally do fall asleep, I fall like a ton of bricks. Then I can't get up in the morning."

"Well, aren't you going to invite me in?" Tiffany asked.

She didn't bother to wait for an answer. She walked right past him into the foyer and then turned towards him.

"You look great," Matt said, both happy and upset to see her.

Matt still was basking in the warm afterglow of his wonderful Saturday with Robbyn and her boys. Consequently, he was a little disoriented -- a condition not enhanced by his grogginess.

"And you look like shit," Tiffany said, giggling. "I'd kiss you, but I bet you haven't brushed your teeth yet."

Matt, whose appreciation of her reaching out to him was growing as he became more oriented, smiled.

"I haven't," he said, "so just give me a hug."

She hugged him. It was an awkward hug for a moment, then a full-fledged hug, punctuated by a passionate kiss -- unbrushed teeth be damned.

"You even taste good with bad breath," Tiffany said.

"I have missed you," Matt said, who actually had missed her -- especially the physical part of their relationship -- despite his strong attraction to Robbyn.

The previous night he had been sure that his relationship with Tiffany was over. Suddenly, he was wavering slightly. Still, he felt he needed time to get to know Robbyn a bit more. He thought it was a bit premature to write off Tiffany entirely because he wasn't totally sure about Robbyn. But then, he wasn't totally sure about Tiffany once her Braxton shoot was over. He wasn't totally sure about anything. It was all so confusing and conflicting.

As for Tiffany, she wasn't sure about Matt either. She still was profoundly hurt over the way he had snapped at her after Timmy had been hit by the pitch; still miffed that he evidently thought her to be somewhat superficial and artificial. But she wasn't ready to throw away everything on what might have been just a knee-jerk reaction out of anger. After wrestling with her feelings and bruised ego for days, she decided to ask him point blank.

She sat down on his family room sofa, and he slumped in a nearby recliner, opting not to sit next to her. His choice of seats surprised her enough that it registered on her face.

"You could have sat down next to me," she said. "You still angry with me because I stayed in New York over the weekend?"

"Well, yeah," Matt said. "But I did call you and text you several times."

"And I called you and texted you," she responded quickly. "I guess we kept playing phone tag."

"I think we could have communicated if one of us really wanted to," he said.

"Are you saying you didn't want to?" she asked, a little hurt creeping into her voice.

"I'm just saying we both were out of touch, and I appreciate you making the first step," he said. Then, smilingly, he added: "Of course, you could have picked later in the day to get in touch."

Tiffany smiled, too.

"Maybe I knew I'd find you in bed," she said, laughing. "Speaking of your bed, there's nobody up there keeping it warm for you, is there? After all, you are the dream guy of Braxton, PA."

"Yeah, I'm a dream guy all right," Matt said, laughing, "which is why give you've been giving me such nightmares."

"Ah, ha! You did miss me," Tiffany said, exulting.

"OK, I did," Matt said, quickly deciding he'd placate her with a confession. "And, OK, I'm sorry. I was wrong. I admit it. In the heat of the moment, and in my concern for Timmy, I lashed out at you and misjudged you. I was upset. So, I said things I really didn't mean. I'm sure you've done that from time to time."

"Never," Tiffany said, teasing him and flirting with him. "Apology accepted. But please know that I'm a person of substance, not some dizzy actress who preens in front of the mirror all day. And please know that I love you, you big lout."

"Flattery will get you everywhere," Matt said, grinning broadly.

"It had better get me in your bed in a few minutes," Tiffany said, adding with a loud laugh: "But you had better brush your teeth first."

"We could skip the kissing and the foreplay and get right to screwing," Matt said, devilishly.

"Pig!" Tiffany yelped.

Matt and Tiffany both missed each other physically, and Tiffany missed Matt on an emotional level. Matt didn't miss her to the same degree on an emotional basis because of Robbyn. And as Tiffany and Matt bounded upstairs to his bedroom, he suddenly found himself conflicted again -- full of a strong physical yearning for Tiffany and full of a strong feeling of guilt that he was cheating on Robbyn. For a man who had essentially been involved in monogamous relationships, it was a dirty, uncomfortable feeling. As Tiffany sprawled invitingly on his bed while he brushed his teeth in his adjoining bathroom, he wondered why he felt so deeply about betraying Robbyn since they had yet to consummate their relationship. His feeling of betrayal toyed with his concentration while making love to Tiffany. For the first time, their lovemaking lacked the crackling fire of intensity that had made their relationship so spectacular. Tiffany's molten desire for him noticeably ebbed as she sensed his passion was more perfunctory than inspired. Matt wanted to be more energized as he caressed, fondled and explored Tiffany's curves and recesses, but it was almost as if his mind and heart were removed from his body. His body was going through the motions, but his mind and heart were strangely detached -- as if someone else was now climaxing in Tiffany while his mind's eye hovered with disinterest above. It had taken Matt considerably longer to come, and Tiffany's love juices were dissipating, making his penetrating thrusts a bit uncomfortable. To help himself come because Matt knew that Tiffany had to becoming sore, he fantasized that Tiffany was a slave woman and he was an evil medieval prince who would have her put to death if she didn't arouse him enough to come. Matt had no idea where the hell that strange and sick fantasy had surfaced from and he didn't want to know. But the fantasy, while necessary, made him feel like now that he had betrayed Tiffany as well as Robbyn. His body may have made love to Tiffany, but his thoughts had made love to a fantasy slave woman.

Covered with a cold sweat as he rolled off of her, he noticed a crushing look of hurt and sadness on Tiffany's face. Then sad instantly morphed into mad.

"You really had to work to come, didn't you?" she yelled, not really needing an answer. She began crying softly. "You don't love me anymore, do you, you bastard?"

This time she and her fragile ego needed an answer.

Matt couldn't give her a direct answer, because he himself wasn't even sure if he loved her. Actually, he knew that he loved her to some degree, but all his possibilities with Robbyn had diffused his focus on Tiffany. The most truthful answer he could give her would to ask her to take a sabbatical from their relationship while he tried to establish a lasting relationship with Robbyn. And if Robbyn and he didn't work out, Tiffany should be willing to jump back to center stage after waiting in the wings. Of course, that was an answer that he couldn't give her without risking sudden castration.

"I don't know what got into my head, but I was kind of distracted," he said, sheepishly.

"Distracted!" she screamed. "Distracted by what? I thought you'd never come. I'm going to be sore for a week. Your heart wasn't in it, was it? Well, I don't want anybody who doesn't want me. Do you know how many men would kill for the privilege to make love to me? Screw you!"

She practically jumped out of bed and angrily got dressed. She was seething inside.

"I think I'm falling in love with Robbyn," Matt said, still lying on the bed.

"So, you screwed her all night before she went home to her kids, huh?" Tiffany huffed. "No wonder you had trouble pulling the trigger. You were fresh out of bullets. You ran dry on come."

"I have never made love to Robbyn," Matt said, quietly.

"Like I believe that!" Tiffany said. "Actually, tell your lies to somebody who cares. I'm out of here. I wanted to give you one more shot, but to be honest, I came here with some reservations that you weren't the guy I thought you were. Well, you aren't. You're out of my life. And I'll soon be out of this crummy little town."

She stalked out of the bedroom, ignoring Matt's pathetic closing salvo of "I'm sorry we didn't work out."

Tiffany was heartbroken as she drove back to her hotel suite. Once again, she had failed to cement a lasting relationship with a man. But she wasn't blaming herself. She totally blamed Matt. Failed relationships were never her fault.

"He's selfish, a damn womanizer!" she screamed to herself while stopped at a red light. Since she was driving a convertible with the top down, her scream was overheard by an elderly couple crossing the intersection on their way to church. The old man and old lady jerked their heads toward the crying Tiffany, their faces embroidered with disgust.

"Where are you folks going to, a coffin fitting?" Tiffany screamed at them, totally inflamed by the sourpuss look on their faces.

"My, my, Elmer, I think that's the movie star who's filming that movie here in Braxton," the elderly lady said, shaking her head.

"I think you're right, Martha," her husband answered. "But I don't think it's a good time to ask for her autograph."

Meanwhile, Matt stayed in bed until for a bit. He was mentally wiped out, and he felt awful about how his relationship with Tiffany had ended. There were elements of him that thought he had to be crazy not to embrace a

Hollywood star like Tiffany and hold on for dear life. But most of him realized that he had done the right thing, that he no longer could be involved with Tiffany and Robbyn. He couldn't stand the conflicting emotions, all the complications. He could envision himself being happily married for life with Robbyn, and he could envision himself being a proud and content stepfather to Timmy and Billy. But mostly he didn't want to think. He just wanted to let go of all the emotional trappings and move on.

It wouldn't take him long to move on with his life. Two hours after Tiffany walked out on his life, Matt's doorbell rang again. It woke him up again. And, once again, there was an attractive young lady at his front door. But there wasn't an exact pattern setting in. The sound of the doorbell startled Matt. His heart skipped a beat for a moment, as he assumed it might be Tiffany. He wasn't sure if his heart skipped a beat out of hope or despair. Still disheveled but with brushed teeth this time, he loped to the front door, half-afraid to open it.

When he opened the door and saw a beaming Robbyn in his face, rapture cascaded through his heart. She was looking quite fit and athletic in her black tennis shorts and white tank top. It was at that very moment that he knew for sure that he loved Robbyn, and that she was the lady he was destined to spend eternity with. As for Robbyn, her beaming smile lost a little bit of its wattage as she noticed how terrible Matt looked.

"Are you sick? You look terrible," she asked, concerned.

"Just had a rough night … couldn't sleep right," he mumbled, ushering her in.

"That's a surprise. I was on Cloud Nine last night, thinking of you. I slept like a baby," she said, regaining her smile. "I hope you weren't having a nightmare about me, uh, about us."

Her smile segued into a look of concern. It was a brief look of concern. Her smile was back and bigger than ever a moment later when she heard Matt say: "I couldn't sleep because I was so excited about us," he said, his quick-witted writer's mentality helping him author what he knew she wanted, needed to hear. "Every time I almost drifted off to sleep, another sensation of excitement about the possibilities of our future flooded my mind and heart."

It was a white lie, the last white lie he would ever tell her, he swore to himself. After all, he was now convinced that he was talking to his future bride.

"You MUST be a writer," Robbyn said, no stranger to the art of word-smithing herself. "That's so sappy. But I'll TAKE IT."

Instead, he took her. He swept her up into his arms and carried her upstairs to his room. This time there was no self-doubt, no inner conflict toying with his mind, diffusing his focus on the adorable, delicious, loving woman in his arms. A tender, romantic lover who reveled in foreplay and stoking excitement before plunging into a crescendo of raw, sexual performance, he treated Robbyn to a sexual and romantic tour de force -– the likes of which she had never experienced with Bob. And Bob was her only frame of reference when it came to sex.

But Bob Baxter was not on Robbyn's mind at the moment. Nor in her heart. The memory of Bob Baxter had been nudged aside by the powerful, physical presence of Matt Meredith.

Matt was reaching the zenith of sexual arousal, and Robbyn, her sexual hormones neglected and in limbo since the death of her husband, matched him every step of the marvelous journey to the deep pleasure only true love can elicit. Matt exulted in the utter responsiveness Robbyn exuded and was thrilled when she took turns being the aggressor and treated his body as if it were a temple she was drenching with intense worship.

When they climaxed, their mutual moans and sounds of pleasure spiked their sexual energy even higher. Robbyn thought her multiple orgasms would never stop. At first, she prayed that they would never stop. Then she prayed that they *would* stop because she thought the incessant waves of sheer pleasure washing over her were going to drive her insane. Robbyn and Matt held each other tightly for almost an hour afterwards, basking in the magnificent post-coital glow known only to lovers who realize they have just had the greatest sex of their lives with the very person they wanted to have it with. During that time, they just hung on for dear life, pausing only to stare with acute wonder into each other's eyes and to occasionally mutter, "Oh, my God."

Speaking of God, they both realized they had just experienced a taste of heaven here on earth.

"You're divine," Robbyn said, stroking Matt's tousled hair as tears of pure joy pooled in her eyes.

"No, *we're* divine," Matt gently corrected her, his happiness glowing from his handsome face.

They both fell asleep. When they awoke two hours later, he no longer was just Matt. She no longer was just Robbyn. Their spirits had been fused. They were Robbyn and Matt, hopefully inseparable for the ages.

Chapter Fifteen

It had been a sublime Sunday for Matt and Robbyn. And for the boys. That evening the four of them went to dinner at a Dairy Queen to celebrate Timmy's successful return to the batter's box.

That afternoon Matt had pitched a round of batting practice to Timmy, who didn't flinch once and who hit the ball just like the Timmy of old.

"I feel fine," Timmy had said during the round. "Just like the beaning never happened."

"Good," Matt had said. "I knew you would be fine, especially when I purposely pitched you high and tight a few times and you didn't step into the bucket once."

After they returned from dinner, the boys watched a Yankees game on television while Matt and Robbyn sat on her small patio.

Matt took a long sip of ice tea and frowned, an expression that Robbyn picked up on.

"What's wrong? Suddenly having second thoughts about us?" she asked, concern apparent in her voice.

"Absolutely not," he said. "I'm head over heels over you and I know I will be forever."

"Forever is a long time," she said.

"Good," Matt said. "I want to be with you a long time. But I have something to tell you. It came to my attention recently that there is a problem with the Emergency Shelter capital campaign. Somebody's been skimming funds, it seems."

"Where did you hear that?" Robbyn asked, shock resonating in her voice. "That can't be true!"

"My boss gave me a tip and I've been working on an investigative piece," Matt said. "I wanted to tell you when we went to the Phillies game, but I didn't want to spoil your day. Our day."

"So, you waited until you got into my pants to break the bad news, huh?" Robbyn said, sounding hurt.

"That wasn't it at all, darling," he said, getting up from his chair and putting an arm around her to comfort her. "I know this could make your job terribly difficult. But it's a story that needs to be told, and hopefully will help restore the funds to the account."

Robbyn sat silent for an eternity. Matt felt as if he were sitting in an electric chair, waiting for the jolt.

"I know you're just doing your job, and it sounds like your story might uncover a theft. But my job will be awful trying to restore the damage. This feel-good campaign won't feel very good at all. How much money is missing? And have you talked to Bob Tolliver and Millie Paxton?"

"I've talked to Bob and board members," Matt said. "Bob and I, and a couple accountants went over the books. It looks like there is a $250,000 shortage. I am going to talk to Millie on Monday. Bob said only he and Millie have access to the funds, and Bob said he hasn't touched the money. And I believe him. He's sick over this. And I want you to know that I am, too, because I know the Shelter does great work and I know this will be a nightmare for you."

"I believe you," Robbyn said. "You're a good man. So, you think Millie is taking the money? Why would she need the money?"

Matt stood up, the anxiety making his legs feel rather jumpy.

"The person who gave my managing editor the tip – a person whose identity even I don't know and a name my boss won't give me -- thinks it's Jimbo Cummings who's been dipping into the funds. Bob thinks Millie is innocent and that Jimbo is taking advantage of her. I think Bob was going to talk to Millie this weekend. I hope he didn't because I would have preferred to talk to Millie first. But out of respect for Bob and the Shelter, I agreed to wait until Monday to call Millie. And then I'm going to call Jimbo. I hope to break the story by Tuesday."

"Tuesday! That doesn't give me much time to get some revised image ads produced," Robbyn said.

"I know," Matt said softly. "But I can't sit on this story. Now that I've stirred up the dust, if I don't break it, somebody at Channel 19 or one of the radio stations will."

"I don't believe this," Robbyn said, slumping in her seat. "This has been a fantastic weekend -- until this."

"I know we're on opposite sides of this to an extent, but in some ways we aren't," Matt said. "I know what a wonderful place the Shelter is. My stories will always affirm that."

"The Shelter will be guilty by association and the capital campaign will be a disaster," Robbyn said. "This sucks. If what you say is true, I feel horrible for Millie. Her reputation will be ruined, too."

"She should have shown better judgment when it comes to men," Matt said.

For a minute, Robbyn gave Matt a cold stare. He almost gulped looking at it and sat down as if to avoid it. Then she smiled warmly.

"I think I have shown good judgment in men, don't you think?" she said.

"Absolutely," Matt said, relieved that the news of his investigation hadn't severed his budding relationship with

Robbyn. But he did realize, as did she, that the Shelter's problem could pose some problems for them as a couple.

"I know this is silly," Robbyn said, finishing her glass of lemonade, "but when people start realizing we are, well, a couple, what will they think of your stories? Will they think that I was one of your sources?"

"Actually, I hadn't even thought of that," Matt said. "You and your ad agency are simply guns for hire that the Shelter outsourced for advertising support. You and the agency aren't a part of the internal workings of the capital campaign's fiscal aspects."

"You're right, I guess I'm just being paranoid," Robbyn said. "I'm also wondering if my boss is going to be upset with me when he finds out I'm dating you. Paul Missonis is not the most open-minded of men. He's old, but worse, he's old-fashioned. He undoubtedly is going to feel that the Missonis Agency is going to get a black eye for being involved with a capital campaign that has financial irregularities. I know we are getting paid by the Shelter, but I know Paul has donated some of our services as part of his contribution to the campaign. He may just pull the agency's support. And he may also think that I've been one of your sources."

"I think you're making a big stretch there," Matt said. "It sounds like you don't want people to know that we're a couple until this whole thing blows over."

"Maybe we should keep our relationship quiet until then," Robbyn pressed on. "After all, you are putting me in an awkward situation here."

Matt was annoyed by what he perceived as an overreaction on Robbyn's part. He should have bit his lip. But he wasn't quick enough to hit the self-edit button.

"Robbyn, it's not like you're the Shelter's executive director or the capital campaign chairman. You're just writing ad copy for an outside agency. You're not involved with any of this."

Robbyn visibly bristled at Matt's comment, feeling as if he had just demeaned her role in the campaign. Now she was the one who stood.

"I know newspaper people think PR and advertising people are shills and sellouts," Robbyn said, an edge to her voice. "But we're more important than you think."

"I never said you weren't important, just that a scandal of this sort shouldn't cast a shadow upon you or your agency," Matt said. "But if you are bound and determined to keep our relationship a secret for now, well, fine."

"Is that too much to ask?" Robbyn asked.

"Of course not," Matt said, before adding with a thick slice of sarcasm: "So I had better leave now. One of your neighbors might see you alone with me here on your patio and immediately call your boss and the district attorney."

"Don't be a jerk," Robbyn said. "Tell me you're not a jerk when stress pops up in a relationship."

"Stress is a state of mind," Matt said, "and I thrive on stress. I'm a deadline junkie. But your stress in this situation, in my opinion, is overstated."

"So, are you leaving now?" Robbyn asked, hoping that he wouldn't.

"Do you want me to leave?"

"Of course not."

"Then give me a kiss and I'll think about it," Matt said, smiling.

Reassured at apparently having survived their first personal crisis as a couple, Robbyn walked up to Matt and gave him a deep, warm kiss that was giving Matt a huge erection until they both heard the familiar voice of Billy Baxter excitedly begin a sing-song chant:

"Mommy's kissing Coach Matt! Mommy's kissing Coach Matt!"

Her face turning ever-darker shades of crimson, Robbyn turned to Billy, his face beaming, and said nervously: "I was just kissing Coach Matt goodbye."

Robbyn felt totally awkward at that moment, although that definitely was not apparent to a young child like Billy. She was not prepared to have her sons know that she had become romantically involved with another man. Upset by the Shelter scandal and Matt's role in breaking the story and embarrassed by having had Billy see her passionately kissing his older brother's baseball coach, for a moment or two the thought of ditching the relationship with Matt flashed through her mind. It just seemed as if the whole thing was getting too complicated for her.

As for Matt, he was praying that Billy hadn't seen his erection, one that was rapidly diminishing.

"Wait until I tell Timmy," Billy screamed with delight. With that, he ran back inside the house. As he did so, Robbyn yelled after him through the patio's sliding screen door: "Tell him what? That I simply kissed his coach goodbye?"

"Relax, Robbyn," Matt said, trying to soothe her embarrassment. "I know this must be awkward for you, but they had to find out eventually. Plus, I think they'll be happy for us. Billy seemed genuinely happy."

"I'm not sure I'm ready for all of this," Robbyn said. "This is just so sudden. With the boys finding out about us and this Shelter story, it's sort of a bit too much."

"So, you're ready to cut and run on what could be the greatest thing to happen to us?" Matt said, his voice rising.

"Bob Baxter was the greatest thing that ever happened to me," Robbyn shot back, shocked at what she was saying.

Shoved into a psychological corner, the words somehow had flown out of her subconscious.

But her words were even more shocking to Matt, shocking enough to eradicate any last vestiges of understanding that he may have held for the sensitivities of her widowhood.

"Fine!" he barked. "Keep on living with a ghost!"

With that, he stomped through the yard and to the driveway, jumped into his car, and sped off.

Stunned, Robbyn began crying hysterically just as Timmy and Billy bounded out onto the patio, their broad smiles suddenly shocked into grimaces.

"You guys were just kissing and now you're crying," Billy said, his confusion increasing the volume in his voice.

"Did you and Coach Matt have a fight over me coming back to play ball tomorrow?" Timmy asked.

Drowning in her embarrassment and unable to stop her tears, Robbyn simply hugged both her boys. More than anything else at that moment, she needed a good hug. Billy started crying as well.

Robbyn dabbed at his tears with a Kleenex and then at hers. The absurdity of the moment finally hit her and she started smiling weakly, followed by a soft giggle.

"We're a mess, aren't we, Billy?" she said soothingly.

"Well, I'm not a mess," Timmy interrupted. "What's going on around here. Billy said Coach Matt might be your boyfriend. Is that right?"

Robbyn looked lovingly into Timmy's eyes and asked him point blank: "How would you feel about that, Timmy? I know in your heart that nobody will ever replace your father. And the same goes for me. But at the same time, it's been four years since Daddy died and it would be nice for you boys to have a father-type figure and it would be nice for me to have a husband someday. But that doesn't mean that all three of us won't always cherish the memory of Daddy."

"Mom, it's all right," Timmy said, sounding all grown up. "I understand. For a long time, I didn't want you to have a new husband and I didn't need a new father. You were our mother and father. But Coach Matt is great, although I'm mad at him right now for making you cry. But I think it would be great if you and Coach Matt got married."

"It would be fantastic!" Billy piped in, the heat of his excitement drying his tears. "Then my new dad could coach me in baseball next year. I bet I would replace Timmy at shortstop when he moves up to the junior league."

Robbyn smiled and hugged both of them again.

"It's way premature to talk about marriage, but I would like to start dating Matt," she said. "Which means he will be spending more time with you guys."

"Cool!" Billy yelled.

"You bet!" Timmy yelped.

"And we weren't disagreeing about baseball or you returning to play Monday," Robbyn said to Timmy. "We had a disagreement about a work situation. One of my ad campaigns and one of his stories are coming into conflict. I'm not going into the details, but Matt and I will work things out."

"You'd better!" Timmy said emphatically.

"Do we have any vanilla ice cream left?" Billy asked, dramatically changing the subject.

As Robbyn was scooping out the last vestiges of vanilla ice cream from the half-gallon container, she swore that she would do everything in her power to make things work with Matt. Her sons' enthusiastic endorsement of her budding relationship with Matt had given her heart the green light to put their romance on the fast track. She just hoped and prayed that her overreaction to his investigative story on the Shelter campaign wouldn't make that green light turn red on his part. She realized now that she had been looking to provoke him because she still had been uncomfortable with plunging forward with the relationship.

Meanwhile, Matt was beating himself up mentally back at home. He realized he had overreacted himself by storming out on Robbyn and leaving her in tears. He didn't usually have such a short fuse, but he had grown exasperated with her. He had felt as if she had been going out of her way to think of possible complications the Shelter controversy would cause their relationship. He had harbored a strong sense that she was looking for ways -- or excuses -- to jeopardize the relationship. He had realized the situation was awkward for her, and there would be some stress on their relationship. But to hide their relationship, to keep it a secret, well, he thought that was more than just a bit much. He also had felt mortified that Billy had walked in on their kiss and prayed that he hadn't seen his erection. That embarrassment had contributed to his hasty exit. But before he could think more about their tiff, his phone rang. When he heard Robbyn's voice on the line, his heart rang as well.

"I'm so sorry for leaving so abruptly," Matt said loudly, excitement coating his words.

"And I'm so sorry for acting like such a jerk," Robbyn said. "I realize you're just doing your job. And I think the real reason I was being so insistent on keeping our relationship a secret was a fear of rushing into things before I -- and more importantly, the boys — were ready for me to have a relationship. But now I realize that I'm more than ready. And so are the boys. I had to explain to them what's up with you and me. And they think it's great. They think you're great. And so do I."

"You just made me the happiest guy in the world," Matt gushed. "And I promise you I will do everything I can to make you and the boys happy forever."

"Ditto!" yelped Robbyn. "And don't worry about the Shelter campaign. I'll do my job and you do your job. And I won't worry about what people think. And from now on, the whole world can know about us! I'm flattered and thrilled to have someone like you. And I'm so sorry about saying what I did about Bob. I'm not the comparative type, and I promise never to compare you two."

"And I'm so sorry about the crack about living with a ghost," Matt said. "That was mean. I'm not normally such an asshole."

"We have such intense feelings for each other, and we have some new territory to explore together," Robbyn said. "So, both of us will have some emotional responses."

"If you were here right now, I'd give you the greatest kiss in history," Matt said, laughing.

"I'd give you more than a kiss," Robbyn said. "I'll leave you with that tempting thought. And please let me know how your conversation with Millie Paxton goes tomorrow."

"I'll call you right after I'm done talking to her," Matt said. "And fill you in after the ballgame. I think Timmy is going to have a great game. I can't wait for him to get back into the swing of things."

"I love you," Robbyn said, her voice almost tingling.

"I love you, too," Matt said emphatically. "With every damn fiber of my essence."

"You sound like a writer," Robbyn fired back, teasingly. "You should be a gushy romance novelist."

"I have no experience with romance," Matt said, laughing.

"Yeah, right, Mr. Casanova," Robbyn said sarcastically.
"I'll always be your Casanova," Matt said.

Chapter Sixteen

Matt was thankful for large favors. Especially when he called Millie Paxton the next morning and discovered that she hadn't spoken over the weekend with Bob Tolliver, the Shelter's executive director. Matt wanted to be the first person to tell her about the capital campaign fund shortage. Not because he relished being the bearer of bad news, but he wanted to hear her fresh reaction ... before she had time to mull over her thoughts or have her response coached and couched by Jimbo Cummings.

"Bob left me a voicemail, but I was out of town over the weekend with Jimbo and didn't get a chance to call Bob back," Millie said sweetly.

Millie Paxton was an adorable person and Matt knew what he was about to tell her would be crushing.

He didn't mince words when he opened with, "Millie, what I have to say you will find devastating."

"This can't be! Oh, Lord, this simply can't be!" Millie yelped upon hearing the full story from Matt. "Are you sure Bob and the accountants didn't miss anything?"

"Unfortunately, we're sure," Matt said. "I wish there was no shortage. I know the Shelter does wonderful work. And I know that Bob is absolutely trustworthy, as are you. I know you are a marvelous asset to this community."

"Don't patronize me or sugar-coat this," Millie said, her voice growing glum. "So, what do you think happened because there's no way anything like this could have happened?"

"I was hoping you could shed some light on this for me before I print this story," Matt said.

"I've been involved in numerous capital campaigns and we have the same fiscal controls on this one like we did all the others," Millie said, becoming annoyed. "This has to be a mistake. This isn't possible."

Millie at that moment in time didn't even factor in the Jimbo Cummings equation. She trusted him implicitly and had solicited his help in this particular campaign to ease the burden on her. It was an informal arrangement, so when Matt asked her who had access to the campaign funds, she didn't even think to mention Jimbo.

So, when Matt specifically asked her if Jimbo had access to the funds or was anyway, either directly or indirectly involved with the campaign, Millie became flustered and denied that he was.

"Oh, uh, why heavens no!" she said, her voice trembling. Then she quickly added, "I don't know why you have to print a story about this. It will destroy the capital campaign. I personally will make up the shortfall if there is one, every penny of that. I will account for the difference. There's no need to write a story."

"I respectfully disagree," Matt said, feeling her obvious pain but sensing that she indeed was lying about the mayor's access to funds. "Whenever the credibility of a capital campaign is in question and when it is documented that a substantial amount like $250,000 is missing, there's a story."

"I thought you were a good guy," Millie said, getting huffy. "But I guess you're a muckraker just trying to sell newspapers. You don't care who you hurt. You don't care if the Shelter and the people it serves are hurt."

"Yes, I do," Matt said. "This is not about selling newspapers. This is about the public trust."

Millie Paxton rarely was a rude person. But she promptly hung up on Matt.

Matt sat in silence at his desk for a good five minutes, feeling pretty lousy about what Millie Paxton was going through. Balancing that, however, was an adrenaline rush. He sensed that his managing editor's source was correct in fingering Jimbo Cummings. The mayor's administration had been rocked by several scandals through the years, but he was such a popular figure with the masses that the popular perception was that he simply was a benevolent scalawag.

Matt was determined to alter that perception.

Moments after hanging up with Matt, Millie was on speed dial to Jimbo's cell phone.

"There's a campaign fund shortage!" she shouted, in tears. "I can't imagine how. Matt Meredith from the *Braxton Bugle* called me. He knows about it. He's even met with Bob Tolliver. He said he and Bob sat down with accountants and we're 250 grand short."

"Now, calm down, Millie," said Jimbo, his voice reassuring. "I'm sure there's some mistake. Some damn accounting mix-up. I'll call Bob and see what's up. Maybe we can clear this up before Meredith runs a story. What did you tell Meredith?"

"That I couldn't imagine how this could happen, if it's true," Millie said, her voice quavering. "Then he asked me if you had access to the funds. I didn't tell him you've been helping me out, since you aren't officially connected with the campaign. So, I told him no."

"Sounds like he's trying to smear the campaign and me and you," Jimbo said, getting angry. "That pretty boy columnist should mind his own business. The nerve of him. Why would he ask such a question?"

"I never told anybody that you were helping me with the fiscal aspects of the campaign," Millie said.

"I guess he wants me to be the fall guy," Jimbo bellowed.

"Do you know anything about this?" Millie asked, growing even more alarmed.

"Of course not, dear," Jimbo said, his voice growing calmer as not to further provoke her alarm. "I may be a politician, but I'm no crook."

"I know, I know," she said. "It's just so unnerving. I'm sorry. I'm not accusing you of anything."

"I know," Jimbo said. "I'll call Bob and get back to you."

As Jimbo hung up, his cell rang again.

"Hello?" he asked, then yelled, "What the hell are you up to and how did you get this number, Meredith?"

"Good morning, your honor," Matt said, semi-sarcastically.

"Screw you!" bellowed Jimbo. "I just talked to Millie. This is bullshit. If there is a shortage with her capital campaign, I'm sure it's an innocent accounting mistake that can be rectified. And if you're trying to tie me into any shortage just because Millie's my girlfriend, well, that sucks. I have nothing to do with that campaign. It's none of my business. And if you smear me or Millie in this, I'll sue your damn paper. Got it?"

"So, you're denying you had access to any capital campaign funds?" Matt asked calmly.

"Of course I am, you freaking idiot!" Jimbo screamed, hanging up.

Matt spent the rest of the day writing his investigative piece on the Emergency Shelter's capital campaign fund shortage. He worked on it as diligently as he had on any story he had ever written. The managing editor, city editor and two assistant city editors pored over every word. Then the copy desk chief gave it a hard edit. They all were confident that the story was structured in proper sequence, and that there were no holes in it or missing facts. Matt strove to point out all the positive aspects of the Shelter in the story. He wrote it simply and directly, foregoing the eloquent phrasing or one-liners that frequently populated his columns. He was precise and to the point. It was a straight news story, so he simply reported the shortage, threw in a bunch of numbers his and the Shelter's accountant had shared with him, and quoted Bob Tolliver and Millie Paxton, including Millie's vow to personally make up for any shortage of funds. He also quoted Shelter board members, some of who swore they would get to the bottom of the matter. Some officials downplayed the repercussions of the shortage on the campaign; others emphatically said the shortage would severely crimp the remainder of the capital campaign. Matt didn't write anything about the mayor in the story. Matt had no proof that Jimbo had taken any money. He also felt it wouldn't be right to print Jimbo's denial about having access to the funds because the mayor had no ties to the campaign, other than dating the campaign's chairperson. Matt would have to hold off on involving the mayor until he got proof that Jimbo actually had taken the funds. And for now, Matt had no idea how he would get that proof. Because, after going over the structure of the campaign's fiscal controls, Matt felt that only Millie and Jimbo knew what really happened.

By the time Matt and his editors had edited and proofed the story and several accompanying sidebar articles and charts, Timmy's first baseball game since his injury was over. When Matt realized he would miss the game, he had called Robbyn at work and at home, leaving voicemails of sincere apologies. He hoped that she and, most of all, Timmy would understand. He also called his assistant coach, Paddy Flanagan, a crusty 73-year-old former Phillies farmhand, and told him he would have to be the head coach.

"And put up with all those damn parents!" Paddy said, laughing into the phone. "Don't worry, Matty. I'll bring home a winner. And if I see Timmy being tentative at the plate, I'll tell him to forget about the beaning and just pretend he's swinging at a big marshmallow out there."

When Robbyn checked her voicemail messages before going to the game, she was hurt that Matt would miss Timmy's first game back. But she could tell from the tone of Matt's voice on his message that it was killing him to miss the game. And she understood that this just wasn't some story that Matt could bang out in a whirl of fingers tapping on a keyboard. Timmy was a little less understanding.

"What could be more important than this game?" Timmy said, the annoyance and hurt evident in his voice. "If we win this game, we're one win away from clinching the division title. It's just a newspaper story."

"It's his job, Timmy," Robbyn said. "And I know he wouldn't miss this game unless he absolutely had to."

"OK," Timmy said, grudgingly.

Timmy's disappointment was short-lived. He hit three homers and a triple, driving in 12 runs, as the Cubs romped 15-2. He was perfectly relaxed and poised at the plate.

"Son, you're gonna be a big leaguer someday," Paddy shouted at Timmy after his last home run.

After the game, Robbyn hugged Timmy and said: "I'm proud of you, Timmy. You were your old self up there at the plate."

"I can't wait to tell Coach Matt about this," Timmy said.

He didn't have to wait long. As soon as Matt and his editors put the Shelter package of stories to bed, Matt drove over to the Baxters. Over dishes of vanilla ice cream, Timmy described his at-bats pitch by pitch to Matt and Robbyn. Billy was part of the audience for a brief period, but quickly grew bored with his brother's tale of triumph and opted to watch television cartoons instead.

"It kills me to have missed your big return," Matt said, tousling Timmy's hair. "You must have been quite the slugger tonight. I wished I could've seen it."

Then Robbyn and Timmy both beamed.

"I videoed all his at-bats on my iPhone," Robbyn said. "Care to watch them?"

"Of course, I do," Matt said loudly. "You guys made my night!"

The three of them sat together on the sofa in the family room, watching Timmy's magical night. Eventually Billy sauntered into the room and joined them.

They were a family.

Matt didn't know what looked prettier -- Timmy's swing on the videos or the expression of joy and contentment on Robbyn's face as she sat with her boys and with her arm around her new man.

For her part, Robbyn was very proud of all her boys, a lineup that now included Matt.

The next morning, however, wasn't nearly as happy for Robbyn. When her boss and ad agency owner Paul Missonis read that morning's *Braxton Bugle*, he was appalled by the Shelter's fiscal crisis and determined to minimize the fallout with an aggressive advertising counter offensive.

"I don't doubt there's a problem with the funds," Missonis, a gruff and decisive man in his mid-sixties, barked to Robbyn. "But I'm sure that will be worked out, especially if Millie Paxton makes good on her pledge to make up for any possible shortage. What we have to do is produce a quick series of ads in print, radio, online, social media and TV acknowledging that while there may be a short-term fiscal problem with the campaign, the long-term global picture is that the Shelter does great work in rescuing folks from the trash heaps of society."

"It's going to be a challenge, but I'm up for it," Robbyn said.

"I want radio spots on the air by tomorrow," Missionis said, "and I want print ads in the *Bugle* in a matter of days. And hopefully we can turn around a TV spot in a week or so. I want it airing during all the Miller Edition newscasts on Channel 19. And on social media today."

"We can do all of that, but it's going to require a lot of work in a short time," Robbyn said.

"Well, you can catch up on your beauty sleep later," Missonis snapped at Robbyn in his less than politically correct way.

Robbyn poured herself feverishly into the project. There were bound to be late nights for the remainder of the week. Already she was worried about missing Timmy's game on

Thursday night and she fretted over the boys being left in the care of Cindy Loeper for a few days. She loved Cindy, but knew she had a tendency to be overwhelmed at times. But Robbyn knew that Timmy would enjoy spending time with Derek Loeper each night.

Predictably, Matt was busy all day and night Tuesday. He spent the morning on WBAM's *Feedback* show, fielding calls from listeners who were either supportive of him doing a public service by pointing out the shortfall or who were angry that he was throwing mud on a venerable and important Braxton institution that had touched the lives of thousands over the years.

The highlight of his session on WBAM was when Millie Paxton called in and once again renewed her pledge to make up for any shortage, even if it did turn out to be the $250,000 amount mentioned in Matt's story. But Millie, who obviously was sobbing while on the air, didn't stop there. She suddenly announced that she was resigning, effective immediately, as the chairman of the Shelter's capital campaign. That blockbuster announcement stunned Matt for a moment. He realized he had just scooped himself by agreeing to appear on the radio. WBAM now got the scoop, not him. But since WBAM was owned by Braxton Bugle Company, it wasn't the end of the world. Still, Matt would have loved to have broken the story. Thinking quickly, he decided to press Millie on any influence that Jimbo Cummings may have had in her decision to resign. But first he decided to flatter her.

"Well, Millie, I think it's unfortunate that you have come to the decision to resign as chairman," he said, comfortingly. "Your contributions to this community in terms of time and treasure have been unparalleled. Nobody has accused you of any wrongdoing in this matter. None of my sources has implicated you in the slightest. Your reputation is above reproach."

"Well, uh, thank you for your kind words," Millie said haltingly. "But this apparent shortage happened on my watch. And I'm ultimately responsible. Shelter officials tried to talk me out of it, but my mind is made up."

Matt decided to jump on Millie's last phrase.

"Did our mayor, Jimbo Cummings, have anything to do with helping to make up your mind?" he probed.

"I resent that, Mr. Meredith," Millie said, her voice rising. "Mr. Cummings has had no involvement with this capital campaign. And while he and I have a personal relationship, I am my own person and I make my own decisions."

After Millie hung up, Jimbo -- who was beside her the whole time -- gave her a kiss. Smiling reassuringly, he said: "You did the right thing, Millie. There's no need to have your good name drug through the mud of a smear campaign.

Nobody in his right mind thinks you're guilty. But Meredith thinks you might be guilty by association because I think he thinks I had something to do with it."

"I still don't know how he knows you were handling the campaign finances for me," Millie said. "Only you and I know that. You didn't tell anybody."

"Of course not," Jimbo said emphatically. "I'm no fool. I think Meredith is just trying to connect me with the shortage because of our relationship and because he's been out to get me for years. I just would love to know who tipped him off to the shortage."

"Who knew there was a shortage if you and I and Bob Tolliver didn't?" Millie asked, tearing up.

"Damn if I know," Jimbo said, giving her a hug. "But I sure as hell will find out."

She couldn't have looked glummer.

After Millie's stunning announcement on the radio, Matt spent the remainder of the day and early evening calling Shelter officials and campaign officials, seeking reaction to her resignation. That was his main story. But he also wrote a sidebar story on Millie herself, filled with quotes from community leaders on her vast accomplishments and on their regrets that her public service had been tainted by the Shelter campaign scandal. Matt also wrote a commentary column, extolling Millie for her wonderful career, but also asking some tough questions about whether she had fallen asleep on her watch. He also was critical of the Shelter and its capital campaign structure, citing a lack of tight fiscal controls. Balancing matters, he wrote an additional sidebar on all the services the Shelter provides, liberally sprinkled with quotes from people it had helped and from community officials.

"You've done a helluva day's worth of work," his managing editor, Ned March, said to Matt as March prepared to leave for the evening.

"It's exhausting but rewarding," Matt said. "It's nice to be a part of substantial, breaking news stories from time to time. You sort of miss that adrenaline rush when you're a columnist."

"Thinking of going back to a beat?" Ned asked, laughing.

"I couldn't afford the pay cut," Matt said.

Fortunately for Matt, he wasn't overwhelmed by Shelter work on Wednesday or Thursday, days spent primarily looking for the smoking gun to nail Jimbo. He did a couple of mundane follow-up stories as well. The important thing was he was home in time to watch the Baxter boys while Robbyn slaved away with her counter advertising image campaign for the Shelter. That way Robbyn didn't have to rely on Cindy Loeper to watch the boys in the evening. Matt took the boys to the movies on Wednesday night. It was nice to spend some time with them out of a sports environment. He didn't want them to think that all he cared about was baseball.

But he and they certainly cared about baseball on Thursday night when Matt was there to coach the Cubs to a 7-4 victory, the one that clinched the regular-season title. Timmy helped out with another homer and two doubles, driving in six runs. Robbyn was upset that she missed the game because of work, but Matt asked Natalie Lane to video Timmy's at-bats on Robbyn's phone.

"I hear you guys are an item," Natalie said to Matt, referring to he and Robbyn. "I didn't suspect you guys were a match. I thought that I was more your type."

Matt smiled.

"Word travels fast, doesn't it," Matt said. "Yes, Robbyn and I are seeing each other. As for you, dear Natalie, I find you to be captivating. But that's the problem. I'd be so enthralled with you I'd never be able to focus on work or on this team."

"You're not that good of a liar," Natalie said, giggling. "But if I can't have you, what the hell, why not Robbyn? God knows she could use the companionship. For the life of me, I can't imagine being horny for all those years. Can you?"

Matt winked, patted Natalie on the back, and said: "Obviously not. At the same time, I can't imagine that you can either."

"No denying that," Natalie said, laughing. "Listen. If you and Robbyn ever get tired of each other, you have my number."

"OK," Matt said, "but I think Robbyn is a keeper."

"If you like the Miss Betty Homemaker type," Natalie said.

"I do," Matt countered.

"Who would have thought?" Natalie responded, trying her best to look wicked. "Oh, well. There's no accounting for some people's tastes."

Robbyn looked absolutely beatific when she watched highlights of the Cubs' championship-clinching victory on her phone with her boys and Matt.

"You guys are something special," she gushed.

That night was sublimely special for Robbyn and Matt as well. After the boys went to sleep, Robbyn and Matt felt comfortable spending some of the night together, with the proviso that Matt leave the house before the boys awoke. They both had the most exquisite lovemaking session of their lives. They rode an awesome wave of untamed passion that churned into cascading pools of pure pleasure. They burrowed into each other, exploring the entire expanse of their bodies with lips, tongues, fingers and writhing limbs.

Drawing upon every ounce of his considerable testosterone levels, Matt's stamina once again was extraordinary. Post climax, they were content to just nestle in each other's arms and stare at each other with utter love and wonder at what they had discovered in each other.

"I love you dearly," Matt finally whispered.

"You're fantastic!" Robbyn said, definitely not whispering. "You screw like a stallion!"

"And you are one hot mare to ride," Matt replied.

Matt laughed so hard that Robbyn had to shove a pillow in his face because she was fearful his belly laughs would wake the boys.

"Now that you've ruined our romantic mood with your gutter talk," Matt said, "how about letting me look at some of the proofs of the print ads you're working on?"

Matt and Robbyn spent the next two hours sprawled on her bed -- revising, tweaking and creating text that would prompt people to still trust the core mission of the Shelter and to reaffirm in them the confidence that any dollar they gave to the Shelter campaign would be worth the investment. It was not an easy task, considering all the publicity Matt was generating about the Shelter scandal, but Robbyn was an expert in pushing all the right emotional buttons. She knew that people gave to a capital campaign because they believed in the organization. But she also knew that the prime reason people gave was because it made them feel good about themselves.

When Robbyn, with a few assists from Matt, had finished revising the ads, the only way people couldn't feel good about themselves for giving to the Shelter campaign would be if they were corpses.

"You do excellent work, Robbyn Baxter," Matt gushed.

"Well, thanks to you, I've been forced to do a lot of excellent work. You're making me work my ass off."

"Well, don't work off too much of that ass," he cracked, playfully slapping her butt cheeks. "I like your ass just the way it is."

"You know," she said, laughing, "even the nicest of guys are pigs."

"Oink, oink," Matt responded, losing all pretext of professionalism.

"On that note, I think our work tonight is done," laughed Robbyn. "Now get your butt out of here. By the way, I enjoy working much more with you than with Paul Missonis or Chad, who has to be the most temperamental designer in the world."

"Want me to kick his ass for you?" Matt said, flexing his ample biceps before putting his golf shirt back on.

"Please stop in my office tomorrow morning and do just that," Robbyn said, grinning.

The next morning Paul Missonis practically kissed Robbyn. She had never seen him look this happy. In fact, she couldn't remember ever seeing him genuinely happy.

"You've done a remarkable job with this Shelter campaign," he said. "The body of multimedia work you've produced has been nothing short of amazing. Effective next week, there will be 50 bucks more a week in your paycheck."

"Thank you so much, Mr. Missonis," she said.

"After all these years, it's time you've called me Paul," he said.

"Yes, sir," she said. "I mean Paul."

"Now that we are on a first-name basis, I've heard that your son Timmy is quite the ballplayer," Missonis said.

"Well, he is having a nice season. He did get beaned during a tournament game and suffered a mild concussion.

Fortunately, he's bounced back and helped lead his team to the regular-season title. Now we have the playoffs and several more tournaments to look forward to."

"He must have a good coach, what with not having, uh, a father around," Missonis said.

"Yes, he has an excellent coach," Robbyn said, not anxious to tell Missonis that Timmy's coach was Matt Meredith.

"Who is his coach?" Missonis asked.

"Well, uh, you're not going to believe this, but his coach is Matt Meredith."

Missonis looked as if he had just swallowed a squid.

"Matt Meredith the columnist?" Missonis replied, sounding shocked.

"The one and the same," Robbyn said, almost sheepishly.

"So, this Meredith is a friend of yours?" Missonis pressed.

"Well, yes, he's my son's coach," she said, softly, then quickly adding, "but I was sure upset with him when he started writing all these Shelter stories. He sure helped create a lot of work for us, and certainly his stories didn't help the Shelter's credibility or the viability of its capital campaign. But I realize he's just doing his job."

"Well, perhaps he should do his job a little less zealously, don't you think?" Missonis huffed.

"Perhaps," Robbyn said. Before she could add anything, Missonis' phone rang. He answered it, began a conversation, then politely waved her away.

Robbyn noted that he didn't smile at her when he waved her away. She could tell that he was less than thrilled to discover that she knew Meredith. She wondered why he would think that was a major problem. But he was such an old fart at times that she wouldn't be shocked to find out that he would consider her to be sleeping with the enemy if he ever found out the extent of her relationship with Matt.

The following weekend Matt and Robbyn and the boys were in Altoona, where the Sorbonne Township traveling team won four games to win its first tournament title of the season. Timmy was sensational in the tournament, hitting six homers, two triples and four doubles to drive in a total of 26 runs. Matt and Robbyn were practically bursting with pride when Timmy was presented with the Most Valuable Player trophy.

"That trophy's almost as tall as you are," Matt joked to Timmy.

"And better looking," Billy chimed in.

Billy's remark triggered a playful punch to the ribs from his older brother.

"See what you do on this team next year, squirt!" Timmy teased Billy.

"Boys, this is not the time to test the boundaries of brotherly love," said Robbyn, ever the dutiful mother.

It was a blissful ride back to Miller County for Matt and the Baxters. They talked about anything and everything as a foursome. And as a twosome, Robbyn and Matt never were at a loss for words.

"I truly think we found something special here," Matt said to Robbyn as he kissed her goodbye after dropping her and the boys off at their house.

"I feel the same way," she said. "You make me feel alive again."

"Ditto," Matt beamed.

But Matt wasn't beaming when he got home and started paging through the Sunday *Braxton Bugle*. Right there on page A3 was a full-page color ad that featured a smiling Millie Paxton handing a check for $250,000 to Shelter executive director Bob Tolliver on the front steps of the Shelter. It was accompanied by a headline that proclaimed: "Our Emergency Shelter Remains in Good Hands!" The accompanying text that put a positive spin on the capital campaign scandal was some, but not all, of the verbiage Matt had helped Robbyn tweak on her bed that night.

Matt kept staring at the ad, sick to his stomach. He couldn't believe that Robbyn hadn't told him about Millie's check presentation. He felt betrayed. Obviously, Robbyn hadn't trusted him enough to confide in him that the check presentation ad was running in Sunday's paper.

After his nausea passed, his emotions got the best of him and he felt more and more angry with her. Since it was late, he decided not to call her about it. His anger increased when he went through his phone messages and heard the voice of his managing editor, Ned March, say semi-sarcastically: "Scooped by an ad agency, were you?"

The first thing Matt did Monday morning was write a quick follow-up story, getting reaction from Shelter and civic leaders to the news that Millie Paxton had made good on her pledge to make up for the Shelter shortage.

The second thing Matt did was call Robbyn at Missonis Advertising.

"I know why you're calling and I'm so sorry," Robbyn gushed into the phone before Matt could say anything beyond "Well."

"I can't believe you kept me in the dark about that," he said sternly. "Didn't you trust me?"

There was an awkward silence for several moments.

"I really can't get into it here," Robbyn said, "but this wasn't about trust. And this wasn't about our relationship. This was about an ad person and a journalist. I know how competitive you are. If I had told you about the ad in advance, your instincts would have compelled you to break the story. You wouldn't have been able to stop yourself. Even if it meant hurting me. I understand that. So, I decided to take the pressure off you, to prevent putting you into a situation where you had to choose between me and my job."

Then there was a long silence. Robbyn braced for the worst. Then she was startled by the sound of laughter pouring into her ear.

"Damn you're good," Matt said. "You're amazing. First of all, that's the best positive spin I've heard in a long time. You did me a favor by not telling me, huh? Well, believe it or not, you're absolutely right. You did. I wouldn't have been able to stop myself from following up on it. I would've been relentless in trying to have a story in to trump the ad. And I would have felt like a louse for doing that to you. But it wouldn't have been personal. And you obviously understand that. But, to be honest, you should feel a little like a louse for keeping it from me. And let's not be naive. You certainly got great impact from the ad and got the Shelter's slant in first."

"I do feel like a louse, and I did get the best of it, didn't I?" said Robbyn, laughing. "Hanging out with you, I'm getting more aggressive."

"In a way, I feel closer to you than ever," Matt said.

"Well, just so you know, part of my decision was self-preservation," Robbyn admitted. "I'm paranoid about Missonis knowing about us. He was asking me about Timmy's baseball team and was surprised to hear that you're his coach. Then he went on to be critical of you for making such a big deal about the Shelter situation. I think he's really going to be pissed if he finds out I'm sleeping with the enemy."

"Sounds like you work for a real prince," Matt said.

"Speaking of his Royal Highness, he's walking toward my desk as we speak."

"Well, you'd better go," Matt said quietly. Then raising his voice, he added: "By the way, you owe me some great makeup sex!"

"We didn't have a fight," Robbyn protested.

"Only because I truly am a prince," Matt said, laughing as he hung up.

"You are a prince," Robbyn whispered into the dead phone line.

Well, if Matt were a prince, he was a prince on a mission. And he knew unless he could prove that Jimbo dipped into the Shelter funds, his story was going to dry up. Especially now that Millie had taken much of the sting out of the public backlash. And Robbyn also had done yeoman's work in muting public outcry with her Shelter image campaign.

After exhausting all his leads, and short of torturing Millie and Jimbo to force them to admit the truth, Matt knew he had only one recourse: Ned March's source.

When Matt told Ned that he absolutely had to talk to the source who had tipped Ned off, March had a pinched look on his face.

"What's the problem? I won't blow his cover," Matt said, annoyed. "The guy talked to you. Why can't he talk to me? Or you can do it for me. Whatever. But I'm at a dead end unless I get more insight into what the hell went down with the mayor and the campaign funds. As you know, if I don't soon get some concrete proof that the mayor did grab the funds, this story is going to die on the vine."

"Obviously, I know that," Ned admitted, still looking stressed. "I was just hoping you could somehow nail the story down without me or you having additional contact with my source. You see, my source was absolutely adamant that you know not her identity."

Matt blinked hard. Twice.

"It's a her?" Matt asked excitedly. "You never told me that before. I had no idea it was a woman. Now, you're sure as hell not going to tell me that it's Millie Paxton, are you?"

"No, because it isn't her," Ned said.

"Well, who is it? Damn it, you can tell me!" an exasperated Matt said.

"OK, even though she made me swear that I couldn't reveal her identity to you or anybody else, I'll guess I'll have to call her. And tell her that unless she gives us something more specific or leads us to something concrete that implicates the mayor, we're at a dead end," Ned said.

"So, call her!" Matt said.

"I will," Ned said sheepishly. "I'll let you know what she says."

"Will you give me her name?"

"Let me talk to her first," Ned said.

"After all, this our newspaper and our big story," Matt said. "What's with you? You aren't being the hard-boiled, hard-ass editor that you usually are."

Ned shot Matt a glance hard enough to hang wash on.

"Spare me the pep talk," Ned said, getting a little steamed. "And never doubt my drive and dedication. If you recall, I'm the one who gave this paper some spine when it needed it. We do more hard-hitting pieces now than we ever did."

"I don't need a history of the *Braxton Bugle* right now," Matt said. "I need you to make a call."

Ned March gave Matt a withering look and abruptly walked back to his office, shutting the door behind him. He took a deep breath, picked up his phone after checking his source's number, and punched in the numbers. While the phone was ringing, Ned still was berating himself for being a wimp, just like he was flogging himself mentally while talking to Matt. He normally wasn't so soft, but his source had melted him when she begged him not to tell anybody her identity, making him swear to specifically not tell Matt Meredith. Ned knew Matt was right, but making this call was one of the hardest things Ned March had had to do in a long time, maybe ever.

His source answered on the third ring.

"Tiffany Underhill," said the sweet voice of Ned March's source.

Chapter Seventeen

"Tiffany, uh, this is Ned March, the managing editor of the Bugle," he said haltingly.

Tiffany's voice suddenly wasn't so sweet as she said: "I told you never to call me, Mr. March. You haven't told Matt Meredith who your source was in the Shelter scandal, have you?"

"Trust me, I haven't," Ned replied. "But he is pressing me for more information. His investigation has come to a dead end. He thinks the mayor is involved, you have told me that the mayor is involved. But without any specific, concrete evidence, we won't be able to print anything about the mayor."

"So, you want me to go on the record?" Tiffany asked. "And why should I do that? I have a reputation to protect. You're lucky I told you what I did. Enough about civic duty. I don't care about your damn little town. In a few days, I'll be out of here forever."

"Why are you so set against coming forward?" Ned asked, trying to gently prod her. "And why are you so set against talking to Matt?"

"Because Matt is a bastard," Tiffany yelled. "He was two-timing me with one of his baseball team mothers. I loved him more than anybody I've ever loved. And he spurned me. Why the hell should I help him now?"

"This isn't about helping him," said a startled Ned. "This is about helping an entire city. About erasing a black eye that the Shelter has gotten from all of this. You don't have to talk to Matt. You can tell me. I'll relay the specifics to Matt."

There was a long pause. The silence was torturing Ned. Finally, he heard Tiffany sigh.

"All right, I'll talk to Meredith," she said simply. "Tell the jerk to give me a call. And do it quickly. Before I change my mind."

As soon as she hung up, Tiffany hated herself for agreeing to talk to Matt. Her resentment toward him was profound. But at heart she was a good person and she wanted to do the right thing. And she wanted to nail Jimbo for being such a pompous ass and for being such a pig toward her. The mayor had drunkenly groped her one night in the Nut Bar parking lot. She had slapped him in the face and he had relented. Prior to that, he had regaled her inside the Nut Bar with how he was responsible for bringing the movie "Drug Town" to Braxton. He had given the movie's producer a $250,000 site fee to bring the production to Braxton. The producer had confirmed this for her but thought the money had come from the city's general fund. But the tipsy Jimbo, trying to impress Tiffany, bragged to her that he had siphoned off funds from the Shelter campaign for the short run, but would incrementally replace the $250,000 over time from the city coffers. He thought it was a stroke of genius. He said he would announce personally at the movie premiere in Braxton that he had brought the film to town and planned on reaping the resultant political benefits.

"Of course, I won't tell folks or Millie how I initially got the money," Jimbo had told Tiffany. "I'm only telling you because you should be grateful for me helping to make you a star. How about fooling around with me?"

Tiffany had thought the mayor was all bluster until he groped her in the parking lot and threatened "to split her apart" with the best sex of her life. Which is when she had slapped him hard, punctuating it with "I don't sleep with fat pigs like you!"

As soon as Ned hung up with Tiffany, he called Matt into his office.

"My source has agreed to talk to you, but she said to call her now before she changes her mind," he said.

"Give me her number and I'll call her right now," Matt said excitedly.

"You already have her number," Ned said, enjoying toying with Matt.

"Don't play games with me," Matt snapped. "Who the hell is she?"

"Tiffany Underhill," Ned said almost too loudly.

Matt's legs seemed to buckle for just an instant, but he quickly regained his balance, if not his sense of respect for his boss.

"You gotta be shitting me!" Matt screamed. "No effin' way!"

"Believe me, it's Tiffany," Ned said, smiling sheepishly.

"You bastard," Matt yelled. "How could you keep that from me?"

"Because she asked me to, and I was respecting a source," Ned said, shrugging.

"Don't give me that journalistic piety," Matt snapped.

"Well, I didn't know you were screwing her and I didn't know you were screwing around on her," Ned said, his temper flaring.

"She told you that?" Matt barked.

"Who else?" Ned fired back.

"I wasn't screwing around on her per se, I just met somebody else I'm going to marry," Matt said, lowering his voice.

"I don't give a damn about your bedroom exploits, Matt," Ned said. "Just give Tiffany a call now and get this story. I want to bury the mayor."

Matt returned to his desk and without hesitation, called Tiffany at her hotel. However, his lack of hesitation hadn't mitigated the sense of dread he felt having to call her. But that dread was riding tandem with a great sense of excitement that he finally had the smoking gun to implicate the mayor in the scandal.

Tiffany didn't even bother to say hello. Her first words were "I don't know why the hell I'm helping you, but I am." She was helping because despite her self-focus, she was a person of considerable character.

"Thank you, I am very grateful that you are," Matt said.

"You sound like you're talking to a stranger," Tiffany snapped. "This is me. Tiffany! The lady whose heart you broke. The lady who loved you like nobody ever will love you. And you threw it away. What the hell is wrong with you?"

"I'm sorry, but Robbyn is somebody I'm going to settle down with," Matt said.

"Spare me the domestic tranquility crap with Mrs. Suburban Housewife," Tiffany said. "Don't mention her again to me. Meet me at the Nut Bar in an hour. We'll have dinner and I'll tell you everything. Then you can pick up the tab, I can punch you in the mouth, and you can have your damn story and the mayor's head on a plate."

She then hung up. Matt sat slumped for a few moments, fully comprehending for the first time how much Tiffany truly must have loved him and how much he had hurt her. For some strange reason, he felt aroused by the passion he had generated in her. He felt he must be some sicko to feel that way. He also felt a subtle sense of betrayal toward Robbyn.

Robbyn, meanwhile, was experiencing some rough moments herself. She was called into Paul Missonis' office and he read her the riot act.

"Why didn't you tell me that you were going out with Matt Meredith?" he asked sharply.

"Who told you that?" she asked.

"Never mind. Are you denying your relationship with Meredith?" Missonis asked, fire raging in his eyes.

"No, it's true," Robbyn said, getting angry herself.

"So why didn't you tell me you were screwing him," Missonis said.

"Because that's none of your damn business," Robbyn yelled.

"I think it is," Missonis said. "I think your relationship with Meredith compromises your position on the Shelter account. It's a conflict of interest. I'm removing you from the account, effectively immediately. And, by the way, you can forget about that raise I promised you. We here at Missonis Advertising don't reward disloyalty."

"Disloyalty! Disloyalty? That's bullshit!" Robbyn screamed. "I've never been disloyal. And I've never allowed my relationship with Matt to compromise my work on the Shelter account. I didn't even tell him about the ad showing Millie Paxton holding the $250,000 check. And he understood later why I didn't. He's a professional, too. It's just that you're such an old fart that you just don't get it. If you don't put me back on the account and give me the raise you promised me, I'm going to sue you."

"You'd be laughed out of court because you have no basis for a suit," Missonis said. "Besides, how dare you threaten me? If you hadn't been such a good worker all these years, I'd fire you right now."

"I dare you to fire me right now!" Robbyn flared.

"I'll pretend I didn't hear that because you'll regret it later," Missonis lectured her. "But don't dare say it again."

In tears, Robbyn made a hasty retreat to the ladies' room.

After Robbyn composed herself, she decided not to quit. But she wasn't sure how to fight back. She called Matt's office phone and his cell phone. Failing to reach him on both, she left voicemail messages on both, urging him to call her back right away. But Matt already had left to meet Tiffany at the Nut Bar and had turned off his cell phone so his interview would not be interrupted.

Tiffany was already waiting for Matt at a back-corner table in the Nut Bar. She was dressed in a jumper and had her hair pinned back in a bun. With a harsh frown on her face, she looked more like a stern schoolteacher than a sexy movie star.

"I really appreciate you doing this, considering the circumstances," Matt said, sitting down.

"Do me a favor and spare telling me how wonderful I am and if it weren't for the marvelous mom you're hanging out with you'd still be with me," she said. "I'm a big girl. I'll get over you."

"I am so sorry," Matt said. "You mean a lot to me. It's just that ... ."

Tiffany cut him off at that point.

"No more personal talk. Do you want to know what I know or what?"

"Of course, I do," Matt said, opening his notebook and getting his small tape recorder ready.

Tiffany then told Matt everything she knew on the record, including the fact that she had lied to Ned March about the mayor having taken the funds to wine and dine another girlfriend.

"I felt bad about that, especially when I was reading your stories and praying that wouldn't wind up in them," Tiffany said. "I just told your boss that to distance the scandal from the movie."

"Did you lie about anything else?" Matt asked, just doing his duty.

"Damn you!" Tiffany snapped. "If I did, I'd tell you. The truth is the mayor told me he skimmed $250,000 from the Shelter capital campaign and used it as a site fee to attract Vintage Studios to film 'Drug Town' in Braxton. Our producer, Marc Goldstein, confirmed this for me. But as I told Mr. March, he thought the money had come from the city's funds."

"So, when he saw my stories in the *Braxton Bugle*, why didn't Marc Goldstein come forward?" Matt asked.

"You'd have to ask him," Tiffany said. "For one, he's not always in town. He has spent most of his time back in Hollywood. For two, not everybody reads the *Braxton Bugle*, especially if you don't live here. Why should Marc Goldstein care about Braxton's emergency shelter?"

"Why should you care?" Matt asked Tiffany.

She paused, then simply said: "Because it's the right thing to do. Besides, the mayor is a pig and a moron who deserves to get nailed in this. If I have to be the hammer in this, I will. Of course, the studio PR people are going to kill me over this."

"Maybe not," Matt said. "All publicity, whether good or bad, captivates PR people."

"You journalists are elitists," Tiffany said, "even small-town guys like you."

She then gave Matt the finger.

"OK, Miss Hollywood," Matt said, flashing a smile in an attempt to lighten the mood.

Matt was feeling great at this moment, knowing that Tiffany had provided him with the smoking gun to implicate Jimbo in the Shelter scandal. Of course, he would try to confirm her story with Marc Goldstein, the movie's producer.

"Do you have Goldstein's number so I can confirm your story?" Matt asked gently.

"Why, don't you believe me?" Tiffany asked. "Do you think I would be so petty as to steer you into a bogus story that could ruin your career?"

"Well, I hadn't thought of that," Matt said, "but now that you have planted that seed, I wonder."

"Then you really don't know me as well as I thought you did," Tiffany said. "We spent so much time talking on the phone, texting each other constantly and bonding our souls during pillow talk that you should have realized how truly wonderful I am and how good we would have been together."

"I thought we weren't going to get personal," Matt said.

"I lied," Tiffany said, flashing a wicked grin.

"No self-respecting journalist is comfortable with a source who lies," Matt said, laughing. "Do you want to order something to eat to go with these peanuts and white wine?"

"This isn't a dinner date," Tiffany said, rather sternly. "This isn't social. This is business. After all, what would your girlfriend think about you having dinner with me?"

"She wouldn't mind if she knew it was business," Matt said.

"Dream on, pal," Tiffany said. "I thought you knew women well. Trust me, she'd be pissed if she knew you were here with me right now, no matter what the circumstances."

"So now that you've told me everything about the mayor and the Shelter funds, do you want me to go?" Matt asked.

Tiffany stared into Matt's eyes, giving him a longing look that came attached with vapor trails of passion.

"I want you to come back to my hotel suite and make love to me," Tiffany said. "But only if you tell me that it's over with you and the Little League mom."

"Her name is Robbyn and I can't tell you that," Matt said. "I think you need a cup of coffee. Three glasses of wine, with only a salad to eat, have gone to your head."

"So, I guess you aren't coming to your senses," Tiffany said, slurring her words slightly.

"I guess not," Matt said.

"Well, then drive me home because I'm in no shape to drive," Tiffany said. "I won't ask you in for a nightcap. I know you're Mr. Monogamy these days."

"How will you get your car back to your hotel?" Matt asked.

"I'm a damn movie star," Tiffany said. "Somebody from the studio will go fetch for me. It's a job perk."

"Silly question on my part," Matt said, settling the bill and ushering Tiffany onto Park Street.

Matt had parked his car across Park Street, right in front of the *Braxton Bugle*. As he opened the passenger door for Tiffany, she lost her balance for a second and grabbed his neck for support. Their faces brushed together and she seized the opportunity to kiss him on the lips. She tried to slip her tongue into his mouth, but he quickly pulled away. But as fate would have it, an upset Robbyn was driving down Park Street on her way to the *Braxton Bugle*, where she hoped to see Matt and tell him about how Paul Missonis had treated her. As she passed the *Braxton Bugle* on her way to the parking lot, she saw Tiffany and Matt kissing. Stricken with shock and disbelief and nausea, she quickly looked away before she could see Matt recoiling from Tiffany. Robbyn then quickly decided to go home, leaving Matt and Tiffany in her rearview mirror. At that moment in time Robbyn decided to leave Matt in her rearview mirror permanently.

"He's a damn womanizer and he'll never change," she yelled to herself. "What a fool I've been!"

Matt, of course, had no idea that Robbyn had passed by while Tiffany had kissed him. On the way to her hotel, Matt politely admonished Tiffany for kissing him, and gently kissed her on the forehead when he dropped her off.

"Again, thanks so much for all your help," Matt said to Tiffany as he walked her to the hotel lobby. "And again, I'm sorry I disappointed you. It's just that my heart belongs to another."

"Sorry about the kiss," Tiffany said. "I'm a little tipsy, and I thought I'd give it one last shot. It's kind of cute you're so faithful to what's her name? Robbyn? You're an idiot, but I wish you a lot of happiness."

"I wish you plenty of happiness as well," Matt said. "Give me a call before you leave town. And I guess I'll see you at the movie premiere here in Braxton."

"And you can bring Robbyn," Tiffany said. "I promise I'll claw out only one of her eyes."

And with a giggle, she was off into the elevator.

Matt was a happy man. He had just gotten the information needed to punctuate the greatest story of his life. And he had just received personal validation that he was over Tiffany and was utterly in love with Robbyn.

Of course, it would be a rather rude shock to Matt when he found out that Robbyn was not exactly harboring loving thoughts about him.

Matt didn't have time to call Robbyn that night. Immediately after dropping off Tiffany, he returned to the office and wrote the story that almost wrote itself. He even was fortunate enough to get confirmation from the movie producer, Marc Goldstein, that the mayor had given him $250,000 for a site fee. Goldstein repeated to Matt what he had told Tiffany: He thought the money came from city funds.

When Matt was done writing, Ned and two copy editors pored over it, tweaking it slightly and rechecking his facts. The story pulled no punches: It said the mayor took the money from the Shelter fund without Millie's or anybody else's knowledge. While it was being edited, Matt repeatedly tried to reach Millie and the mayor for a comment. He couldn't reach them and he didn't want to tell them what he knew on a voicemail. He did get a hold of Bob Tolliver, the Shelter's executive director, who expressed the proper outrage and remorse, being astute enough, of course, to point out that the mayor's action, if true, certainly absolved the Shelter of any malfeasance.

"Well, I guess we will have to let the story go even without comment from Jimbo or Millie," Ned finally said as the deadline drew near.

"Damn right we are," Matt said. "Jimbo will just deny it and Millie wouldn't comment anyway. Whatever they have to say will make for a good follow story in the next day's edition."

Matt went back to the Nut Bar for one quick beer before last call. Ned went with him, even though he no longer drank.

"We nailed that bastard," Ned said in triumph, raising his glass of Coke to Matt's glass of beer.

"Thanks to Tiffany," Matt said. "The movie star I spurned."

"You gotta be out of your mind," Ned said, laughing. "I hope you don't live to regret dumping her."

"Don't worry, I won't," Matt said, confidently. "I've found the woman I'm going to marry. I need to introduce you to Robbyn. She's wonderful."

Of course, when Matt arrived home, he was shocked when one of his voicemail messages was from Robbyn. She was crying on the message, which simply said: "I can't tolerate a womanizer. We're finished. Don't ever call me again. And I mean it. If you come near me, I'll get a protection-from-abuse order filed against you."

Matt sat down in stunned disbelief after playing Robbyn's voicemail message for a third time. He felt queasy in his stomach and weak in his knees. He felt a deep ache in his chest. He had absolutely no idea what had prompted such a vicious message. He was dying to call her but wanted to get his wits about him before doing so. He couldn't imagine what had prompted such a response from her. Then it dawned on him, a crushing thought that leveled him with all the impact of a high-rise building toppling upon him.

"She must have heard about me having dinner with Tiffany," he said so loudly that he startled himself. And then even louder, he added: "What else could it be? But how did she find out?"

He quickly dialed Robbyn's cell, confident that a simple explanation of why he and Tiffany had dinner would immediately give Robbyn a profound change of heart. Robbyn didn't answer, her phone kicking into voicemail. Since it was 3:30 in the morning, he knew she was home. And if she was asleep, he would be surprised. He decided to leave a quick message.

"Robbyn, I have no idea why you are so upset," he said frantically. "I know it's late. But I just have to talk to you. Whatever you think of me at this moment, it has to be a misunderstanding. I've been totally faithful to you. And I know I have the reputation for being a womanizer, but that label has been way overblown. I love you and miss you. Please don't shut me out of your life. And if you're upset because you found out that I had dinner at the Nut Bar with Tiffany, it was all business. She, believe it or not, was the final piece to the puzzle in my fingering the mayor as the culprit in the missing Shelter funds. If you don't believe me, read all about in the *Bugle* tomorrow. I interviewed her, then spent the rest of the night working on the story. I just didn't have a chance to call you. So, if you're awake, please call me back now. I promise you won't be sorry."

Robbyn, meanwhile was awake. She was sitting in bed with the lights out. She was out of tears, but her heart still ached. She still loved Matt but was afraid that he always would have more than an eye for other women. Consequently, she didn't think she could ever be totally sure of his fidelity. And she couldn't tolerate living with that uncertainty. She saw no resolution, no hope for patching things up. She saw Matt kissing Tiffany, and therefore Matt's excuse of a dinner meeting for the Shelter story didn't ring totally true to her. Her feeling was that Matt may have met Tiffany for newspaper business, but the dinner had ended with monkey business. She had seen that with her own eyes. And she had no intention of calling Matt back. Not now, not ever. In fact, she had no intention of ever speaking to him again. The Cubs' first league playoff game was that night, and she already had made up her mind to completely ignore him. Of course, she still had yet to figure out how she was going to explain this to her boys.

Not surprisingly, neither Robbyn nor Matt fell asleep that night. And both were facing full days. But matters of the heart, especially grief-stricken hearts, often intrude on everyday realities. Even on critical everyday realities.

Robbyn was an irritable mess when she arrived at work the next morning. She certainly was in no mood to tolerate any friction from Paul Missonis, who had been so harsh to her the previous day. Besides, after reading Matt's account that morning in the *Braxton Bugle* of the mayor's involvement in the Shelter campaign scandal, she was determined to return to the Shelter ad campaign. So, she approached Missonis in his office, claws ready.

"I don't give a damn what your boyfriend says about the mayor, you're not getting back on the account," Missonis said with a severe edge to his voice. "This isn't about the mayor or whoever took the damn money. This is about you being intimately involved with an account and being disloyal to me and this agency by being intimate with a newspaper reporter covering the scandal."

"You have no grounds to make such a sexist decision," Robbyn said. "I've been a star here, a top producer, and you're treating me like some high school girl in the 1950s. Besides, Matt no longer is my boyfriend."

"I'm treating you like a professional," Missonis retorted. "And the bottom line is, I'm the boss. Again, you're lucky I didn't fire you. And now that Meredith has dumped you, you want back on the Shelter account."

Robbyn could feel the anger splashing up her spine and spilling over into her brain. Normally a person with good patience, she was a slave to her molten emotion at this particular moment. Consequently, the words fired from her lips before even she knew she was saying them.

"You're an ignorant old asshole! I can't stand even looking at you, let alone working for you anymore. You've screwed me out of a raise. You'll hear from my attorney. And I quit. You can shove this job up your shriveled ass. And when I get a job with another agency, I'm reaching out to all my current clients."

"You don't have the balls!" Missonis flared, going for the jugular, which she did have.

"I may not have balls," Robbyn snapped back, "you sexist pig! But I've got plenty of stones. I'm gonna burn you. And you, sir, don't have the fucking balls to stop me, you bastard!"

Paul Missonis' arteries were clogged with venom at that juncture. Which must have restricted the blood flow to his brain, because the only response he could muster was: "You damn bitch! You're fired!"

Robbyn stormed out of his office, ran over to her desk, and began to violently pack up her things.

"What the hell is going on here?" asked an alarmed Chad, her primary designer.

"I quit!" Robbyn said loudly. "I can't stand the old man any longer."

"Man, that's awesome," Chad said. "But where are you going to work?"

"I've got plenty of contacts," Robbyn said defiantly. "I'll find something soon."

"Well, keep in touch," Chad said, showing uncharacteristic compassion by putting a hand on her shoulder. "And if you get a good opportunity and they need a good designer, call me."

"Yeah, right," Robbyn snapped, sticking to her assault mode. "You're a pain in the ass! Why would I ever want to work with you again?"

"Because I'm good and you damn well know it," Chad said cockily, even though he was taken aback by Robbyn's aggressive manner.

"We'll see," Robbyn said, "but only if you help me carry my damn things to my car."

"Well, I do admire your spunk," Chad said. "So, lay your junk on me."

"Thanks," Robbyn said, kissing him on the cheek.

The enormity of what she had done really only hit Robbyn while she was driving home. She was glad she had done what she had done, but she now suddenly found herself to be the unemployed mother of two growing sons. Two sons with big appetites for food, sporting equipment and video games. She could feel the panic exploding throughout her body. Her first impulse was to call Matt, one that she quickly squelched.

Matt had awoken heartsick that morning, prompting another call to Robbyn and another voicemail message, imploring her to call him back. Now panic was starting to take residence in Matt's psyche. He was beginning to become alarmed, thinking that somehow either Robbyn had seen Tiffany kissing him on Park Street or else somebody else had seen the kiss and told Robbyn. Explaining that kiss, even if it had been Tiffany's initiative, would definitely be a hard sell to Robbyn in her present state of mind. And he definitely didn't want to ask Tiffany to explain that to Robbyn.

So, a distracted Matt was appalled upon reaching the office when he found a note from Ned, requesting him to make an appearance on the radio show *Feedback* on WBAM and field questions about his Shelter story.

"Man, I'm in no mood for this," Matt told Frank Funk, the show's host, moments before going on the air.

"Why the hell not?" Funk said, somewhat surprised. "You've just written a blockbuster story that has shaken City Hall. Why not milk it for all it's worth?"

"Well, you see, I'm kind of, uh, hung over," Matt lied.

"Celebrating the big scoop at the Nut Bar, huh?" Funk said, laughing. "Some Braxton journalistic traditions never die."

Once they opened the *Feedback* talk lines, there was an onslaught of calls that labeled the mayor a crook and requested his immediate resignation. Many of the angry callers also demanded that the movie producers give the money back to the Shelter. But the show really heated up when Mayor Jimbo Cummings himself called and got into an angry exchange with Matt and Frank Funk.

"Do you deny the story, since you didn't have the courtesy to return my repeated calls last night?" Matt asked in exasperation after hearing the mayor spew endless rhetoric about a manufactured witch hunt by the media, spliced with countless recollections of all the esteemed, honorable achievements he had accomplished on behalf of the beloved citizens of Braxton.

"Of course, I do!" Jimbo huffed.

"Well, the movie producer confirmed that you gave him a $250,000 site fee for 'Drug Town' and Tiffany Underhill said you told her that the money came from the Shelter capital campaign funds you skimmed behind your girlfriend's back," Matt hammered home.

"She's making that up!" Jimbo screamed.

"Are you calling Ms. Underhill a liar?" Matt pressed on.

"Damn right, the bitch is lying," Jimbo yelled. "Besides, what kind of source can your girlfriend be?"

"Girlfriend?" Matt asked quietly, alarm bells already ringing inside his head.

"I've seen you and Tiffany all lovey-dovey at the Nut Bar," the mayor bellowed. "She made that story up about me taking funds from Millie and the Shelter because she's involved with you and just trying to help you get a big scoop. But you can't lie to the citizens of Braxton. I'm innocent. Pillow talk between you and Tiffany won't bring down my administration. I'm going to file a libel suit against you and your damn newspaper."

Matt sat silent for a moment, as Fred Funk stalled for time by giving a quick recap of the mayor's allegation.

"Well, I just want our listeners to know that I was involved with Miss Underhill, but we no longer are involved," Matt said, wishing he was lying in a ditch somewhere. "She came forward as a source in this important story to our managing editor, Ned March, not me. Her insight to this story has nothing to do with her previous relationship with me. When the mayor revealed to her what he had done -- and she indicated that the mayor's intentions toward her definitely were less than honorable that night -- she felt compelled, as a matter of civic duty, to come to the newspaper with her story."

"What are you talking about?" an angry Jimbo interrupted. "I never displayed any less than honorable intentions toward Tiffany Underhill."

"That's not what she has told us," Matt said. "She said you hit on her big time in a drunken fashion."

"That libel suit just got bigger!" Jimbo bellowed. "You're thinking and talking like a jealous boyfriend there Matty boy. Afraid I'm gonna steal your girlfriend? Well, who needs her? My friend Millie Paxton is one of our community's brightest lights, a concerned citizen of considerable magnitude. Why would I compromise that with one of your leftovers, Mr. Meredith? And I deeply resent the implication that I was intoxicated."

"You took the money and you damn well know it," Matt said, succumbing to his rage. "Cut the crap and confess. You pulled off a grandstand play to get the movie people in town, thinking you could reap all the political benefits. You figured nobody would miss the money from the Shelter campaign and that you somehow would replace it, either from city funds or from Millie's funds."

"How dare you!" Jimbo shouted at the top of his lungs.

His anger crackled through the phone line.

"Because I know you did it," Matt said calmly. "And it has nothing to do with anybody's girlfriend. Facts are facts. Just admit it and be a man about it."

Matt expected Jimbo to hang up and stonewall him until the district attorney looked into the matter.

So Matt suddenly was nearly shocked off his chair when the mayor simply said in an understated voice:

"OK, you bastard. You got me. I did temporarily borrow some Shelter funds for the greater good of the city. I was going to definitely repay the 250 grand from city funds. It was a brilliant ploy on my part to shed much-needed publicity on the alarming drug problem eating at the core of our city. I should be given an award for this, not asked to resign."

"I'm sure the district attorney definitely will disagree, Mr. Mayor," Matt said triumphantly. "Thank you for giving *Feedback* this incredible scoop. Don't forget to read my incisive follow story in tomorrow's *Bugle* as well as my column calling for your resignation."

Jimbo, just now realizing that he had been baited into admitting his crime, amped the volume in his voice and uttered "the good citizens of Braxton know my heart was in the right place and know I never would have permanently deprived the Shelter of their much-deserved funds" before hanging up.

Driving home in tears after quitting her job, Robbyn listened to Matt and the mayor on *Feedback* in stunned silence. The mayor's remarks about Matt and Tiffany served to profoundly stiffen her resolve to never talk to Matt again.

Tiffany Underhill had read Matt's story in the *Bugle* that morning and was pleased with it. She also noticed the pullout box promoting Matt's appearance on *Feedback*. It was a show she had bittersweet emotions about after Matt signed off. She was thrilled that the mayor had admitted his involvement on air, but disgusted that her personal relationship with Matt was discussed on air. She felt cheapened by those comments, as if she only had come forward with her allegations about the mayor because of her relationship with Matt.

Matt, too, left the radio show with profoundly bittersweet emotions. He was embarrassed by having his personal relationship with Tiffany drawn into the discussion. He was angry that he had scooped his paper out of the mayor's admission of guilt in the Shelter scandal. But he was thrilled that the mayor had admitted his guilt.

When Matt arrived back in the editorial office, he found Ned to be extremely happy.

"I don't care that we were scooped by WBAM," he said. "What the hell, we are owned by the same company. Plus, everybody who heard the show will your read follow-up story tomorrow."

"I guess you're right," Matt said. "How did you feel about Jimbo bringing up my past relationship with Tiffany?"

"Hell, I think it's good for your reputation as a man about town," Ned said, laughing. "It didn't bother me. Hopefully it didn't bother your new girlfriend."

Ned saw Matt's face turn ashen.

Ned's comment hit home big time with Matt.

"God, I hope Robbyn wasn't listening," Matt said. "But I imagine she was. And she's already upset with me. Sometimes a guy can't win."

"You won big time today, big fellow," Ned said. "Now knock out a killer follow story and write a compelling column calling for Jimbo's resignation. We'll run both of them on Page One. And when you're done with that, WBRA-TV will be here at 4 to tape an interview with you for its Miller Edition newscasts tonight at 5:30 and 10:30."

"As long as I'm done by 5," Matt said. "My baseball team has its first playoff game tonight."

"Talk about having the proper priorities," Ned laughed. "But an old pro like you should be done by then."

Matt was a very fast writer who could keep the words flowing. But when he sat down to write, he developed a mini-writer's block because he kept getting distracted by thoughts of Robbyn and Tiffany, wondering if they listened to *Feedback* and what their reaction was. More importantly, he was afraid that Robbyn had left him permanently.

But once Matt regained his focus and zoned in on his story and column, his prose found a life of its own and flowed quite nicely. Making matters go even smoother was that every source he called for a follow-up quote was available, setting a personal record. When it came time to write his column, Matt was in a groove. His eloquent words described how the mayor had betrayed the public trust, forming a compelling argument for the mayor's resignation.

"Fantastic job on both stories," Ned gushed to Matt after editing them. "Damn, you are good! It's a good thing I overpay you and indulge you or you would have jumped to the *Philadelphia Inquirer* years ago."

Right before Matt was to be interviewed by WBRA-TV, he received a call from Tiffany.

"I just wanted you to know that I thought you did a great job with your story this morning and I thought you handled yourself quite well on the radio," she said. "But I wasn't thrilled to hear the mayor discuss us."

"I know, I thought it was terrible that he did that," Matt said. "I felt badly for you. He was angry and desperate. By the way, I can't thank you enough for what you did. If you hadn't stepped forward and alerted Ned about this, we probably never would have been able to prove that the mayor skimmed funds."

"You're welcome, but I didn't do it for you, I did it because it was the right thing to do," Tiffany said. "Of course, the studio PR people loved it, too. All those syndicated Hollywood-celebrity TV shows are all over it. I'm sure they will be calling you for a comment. And it's going viral on social media. By the way, I told several celebrity TV reporters what a great journalist and guy you are and that you and I remain good friends."

"I would like to remain good friends," Matt said. "I'm sincere about that."

"Me, too," Tiffany said. "Of course, you had better run that by the Mrs. Mom who stole you from me."

"Well, she's not talking to me right now," Matt said. "Wants nothing to do with me. I think somebody told her I had dinner with you or somebody told her that you and I were kissing on Park Street."

"I, um, sorry about that," said Tiffany. "I lost control. You know ... well, I'd better not say it."

"Come on, say it," Matt said, his curiosity definitely tweaked.

"Well, you see, OK, I love you, you bastard. And I pray every night you'll come to your senses and come back to me. Damn it, we're good together. You're everything I ever wanted in a guy. And you're cool enough and secure enough not to let my career and celebrity get in the way."

"I appreciate you saying that," Matt said. "I really do. Just let me say that you were superb to me, and I treated you like hell. I just followed my heart in another direction. It was nothing against you."

"Well, here's hoping you make a quick U-turn," Tiffany said, "and realize what you've walked away from in me."

"Stranger things have happened," Matt said, still stringing her along.

"Call me tomorrow?" Tiffany said, hopefully.

"I will," Matt said.

When Matt hung up, he had no idea why he said that. Part of it, he rationalized, was because Tiffany had such strong feelings for him. And part of it, he further rationalized, was because he was uncertain about his future with Robbyn. She seemed to be so preoccupied with his reputation as a womanizer, a reputation he felt was terribly undeserved.

After talking to Tiffany, a somewhat distracted Matt was interviewed in his office by WBRA-TV. Then, just as he was scrambling to leave to get home and change for the Cubs' playoff game, he got a call from "Hello Hollywood!" concerning the mayoral scandal and Tiffany's role in it. He really poured it on thick in praising Tiffany's good citizenship and tried to deflect probing, tabloid questions about their relationship.

Once done with that, he zipped home, quickly changed into his coach's gear, grabbed a granola bar and some fruit punch, and zipped over to the ballfield to line the baselines and conduct pre-game practice.

The Cubs won the game easily, 8-2, over the Mets. Timmy didn't have one of his blockbuster games, but still managed to hit two doubles and drive in three runs. He also made two nifty plays going into the hole at shortstop. Matt found it to be interesting that Robbyn sat on the top row of the bleachers, looking sullen despite the resounding victory. Whenever Matt gazed in her direction during the game, she always had her eyes averted. They didn't make eye contact once. And when the game was over, Robbyn had disappeared.

"Great game, Timmy," Matt said following his post-game address to the team. "You looked like Derek Jeter going into the hole. By the way, where's your mom?"

"She said she had a meeting after the game with somebody, so Mrs. Loeper is driving Billy and me home," Timmy said.

"A night meeting?" Matt asked, sounding skeptical.

"She's looking for a new job. She quit her job today," Timmy said. "She got into a fight with her boss."

"Oh, no," Matt said, feeling awful and responsible. He instantly knew that her fight with Paul Missonis had to have something to do with the Shelter scandal.

"What kind of fight?" Matt asked.

"I don't know," Timmy said. "Just a fight. But I know Mom is upset and was crying when she told me about it. That's all I can say. Besides, she told me not to tell you."

"Why would she say that?" Matt asked.

"She wouldn't tell me," Timmy said. "But I think she's mad at you."

"But why?" Matt asked.

"Don't know why. She didn't say why. I just sensed it. Why don't you ask her?"

"Believe me, I will," Matt said.

"Come over to the house tonight and watch the Phillies game with Billy and me," Timmy said, getting excited. "And bring some ice cream cones."

"I'm not sure that's a good idea tonight," Matt said. "But maybe another night."

The disappointment in Timmy's face haunted Matt.

"I wish you could live with us every night," Timmy said.

"Well, maybe someday," Matt said, forcing a grin.

"But Billy and me want Mom and us to live with you at your house because you have a swimming pool," Timmy said.

Matt laughed. It had been the first time he had laughed in what seemed to be an eternity.

"We'll have to work on that, slugger," Matt said, tousling Timmy's hair affectionately.

Matt drove home and poured himself a stiff Scotch. He felt awful that the Shelter scandal evidently had led to Robbyn losing her job. He was dying to find out the details of what happened and to express his deepest regrets to her. But he figured she wouldn't dare answer his phone call. Nevertheless, he called her cell and once again got her voicemail. He felt so frustrated by his inability to communicate with her. He was beginning to despair of ever reestablishing a relationship with her. And somewhere deep in his psyche and heart he was wondering why he still felt ties to Tiffany ... ties that were stronger than he cared to admit. His Scotch led to another. Professionally, he had never been higher. Personally, he had never been lower.

Chapter Eighteen

As soon as Timmy's playoff game was over, Robbyn had zipped home to change into one of her demure but professional business suits. She had been fortunate to land such a quick meeting with Robert Thaxter, the owner of Thaxter Advertising, and she wanted to take full advantage of it. Robert Thaxter had tried and failed to recruit Robbyn several times over the years to join his expanding advertising and public relations firm as a copywriter. When Robbyn had called Thaxter that afternoon and told him that she had left Missonis Advertising following a dispute with Paul Missonis over the Braxton Emergency Shelter account, she was surprised that Thaxter had agreed to meet with her so quickly. And she was as equally surprised to hear that he wanted to meet over dinner and drinks at Diamond's, a popular steakhouse in Sorbonne Township. It wasn't that she feared that Robert Thaxter harbored any untoward intentions toward her, intentions of a personal nature. Thaxter was a silver-thatched, distinguished gentleman in his late 50s who was happily married with seven children and was a deacon at St. Michael Roman Catholic Church in Sorbonne Township. Still, she felt just a twinge of discomfort about meeting him over dinner.

When Robbyn arrived at Diamond's, Robert Thaxter already was seated at a table, waiting for her. He was sipping a large glass of ice tea, topped off with three lemons.

"Good evening," he said, rising from his seat to shake her hand. "I appreciate you meeting me here. I'm leaving for France for a week's vacation tomorrow and I wanted to speak with you before I left."

"Well, I appreciate that," Robbyn said. "I'm not interfering with your packing?'

Robert Thaxter laughed so hard that his Adam's apple appeared as if it were playing Ping-Pong between his chin and necktie.

"My wife has been packing for weeks," Thaxter said. "We have so much luggage now that we should simply move our house to France. I think that would be simpler."

"I always overpack myself," Robbyn said.

"Anyway, so you and Paul Missonis had a parting of the ways, so to speak," Thaxter said gently.

"Well, I wound up quitting in a huff," Robbyn said. "As you know, I was working on the Shelter account. I thought -- and Paul Missonis thought -- I was doing an admirable job in a difficult situation. The capital campaign scandal made the Shelter a tough sell, but we were happy with our ad campaign."

"I thought you did a great job," Thaxter said. "You always do a great job. Which is why I'm thrilled you're suddenly on the job market. I know today must have been traumatic for you, but this story could have a happy ending."

"Well, hopefully it does," Robbyn said. "I've always tried to be a true professional and I've never been a disruptive employee. I want you to know that. But when Paul Missonis accused me of disloyalty because I was dating Matt Meredith while working on the Shelter campaign, it was tough to swallow. Especially when he canceled a raise he had promised me and took me off the Shelter account."

"You're dating Matt?" Thaxter asked, his brown eyes lighting up.

"Well, I was," Robbyn said.

"I'm sorry to hear that you broke up," Thaxter quickly said, surprising Robbyn. "I know Matt very well. He's a great guy. A member of our parish. He rarely misses Mass even though he has a less-than-normal schedule. He even contributes to our parish newsletter at times. My wife, Betty, and I have him over to the house for dinner at least once a month. Our kids love him. Especially our older daughter, who thinks Matt is quite the hunk. But what Betty and I love about Matt is that he's such a fun guy, and always the perfect gentleman. My wife has been trying to marry Matt off for years."

"Well, it's not like he hasn't dated a lot of women over the years," Robbyn said. "He must be very picky."

"You would think," Thaxter said as they ate their salads. "But I don't think his standards are off the charts. At least from what he has told my wife and me over dinner on many occasions. It's true that he's dated a lot of women and has this reputation as a ladies' man, but I can honestly say that I've never known Matt to date more than one woman at a time. And there are periods of time when he's not dating anyone. Matt said he simply is looking for a woman who loves kids, who has a sense of humor, and who loves him. I know Matt would love to get married and have kids. He just hasn't found his soul mate."

"Well, he didn't find one in me," Robbyn said, her mind preoccupied over whether she had judged Matt too harshly. But then, she thought, maybe Matt was the biggest bullshit artist of all time and had everyone snowed, including Robert and Betty Thaxter.

"Well, from what I know about both you, I would think you two would be great for each other," Thaxter said. "I'm sure my wife would, too. But there's no accounting for affairs of the heart. So, let's talk advertising."

As Robbyn nibbled at her swordfish and Thaxter attacked his sirloin, they agreed that Robbyn would start work the following week as a copywriter for Thaxter Advertising. And her starting salary would be $200 a week higher than her salary at Missonis Advertising.

"I lost a copywriter to a New York firm last week," Thaxter explained, "and that's why I was so anxious to hire you before somebody else in town gobbled you up. I like your style. You will have plenty of creative control. At Thaxter, we don't stifle our creative people by being nit-picky."

"This sounds too good to be true," said Robbyn, who was elated over her new position but still haunted by Thaxter's ringing endorsement of Matt.

"Well, just as a signing bonus, you also will start with four weeks' vacation a year," Thaxter said, beaming. "Normally new employees get just one week the first year, and then two weeks for the next two years. But I know you have two boys to take care of, and we at Thaxter encourage family values. Your title will be senior copywriter. Welcome aboard!"

Robbyn and Robert Thaxter had a stimulating conversation over dessert on the accounts that she would be working on until he returned from vacation.

When they rose from their table, Robbyn took Thaxter's hand and gave him a hearty shake while leaning over and kissing him on the cheek. As she did so, Tiffany Underhill and Bronk Cassidy just happened to be walking by their table en route to a late dinner. It had been Bronk Cassidy's final day of shooting on location in Braxton, and her leading man was treating Tiffany to a farewell Miller County dinner.

Tiffany saw Robbyn kiss Thaxter on the cheek, and promptly remarked aloud with just the right touch of sarcasm as she walked by. "Well, I wonder what dear Matt would say if he knew that Miss Sally Hometown was stepping out on him and kissing another man in public. My, my!"

Robbyn blushed a deep crimson. Robert Thaxter looked as if he had just swallowed an entire cow and it had stuck in his throat. Tiffany wore a smile glittery enough to post on a movie theater marquee. Only Bronk Cassidy wore a nondescript facial expression.

"Don't mind Tiffany," Cassidy said with a laugh. "She's just jealous that she lost her newspaper columnist to a Miller housewife. Not good for her Hollywood ego."

"Oh, hush, Bronk," Tiffany said as she and Cassidy sauntered off to their table.

"I'm so, so sorry," Robbyn said to the mortified Robert Thaxter.

"Well, I must say perhaps Matt does get around more than I thought," he said, managing a weak smile. "Wasn't that the actress who's been filming that movie in Braxton?"

"The one and the same," Robbyn said, also smiling weakly. "She's why Matt and I no longer are together."

"It sounded like you're the reason why she and Matt no longer are together," Thaxter said, regaining his composure. Then, with a wink, he added: "Perhaps Matt should spend more time in church."

"Matt is a great guy, but I don't believe he's the altar boy you think he is," Robbyn said, giggling lightly.

"Whatever," Thaxter said, shaking Robbyn's hand again. "Enough about Matt. I just want you to know that we're thrilled to have you at Thaxter. And your personal life is your personal life. Unlike Paul Missonis, I won't ask you who you're dating."

"I appreciate that," Robbyn said. "Thank you so much for the opportunity. I won't let you down. And thanks for dinner. It was delicious. I had a great time."

As Robbyn and Thaxter left the restaurant, he escorted her to her car and simply said, "Good night and good luck. I'll let my secretary know you are starting next week."

"Have a wonderful vacation in France," Robbyn said sweetly.

As Robbyn was driving home, her thoughts were scrambling wildly through her brain. She was thrilled about the job; appalled by the interlude with Tiffany in front of Robert Thaxter; and terribly confused on whether Matt was or wasn't involved with Tiffany. And more than ever, she was terribly confused on just what sort of person Matt Meredith really was. The bottom line was that she loved him. But could she -- could any woman -- ever be totally secure that he truly loved her and would never focus on another woman? She also was tormented by the fear that she was being a drama queen and somehow exaggerating Matt's exploits with women.

Chapter Nineteen

Matt felt as if his life had been thrown into a vortex of cascading events. His personal life and his professional life seemingly had left him little time for any real life.

Professionally, he was being hailed as a hometown hero. Bob Tolliver, the Braxton Emergency Shelter executive director, was so pleased that Matt's investigation of the capital campaign scandal had exonerated Shelter officials that they presented Matt with an award. The award presentation was televised live on WBRA-TV and the *Braxton Bugle* ran a photo of the presentation and a small article on the front page.

Matt's voicemail and email messages were enormous and the vast majority of them were highly favorable. Only a handful of them accused of him crucifying the mayor and not giving Jimbo a chance to repay the funds, as he said he intended to do.

Then Jimbo announced his resignation in a simple one-page letter that his administrative assistant sent to all local media outlets, with the exception of WBAM and the *Braxton Bugle*. But Matt's vast network of contacts tipped him off to the letter, and he and the *Bugle* were not scooped.

Jimbo's resignation received a massive treatment in the *Bugle* the next day, including a biting column by Matt that elicited a firestorm of favorable response. Of course, the stories and column included no quotes from the mayor, who ignored all of Matt's phone calls. But the newspaper did publish the mayor's letter in full despite the venom Jimbo displayed toward the *Bugle* in his reasons for resigning. "Our muckraker local newspaper has rendered me ineffective as mayor," Jimbo wrote in his letter. "I am saddened by my loss. But I feel even sadder for the loss suffered by the community, which will be deprived of my leadership. My tenure in office speaks for itself."

When Matt and his editors first read that line by the mayor, their ribs almost cracked with laughter.

"What a bozo he is," said, the venerable city editor.

Two days after Jimbo's resignation, Matt, in a Page One exclusive, broke the story that the Miller County district attorney's office was going to file criminal charges against Jimbo.

Matt was like a man possessed. He wrote every conceivable follow-up story and some that wouldn't have been conceived by a journalist with less instinct and energy. The whole Shelter scandal had evolved into Matt's finest collective body of work.

Personally, the only stability in his life came as a baseball coach. His Cubs, led by the pitching, fielding and hitting prowess of Timmy Baxter, won two more playoff games to win the Sorbonne Township title. The only down note -- and it was a major one -- of the baseball experience was that Robbyn totally avoided speaking to Matt throughout the playoffs and the ensuing victory celebration at a local Dairy Queen. It was terribly awkward for both of them, as well as for Timmy, and to a lesser degree, Billy.

"Mom really must be pissed at you," Timmy said to Matt between scoops of ice cream at Dairy Queen.

"You shouldn't be using the word *piss*," Matt said, "but I must admit it seems quite appropriate. She is pissed big time at me."

"Billy and I keep going to bat for you," Timmy said, "but we've been striking out big time."

"I appreciate your help, partner," Matt said, smiling for the first time at the party. "I've been striking out big time with your mother as well. I tried to talk to her right after the game. But it went nowhere. All she said was, 'Please don't talk to me. It's over.' I guess it is."

"Don't say that!" Timmy said, his eyes tearing up.

"Well, don't think about it now," Matt said. "We just won the championship. Let's enjoy this. And even if I don't wind up with your mom, you and I, and Billy, always will be friends."

"I want you to coach me forever," Timmy said.

"Good! I'll remember that when you're playing with the New York Yankees," Matt said, laughing. "I've always wanted to be a major league manager."

Timmy laughed and shoved some more ice cream into his mouth.

Robbyn seated herself with Billy and the Loepers in a corner at Dairy Queen, deploying careful geographical logistics to avoid getting near Matt. Her emotions and inner conflict were massive. She would look at Matt and want him to ravish her. Then she would look at Matt with her mind's eye and see him with Tiffany and a whole army of women in bed. She no longer trusted and respected Matt. But she still loved him and lusted for him. Her emotions felt as if someone had stuck them in a dryer and they were destined to spend eternity tumbling over and over. It was a nauseating feeling, one that left her life in a wobbly situation.

Meanwhile, Matt would look at Robbyn and wonder why. He had no idea how little she thought of him now. He had no idea that she had this vivid image of him as rogue playboy flashing constantly in her mind. As the victory party at Dairy Queen was winding down, Matt impulsively decided to make one final pitch for Robbyn's love. He quickly walked over to her table while she was engaged in conversation with Cindy Loeper, leaving her no time for a sudden exit.

Suddenly, he was in her face as he sat down at her table.

"I don't remember inviting you to sit down," Robbyn said quietly and without emotion -- although her conflicting emotions were churning inside her.

"Come on, Robbyn!" an exasperated Cindy said.

"This none of your damn business, Cindy," Robbyn snapped.

"Well, EXCUSE ME!" Cindy yelled, walking away from the table and leaving Matt alone with Robbyn because Billy Baxter and Derek Loeper now were standing in line for another round of ice cream treats.

Natalie Lane, sitting at an adjoining table, quickly jerked her head toward Matt and Robbyn upon hearing Cindy's outburst.

Robbyn felt Natalie's gaze upon her and quickly fired a nasty look at her.

"Stay out of this, Natalie!" Robbyn barked.

"Look at who's become a real bitch!" Natalie fired back. "Don't get your panties in an uproar!"

"I guess this was a mistake," Matt said softly to Robbyn.

"You and I ... the whole damn thing was a mistake," Robbyn said defiantly, her tears now flowing. "You're a ladies' man. And you're not fit to be my husband. So, stop wasting my time."

With that, Robbyn quickly arose from the table and walked outside to her car.

"Trouble in paradise, Coach?" Natalie yelled over to Matt.

"Don't push the wrong button, Natalie," Matt said, his face a mask of confusion and anger.

Matt's pitch for love had sailed high and wide. The ballgame for him and Robbyn apparently was over.

When Matt got home that night, there was a sweet message from Tiffany on his voicemail. Her voice never sounded so good, so utterly intoxicating. There was no doubt in Matt's mind that Tiffany loved him. That was becoming more and more apparent to him. There was no doubt in his mind that Robbyn was a better fit for him and his lifestyle. But he now doubted that the Robbyn he knew still existed. She now had developed this acute disgust and mistrust concerning him, and he no longer harbored any hope of reestablishing a relationship with her.

He decided to move on with his life, and it was obvious to him now that the direction pointed directly at Tiffany. He didn't need a compass to figure that out. But what he couldn't figure out is if he could tolerate long-term Tiffany's penchant for being all about herself. He had come to realize that down deep that Tiffany was a good-hearted person. But her mindset as an actress had given her an inner focus that might be difficult for him to live with. And he sometimes wondered whether her strong affection and feelings toward him weren't fostered by her strong ego-driven competitive nature.

Still, whatever her underlying motivation, he had to admit that he found her physical charms to be irresistible. And he had to admit that if you were going to be involved with a film star, you had to accept that some ego would be part of the equation. He decided to give Tiffany a call in the morning. He hit the sack, but he didn't have a restful night.

When Tiffany heard Matt's voice the following morning, her spirits couldn't have been higher if she had just seen her name displayed in neon on Times Square.

"Why, Matthew," she purred, "I'd love to have dinner with you tonight. But may I ask: Is this business or pleasure?"

Matt's belly laugh jolted Tiffany on the other end.

"Well, I wasn't ready to bring up the pleasure part, but the dinner invitation sure wasn't about business," he said. "You know I do have a life beyond being a newspaper man. I'm not always on the prowl for a story."

"No, but you're always on the prowl," Tiffany laughed. "But somehow I suspect your days and nights on the prowl might be over."

"Well, again, I'm not the wolf or pig some people think I am," Matt said. "Just say that perhaps I'm ready to make that U-turn and get back with a certain sizzling actress with a heart of gold."

"Talk about typecasting," Tiffany purred. "You're labeling me. I'm just the sweet girl next door who somehow found herself in front of a camera."

"Yeah, right," Matt said. "We'll talk more. I'll pick you up at 6 and we'll eat at the Nut Bar."

"Sounds like a plan," Tiffany said.

After she hung up, Tiffany felt like a conquering heroine. Her conquest was back in the fold. And she was determined to make sure that Matt Meredith remained in the Tiffany Underhill Empire.

Which is why they had an evening they write romance novels about. They had a delightful dinner at the Nut Bar. He had filet, she had tuna. He had two glasses of Merlot. She had one glass of sherry. After dinner and drinks, they went to Matt's house and had a naked moonlight swim. Then they made love on a large blanket by Matt's pool, once again utilizing their fit bodies to mine mounds of exquisite pleasure while the stars in the sky gazed down upon them.

After they had drained every ounce of sexual energy in them, an exhausted but exhilarated Matt caressed and fondled the gleaming Tiffany and said: "If I die and go to heaven, I won't be any happier than I am at this moment."

"Ditto, big guy!" Tiffany said with a Hollywood smile. "Me, too."

Indeed, Tiffany once again felt like a leading lady. She didn't care that she and Matt most likely would wind up having a bicoastal romance. She wanted him to be her leading man. And she would smother him with so much love and affection and attention that he wouldn't even think to look at another woman while she was off somewhere shooting a movie. And if she could convince him to quit the *Braxton Bugle* and move to L.A. and become a screenwriter, so much the better. After all, she knew a few producers who would be agreeable to reading a script by an aspiring screenwriter. Of course, this wasn't a topic that she was quite ready to broach with Matt. She knew how deeply ingrained he was in Braxton and with the *Bugle*. His town and his newspaper defined him. An uprooting to another locale, even as one as enticing as Hollywood, wasn't something he would do without a lot of convincing.

But as Tiffany had learned over the years, she could be quite convincing. Especially when it came to men.

But she swore to herself that she would be prudent with Matt. Tiffany knew that her self-focus had terminated more than one serious relationship. She was determined not to jeopardize this relationship. She had worked so hard and had swallowed her pride to reclaim him. She had been instrumental in him landing the biggest story of his life. Granted, she came forward to Ned March partly out of civic duty and partly out of her anger toward the mayor. But the primary reason she had provided Matt with his smoking gun to crack the Shelter scandal story was to ingratiate herself with him, even if it was subliminal.

As for Matt, he had finally written off Robbyn as a lost cause, which had thrown him back into Tiffany's arms. He truly did care about Tiffany, even thought he loved her. He had come to realize that you could love two people at once.

And although his love for Robbyn had seemed more lasting and deep to him, he had found her behavior to be bizarre. He ultimately felt that she would bring more emotional baggage to a relationship than he could handle. He had decided it would be easier to deal with Tiffany's career and self-focus than it would be Robbyn's sensitivities. And he couldn't deny that Tiffany's considerable physical charms were incredibly enticing. Which is why he proceeded to make love to her once again by his pool, followed by another moonlit naked swim.

Tiffany served breakfast in bed to Matt the next morning. Of course, for Matt, that simply meant a bowl of Wheaties, a glass of pineapple juice, and a cup of coffee. Tiffany just had a cup of coffee and a granola bar.

"So, when does your filming wrap up here?" Matt asked, not wanting to know the answer if that time was soon. "We wasted a lot of time being apart while you've been filming here. And now that we're back together, I don't want to hear that you're leaving for Hollywood in two days."

Her smile was so wide you could have hung draperies on it.

"It's so touching to hear you say that," she said, cocking back her head and hair provocatively. "Well, unfortunately, I have to leave tomorrow."

"You're kidding me," Matt said, looking crestfallen.

"Afraid so," Tiffany said softly. Her lovely features had shrunk into a gloomy mask.

Suddenly her features dramatically brightened into a rainbow of joy.

"Got ya!" she yelped in triumph. "I was just kidding you. I'm here for at least 10 more days!"

"Man, I believed you," Matt said. "You had me going there. Don't mess with me like that."

"Well, I *am* an actress," she cooed.

"That you are," he said, smiling. "And I'm a columnist. Which means I make my own hours. So today I'm not working if I don't feel like it. And I don't feel like it. Let's spend the whole day hanging out. You don't have to be on the set, do you?"

"Not today," Tiffany said, delighted he was putting work aside to be with her. "It's your lucky day!"

So, they spent the day shopping, visiting the local museum, strolling in city park, eating at an outdoor cafe in an upscale suburb of Braxton, and driving through the Amish countryside in nearby Lancaster County.

That evening, while driving back to Matt's house after a luscious dinner at an out-of-the-way French restaurant in the Miller County countryside, Matt asked simply:

"So, what's up with us after you leave town?"

"Nothing changes," Tiffany said almost too loudly. "I spend time here with you as much as possible. You make your own hours, so you spend some time with me in California. We have long-distance phone sex. And ultimately, well, who knows? We live here full-time when I'm not filming. Or, well, you become a full-time screenwriter and live with me in Beverly Hills. Of course, we should get married somewhere along the way."

"Wow, your brain has been working overtime, hasn't it?" he teased her, playfully tousling her hair. "Well, the marriage works for me. You living here works for me. Us being bicoastal semi-works for me. Me leaving Braxton to write screenplays in Hollywood? Well, I'm not so sure. You know, I love what I do. And what I do I do best here. Being an actress, you don't have to live on the West Coast. You just have to show up on location wherever you're filming."

"Well, yes and no," Tiffany said. "It's nice to network and *be* there. That's how the business works. I can't leave everything up to my agent. Of course, if I become a superstar, I could live on the moon and still land parts."

"Well, before we get too immersed in all the details of our future, why don't we just take it a day at a time and build our relationship from there," Matt said.

"I don't think I can bear being separated too frequently from your sexy body," Tiffany said, playfully pinching his ear lobe. "But philosophically I agree with what you're saying."

Their minds being in agreement, they then opted to have their bodies in tandem as well when they returned to Matt's house. Some couples are good only at coupling. As Matt fell asleep that night in Tiffany's arms, he was starting to think that he and Tiffany could have a lot more in common than just their bodies. As Tiffany fell asleep that night, her only reservation about Matt was whether his own independence and career focus could ultimately mesh with hers. Since she still was in an exquisite post-coital glow, she didn't think that was that compelling of an issue. She figured she probably would have that issue with most men of substance and consequence, men who didn't have Matt's looks, sense of humor and sexual prowess. But she did wish that Braxton wasn't so far from Hollywood.

Meanwhile, as Robbyn Baxter fell asleep that night, she did so with some pangs of regret over her failed relationship with Matt. She missed elements of him terribly -- his sense of humor, his companionship, his great relationship with her boys, and, certainly not the least, their wonderful sex life. But at the same time, she felt a great sense of relief that she hadn't rushed into a mistake that she would live to regret. She was utterly convinced that Matt had a roving eye and that she never would totally trust him to be faithful. She felt that Matt was a great guy who was totally focused on her when they were together. Yet she also felt that he was a hopeless hound by nature, one who would never be put on a leash by any woman.

Chapter Twenty

Matt decided to take a week's vacation now that his Shelter and mayoral journalistic adventures had concluded. But the real reason he opted for some time off was to spend as much time with Tiffany as possible while she was still in town. Since Tiffany's location shots also were winding down, she managed to have considerable time off each day to spend with Matt. They both had the same motive: Get to know one another as much as possible. Tiffany found Matt to be everything she ever wanted in a man. She wasn't the least disappointed in him as they spent more time together. In fact, she grew to love and like him a bit more each day. As for Matt, he discovered that he truly enjoyed her company. But he became increasingly aware that Tiffany's conversation generally centered on her. Even when they were planning fun activities together, he always was asking her what she would like to do. And she rarely asked him what he would like to do because she was too busy telling him what she wanted to do. He also realized that when they were having a serious discussion, she was quite forceful in her views and seemed to be one of those people who knew the answer to everything. However, Matt felt that he might be somewhat unfair to her in his evaluation because he was so conscious of looking for flaws. He had spent years looking for the right person to share his life with, and now he just wanted to be sure. At the same time, he didn't want to be so anal that he was looking for a speck of dust on a Porsche. Granted, Tiffany and Matt were doing fun things, and there hadn't been any stress-related issues that go hand in hand with living with a person. Matt was aware that Tiffany's self-centered nature could easily morph into pure selfishness if he was encountering a crisis and she was too distracted by herself to be supportive of him.

While Matt had freed himself of work-related issues for a week, he still had some baseball duties. The Cubs had won their league championship and their season was over. But the Sorbonne Township traveling team still had a couple of tournaments on its schedule. In fact, the team would be in Wilmington, Delaware that upcoming weekend. Matt wondered if Robbyn would be there. He assumed she would be because of Timmy, but there always was the possibility that Robbyn could have Cindy Loeper take Timmy along with her son Derek. After Robbyn's rude behavior toward him at Dairy Queen, Matt was prepared to ignore Robbyn. He had resolved to be civil to her if she was in turn, but that was all.

She had truly hurt his feelings in such a severe way that she had effectively turned off his feelings for her. That, in turn, had opened his heart once again for Tiffany. However, Matt desperately missed Timmy and Billy. They had become almost like his own sons and he missed hanging out with them. Since the Cubs had finished their season and since the traveling team hadn't yet practiced for the Wilmington tournament, he hadn't seen Timmy since the night the Cubs won the league playoff title. The same epic night that Robbyn had been so demonstrative in squelching any desire he had for her. Matt was relieved that Tiffany would not be accompanying him to Wilmington. She had a publicity appearance in Manhattan that Saturday. Which was convenient for both of them since neither wanted to relive or rehash what had transpired the last time she went to a tournament and a "Hello Hollywood!" camera-distracted Timmy wound up getting hit by a pitch.

Since she couldn't make the tournament, Tiffany decided to stop by and watch the Sorbonne team practice that Thursday. She wanted to surprise Matt and take him out to dinner. Since practice already was in progress upon her arrival, her short shorts and tight pink tank top elicited some pronounced rubbernecking and stares from players, coaches and parents of both genders.

Matt, who was pitching batting practice, was not pleased by her choice of outfits. Nevertheless, he was glad to see her. Despite her penchant for drawing attention to herself, Matt was enraptured by her charms.

Robbyn, who was sitting in the stands with Cindy Loeper, actually was glad to see Tiffany. Robbyn had been second-guessing herself about terminating her relationship with Matt. But one look at Tiffany sauntering toward the third base line instantly eradicated any regrets in Robbyn's heart and mind.

"Look at that slut," Robbyn said sharply to Cindy. "She deserves a pig like Matt. I'm so glad I found out about what he's really like before it was too late."

"Ah, you're just jealous," Cindy said lightly, trying to diffuse Robbyn's malice.

"I'm way past being jealous," Robbyn said. "Believe me, I'm glad it's over. I'm over him. I just wish I could find someone who was just like him, but someone who can keep his dick in his pants and out of every cute woman he bumps into."

"My! My! What a crude mouth!" a truly surprised Cindy exclaimed. "What's gotten into you, Robbyn?"

"You lie down with a pig and you start talking like one," Robbyn said.

"Enough said," said Cindy, not wanting to hear anymore.

Besides, Cindy wanted to focus on Tiffany and her interaction with Matt. But Matt was preoccupied with practice, so an amused Cindy and a frowning Robbyn watched Natalie Lane approach Tiffany.

"Oh, man, look at Natalie pushing out her boobs, trying to match Tiffany," Cindy said, giggling.

Even Robbyn had to snicker, adding sarcastically: "Well, one slut to another."

"I'm Natalie Lane," she said to Tiffany without introduction. "So, you are friends with our coach, huh? My son, Mikey, was added to the tournament team for this weekend. So, will you be going to Wilmington with us?"

"I'm Tiffany," she said in response. "Well, I have to work this weekend, so I won't be in Wilmington. But nice to meet you."

"So how did you hook up with Matt?" Natalie asked. "He's quite the man around town, but rather particular. I'm not terribly surprised he fell for you."

Tiffany smiled.

"Well, I don't discuss my personal relationships with total strangers. But I met Matt during an interview for his column and TV show. And we became friends."

"Good friends, huh?" Natalie asked.

"You could say that," Tiffany said.

Tiffany checked out Natalie's sexy shorts and blouse, her abundant brown curls and equally abundant curves, and was piqued by curiosity.

"So, tell me, Natalie," Tiffany said sweetly. "Are you and Matt good friends?"

"Well, unfortunately, we're not," Natalie said. "I hate to admit this, but it wasn't because I didn't try."

"Well, no offense, but I'm glad to hear that," Tiffany said, splashing a bit of a Southern drawl on her words. "Because if you and Matt had been an item, well, there wouldn't be room for little old me in his life, now would there?"

"I, uh, guess not," replied Natalie, not exactly sure about whether she had just been insulted or complimented. It was at that point that Natalie excused herself. And it was at that point that Tiffany grew even more comfortable with Matt. She figured that if he had resisted the obvious physical charms of the hot but hardly classy Natalie Lane, he couldn't be the womanizer some folks portrayed him as.

Tiffany waved at Matt, who took a break during batting practice to walk over for a quick chat.

"I wanted to surprise you," Tiffany said. "I won't get in the way. I'll sit in the stands and wait for you."

"This is great," Matt said, lying. Internally, he was wondering what Robbyn was thinking. Which he found to be a strange, awkward feeling considering that he had written off Robbyn and ushered Tiffany back into his life. But it was a feeling he couldn't deny.

"Wouldn't it be great if I went up into the bleachers and struck up a conversation with Robbyn?" Tiffany teased.

"Well, not really," Matt said, unsuccessfully trying to transform his grimace into a smile.

"Just kidding," Tiffany said. "I'll sit on the bottom row and just keep to myself."

"Just stay away from the fathers," Matt whispered. "Their wives don't exactly look like you."

"I would think they would be friendlier toward me than their wives," Tiffany said through soft giggles.

"Well, I had better get back to my job," Matt said. "If you get bored and can't hang until after practice, just drop by my house and hang out. This could take another 45 minutes."

"I could use 45 minutes to just sit and relax while I scope you out," Tiffany said, smiling as she turned and walked toward the stands.

As Matt headed back to the pitching mound, Timmy Baxter, who was fielding batting practice grounders at short, jogged up with a sad look on his face.

"Coach, it was great seeing you tonight," Timmy said glumly. "Until that actress lady showed up. Are you with her again? And what about my mom?"

Matt was embarrassed by his questions. But he didn't want to be insensitive to Timmy.

"Well, Timmy, this really isn't the time or the place," he said. "But, yes. I'm back with Tiffany. And that has nothing to do with your mom. She doesn't want anything to do with me. Doubt if she ever will."

While Matt was saying that, he knew Robbyn had everything to do with his return to Tiffany. Because he wasn't in denial. He knew that if Robbyn hadn't so vehemently spurned him, he wouldn't have restored his relationship with Tiffany. But he was OK with that because he figured Robbyn was part of his past and that he now had an exciting if uncertain future with Tiffany.

"I hate that you and my mom are apart," Timmy said. "I don't understand."

"Relationships are hard to understand," Matt said. "When you get older, we talk about it over a few beers. But for now, I have to finish batting practice or you guys will be here all night."

"Being here is better than being home," Timmy said, "because my mom is grouchy these days. I think she's mad at you, but I think she misses you, too. Women are weird."

"Uh, yes they are," Matt said softly, distracted by the notion that perhaps Robbyn did miss him despite her blatant malice towards him.

Matt resumed throwing batting practice, alternating between-pitch glances at Tiffany and Robbyn. Tiffany looked radiant; Robbyn looked depressed. Both looks stimulated Matt, which he found disturbing. He mentally castigated himself for being weird as he threw a pitch in the dirt at the feet of Derek Loeper.

After the team finished batting practice, Matt was preoccupied hitting ground balls during infield practice. So, he didn't notice Tiffany migrating to the top of the bleachers and sitting right next to Robbyn and Cindy. It would be an understatement to say that Robbyn and Cindy just about swallowed their teeth when they saw Tiffany approaching them.

Robbyn was usually a classy lady, one who normally wasn't rude or crude to people. But she also was spunky and spirited when she had to be. And she took Tiffany's appearance as an insult.

"What the hell do you want?" Robbyn snapped as Tiffany sat down next to her, smiling and looking buoyant.

Cindy cringed as she heard Robbyn's question stab the air.

"I just wanted to chat, darling," Tiffany said lightly, "and to say I have no hard feelings."

"Well, I'm sure as hell not your darling," Robbyn said. "And I could give a shit what your feelings are. I don't care about you. You're not even on my radar screen. What happened between Matt and myself doesn't concern you. I broke up with Matt. He's not the man I thought he was. And if he's with you now, I don't care. Hell, he'll probably be with somebody else by next week."

Cindy couldn't help but giggle.

Tiffany wasn't giggling. But she was frowning as she said: "I know you're a single mother in a small town, so your take on relationships may not be as cosmopolitan as mine."

"Spare me that big-time Hollywood goddess bit," Robbyn said, again to accompanying giggles by Cindy.

Then Cindy yelped: "You go, girl!"

Tiffany flashed a look of annoyance at Cindy, but otherwise ignored her. At this point, Robbyn wasn't even looking at Tiffany.

"Leave me alone," Robbyn said harshly. "I'm here to watch my kid practice. I'm not here to make small talk with some Hollywood slut."

"You're just jealous because you couldn't compete with me," Tiffany said. "How could you? You're pretty and built, but look at who you are and who I am. It was no contest!"

Robbyn laughed but didn't look at Tiffany.

"You're pathetic," Robbyn said. "Your ego must have been killing you when Matt left you for me. Dumping you for a nobody. Well, you may appear in movies. But I find you to be so damn shallow. And I know you think I'm just some single mother, but I happen to be a person of consequence and substance. A person who is good at her job, an advertising position that I utilize to make a difference in this community. So, you know where you can stick your Hollywood attitude. I am not at all impressed with you."

Tiffany hadn't realized she would be getting a tiger by the tail when she had sat down. Now, she was angry because Robbyn had touched a nerve in her notoriously fragile psyche.

Just as Tiffany was about to scream at Robbyn, she caught Matt's eye down on the field. Matt had just moments before noticed Tiffany sitting with and talking to Robbyn. The sight of them together all but gave him cardiac arrest. He literally stopped breathing for a moment or two. He couldn't imagine why Tiffany had ventured up there. Actually, he could. He figured correctly that Tiffany went up to Robbyn to gloat and rub it in. He was so angry with Tiffany that he could hardly control his rage.

He stood there transfixed for several moments until Timmy's yell of "What's up, Coach?" startled him.

"Uh, nothing," Matt said.

That's when Timmy looked up at the bleachers and saw his mother talking with Tiffany.

Timmy walked over from shortstop and said to Matt: "That's kind of awkward, the two of them talking. Do you think they'll get into a fight?"

"I'm not worth fighting over," Matt said, forcing a smile. "Let's finish up here. Get back to short."

After Tiffany had caught Matt's eyes, the words that were going to come screaming out of her somehow got stuck in her throat. So, she literally bit her tongue. After dabbing at a speck of blood on her tongue with a finger, she stood up and towered over the seated Robbyn. At that point, Robbyn resumed eye contact with Tiffany.

"Just let me say that your perception of Matt is totally off base," Tiffany said. "He is not some slob who screws anybody with a pulse. He's an attractive guy, a guy with a sense of humor. He's every woman's dream, which is why he hasn't been exactly celibate. But he is not a pig. And he can be faithful."

Robbyn's eyes were saucers of surprise as she listened to Tiffany's endorsement of Matt.

Robbyn's eyes got even wider as Tiffany bent over and whispered into her ear:

"You blew it. You were just what he was looking for. But you were too damn prissy. He loved you more than me. I know that. But you killed that love he had for you. It's gone. Which is why I have him back. I know that. I'm not an air-headed actress. But now I have him back. And you're not getting him back."

Tiffany then pranced down the bleacher steps, wondering if she should have admitted that to Robbyn. Her motive in telling her that was to torment Robbyn for life, to torture her with the knowledge that she had misjudged Matt and had walked away from the love of her life.

"I'm an asshole," Tiffany uttered to herself under her breath as she walked toward the field. "I embarrassed myself. Big time."

As she drew near to the field, Tiffany simply yelled to Matt: "I'll be at your place."

Matt simply nodded, still churning inside over his curiosity over what had transpired between Tiffany and Robbyn.

Most of the eyes on the field and the bleachers gazed upon Tiffany's lithe figure as she sauntered toward her car in the parking lot. But not Robbyn's. And not Cindy's. Robbyn was simply staring ahead into space. Cindy was staring at Robbyn, imploring her to share with her what Tiffany had whispered to her.

Finally, after what had seemed like an eternity to Cindy, Robbyn turned to Cindy. Cindy blinked in disbelief. Robbyn's face had turned radiant.

"She just told me something that will change my life," Robbyn said with reverence in her voice.

"What?" Cindy screamed loud enough to elicit startled stares from half the people in the bleachers.

"She told me that Matt really isn't a hopeless womanizer. Not at all!" Robbyn said so excitedly that her phrases came out in torrents. "And she told me that he really loves me. Really loves me! He only went back to her because he figured I'd written him out of my life for good."

"Tiffany told you that?" Cindy asked incredulously, the volume of her words still turned on high.

"Absolutely!" Robbyn said through a smile so wide that her vocal cords could practically be seen throbbing with animated delight.

"What an idiot that Tiffany is!" Cindy said, giggling and shaking her head. "Now what are you going to do? I mean, it's not like Matt and Tiffany broke up. I imagine she and Matt might be, well, sort of intimate tonight."

"I don't even want to think about that," Robbyn said, her smile suddenly vaporizing. "But this will be their last night together!"

Robbyn spat out those last words with ferocity.

"Well, what are you going to do to get him back?" Cindy asked, her mind racing with possibilities.

"I have no idea," Robbyn said giddily. "But I'll think of something."

Matt was dying to know what sort of conversation had transpired between Robbyn and Tiffany. So, he wrapped up practice 10 minutes early, telling the boys they were sharp and he was cutting practice short as a reward. He couldn't wait to get home to ask Tiffany what was discussed. Of course, he never even thought of asking Robbyn what was said. So, he was utterly shocked when, looking up after putting some bats in a bag, he found Robbyn standing behind him.

"Startled you, huh?" Robbyn said, beaming.

Matt blinked in disbelief. Robbyn's sudden friendliness toward him was way out in the margin and his mind was scrambling to fathom how he and she suddenly got on the same page -- at least in terms of having a conversation.

After several moments of awkward silence while Matt struggled to get his wits about him and while his emotions once again spun in a conflicted fashion, he said: "Of course, you did. I don't get it. You don't want anything to do with me. And now you are gushing this big smile and talking to me. Who's crazy here? You? Me? Or both of us?"

"Both of us," Robbyn said softly. "Listen, I know you must think I'm crazy. But I'm not. Just let me explain. I know you're evidently back with Tiffany, but I need to talk to you. Is tonight good?"

"What the hell did you and Tiffany talk about?" Matt said, confusion assaulting his state of mind.

"I'll tell you if you'll have a drink with me tonight," Robbyn said, layering her words with a subtle but intoxicating come-hither charm.

Matt hesitated, cleared his throat -- which suddenly had grown drier than the infield dirt on the Sorbonne Township practice field -- and said: "Well, uh, I sure would like to. But, you know, Tiffany ...."

"Tiffany is waiting for you, right?" Robbyn said, picking up the narrative in a cheerful tone that seemed out of sync with the text of her words. "I understand. How about tomorrow night? Say 7 or so at the Nut Bar?"

"Oh, man!" Matt said, pounding a bat into the dirt. "You're something else. You're toying with me, right? I thought you were finished with me because you think I'm an unfaithful cad or something."

"I don't even know what you mean by cad," Robbyn said, laughing. "Just say it turns out that I misjudged you. I'm sorry. I loved you so much I wanted you to be perfect. Well, you're not. But I'm not either. And I love you. And I want you to marry me. Do you want me to get on bended knee here and ask you to marry me?"

Matt laughed. Hard.

"This is bizarre," he said, shaking his head. "Are you kidding me? What's the deal here? What the hell did you and Tiffany talk about?"

"Ask her tonight," Robbyn said, smiling. "And enjoy your last night with her. And be at the Nut Bar tomorrow night. If you're not, you'll live to regret it. Big time. Trust me."

With that, she leaned over and kissed him gently on the lips. Then she turned delicately away and walked toward Timmy and Billy.

Matt's head was spinning. He didn't know what to think. He did think that he needed a quick drink. And he needed to get home to find out from Tiffany what she and Robbyn had talked about. But he wasn't going anywhere at the moment. He had an erection that was as big as a baseball bat. OK, a miniature baseball bat. Fortunately for him, he had the team bat bag to hold in front of him while his penis slowly went soft.

"Are you and Matt getting together again?" Timmy excitedly asked his mother.

"I think so," Robbyn said. "I hope so."

"So do I!" yelled Billy.

"Well, let's go to Burger King to celebrate," Timmy said.

"It's a date," Robbyn said.

She then looked over her shoulder back at Matt and saw him standing there all by himself, holding the bat bag in front of him.

"See you tomorrow night," she yelled back at Matt as she waved goodbye.

"I'll be damned," Matt said to himself.

Besides his penis, Matt at that moment didn't know what was up with his life. But he was dying to find out.

When Matt got home, Tiffany was having a glass of wine poolside. He was surprised to see her with a glass of wine. He had never seen her drink alone before.

"Rough day?" he asked.

"Why?" she said, looking damn hot in her white bikini that perfectly showcased her tan.

"I didn't think you drank alone," he said, smiling.

"Well, it's not something I've made a habit of," she said, smiling. "Come here. I could use a kiss."

Matt leaned over as she reclined on a lounge chair and kissed her gently on the lips with closed lips. But Tiffany forcefully stuck her tongue into his mouth and kissed him passionately. Matt joined in the passion, but his mind was back to its guilty flashbacks of betraying Robbyn. Her talk with him after practice had put him back at square one in his relationship dilemma.

Before their hot kiss evolved into foreplay, Matt pulled away, using the excuse that he too needed a drink.

"Let me get a glass of wine and refresh yours," he said smiling, "before we resume enjoying each other."

"Sounds like a deal," Tiffany said.

While Matt went inside to fetch the chilled bottle of white wine, Tiffany mulled over what she wanted to tell him concerning her conversation with Robbyn. She knew that Matt would ask her about it, and she was wrestling with how honest she wanted to be with him. As Matt returned with the bottle of wine, Tiffany made a snap decision to fudge the truth. She had lost him once. And she had made a possibly severe tactical error in telling Robbyn that Matt really was a faithful sort of guy and that he actually loved her more than she. Tiffany still was kicking herself over what she had said; hence, her eagerness to have some wine to take the edge off her anxiety.

"So, what did you and Robbyn talk about?" Matt asked quietly in an unsuccessful attempt not to bring too much drama to his query.

"The Shelter scandal," Tiffany said, also trying to lighten the mood.

"Yeah, right," Matt said, sitting in the lounge chair next to her.

"We talked about you, silly," Tiffany said, reaching over and running her fingers through his hair.

"What about me?" Matt asked, adding in a teasing voice: "You're really going to make me pry this out of you, aren't you? Gonna make me work for this. You're enjoying this. Knowing I'm dying to know."

"We talked about what a bastard you are," Tiffany laughed. "She said she was glad to be rid of you and that she feels sorry for me because now I'm stuck with you again."

Tiffany stuck out her tongue playfully.

Matt, his ardor for Tiffany somewhat doused by his conversation with Robbyn, was having his torch for Tiffany re-lit by her provocative, sexy manner. *Is it possible to love two women?* was a question that was assaulting Matt's conscience at the moment.

"Come on, I'm serious," Matt complained softly. "Don't mess with me."

"I just told her that I hoped that there were no hard feelings between us," Tiffany said, altering the dialogue she actually had with Robbyn. "I told her you weren't a bad guy, but that you and I are just a better fit than you and she were."

Matt arched an eyebrow in disbelief, figuring that Tiffany was putting a spin on her conversation with Robbyn.

Tiffany picked up on his look, read his doubting vibe, but nevertheless pressed on in what she hoped was a subtler fashion.

"OK, I told her that you weren't the womanizer that she apparently must feel you are," Tiffany said, telling the truth. But then she segued to the fiction by adding: "To be honest, she said that she always would have doubt in her mind about your ability to be faithful. That she could no longer see herself in a relationship with you. And I told her that was no longer her problem. That you would be faithful forever to me because you're mine and I wasn't going to lose you to any woman anywhere."

"To which she said what?" an anxious Matt asked.

Tiffany sensed Matt's anxiety and noticed a cynical look in his eye. But she had gone too far to revise her script now.

"She wished us good luck and said she hoped to at least be with friends with both of us, especially since her boys think so much of you."

Matt didn't respond. At that moment, he didn't know what to respond. His only thought at the moment was that Tiffany wasn't quite as good an actress as she thought she was.

After a long, awkward pause in which the sound of silence was deafening in serving as the bass line to high anxiety, Matt decided to come clean. His heart was being crushed by the vise of being caught between two women.

He refilled both of their wine glasses, sighed, and looked intently into her eyes.

"Tiffany, I think you may have put a bit of a spin on your conversation with Robbyn, but that's OK," he said softly. "I understand. I'm flattered that you're fighting for me. I don't want you to fight for me."

"What did you just say?" she asked, alarm coating her voice.

"Let me finish," he said quickly. "Someone as beautiful as you, someone who loves me as much as you do, shouldn't have to fight for me."

"Well, thank you," she said, smiling with relief.

Matt didn't return her smile. Tiffany picked up on that immediately, freezing the smile on her face.

"Let me finish," he repeated. "I should have absolutely no reservations about our relationship. But I have two problems."

"What problems?" Tiffany said sharply, gulping her wine.

"The first one is relatively minor," Matt said softly. "I've discovered that you're somewhat self-centered, a trait that could get old with me down the road."

"I am not!" she protested, standing up.

"You don't realize it, honey," he said, "but you are. I blame your celebrity status for that. It's understandable. And I can live with that."

"So, Mr. Perfect, what's the other damn problem?" she asked, her irritation and anxiety igniting the embers of impeding anger.

Matt drained his wine glass and poured himself another.

"This is my problem, not yours," he said quietly. "I'm in love with two women. I love you. And I love Robbyn. I can't help myself."

"Well, screw you!" she said sharply. "I just got done telling her that you're not a pig, not a womanizer. What the hell was I thinking? You can't keep your dick in your pants, can you? I thought there were Romeos in Hollywood. Well, they've got nothing on you, buster!"

"You know, I've been in monogamous relationships my entire life," Matt said, standing up. "Until you and Robbyn came along. And since you and I and she and I have had alternating breakups, technically I've been monogamous with both of you."

Tiffany burst out with a sarcastic laugh of considerable volume.

"Talk about splitting pubic hairs, you bastard!" she yelled. "The nerve! You've taken turns banging both of us. And now you're supposedly in this psychological mess, trying to choose. Well, I don't think you want to choose between us. You like screwing both of us."

"That's not true," he said calmly, as he gently put his arms around her.

"Don't touch me!" she said with anger, backing away from him. "Don't *ever* touch me again! I never want to share you with anybody. You're not worth it. Who the hell are you to treat me like that? Or her. I'm done with you! And she should be done with you if she has any brains."

"I truly am conflicted and confused," Matt said.

As soon as the words slipped through his lips, he realized how lame they sounded.

"Fuck you!" Tiffany flared. "You're pathetic. You're two-timing two women and you tell *me* that I'm self-centered? Your brain must be up your ass. No, I got it! You're thinking with your dick, you bastard!"

She then ran into the house and zipped upstairs to gather her belongings.

Matt stood numb for a moment. He was transfixed by indecision. He didn't know whether to chase after her or not. Paralyzed by analysis, his thoughts playing Ping-Pong on the pros and cons of the two women who had tugged at his heart, he remained there. If was as if subconsciously he was choosing Robbyn and allowing Tiffany to flee from his life.

Tiffany, startled that Matt didn't chase after her, angrily ripped her clothes from his closet and sprinted down the steps. In her haste to run away from Matt's life, one of her dresses slipped from the bundle of clothes she was carrying and got tangled in her feet. She tripped, lost her balance, and fell down the bottom third of the steps. The sound of her tibia breaking sounded like a tree branch breaking. The pitch of her scream pierced the quiet of the evening, startling Matt out of his statue impersonation. Tiffany's scream segued into loud cries for help as Matt raced to her rescue. He found her at the bottom of the stairs, convulsed in sobs and tears, distracted by pain.

Matt rushed up to her and frantically yelled, "What's wrong? What's wrong?"

"I tripped over my damn clothes," Tiffany shouted between sobs, her face wet with tears. "I think I broke my ankle. It's killing me. It's all your fault, you monster!"

That having been said, she angrily flailed her arms at him in frustration and desperation.

Matt, after taking a few slaps to the face and shoulders from Tiffany, bent down and saw that her left ankle was terribly swollen.

"I'm so sorry," he said. "I did this to you. You're right. Let me get you to the hospital."

"Don't touch me! Don't touch it! Just leave me alone!" she yelled, crying and screaming hysterically.

Matt, his already battered psyche wrought with guilt, ignored her and delicately but swiftly lifted her up and put her over his shoulder, her midsection cradled across his left shoulder. The movement startled her and sent waves of pain shooting through her ankle. Angry, she began pounding on his back.

"Stop that!" Matt shouted. "You'll make me drop you and you'll hurt yourself worse. I know it hurts, baby, but you need help fast. I'm taking you to the hospital now."

Ignoring her protests, he walked out to his car in the driveway, thankful he hadn't put it in the garage. Otherwise, he would have had less room to maneuver. Somehow, someway he managed to open the back door and lower her and drape her sideways across the back seat. At least she had ceased punching him while he did so. He drove her to Braxton Hospital, about 15 minutes away. Each time he made a turn and came to a stop, she yelped in pain.

During the trip, he kept saying soothingly, "You'll be all right, you'll be all right. Just stay calm, baby. I know it hurts. Just stay calm, baby."

And she kept crying and screaming, "Don't call me your baby! And see what you did to me! We're finished! Forever!"

When Matt pulled up to the emergency room, he parked illegally right in front of the doorway.

"What the hell do you think you're doing, buddy?" a security guard yelled at him.

"My girlfriend broke her ankle and I'm taking her in," Matt snapped back at the security guard.

Matt didn't even wait for a reply, quickly adding: "Get some help or get lost. I need help getting her out of the car."

The security guard, a rotund middle-aged man whose waist size was a close match for his IQ, said nothing. Seeing Matt's size as he exited his car, the guard obediently helped Matt extricate a sobbing Tiffany from the back seat.

Matt lifted her into his arms, and she immediately began punching him again, yelling at him.

"You didn't do this to her in a fight, did you?" the security guard asked, playing the role of detective.

"Don't be an idiot!" Matt snapped. "She's just in pain. She broke her ankle falling down the stairs."

"Did you push her?" the guard asked.

"Get a wheelchair or get the hell out of here!" Matt screamed.

While the guard ponderously walked away to get a wheelchair, Tiffany, still perched across Matt's left shoulder, suddenly laughed. The security guard's questions had sparked a thought in her pain-addled, vengeful mind.

"Hell, I could tell them you pushed me down the stairs," she said, almost in manic glee. "Imagine that police story in the pages of your damn *Braxton Bugle*! Wouldn't your managing editor, Ned March, love that?"

"Tell them anything you want," Matt said, so upset with himself that he frankly didn't care what happened to him because of her fall. "I just want to get you out of this pain."

"Well, why don't you shoot me?" she yelled sarcastically, just as the security guard returned with a wheelchair.

Her question struck a chord in the security guard, a policeman wannabe.

"I'm starting to think you abused your lady friend here, pal," he said, returning to his tough-cop bit.

"I didn't, but frankly I don't a damn what you think, you fat fuck!" Matt said.

His anger now had gotten the best of him. He was sick of the security guard. He was sick of being caught between two women. He was sick of himself. And he was heartsick that Tiffany was in such distress. Despite his anger, he gently lowered Tiffany into the wheelchair and whisked her inside. He took her immediately to the front desk.

"I have a lady with a possible broken ankle," he said calmly as Tiffany sat sobbing in her wheelchair, her face in her hands.

"Well, I'll take her back to a waiting room and then I'll get some information from you," said a stern-looking nurse.

The nurse walked around the desk to wheel Tiffany inside.

Before the nurse reached Tiffany, Matt bent over, and whispered into her ear: "I'm so sorry. I didn't mean for this to happen. I was just trying to tell you what was going on with me. I realize now I don't deserve either one of you."

Tiffany gazed up, looked forlornly into his eyes, and simply, softly and profoundly said: "I deserved better from you. And so did Robbyn."

Matt stood there stricken. Tiffany's words had shot through his heart. He suddenly felt like the most selfish bastard in the world.

As the nurse wheeled Tiffany away, Matt could hear Tiffany, between sobs, telling her: "You don't need any medical insurance information from him. I'm single. I have my own insurance. Just tell him to go away. Far away."

But Matt couldn't go far away. He couldn't go anywhere. He felt like such a louse. He didn't think it would be right to leave, even though it was quite obvious that Tiffany didn't want him there. He sat forlornly in the emergency room waiting room, beating himself up for how he been involved with Tiffany and Robbyn. He didn't think he was a bad guy, and he didn't intentionally try to lead each of the women on. He simply had been attracted to both of them. And he simply had had issues with both of them, triggering his see-saw relationships with both of them. He tried to justify his actions by dwelling on the fact his sexual encounters with Tiffany and Robbyn had been sequential, not simultaneous. At least in the strictest sense of time management. Nevertheless, Tiffany's stinging rebuke right before she was wheeled away about how she and Robbyn had deserved better from him kept echoing in his ears and pinballing through his conscience. Matt sat there castigating himself mentally until he fell asleep. He slept through the arrival of a flunky and publicist from Tiffany's movie studio. And he slept through Tiffany's departure from the hospital after she had had her fractured left tibia put in a cast that ended just below her knee. When he awoke and found that Tiffany had been discharged and had left with studio personnel, he wasn't surprised that she or her staff hadn't awakened him and said goodbye. In fact, he felt relieved. As bad as he felt about hurting her, he sensed that it was best that they were going their separate ways. As he drove home, feeling tired and depressed, he knew that she would have been high maintenance. And her self-focus eventually would have blinded him to her considerable attributes.

Meanwhile, he was intrigued by Robbyn's renewed interest. But at the moment, he hated himself. So, he found it difficult to believe at that particular moment that anybody could love him. Still, he knew that Robbyn was expecting to see him tomorrow, and he wondered if he should show up. He was at the point where he wondered if he should love anybody at all. Matt knew that he hardly had been an angel at times. But still, at his core, he always had thought he essentially was a quality human being. A man with integrity. A man of substance. A man of commitment.

Now, his self-perspective had been especially shaken by Tiffany and also a bit by Robbyn. As he went home to bed, he just wished he could recover the old Matt, the self-assured newspapermen who enjoyed working and who enjoyed having a good time. And now, as he drifted off to sleep, he realized he needed an anchor in his life besides his job. He needed a wife and a family. He needed Robbyn, Timmy and Billy!

When Matt awoke from his four-hour sleep, he felt refreshed. As he showered, shaved and shampooed, he felt more determined than ever to claim Robbyn and her boys as his own. He felt as if he had chosen to coach Little League baseball for a reason -- and that reason was to coach kids to fill a void in his life. He loved children and always had wanted to be a father. Now, he felt, he had hit a triple. Now only was he destined to have two boys of his own in Timmy and Billy, he was destined to have the wonderful wife he always had wanted but had found so elusive.

"You're a damn lucky guy for being such a jerk," Matt said to himself as he inspected himself in the mirror. "Now get your act together and sweep Robbyn off her feet tonight!"

Chapter Twenty One

Matt arrived at the Nut Bar at precisely 7 p.m., the time of his date with Robbyn. As he entered the bar area, scanning the adjoining tables for Robbyn, he immediately felt a shiver of annoyance flash down his spinal column. Seated at the bar were Jimbo Cummings and Millie Paxton. He was hoping they hadn't noticed him. But his luck wasn't that good.

Jimbo, intoxicated, saw Matt standing there and immediately felt compelled to bellow to all the patrons at the end of the bar: "There's the bastard who ran me out of office! I hope you can sleep at night, you prick. This city will never be the same without me."

Matt stood there in silence, gazing at Jimbo, who was rising from his barstool.

While he did so, Millie Paxton tried to hush her boyfriend, telling him: "Just sit down, Jimbo, and ignore him. He's not worth getting your blood pressure up."

But Jimbo ignored her advice. He stumbled toward Matt, pointing a finger in his face and saying: "You made a big deal out of nothing. And now that pipsqueak district attorney we have is pressing charges. You just wanted to make a name for yourself. Why, I ought to ... ."

Before Jimbo finished his sentence, he tried to finish off Matt with a big right hand. But his alcohol-affected reflexes were no match for Matt's. As Jimbo's punch neared Matt's head, he easily ducked the blow. But the man who had just walked in behind Matt wasn't so fortunate. Jimbo's punch smacked the gentleman right in his left eye, leaving a welt that surely would soon become a nasty black eye. The man yelped in pain and fired his own right hand at a startled and disoriented Jimbo. The man's right hand caught Jimbo on top of the head, dropping him to the seat of his pants into a pile of peanut shells. As Jimbo sat there stunned, Millie left her stool and knelt beside him, comforting him. Bar and restaurant patrons who witnessed the bizarre fight at first were too startled to react. Once they had digested the sight of seeing two elderly men duke it out, they began laughing and joking as they replayed the pugilistic scene in their minds and with their gossipy tongues, tweets and Facebook messages.

As for Matt, he was shocked to see that the man who took Jimbo's right cross and countered with his own was none other than Robert Thaxter, Robbyn's' new boss. Matt hadn't yet had a chance to say anything to Robert Thaxter, who was busy being scolded by his wife, Betty, a prim and proper lady who was embarrassed by having her husband involved in a barroom brawl.

Matt stood in the middle as Millie comforted but chastised Jimbo and as Betty Thaxter bawled out Robert. Feeling awkward, Matt approached the Thaxters and simply said: "I'm so sorry you walked into that punch, Bob."

To his surprise, Bob Thaxter, already getting a shiner, laughed and said: "Did you see my counter? I used to box in the Navy, you know. And you know what? I enjoyed that! I've wanted to punch out that clown for years."

"Now, Robert!" snapped Betty. "That's enough of that!"

"What was all that about?" Bob Thaxter asked Matt. "Is our ex-mayor still holding a grudge against you?"

"Obviously," said Matt, grinning and looking self-conscious as he shot a glance over to Jimbo, now was on his feet.

To his credit, Jimbo Cummings walked over to Robert Thaxter, completely ignoring Matt.

"I'm sorry, fellow," Jimbo said to a smiling Bob Thatcher. "I didn't mean to punch you. I was aiming at this hack journalist."

Jimbo shot a wicked glance at Matt and then focused once again on Thaxter.

"I know we've met, and I think you're in advertising," Jimbo said, slurring his words.

"My name is Thaxter," Bob said, "and if you sue me for hitting you, I'll personally punch you again."

Thaxter punctuated his threat with a belly laugh, much to the chagrin of his wife.

"No need," Jimbo said, rubbing the top of his head. "You just swung in self-defense. If I do any suing, I'm gonna be suing Meredith here for libel. But for now, I'm out of here. We're leaving, Millie."

Millie, mortified by what she had just witnessed, apologized to the Thaxters profusely as she escorted Jimbo out of the door. She didn't find time to say anything to Matt.

"We came for dinner, not to get involved in a brawl," Betty said. "Let's get a table. Why don't you join us, Matt? We can share our short stay in Paris with you."

"Actually, I'm meeting someone here for dinner," Matt said. "She works for you, Bob. Her name is Robbyn Baxter."

Both Bob and Betty Thaxter smiled delightedly when they heard Matt mention Robbyn's name.

"That's wonderful," Betty said. "We think the world of Robbyn. The four of us must have dinner together."

"Well," Matt said, trying not to be impolite as he tried to think of an excuse. He wanted to have Robbyn to himself for dinner.

"No ifs, ands or buts," Bob Thaxter shot back before Matt could say anything else. "It's a foursome. Let's grab a table before Robbyn gets here. And before somebody else takes a punch at me."

"I'll have a waiter fetch you some ice for that eye," Betty said, looking at the angry blotch around her husband's eye.

As she said so, Robbyn walked in and immediately saw the three of them standing there. Her heart sank. As much as she enjoyed the Thaxters' company, she, too, wanted to be alone with Matt for dinner. But then she saw Bob Thaxter's angry eye.

"Oh, my God!" she said. "What happened, Bob?"

Bob Thaxter laughed heartily.

"Well, our former mayor took a punch at Matthew here," Bob said ebulliently, enjoying his freshly minted war story. "But Matt had the foresight to duck. Betty and I had just walked into the place and I walked blindly into a sucker punch. Fortunately, I used to box and I immediately fired my own right cross at Jimbo. I decked him right on his ass in a pile of shells. Perfect!"

"Now don't gloat over a schoolboy stunt, dear," Betty said. But her tone was softening as she saw how much her husband was enjoying this unexpected shot of macho testosterone in his life. "You're much too old for this."

"Nonsense," Bob said, grinning broadly.

Robbyn looked at Matt for the first time and gave him a smile warm enough to melt the polar caps left untouched by global warming. Matt returned the smile with one so bright it gave her goose bumps.

"I promise you I was behaving myself," Matt said to Robbyn. "Jimbo was the guy causing trouble. I was just looking for you."

"I'm sorry I missed all the drama and excitement," said Robbyn, adding with a laugh: "I'm not used to going out to dinner with brawling men."

"Well, let's get a table and some ice for Bob before he is a one-eyed wonder," Betty joked.

Betty Thaxter was delighted that Matt and Robbyn were seeing each other. She was a big fan of both and felt they could be a perfect couple. She had been trying to marry Matt off for years. She had immediately grown quite fond of Robbyn, so she was hoping to be a matchmaker for both. And now that she had discovered that Matt and Robbyn might be a couple, she was dying to find out more about them.

As dinner progressed, and as Bob Thaxter took breaks from eating his steak to put ice on his swollen eye, the conversation was difficult for Matt and Robbyn. Betty kept asking questions about their relationship, and Matt and Robbyn kept putting a positive spin on it, trying to be nice without revealing any details about the strain Tiffany's presence had put on their on-again and off-again relationship. And they certainly didn't want to reveal that this was their first date after a less than cordial breakup.

Matt and Robbyn managed to craft enough creative and light-hearted conversation about the joys and splendors of their romance to satisfy the curiosity of Betty, who, unlike her husband, didn't have a clue about the Robbyn, Tiffany and Matt triangle. Robbyn sensed how much the Thaxters thought of Matt. And Matt sensed how much they thought of Robbyn. Such a feeling on both their parts reinforced the notion that both of them must be somewhat special and it was time to focus on the positive aspects of their relationship. Both Matt and Robbyn were hoping that the Thaxters wouldn't make it a late night, giving them ample opportunity to re-ignite their relationship.

So, Matt and Robbyn were acutely disappointed that after dessert and coffee, Bob Thaxter ordered four glasses of champagne.

"I don't want to be late for work tomorrow," Robbyn said teasingly as she protested the champagne order.

"Don't worry about it," Bob said, smiling broadly. "I'm the boss. And besides, I may not go into the office. This eye may make me look like some sort of rogue."

"You definitely will be in the office bright and early," Betty said, giggling. "You can't wait to tell everybody at work what a stud you are. You're the guy that knocked big Jimbo on his ass."

Betty Thaxter's use of the word "ass" had all four of them laughing.

"Wow, aren't you getting racy?" said Bob.

"I'm shocked," Matt said. "I've never heard you say anything like that before."

"Just don't tell the monsignor," Betty said, still giggling.

"Your secret is safe with us," said Robbyn, looking radiant despite her longing to be alone with Matt.

Matt was trying hard to conceal his impatience.

When the champagne arrived, Bob Thaxter raised his glass and the other three fell in lockstep.

"Here's to two of the brightest and best young people Betty and I have been privileged to know," he said, suddenly reverential and solemn in tone. "Betty and I are thrilled that you are dating. Not to put any pressure on you and not to jinx anything, but we think you two are perfect together. Isn't that right, Betty?"

Robbyn blushed and Matt sat there wearing a goofy smile on his face.

"Definitely!" Betty said excitedly. "It's awesome that you are together. We think so much of both of you. Now let's share a toast. And then Bob and I are going to go home and take care of his eye and leave you two lovebirds alone."

As they clinked champagne glasses and drained them, Robbyn had tiny tears trickling from her eyes. Matt had moist eyes. Bob and Betty had pride gleaming from their eyes. Of course, it was difficult to see the pride emanating from Bob's black eye.

After the Thaxters left the Nut Bar, Matt and Robbyn sat there for several moments, simply smiling and grinning at each other.

"You know, if I wrote a book about us, it would sound too contrived even for fiction," Matt said, laughing softly.

"Sometimes I think we look so closely at a person that we fail to step back and see the whole picture," Robbyn said, shifting to a serious demeanor. "I think that's what I did with you. I got a perception of you, one narrow in focus, and it blinded me to all of your good qualities."

"I did the same thing to you," Matt said. "As you know, I thought you were a bit strange when we first met. Aloof, distant and hung up. I didn't realize you were wrestling with the concept of dating again. I prejudged you. I was insensitive."

Robbyn smiled. And then shook her head.

"Tonight isn't about what we did wrong," she said forcefully. "Tonight is about starting over. We've got a fresh start at being us. Let's make it memorable!"

"You've got a date, young lady!" Matt fired back with gusto.

"Well, make it quick," Robbyn said, smiling. "I've got two kids to get home, too."

"Ever the incurable romantic," Matt said, grinning as he rose and took her hand. "We're out of here."

Robbyn assumed that Matt was going to take her to his home for a quick sexual interlude. Indeed, she was looking forward to consummating the renewal of their relationship.

So, when he proceeded to drive into the grounds of the nearby Braxton Museum, she was surprised.

"What are we doing here?" she asked, somewhat disappointed. "I thought we were going to your place."

"Not tonight," Matt said, smiling. "I wanted tonight to be special. You and I are going to sit on a bench near the babbling brook, sit and kiss under the stars, and watch the ducks swim by as we whisper sweet nothings into each other's ear."

"How romantic!" she said, her heart racing.

For 75 lovely minutes scripted from the pages of Romance 101, they sat by the gurgling brook on this gorgeous star-filled night. They talked about the boys. They talked about baseball. They talked about their jobs. They talked about their dreams. They talked about each other. They talked about what being a couple would mean to them. They also kissed and fondled and cuddled until the passion in their hearts and bodies could no longer be contained. The fire in their loins raged into an inferno, a heat that had been chilled way too long, and there was no humanly possible way they could put that passion on hold. They couldn't keep it in check until they drove to Matt's house. There was no keeping their craving and need for each other under control. So, like a couple of lusty teen-agers throbbing with the molten emotion of the moment, they scrambled into the back of Matt's car and still were pliable and flexible enough in the cramped quarters to achieve orgasms without tearing ligaments and destroying cartilage.

When they had expended themselves, they clung to each other tenaciously in breathless and silent rapture.

"I hope we didn't offend the ducks," Matt finally said, laughing.

"I will never forget tonight," Robbyn said. "And I'm sure the ducks won't either. Of course, I definitely will remember tonight tomorrow morning when my back does its impersonation of a mangled train wreck."

Matt laughed and said: "We all pay a price for love. I think I have brush burns on my knees from rubbing against the leather seat."

"Well," Robbyn laughed, "we'd better put our clothes back on to cover up your brush burns. And before some overzealous security guard arrests us for indecent exposure and public lewdness."

"Yeah, I'm not sure Betty Thaxter would be OK with that," Matt said playfully.

"You mean the Betty Thaxter who let her hair down tonight?" Robbyn replied, continuing the banter.

"She let her hair down and you let your pants down," Matt snapped back.

"Hell, so did you," Robbyn said.

"Good point."

The look on her face, even in the darkness, captivated him. He gave her a kiss deep enough to be felt throughout her body and limbs, leaving her limp and breathless with love and excitement.

When he finally pulled away from her so she wouldn't suffocate, she smiled, her eyes glistening.

"If I didn't have two boys, I'd be here all night," she said.

"And I'd be too tired to go to the tournament this weekend," he joked. "What a weekend this is going to be. The four of us. And baseball."

"Sounds like quite the double play to me!" she said.

He then hugged her so sweetly she began tearing up even more so. And then warm tears of joy cascaded down her face when he whispered delicately into her ear, his breath echoing into her eardrum.

"I swear no wife of mine will ever, ever have to worry about my fidelity," he whispered dramatically. "I stake my soul on it."

She pulled away and stared into his eyes.

"Wife? Is this a proposal?"

"Yes," he said sweetly. "I'd get down on bended knee, but I'm already on my knees in this back seat."

She gave him the sweetest kiss of his life, pulled her lips free, and used them to say emphatically: "The answer is yes, Mr. Meredith. A *resounding* yes! Besides, you need to make an honest woman out of me. A mother of two growing boys is too old to be screwing around in the back seat of a car on museum grounds."

"Where the hell is your sense of romance and adventure?" Matt asked, feigning shock.

"I have all the romance I need with you by my side," she said.

"Flattery will get you everywhere," he said before getting serious. "I can't wait to tell the boys about us. Should we do it together or do you want to do it?"

"We will tell them together," she said. "From now on, we're a couple and you are as much a part of their lives as I am. They're gonna love you as a dad."

"I already love them," he said, choking up.

"I know," she said. "But we have to go. I have to get home. And out of this back seat. My back is killing me. I don't want to have to go down the aisle in a wheelchair."

Matt laughed loud enough to wake up any sleeping squirrels on the museum grounds and then proceeded to drive Robbyn back to the Nut Bar to pick up her car, barely able to keep his eyes on the road because he couldn't stop looking at her. Men fall in love with their eyes, women with their ears. And as they chatted away on the ride home, Robbyn once again rejoiced in the splendor and beauty of the words with which Matt spoke to her and marveled as well over what a keen listener he was as well.

Chapter Twenty Two

Matt and Robbyn decided to tell Timmy and Billy about their wedding plans while traveling to Wilmington, Delaware for the baseball tournament in which the Sorbonne Township traveling team was participating that weekend.

They had just crossed the state line into Delaware from Pennsylvania early Friday evening when Robbyn whispered to Matt, who was concentrating on rush-hour traffic: "Should we tell them now?"

Matt smiled and replied: "Might as well since we've got a captive audience. Once we get them out of that back seat, we won't have their attention. Baseball and their buddies will be taking up their time."

Robbyn, who couldn't keep the news to herself any longer, quickly whirled around to face her sons.

"Matt and I have something to tell you guys," she said excitedly.

"Are we finally getting a puppy?" asked Billy with animation.

"Yeah, a real big dog," Matt couldn't help chiming in.

"Stop!" Robbyn said playfully.

"So, what's up, Mom?" asked Timmy, tearing himself away from his *Sports Illustrated* magazine.

"Well, Matt and I have some good news for you," Robbyn said, then pausing for effect. "We're in love!"

"Awesome!" Billy chirped.

"That's great, but I hope you guys don't break up right away," Timmy said.

Robbyn and Matt weren't expecting to hear one of the boys questioning the duration of their relationship. Robbyn's smile disappeared for a moment and Matt winced.

"We won't, buddy," Matt said emphatically. "Your mother and I are in this for the long haul. After all, we have to stick together so we're both around to watch your kids play in baseball tournaments."

"Absolutely," Robbyn seconded.

"Cool," Billy said.

Robbyn and Matt glanced at Timmy, awaiting his response. None was forthcoming until Robbyn prodded him.

"How do you feel about this, Timmy?" she asked reluctantly.

She knew only too well that Timmy, while seldom verbalizing it, still harbored a deep sense of loss over his father.

"I just hope Matt doesn't die like Daddy did," said Timmy, tearing up.

His sad tone triggered a few tears from Robbyn as well.

"Well, hopefully God will grant all of us a long life," Robbyn said softly. "It's just that God needed Daddy to be in heaven with Him."

"God has plenty of souls in heaven with Him," Timmy said. "Why did he need Dad with Him now? He could have waited until Daddy was real old to make him die."

Robbyn had heard Timmy ask that same haunting question several times. She always had been very comforting and reassuring to her son, since that same question had torn at the fabric of her serenity for years as well.

But now Matt was in her life, and she wanted him in her sons' lives as her husband and their stepfather.

"It's not our place to question God," Robbyn said with a voice that was almost sermon solemn. "He has a plan for all of us. I miss your father terribly. Always will. But he always told me that if something ever happened to him, he wanted me to remarry if I found a man whom I loved and who you boys would love. And I, we, couldn't have found anyone better than Matt. He's truly a blessing from God."

"It's like Matt is pinch hitting for Daddy," said Billy.

"Yeah, right, that's it," said Timmy excitedly.

"I can never replace your father," Matt said. "From what I hear from you and your mother, nobody will ever replace him. And I won't even try. All I can do is promise you that I always will love your mother. I'll always love you. And I always try my best to take care of you. And I promise you that we'll have a lot of fun."

Matt pulled over to the side of the road and stopped the car.

He turned fully toward the boys in the back seat and simply said, "I'm going to marry your mother."

Robbyn leaned over and kissed Matt gently.

"Do we call you Dad now?" Billy asked.

"No, Billy," Matt said gently. "I'm not your Dad. You have a Dad. And his name was Bob. Just call me Matt."

"So, when are you guys getting married?" Timmy asked.

"We haven't set a date," Robbyn said. "But probably around Christmas."

"Cool," said Billy, using his favorite word.

"We're thinking of either buying a new house or moving into Matt's house after we're married," Robbyn explained.

"I like Matt's house," Timmy said. "Especially the pool."

The remainder of the trip to Wilmington was a joy ride bursting with family values. The foursome bantered and joked, but also chatted with delight about the future possibilities of being a family.

The only blemish on this happy landscape was that Matt still harbored guilt feelings over being torn between Tiffany and Robbyn. And he certainly felt guilty about what had led to Tiffany fracturing her left ankle. He, of course, had told

Robbyn what had happened and Robbyn, while feeling sorry for Tiffany, did emphatically tell Matt that her fall down the stairs was not his fault. And Matt had told Robbyn that he had sent a get-well card and flowers to Tiffany's hotel suite. Matt had not written anything on the card except for the word "Sorry" and his name. That was it. He had not told Robbyn that Tiffany had responded to his card and flowers by leaving a blistering, angry message on his cellphone.

The message, with a malicious hiss, said: "You broke my heart. You broke my ankle. Now, I hope she breaks your heart. If you have one, you fucking bastard!"

Matt had played that message three times on his voicemail and countless times in his head. He felt great remorse over what had happened to Tiffany. Guilt gnawed at him up for mistreating Tiffany and leaving her a very unhappy woman. Guilt always had been a frequent companion of his. He blamed it on his Catholic upbringing. He had wished for years that he could be more laid-back, more devil-may-care and cavalier in his approach to life. The irony was that he often gave the impression that he exactly was that way. Indeed, he wished it could be that way. After all, it would have been infinitely more pleasurable and infinitely less stressful if he were selfish and superficial. Especially when he was juggling Robbyn and Tiffany in his life. Now Tiffany was out of his life, Robbyn was in his life, and Matt was hoping that the drama was out of his life. Or at least the major drama. There always would be drama. Like how with separate rooms, one for him and one for Robbyn and the boys, he would manage to make love to Robbyn this weekend.

As they continued their drive, thoughts of Tiffany ebbed in the background as the lovely woman beside him filled his senses in a way no other woman ever had. He couldn't pinpoint why; he could just feel it and savor it. And he found a remarkable contentment in having acquired a ready-made family. He had been single for too long. He was thrilled by his newly minted status as a family man.

As Matt, Robbyn and the boys pulled up to their motel in Wilmington, he essentially felt at peace with his life. He realized that a life with Robbyn and the boys would make him the happiest.

"See you at the team dinner," Matt said to Robbyn after they hauled their luggage to their rooms. "I need to meet with the other coaches to discuss lineups and our pitching rotation. Of course, I'm sure Timmy will be our pitcher in the opening game tomorrow morning."

"He'd better be," teased Robbyn, "especially if the coach still wants to sleep with his mother."

"You're wicked," Matt said, smiling.

They smiled the radiant, intimate smile of lovers at each other. It was a tender moment, one they both hoped to reprise time and time again for an eternity or two.

The Sorbonne Township tournament team's opening game that Saturday morning was a heartbreaker. They lost 5-4 as Timmy wasn't his usual dominant self. He was pressing, which fouled up his pitching mechanics and gave him control problems. He walked seven guys and gave up two home runs. Timmy also wasn't his usual force at the plate.

He managed one measly infield single in four at-bats, striking out three times. Timmy was glum and angry after the game, and no pep talk from Matt could cheer him up.

"Hey, even the great ballplayers have off days," Matt said, tousling Timmy's damp hair after the game. "Forget about it, slugger. We'll win the second game."

"I sucked," Timmy snapped. "I choked."

"You're the heart and soul of this team," Matt said.

"Well, then we're dead," Timmy said sadly.

"Knock off that kind of talk," Matt scolded him. "Take your lumps and forget about it. You can't dwell on bad games. Just learn from them. You were trying too hard. You were swinging for the fences on every pitch. Just try to meet the ball. And when you were pitching, you were aiming the ball, not throwing it. You tried to compensate by being too fine with your pitches."

"Whatever," Timmy said dejectedly, tuning out Matt's advice.

"Timmy will bounce back this afternoon," Robbyn said to Matt during lunch. "He's a kid. He was too anxious. He let the pressure get to him. But he'll get over it."

"I guess you're right," Matt said. "He was trying too hard. I guess we coaches built that Millwood team up too much in our pre-game talk. Timmy must have thought we were facing the New York Yankees."

Timmy got in trouble with Robbyn minutes after the team lunch when he punched Billy in the arm because his younger brother was teasing him about his lousy game.

Before the start of the second game, Matt simply told Timmy to "relax and forget about the first game."

At least Timmy didn't get shelled in the second game. Of course, he didn't pitch. He played shortstop instead.

And he didn't strike out three times. Just twice. And he did manage to hit a run-scoring double and a two-run single. But Sorbonne lost 6-5 to Collegeville, which scored the winning run in the last inning when a ball went between Timmy's legs at short. The error knocked Sorbonne out of the tournament and shattered Timmy's ego. He was inconsolable after the game. Robbyn, Matt and the other coaches, Billy and many of Timmy's teammates tried to console the weeping Timmy. However, one of Timmy's teammates was not so kind. Butch Miller, their overweight and overbearing first baseman who talked a better game than he played, was terribly jealous of Timmy's superior athletic skills. Butch made a crack to Timmy that "the only reason they let you pitch and play short is because your mom is going out with the coach."

Timmy's response was to kick Butch in the shin, who screamed in pain. Then Butch slugged Timmy in the face, giving him a bloody lip.

One of the other coaches, who heard what Butch had said, broke up the fight, saying: "Knock this off. We lost. And we all lost! We lost as a team, not just Timmy, who is an outstanding ballplayer."

When Matt and Robbyn learned the content of the remark that had precipitated the scuffle between Timmy and his tormentor, they felt genuinely guilty about their relationship having an impact on Timmy.

"Sorry my relationship with your mother put you in a tough spot," Matt said quietly to Timmy as he wiped blood from his face. "It's been a tough day, and you didn't need to hear that."

"I should have punched him back," Timmy said, blood still oozing from his lip. "But the day I had, I probably would have swung and missed."

Matt smiled and patted Timmy on the shoulder.

"I'm glad you still have your sense of humor," Matt said. "And you're still a heckuva ballplayer. We all have our bad days."

"That's right," said Robbyn, dabbing with a napkin at the blood on Timmy's chin. "You're good and don't forget it. How's your lip feel?"

"It hurts, Mom," Timmy said. "But could you guys give me a little space?" He lowered his voice to a whisper, adding: "The guys are watching. Don't make me look like a baby."

Robbyn and Matt both patted Timmy on the shoulder and walked away.

"After the day he had, he didn't need to have our relationship cause him additional grief," Robbyn said to Matt.

"I know," Matt said. "I know. But he's hardly the first kid to play ball who had his teammates accuse him of receiving preferential treatment from the coach. He'll get over it. He should have walked away instead of kicking him. But he's a kid. And kids do that."

He put his arm around her to console her. But she quickly squirmed free.

"Let's not reinforce our relationship for the whole team to see," she said.

"You're too sensitive," Matt said. "You should lighten up. Boys will be boys."

"I guess you're right," Robbyn said. "Let's get the boys and our stuff and get out of here. I can't wait to get home."

It was a long ride home to Braxton. Timmy, despite a cheery pep talk from Matt that warmed Robbyn's heart, remained grouchy and glum. He picked two verbal sparring sessions with Billy on the way home, both of them heated enough to prompt strong verbal rebukes from Robbyn. Matt, too, told Timmy to knock it off. As the freshly minted boyfriend of the mother, Matt felt he needed to get involved in discipline. Billy, meanwhile, couldn't resist making a few cracks about Timmy's poor play. A good athlete in his own right, Billy, nevertheless, always had been the younger brother of the star athlete -- not a comfortable spot for a young boy to occupy. So now that Timmy had experienced some splashes of athletic mortality, Billy took advantage of the opportunity until Robbyn and Matt chastised him.

Robbyn was in no mood for idle chitchat. She was very quiet on the ride home. She was heartbroken that Timmy felt such embarrassment. In her mind, she tried to keep youth athletics in perspective. But in her heart, she felt so badly for her son. Matt, meanwhile, knew that Timmy would get over the disappointment. In fact, he realized that the sobering experience would prove beneficial in the long run for Timmy, who had experienced quite a run of athletic success. Matt knew that being a star every day was unrealistic. And he also knew that it was important to learn how to handle defeat and cope with personal failure. He too was quiet on the trip home. He was down because the tourney had ended so abruptly and he was depressed by the tension in the car. And he wasn't too thrilled that his vacation was almost over and that he would be back in the office that Monday. But Matt wasn't the sort of person to remain depressed. He fundamentally was a positive, upbeat person. So, as they neared Sorbonne Township, he decided to cheer everyone up in a grand manner.

"Enough feeling sorry for ourselves," Matt said. "It was only a baseball tournament. It's over. Behind us. Let's go out for some steaks and French fries. We need to just laugh and hang out. What do you say, gang?"

"All right!" yelled Billy.

"Well, OK," said Timmy, flashing his first smile all day.

"I don't know, I'm sort of tired," Robbyn said.

But Matt was determined to have the day end on a positive note and wasn't about to allow Robbyn to stick a pin in the balloon of happiness he was trying to launch.

"Come on," Matt said pleasantly. "You get into the spirit of a good time, now can't you?"

"OK," Robbyn said, not wanting to disappoint her boys. "But it's your treat!"

"Of course," Matt said. "Big steaks all around!"

"Will we still have room for ice cream?" Billy asked.

"Steak without ice cream just doesn't cut it," Matt said, patting Robbyn on her leg. "The four of us have a lot to look forward to. The time to start enjoying life as a foursome is now."

Robbyn looked over at Matt and fell in love all over with him. She knew that there always would be bumpy rides in life, with or without Matt. But at least he had a hearty appetite for life. And she found that to be quite comforting. Robbyn realized she needed to lighten up and enjoy her new life with Matt more fully and to stop reverting back to being the repressed widow. Her new life was dawning as bright as a sunrise and she needed to let the sun set on her years of stunted emotions.

Chapter Twenty Three

Tiffany's days in Braxton were drawing to a close. The "Drug Town" location shoot in the city was almost over and she couldn't wait to get back to California. The final days of shooting had been a hassle as camera angles had to avoid the cast on her left ankle. The producer and director had discussed incorporating her fractured tibia into the script but had opted not to. They thought since the filming was almost wrapped up, it would be easier to shoot around her ankle. Tiffany's last days in Braxton had been depressing. She was a mess over Matt. She was so angry with him for dropping her in favor of Robbyn that she had grown to almost hate him. She just wanted to be done with his memory but felt she couldn't accomplish that until she was back home in Hollywood. Not normally a mean-spirited person, she found her mind wandering toward thoughts of revenge. She wanted to hurt him as much as he had hurt her. She thought the cruelest way to hurt him was to hurt his credibility as a journalist. As she sat in her trailer one afternoon during a break in shooting, she mulled how she could break him. And then it came to her. She had delivered the smoking gun to him in the Shelter scandal story by handing him Mayor Jimbo Cummings' head on a platter.

Her words had implicated the mayor. Now she pondered taking back her words. Could she un-ring the bell? That's what she would ask herself. Of course she could, she told herself. After all, she was an actress. She could tell them she had made up the whole story about Jimbo. She could tell them she had done so because Matt had coerced her into lying. She could add fuel to the fire by adding that she had been the victim of an abusive relationship with Matt, who had threatened to maim her face if she didn't help him frame the mayor. Such a plot filled Tiffany with a perverse pleasure. But she agonized over the potential fallout. Such an admission would generate harmful publicity, possibly damaging her budding career. Still, she rationalized, any publicity was good publicity. And such a story would create a tabloid and social media frenzy, stoking "Drug Town" and her career with the white heat of juicy gossip. *Do I dare?* That's what she kept asking herself. She bounced the question around her mind until it grew a mind of its own and spun out of her control.

To even her surprise, the tale spun right from her lips during a live interview the Monday after the Wilmington baseball tournament with WBRA, the local television station that was doing a piece on her as the "Drug Town" filming wrapped up in Braxton.

"So, what the most memorable part of your stay in Braxton?" the WBRA reporter asked innocently.

Tiffany, without warning, shifted into an acting performance worthy of an Academy Award. Her eyes welling up to the point where the moisture was beginning to smudge her mascara, she told the reporter that her stay in Braxton had been a hellish existence. Without mentioning Matt's name, she said that she had fallen into an abusive relationship with a star local newspaper columnist, who had forced her into lying about the mayor's participation in the Braxton Emergency Shelter capital campaign scandal. Her tears now trickling down her face, she told the reporter a tale of sleepless nights wracked with guilt feelings over the mayor's forced resignation. And then, with considerable dramatic flourish, she said she couldn't wait to leave Braxton for good because she literally feared for her life and was about to file a protection from abuse order against the *Braxton Bugle* columnist.

"Are you referring to Matt Meredith, the *Bugle* columnist?" the young reporter asked so excitedly that his words almost crashed into one another.

"Yes," Tiffany said in a hushed tone before breaking down crying.

When the startled reporter threw it back to the news anchor in the WBRA studio, the anchor excitedly remarked: "Well, tonight's top story came in the middle of our newscast. We hope to have a reaction from former mayor Jimbo Cummings and *Bugle* columnist Matt Meredith tonight at 11. Don't miss it!"

Matt still was in the office during WBRA's newscast that Monday evening. The *Bugle* staffer assigned to monitor the contents of the newscast immediately called Matt over to watch the interview with Tiffany once he realized what she was accusing Matt of. Matt watched the emotional Tiffany lying so convincingly on screen and his heart sank. It was her word vs. his word, and in the realm of public opinion, it was difficult for a man to fight the perception of abuse. Especially when the accuser was a celebrity who looked as good and acted as well as Tiffany. And Matt knew that it was only a matter of minutes before Jimbo would capitalize on the situation. He knew that the former mayor would recant his confession, claiming he only confessed because he knew it was his word vs. Tiffany's word. He knew the mayor would say that it was a battle he couldn't win, so he opted to take the high road and spare the Shelter and Millie Paxton further embarrassment. Matt proved to be quite a prophet. That's exactly what Jimbo said on the 11 p.m. news on WBRA. And he said so with a weeping Millie Paxton by his side.

"I feel vindicated by Miss Tiffany Underhill's admission," Jimbo said, pouring it on thick enough to get an acting job in a B movie. "She is a brave woman to do so. I wish her God speed." He paused for a moment, smiled broadly and said: "Of course, I wish she had come forward while I was still mayor. Now I have to discuss with legal counsel whether I can rescind my resignation and get my old job back. Since our acting mayor is a friend of mine, I'm sure he won't mind returning to his previous position as City Council president."

Jimbo was smart enough not to mention Matt's name during his interview.

WBRA aired Matt's denial right after the mayor's appearance. Matt simply said that he stood by all his stories and columns concerning the Shelter scandal. He said Tiffany Underhill indeed had told his managing editor, Ned March, and himself that Jimbo Cummings had admitted to her that he had lifted $250,000 from the Shelter funds. And Matt pointed out that the mayor had ultimately confessed.

Matt said it was unfortunate that Tiffany was recanting her story and that the mayor was capitalizing on her revision. Matt said he believed Tiffany's original assertion to be true, but he would not speculate on why she would have changed her story. He emphatically denied abusing her.

When the WBRA reporter pressed Matt on his broken relationship with Tiffany, Matt simply said, "No comment."

Shelter officials declined to comment on the story.

After consulting with Ned March, Matt decided to kill his scheduled Tuesday column and wrote a fresh one on Tiffany's change of heart. In the column, which the *Bugle* ran on Page One, he simply affirmed his belief in Tiffany's original assertions about Jimbo Cummings. He made no value judgments on her change of heart in his column. He also pointed out that although the Shelter scandal was essentially a one-source story, all the Shelter's internal controls seemed in place and the only logical conclusion was that the mayor had taken advantage of his girlfriend's access to the capital campaign funds. Matt knew that this sounded a little flimsy, but he and Ned March felt they needed to hang their body of work on more evidence than Tiffany's suddenly tainted word. And they felt that the mayor's resignation had proven them to be correct.

The reaction the next day was startling. Many of those who had seen Tiffany's acting performance on WBRA believed her story. They flooded the *Bugle* with emails and phone calls, demanding that Matt be fired. City Hall also received a number of calls, demanding that Jimbo Cummings be reinstated as mayor now that he had been exonerated. However, many of the people who had not seen Tiffany's interview on WBRA but had read Matt's column sided with him in their emails, texts and phone calls to the paper. Evidently, Tiffany had done a great acting job in selling her change of heart. But apparently you had to see her performance to buy her story. And if you did, her on-air performance was likely to sway your opinion more effectively than Matt's column.

"This is disparity in reaction is amazing," Ned March said to Matt that Tuesday afternoon in the *Bugle* office. "She can't be that good of an actress."

"She normally isn't," Matt said. "But she had superior motivation in delivering the performance of her lifetime: She hates my guts. Which is why she said I abused her."

"Perhaps you shouldn't have broken up with her until she left town," Ned joked.

"I know you're joking, but perhaps you're right," Matt said glumly. "She sure did a number on my and the paper's reputation. And it pisses me off that Jimbo is going to be the prime beneficiary in all of this."

"No way in hell he gets his job back," Ned predicted. "Once the emotion and drama of Tiffany's story ebbs, any clamor to restore him to office will subside."

"I don't know," Matt said. "People around here know he's a louse. But he's been a lovable louse. They tolerate his mistakes because he's our town's amusing caricature of an old-style politician."

Matt went to Robbyn's to have dinner with her and the boys since rain had washed out the baseball traveling team's scheduled practice. Dinner was spent watching portions of several Hollywood tabloid shows that had extensive coverage of Tiffany's WBRA interview. They treated the story sensationally, naturally, but also were quite supportive of her.

"I'm sure this will elicit more texts, emails and phone calls to the editor," Matt said as he poked at his meat loaf. "And I'm being savaged on Twitter and Facebook."

"Don't let it get you down," Robbyn said. "People with any intelligence will realize she's lying."

"You're giving people too much credit for having intelligence," Matt said, smiling weakly. "Any chance Bob Thaxter will hire me at the ad agency?"

"I couldn't work with you," Robbyn teased, smiling. "You're too egotistical. Of course, you always could be my secretary."

"I'm not good at making coffee," Matt said. "Where did the boys get to?"

"They were bored watching these shows, so they went up to Timmy's room to play video games," Robbyn replied.

Matt stood up, walked over to Robbyn and put an arm around her shoulders.

"This is a tough time for me," he said. "But it's nice to have someone like you to share it with."

"Thanks," she said. "I guess misery loves company."

"I guess," he said, smiling before kissing her forehead tenderly.

"You'll get through this," Robbyn said. "But it's a shame your reputation is taking a hit, professionally and personally."

"I guess it goes with the territory," Matt said. "And I thought my biggest anxiety this summer would be coaching Little League baseball and dealing with all the parents."

"Little did you know you'd wind up stuck with one of the parents," Robbyn teased.

"I took one look at you and knew I would," he said, laughing softly.

"Took you awhile to get it straight, now didn't it?" she asked before rising from her chair to kiss him.

"Hey, nobody said I was smart," he said. "Just ask some of my readers. Still, I hate having my integrity questioned. I've worked hard over the years to build it and establish my credibility as a journalist. And now to have her accuse me of being abusive, of threatening her with physical harm unless she lied to help me frame the mayor, well. And to have people believe her just because she's attractive and an actress, that's tough to live with."

"Some people are superficial, gullible and star-struck," Robbyn said. "You know that. But not all people will believe her just because she's a celebrity."

Meanwhile, Tiffany was experiencing some regrets about recanting her story. Several reporters from national magazines and trade papers grilled her on her credibility and gullibility. Studio executives had a mixed reaction -- they loved all the publicity. But some felt the added PR would be just a temporary positive bump, and ultimately her change of story would have a negative impact on public perception of her integrity. Already privately questioning her integrity was "Drug Town" producer Marc Goldstein, who had received the $250,000 site fee from Jimbo Cummings and wondered where that money had come from since it already had been established that it hadn't come from city funds. When Tiffany recanted her story about Jimbo and the Shelter, Goldstein was stunned. He equally was stunned why nobody in the media, with the exception of Matt Meredith in the *Braxton Bugle*, hadn't asked where the money did come from. Matt had broached that very question in one of his follow-up columns and one of the *Bugle* reporters had confronted Cummings with that very question. Jimbo's "no comment" had been his only response. Marc Goldstein didn't want to cause any waves while shooting was wrapping up and before the film was released, but he was wary of ever using Tiffany in a future film. Yet he didn't convey that to her just in case her career took off. After all, Goldstein may have thought Tiffany to be unstable, but so were plenty of marquee Hollywood actresses. And if she was golden at the box office, she was golden with Marc Goldstein.

What really was giving Tiffany second thoughts about changing her story was the barrage of phone messages from Jimbo Cummings, thanking her profusely for coming to her senses and inviting her to dinner to celebrate. She thought either he was the dumbest man she had ever met or the most brazen. Or a blatant combination of both. He had to be in denial, she thought, about his culpability in the Shelter scandal. Or otherwise he was completely amoral. So, she was tempted to recant her story. But she knew that she couldn't, that she would look like a complete fool if she did so. TV, tabloids and social media would eat her up and spit her out. Her credibility would be toast. And burnt toast never is on the menu on Hollywood casting calls. Her career would be toast as well. Still, she did feel a certain sense of gleeful satisfaction for putting Matt through so much turmoil. He had hurt her deeply, and she was enjoying some measure of revenge. But she wasn't enjoying a full measure of revenge -- or at least enjoying it fully. There still were morsels of her being that held great affection for Matt. Tiffany did harbor some bittersweet feelings about besmirching Matt's reputation in his hometown. She found her mixed feelings to be somewhat ironic, considering that Matt had spent considerable time having mixed feelings about her. She was just grateful that tomorrow would be the final day of location shooting. She couldn't wait to take her broken heart home.

The final day of a location shoot usually is a happy day for movie crews who are anxious to get home. But for this day in Braxton for Tiffany, it was a day of pure, unadulterated joy. Saddled with the emotional baggage from her breakup with Matt as well as all the angst accompanying the Shelter scandal, she couldn't wait to leave. Her bags already were packed. She would be flying home the next day and couldn't wait to put Braxton 3,000 miles behind her. Of course, she did have some fond feelings for Braxton because she hoped that "Drug Town" would be the vehicle that would drive her celebrity to the pantheon of hot young movie stars. Tiffany kept to herself most of the day, holed up in her location trailer between shooting scenes. She was in no mood for idle chatter with cast members or production personnel. She spent the time in her trailer packing up her personal belongings. Still, her mind kept focusing on the anguish of her stay in Braxton, distracting her from completely focusing on packing. So, she failed to notice that she had left a $10,000 pair of diamond earrings in one of the drawers built into the trailer. After saying her farewells to everyone on location, she returned to the Homewood Suites for what she had hoped would be a quiet evening. Indeed, she wasn't even planning to go out for dinner. She was content to munch on some fruit and granola bars and sip some white wine. She wanted to go to bed early because tomorrow couldn't come fast enough for her. Bored with her collection of smooth jazz CDs and what was available on television, she began taking inventory of her jewelry when she realized that her favorite pair of diamond earrings was missing. In a panic, she began rifling through all her packed bags, frantically searching for them. Growing ever more impatient, she started to vent verbally. And she spiced her monologue to herself with several choice phrases of vulgarity and profanity -- uncharacteristic for her. Her nerves definitely were ragged at this point. But then a sense of relief washed over her anxiety.

"The damn trailer," she announced to herself. "I must have left my earrings in the damn trailer."

Tiffany assumed the trailer still was on location. And she still had a key, having forgotten to turn it in to the studio staff in her scrambling haste to depart the location venue. Not wanting to bother anyone from the studio, figuring they all were out getting drunk or laid or a combination of both, she decided to drive to the trailer herself in the hope her diamonds were there. She gave

little thought to the fact that the trailer location at Front and Elm streets was dangerous at night. Actually, it was even dangerous during the day when the area wasn't teeming with movie people. Front and Elm was notorious for drug trafficking and drug-related shootings. Turf wars between dealers and gang members frequently erupted in gunplay and murder. Even robustly stepped-up local and state police intervention had failed to stem the tide of drive-by shootings and lawlessness in the "bad lands" of Braxton. Having spent months filming "Drug Town" gave Tiffany a strong base knowledge of how dangerous Braxton was in certain drug areas. But intense thoughts of safety and danger weren't high on her radar screen that night. She was too preoccupied with getting her diamonds from the trailer. Of course, she wasn't totally oblivious to the perils of downtown Braxton after dark. But she figured if she parked right next to the trailer, she would be fine. Annoyed that she had to leave the seclusion of her hotel suite, she hopped into her rental car and drove to Front and Elm streets. That was her destination, but it wasn't where she wound up. Her rental car, or more specifically, her rental's fuel line, had other ideas. The fuel line went bonkers, rendering her car inoperative at Buttonwood and Elm streets, two blocks of high anxiety from her trailer.

Fear can instantly bathe a person in a cold sweat. Which is exactly what happened to Tiffany. Agitated by panic, she frantically tried to restart her stalled car. But it wouldn't turn over.

"Damn it! Damn it!" she screamed in frustration at the steering wheel. The steering wheel, which had nothing to do with the car malfunctioning, ignored her desperate cries.

Fortunately for Tiffany, her windows were up because she had the air conditioner running. So her screams were not heard by several unsavory characters perched on a street corner a block away. They were drug dealers selling cocaine and heroin to users. With the air conditioning off because the car's engine wasn't running, perspiration began to bubble on the anguished face of Tiffany Underhill. Fearful that the dealers might mistake her parked car for someone waiting to make a drug buy, Tiffany grabbed her cell phone and punched the numbers of four studio associates. None answered, either having left town already or out celebrating their last night in town. Getting nauseous and having to go to the bathroom in the worst way, she considered her options. Realizing she had none, other than to try to flee on foot and that seemed to be ill-advised and impractical because of her broken ankle, she reached out for a lifeline she didn't want to grab. The only other person she had a phone number for in Braxton was none other than Matt Meredith. Of course, if Tiffany had been thinking clearly, she simply could have called 9-1-1. But in times of desperation, logical thought frequently suffers acute lapses.

Stoked by dread, she made the call to Matt and prayed that he would answer. Matt and Robbyn were in her living room drinking ice tea and talking excitedly about their future together when his ringing cell phone brought them back to the present.

"You're where?" Matt said, concern evident in his voice. "What are you doing there? ... OK, don't panic. Relax. ... Buttonwood and Elm? Keep your doors locked. I'll be there in five minutes."

"What's up?" Robbyn asked nervously.

"It's Tiffany," Matt said, hating to admit it was Tiffany to Robbyn but realizing, under the circumstances, he had to admit who it was and be on his way. "Her car broke down near her movie trailer on Elm Street. She can't get a hold of anybody else apparently."

"I hope she's not playing games with you," Robbyn said, her voice chilled in tone.

"I don't think so," Matt said. "She sounds scared as hell. Says there seems to be some drug dealers hanging out on a nearby street corner."

"Well, remember that she's quite the dramatic actress, now isn't she?" Robbyn said sarcastically.

"I gotta make sure she's OK," Matt said, headed toward the front door. "Please understand. You're mine. But I'll never forgive myself if she's telling the truth and something tragic happens."

"I know, I know," Robbyn said, scurrying to Matt and hugging him. "Just be careful. That's a bad neighborhood for anybody, even big tough guys like you."

Matt smiled, kissed her on the forehead, and sprinted to his car in the driveway. As Matt zipped onto the bypass headed into town, he prayed that Tiffany wasn't playing games. But he prayed even more fervently that she wasn't in real danger if she was telling the truth. As Matt drove to Buttonwood and Elm, Tiffany sat frozen in her locked car, paralyzed by fear. Her lips started quivering when she noticed two swarthy men approaching her car. They approached her cautiously until they drew near her car and noticed that she was a beautiful young woman in an obvious state of agitation. One of them walked right up to the driver's door, knocking on the glass and motioning for her to roll down the window. With her car conked out, Tiffany couldn't have lowered the electric window if she had wanted to. And there was absolutely no way she wanted to. So she just sat there, petrified, looking blankly straight ahead. For what seemed an eternity. Actually, only a minute or two later, the younger, thinner man knocked on the driver window again ... but this time he used the butt of his handgun. Tiffany instinctively flinched and shot a glance of pure terror at him. Excited by the fear he was causing her, the drug dealer then smashed the window, sending shards of glass all over a screaming Tiffany and the front seat. Seconds later, Matt drove up the street. He recognized Tiffany's rental car and saw the man with a drawn gun at her door. The dealer, apparently thinking Matt was an undercover cop, turned and started firing his weapon at Matt's approaching car. Matt immediately floored it and ran the man over with his car, breaking both his legs. Matt stopped the car and got out of it to rescue Tiffany, who, scared out of her wits, remain transfixed in her car. Matt could hear the cries of the dealer he had run down as he scampered past him toward Tiffany's car. As he did so, the other drug dealer opened fire on him, but missed. Matt dove to the street, right next to the handgun dropped by the man he had run over. Another shot ran out, hitting Matt in his upper right arm. In a flash of anger and survival, Matt grabbed the handgun with his left hand and returned fire, shooting the second dealer in his right leg. Matt, dripping blood, rose and ran to Tiffany's car.

"Come with me," he shouted. "Quick! We gotta get out of here."

Tiffany looked at him with a look of bewilderment. Her lips parted, but no sound came from them. Holding the gun in his right hand despite the gunshot, he used his good left arm to pull the transfixed Tiffany from the car. As they were headed toward his car, a police cruiser with a blaring siren and flashing lights and responding to the sound of gunfire, appeared on the scene. The two police officers saw two men on the ground and saw Matt brandishing a gun while having Tiffany in tow, and at first fingered Matt as the bad guy in their minds. They popped out of the cruiser, weapons pointed at man.

"Drop the gun, put your hands up and let the lady go!" one cop barked.

"I'm not the bad guy here, Bill," Matt said calmly. "It's Matt. Matt Meredith."

"What the hell happened here, Matt?" asked the cop. "Did you shoot these two guys?"

The cop walked up to Matt while the other police officer called for ambulances for the two drug dealers, who were screaming out in pain, and Matt, stoic about his bullet wound but pissed nonetheless.

While waiting for the ambulances to arrive, Matt was grilled by the two police officers, who knew him. As the two officers took notes for their report, they seemed satisfied that Matt was telling the truth. As the cops spoke to Matt, he sat on a curb, with a still very much shaken Tiffany hanging on in silence to his good arm. When the ambulances arrived, their sirens and flashing lights punctuating the night with noise and color, one of the cops and Tiffany helped Matt to his feet.

Trying to lighten the moment, one of the police officers said to Tiffany: "Your boyfriend here evidently is a real knight in shining armor. Got himself shot taking out a couple dealers in coming to your rescue."

Tiffany was in no mood for light moments. She started sobbing.

"I'm sorry I said something to upset you," the cop quickly added.

"He was sure was gallant," Tiffany said softly. "But he's no longer my boyfriend. Just a friend."

"It takes a real friend to take a bullet for you," the other police officer said.

"Especially when his friend has been cruel to him," Tiffany said.

As the two officers left Matt and Tiffany's side to oversee the drug dealers being loaded into ambulances, Tiffany looked up into Matt's eyes, then kissed him delicately on the forehead.

"You have no idea how grateful I am to you," she said, crying. "You saved my life. I was so scared. I didn't want to call you. I didn't deserve your help because I recanted my story. I've screwed your reputation around here. But I swear

I'll tell everyone I lied, even if it makes me look like a fool. It was ... it was just that I was so angry over losing you. But you were right. Robbyn is a better fit for you. I don't deserve somebody like you anyway."

Matt patted her gently on her right shoulder with his left hand, smiled and kissed her on the cheek.

"That's not true," he said. "You are a special person, and I did jerk your heart and emotions around. I didn't mean to ... I was just caught between two women who I loved. It is possible to love two people simultaneously. But you can't. You have to make a choice. I've made mine. It's Robbyn. We're just a better fit lifestyle-wise. But that doesn't mean that I don't love you, have feelings for you."

"I know," she said. "I know."

"You are worth taking a bullet for," Matt said, smiling.

One of the ambulance personnel came up to Matt and put a tourniquet on his upper right arm, which had just suffered a flesh wound, the slug merely taking a small chunk from his triceps muscle.

"I just hope that the bullet didn't take away my fastball," Matt added.

Before Matt climbed into an ambulance, he asked Tiffany if she wanted him to call her a cab on his cell phone since the police wanted to keep his car and her disabled car at the investigation scene.

"Are you nuts?" she asked. "I'm going to the hospital. You went with me when I broke my tibia. Now I'll return the favor."

"Do you want me to skip out on you if you fall asleep in the waiting room?" Matt said.

"I'm sure you won't," Tiffany said, smiling wanly as she joined Matt in the back of the ambulance. "Not if you want me to come to your office and give you an exclusive on what a liar I am and that the ex-mayor did too take the Shelter funds."

"You may have to type the column for me," Matt said. "I have only one arm."

"I may need work as a secretary since my film career likely is kaput," she said, laughing.

"Are you insane?" Matt said. "Do you realize the kind of publicity you're going to get out of this? 'Drug Town' film star almost gets whacked in Drug Town and is saved by a crusading columnist and ex-boyfriend? The tabloids, social media and ticket sales will go crazy!"

Tiffany fondly tousled Matt's hair and said: "Journalistic cynics like you are going to think we contrived this whole thing. But you couldn't make something like this up, could you?"

"Actually, I could," Matt said, "but I wouldn't if it meant getting shot."

A look of anguish engulfed Tiffany's face again.

"I'm so terribly sorry about that," she said.

"And I'm sorry about your tibia," he replied.

In a slightly awkward moment for Matt, he felt he had to call Robbyn on his cell before the ambulance arrived at the hospital.

With Tiffany sitting next to him, he gave Robbyn a calm, quick synopsis of what had transpired.

"Oh my God," Robbyn kept screaming. "I'm coming down there to see you."

"That's OK," he said, trying to act macho but also shooting a guilty glance at Tiffany.

Actually, Matt really did want to see Robbyn, wanted to hold her and tell her how glad he was to still be alive. Although he didn't mention it to Tiffany or the police, the whole incident had been scary for him as well. But while it was transpiring, he had just reacted. Now that it was over, he realized how fortunate he was not to have been seriously wounded or killed.

His bond with Robbyn ultimately proved stronger than any feelings of awkwardness he may have harbored concerning Tiffany's presence at the hospital.

"If you can get somebody to watch the kids, I'd love to see you," Matt said, amping the volume to prove to himself as well to Tiffany that his heart finally belonged to Robbyn.

"I'll call Cindy Loeper," Robbyn said. "I'll be right there."

"Drive carefully, honey," Matt said. "Yes, I love you, too."

After Matt hung up, he looked at Tiffany and smiled sheepishly.

"Sorry you had to hear that," he said.

"I understand, I finally get it," she said. "You guys belong together. Don't worry about me. I'm a survivor. Of course, I wouldn't have survived tonight if it hadn't been for you."

"You know, when it came to the two of us, neither one of us ever thought rationally," Matt said. "For instance, maybe it was destiny that drew us together tonight. But I don't know what you or I was thinking. Why the hell didn't either one of us think to call 9-1-1 and have the police dispatched immediately to the scene?"

"I never even thought of that," said Tiffany. "What a fool. But I kind of like that you were the one to save me. Of course, I wish you hadn't been shot."

"I should have thought of calling 9-1-1, being a newspaper reporter and all," Matt said. "Maybe subliminally I wanted to be the guy to rescue you. I don't know."

Tiffany leaned over and kissed him on the lips.

"That's the last time I'll ever do that," she said. "But I needed to do that."

Tears welled in her eyes and the moisture must have been contagious because it migrated to Matt's eyes as well.

"I needed you to do that," he said fondly.

When they got to the hospital emergency room, Tiffany dutifully sat in the waiting room while a doctor attended to Matt. She fitfully looked through dated magazines, wondering when Robbyn was going to show up. Despite what she said to Matt, she did feel awkward about Robbyn. Tiffany actually liked her, but the fact that they both had been rivals for Matt's affections was something that always would be there between them.

Tiffany, however, felt terrible for feeling awkward about Robbyn a few minutes later when Robbyn rushed into the ER waiting room and immediately jogged up to her.

"You poor dear," Robbyn said, sitting down next to Tiffany. "What an ordeal. You must have been so frightened. Thank God you weren't hurt."

Needless to say, Tiffany was rather surprised but touched beyond words by the genuine, heartfelt concern Robbyn displayed for her.

"You truly are a doll," Tiffany said. "Thanks for your concern. And I want you to know that I'm sick about Matt getting shot. It was my fault. I should have called 9-1-1. I didn't think. I couldn't think of who to call and Matt's number popped into my head. I was in a panic. And I felt so lousy about recanting my story about Jimbo and causing Matt so much grief."

"Well, you compromised his credibility," Robbyn said. "That was awful of you."

"I know, I know," Tiffany said. "But I'm going to tell everybody that I lied. I already told Matt I'm giving him the exclusive story and then I'll talk to the local TV and radio stations and to all the tabloids. Matt will get his good name back."

"Glad to hear that," Robbyn said.

"And I'm glad Matt has you," Tiffany said, "and I mean that sincerely. You're special. He's special. Please be good to him."

"Well, you take care," Robbyn said. "I want to go back to see him."

"I'll be here when you guys get back," Tiffany said. "I want to make sure he's all right. That's the least I can do since he saved my life."

As Robbyn walked to the ER desk, she had the fleeting thought that perhaps the harrowing experience that Tiffany and Matt had just shared would somehow bring them back together. After all, there was a certain kinship and bonding inherent in going through something like that together, especially when they had been in a relationship. But that thought quickly vaporized in her mind and heart when she saw the look of pure, unadulterated joy radiating on Matt's face when she walked into the small room where a physician assistant was bandaging his arm.

"Hey, gorgeous, I can't take out the trash for some time," he joked as she walked over and proceeded to give him a deep kiss and a hug.

"You guys should get a room," the physician assistant said with a laugh. "But don't squeeze his arm too tightly. It'll start bleeding profusely."

"Sorry," Robbyn said, smiling. "I'm just glad to see him alive and in one piece. How is it?"

"Well, I don't think he'll be pitching batting practice anytime soon," the physician assistant said. "But he'll be just fine. The bullet just clipped his arm. You know, if Matt didn't have such a muscular arm, it may have missed him completely."

"So much for lifting weights," Matt said.

The physician assistant excused herself to do some paperwork on Matt.

While Matt and Robbyn waited for him to be discharged from the ER, Robbyn and he embraced gently and kept exchanging kisses.

"You did a brave thing tonight," she said. "I'm very proud of you. You're a hero. My hero. But I would have killed you if you had been killed."

She laughed.

"That would have been redundant," he said, smiling.

"Seriously, this was so dangerous," she said. "Why didn't you just call 9-1-1 and send the cops? Was it because it was Tiffany?"

She had asked the question but wasn't sure she wanted to hear the answer.

"To be honest, for some stupid reason I didn't even think to call 9-1-1," he said. "Was it something Freudian because it was Tiffany? Perhaps so. But it wasn't because I wanted to reconcile with Tiffany. I'm way over that. Maybe it was simply because I care for her and she was in danger. I wanted to help. I would have done it for anybody I cared about it. Hell, I would have done it for anybody. Of course, for just anybody, I probably would have thought of calling 9-1-1."

"I'm sure you would have," Robbyn said. "But I want you to know that I'm also thrilled that Tiffany is fine."

"Just so you know," Matt said, "nothing that happened tonight has changed anything. I care about Tiffany. But you are my lover and I don't ever, ever want you to have to wonder about my fidelity and commitment. You're mine forever."

His kiss resounded to the depths of her soul. While he was so doing, a nurse walked in to give him some pain medicine.

"You know, kisses like that probably work better than these pain killers," she said after clearing her throat. "My husband hasn't kissed me like that since our honeymoon. He's too busy watching NASCAR races."

Robbyn drove Tiffany and Matt home, dropping Tiffany off first, of course. Matt was pleasantly surprised how casual and comfortable the conversation in the car was.

Tiffany thanked Matt several times for saving her and told him she would be in his office at 10 the next morning to recant her story for his column. She promised to delay her departure for home so she could clear his name by appearing on local TV and radio and with the national media and tabloids. Matt and Robbyn were both particularly touched by her apology to Robbyn.

"I know I hurt Matt by changing my story about Jimbo, and I know I hurt you as well," Tiffany said to Robbyn. "I'm sorry. I don't deal with rejection well. I guess like all actresses, I'm insecure when you come right down to it. I was pissed at Matt. Now I feel like the biggest heel. He saved my life. But more than that, he's a good guy and he didn't deserve what I did to him. And you're so sweet. I can see why he fell in love with you."

Robbyn was grateful that Tiffany said that while she was approaching a stop sign. Because the comment stunned Robbyn enough to definitely distract her driving. At the stop sign, she turned around to look at Tiffany in the back seat.

"You have no idea how great it was to hear you say that," Robbyn said. "Thank you."

"Thank you," Tiffany said. "I'm glad we've finally put this love triangle behind us. I just need to chill out now that the movie shoot has wrapped and relax at home."

Tiffany kissed both Robbyn and Matt lightly on the cheek when they dropped her off at her hotel.

"You, buster, are a hero but you're a dumb hero," Robbyn politely scolded Matt as they drove to his house. "You could have gotten killed tonight. That's why they pay policemen to take the risks."

"I know," Matt said. "I'm sorry. And thanks for coming for me."

"What do you think, I'm dumb, too?" laughed Robbyn. "Leave you alone at night with Tiffany after you rescued her? I hesitate to think to what degree she would have been willing to express her gratitude to you if I hadn't been there."

"Yeah, right," Matt said. "Nothing like hopping in the sack with a bullet hole in your arm. Of course, if you're in the mood tonight, I'm sure we could work something out."

Robbyn said, kindly: "I don't think so. I think you need to get some rest. You sure you don't want to come to my place and stay in the guest bedroom?"

"No, I don't want the boys to think I'm hurt that badly," he said. "Just tell them tomorrow that I got winged in the arm. And tell Timmy that I won't be pitching batting practice the rest of the year. But otherwise I'm fine. My only issue is how to shower without getting my wrapped arm wet."

"Do you want me to help you shower tonight?" Robbyn asked, giggling.

"That would be nice ... and necessary," he replied.

"Yeah, you are kind of dirty and sweaty," Robbyn said. "I always thought it would be romantic to shower together. But I never thought our first shower together would happen with you nursing a gunshot wound."

"The life of a macho newspaper columnist," Matt said.

Actually, their shower together hardly was romantic. Robbyn joined him the shower stall and was gingerly helping him soap up, being careful to keep his right arm away from the cascading faucet water. But when Robbyn was helping him towel off after the shower, they both got aroused by her wiping his body. Matt kissed her passionately on the lips and one thing led to another. Matt and Robbyn wound up in bed, with Robbyn on top so that Matt's injured arm could rest on the bed. After all, one-armed people do manage to have sex. And Robbyn and Matt had a sexual encounter as explosive as a bullet exiting a chamber. It was as if Matt's brush with danger had subliminally released previously locked-up passions in both -- he subconsciously because he still was alive and she because he WAS alive. They started off deliberately, laying the kindling for what would prove to be a roaring inferno. They then segued to a deep, thrusting sexual rhythm that was almost barbaric in its symphonic intensity. If their moans of pleasure hadn't been so percussive, both could have sworn they literally heard cymbals crashing. After they had spent themselves, glistening in sweat as they relaxed in bed, Robbyn playfully mentioned it was time for another shower.

"Yeah, right," laughed Matt. "You'll start soaping me up and guess what? We'll be right back here fooling around?"

"You're right," she giggled. "Let me just towel you off and I'm out of here. You need your rest."

"Yeah, it's not every night that I get shot," he said. "Of course, if I got shot every night, my body would look like Swiss cheese."

Robbyn's face took on a serious demeanor as she said: "I know you're making light of all this. But tonight was a very scary situation. You could have been seriously injured or killed. Please, please, Matt, take care of yourself. I've already lost one great man. I don't want to lose another."

She began crying as the anxiety and tumult of the day caught up with her. Matt hugged her with his good left arm and kissed her tenderly on the lips.

"I promise you I will live to be 101," he said, smiling. "But you have to promise me you will live at least one day longer than me. No way do I want to lose you."

She kissed him back, then said: "You know, I'll probably look like hell when you're 101. You sure you will still want me?"

"What choice will I have?" he joked. "I'll be 101."

The next morning Matt awoke bright and early. His arm didn't hurt him all that much. He was fortunate it had only been a flesh wound. The first thing he did was check his freshly arrived edition of the *Braxton Bugle*. He was curious to see if there was a news item about the shooting incident he and Tiffany had been involved in. Apparently the *Bugle* police reporter didn't yet know who the principals were when he filed a short story on deadline about the shooting incident. Besides, shooting incidents in downtown Braxton were so common that they now had the news value of "Dog Bites Man." Of course, Matt knew that the story would become much bigger in the local and national media once they discovered that Tiffany Underhill, the star of "Drug Town" and noted whistleblower on civic corruption, was a leading character in a real-life shooting incident in the real-life "Drug Town."

But even Matt didn't realize how immense the firestorm of publicity surrounding the event would become. Local radio stations began airing reports that morning, and soon area television stations began calling Tiffany, her studio, Matt and the *Bugle*.

Matt and Tiffany shunned the media because, true to her word, Tiffany reserved her comments for a *Bugle* exclusive.

The *Bugle* ran a large Page One story on the incident, with a major sidebar column by Matt in which Tiffany admitted she had lied when she retracted her allegations about Jimbo Cumming's culpability in the Shelter scandal. Matt and Tiffany were quite candid in the column that Tiffany's motivation was jealousy and revenge toward Matt because of their failed relationship. It turned out to be the most personally heart-wrenching column Matt had ever written. As he agonized over every word, every phrase, every sentence and every paragraph, he was motivated by two things: Don't embarrass Robbyn and restore his credibility. It was a very delicate balancing act.

But he was a writer and pulled it off adroitly. Robbyn thought he did a grand job and was thrilled that his credibility had been restored. And Robbyn thought Tiffany came across as a sympathetic and courageous figure. Matt was utterly relieved that Tiffany echoed Robbyn's sentiments. And Matt was genuinely pleased that his editors and the management at the *Bugle* were effusive in their praise of the column.

The story then exploded. Tiffany and Matt were everywhere together — on the local television station, WBRA; on Philadelphia television stations; on network newscasts and morning shows; on various syndicated

entertainment shows; and even on the cover of *People* magazine. Tiffany and Matt had become America's couple even though they no longer were a couple. Of course, Robbyn was hardly neglected by the media. They jumped all over her angle of the story, often casting her in the role as the "other" woman. Needless to say, the media onslaught was awkward for Matt, Robbyn and Tiffany. However, at least for Tiffany, all the publicity was a tremendous boost to her career. In fact, the studio accelerated the post-production of "Drug Town" to catch the tidal wave of media exposure.

Tiffany and Robbyn remained cordial throughout the period of the media blitz, but the stress and strain of the situation did generate some understandable friction.

Robbyn, although she was careful not to express it too forcefully to Matt, became resentful of Tiffany. She felt that Tiffany was exploiting the situation to reap maximum benefit. Even though Tiffany's studio and agent were the catalyst for much of the media opportunities, Robbyn felt that Tiffany was too amenable in grabbing every moment of spotlight exposure. Robbyn also felt that Matt should have declined some photo ops and interviews as well but was afraid to disappoint Tiffany. This, in turn, created tension between Matt and Robbyn. Their relationship was now rock solid and seemed secure enough to survive any number of fissures that life seems to throw at couples in love. Nevertheless, the whole post-shooting publicity fallout was not the ideal environment for a couple balancing careers, wedding plans, two children and a new life. And Robbyn was somewhat resentful of the time Matt wound up out of town with Tiffany during the height of the media blitz. Matt's attempt to appease her by telling her it was good publicity for his career and the *Braxton Bugle* proved unsuccessful.

"It's promoting her career, her movie," Robbyn snapped at Matt. "Not yours. When all of this is said and done, you'll still be a columnist for the *Bugle*. Are you getting a pay raise from all of this?"

"Well, first of all, I love working for the *Bugle*," Matt said. "So that's not a negative. Am I getting a raise? Not specifically for this. I'm already the highest-paid writer in the history of the *Bugle*."

She sensed that she had bruised Matt's ego, so she just shut up.

Robbyn's resentment toward the Tiffany-Matt road show abated somewhat when late in the summer Matt received a five-figure advance from a New York publishing house to write a book about his entire experience with Tiffany, "Drug Town," the Shelter scandal, the toppling of the mayor, and the inner-city shootout with drug dealers.

"Just so there's no shot of you two embracing on the cover," Robbyn said.

"It's not a romance novel," Matt said.

"Well, it's not a novel," Robbyn said, "but it had better be romantic, as far as you and I are concerned. But spare the sexual details when it comes to us."

"So, it's OK to write about my sexual escapades with Tiffany?" Matt asked with a massive grin and just the perfect touch of amusement.

Robbyn's response was to playfully toss a glass of water in Matt's face. She had grown a tad more comfortable with the Tiffany-Matt celebrity couple thing after the three of them had attended a publicity event in Manhattan. It had become quite clear to Matt and Robbyn that the newly adorned trappings of fame had rendered Tiffany even more self-focused.

Indeed, Tiffany, despite being thrown into a media celebrity cauldron with Matt, had lost most of her feelings for Matt. Granted, she felt extremely grateful to him for his heroic efforts in the shooting incident. And she certainly was savvy enough to realize that he had been a prime catalyst in providing her with tremendous career leverage. But her romantic interest in him had waned. Indeed, as the media interest in them waned, Matt was spending most of his time back home while Tiffany made the Hollywood party scene. The media began focusing on the men she was dating in

Tinseltown. In fact, *People* magazine ran a photo of Tiffany arm-in-arm with a handsome male model.

After seeing that photo, Robbyn had remarked with great pleasure to Matt: “Well, stud, I guess you’re stuck with me now.”

Chapter Twenty Four

As autumn rolled into Miller County, life was settling into a more structured pattern for Matt and Robbyn. The traveling tournament baseball season had concluded with yet another tourney title for the Sorbonne Township team, with Timmy once again the MVP for his exploits on the mound, at the plate and at shortstop. Billy, too, had concluded his baseball season in fine style and eagerly was anticipating playing with Timmy the following summer with the Sorbonne Township Cubs. Matt, whose batting practice duties had been ended by the bullet wound in his pitching arm, already had agreed to coach the Cubs again. He knew his time would be limited somewhat by the book he now was authoring but hoped to have much of it written by the ensuing season. Matt and Robbyn immersed themselves in the regular routine of their jobs but found much preoccupation with wedding plans and house hunting. They planned to be married on the day after Christmas, a church wedding followed by a modest reception that was getting bigger than both of them had anticipated. But both knew so many people in the community that it had proven fruitless to keep the reception small. Robbyn was taking care of most of the wedding plans, which pleased her. But what pleased her even more was Matt's willingness to join her in the search for a new home. Matt avidly read the classified real estate ads in the *Braxton Bugle* as well as meeting routinely with Robbyn and their Realtor. Matt and Robbyn both thought it imperative to establish their lives as a foursome in a new home, to better solidify -- especially in Timmy and Billy's minds – their new life together. Matt and Robbyn both wanted to stay in Sorbonne Township for the sake of the boys' schooling and baseball. They wanted a five-bedroom home with a big yard and pool. It would easily be a half-a-million-dollar home or more in a modest retail market, but with the sale of their respective homes, their combined incomes and the money Matt had wisely invested over the years, it was a nut they felt they could comfortably cover.

Matt and Robbyn were convinced they had made the right choice in a mate. Both were extremely happy, taking delight in each other's company. They both enjoyed many of the same interests and both took pleasure in the little joys of life without allowing the occasional travails to alter their naturally optimistic mental landscapes. And spiking their happiness even more was the wonderful relationship they shared with Timmy and Billy. The boys had seamlessly accepted Matt into their lives. They spent a lot of time with Matt at his home. And when they weren't there, Matt was at their house. They loved to watch sports together, go to movies together, and play together ... whether it was playing catch, playing two-hand touch football, wrestling in the living room, golfing, bowling or hanging out at the mall. The addition of such a loving and powerful male role model in her boys' lives made Robbyn love Matt even more deeply. And now that the media blitz concerning the shooting had subsided, Robbyn was thrilled that life had become relatively more normal for herself and her family. Which is why she wasn't looking forward to the grand premiere showing of "Drug Town" set for Braxton the Friday before Thanksgiving. She knew all the pomp and circumstance would throw her and Matt's lives into a media fishbowl again ... and would bring the return of Tiffany to town.

While she no longer viewed Tiffany as a threat to her life with Matt, she still would have preferred if Tiffany would remain in Hollywood and only appear in their lives on the movie and TV screen. And, if truth be told, Robbyn was hoping that "Drug Town" would have a short shelf life in movie theaters. It was not a feeling based in malice. It simply was a wish to bring closure to the movie and allow her and Matt to focus on their wedding.

Of course, Robbyn's preoccupation with house hunting and the upcoming wedding invariably triggered flashbacks to when she and Bob Baxter were making their wedding plans and hunting for a home. Sometimes, in the quiet of night in the moments before falling to sleep, she would reflect on her life with Bob -- and, if truth be told -- still suffer a pang or two of guilt over whether she was being unfaithful to his memory. But such thoughts were fleeting, mostly because she knew that Bob was a totally unselfish man and would want her to start a new life for her sake as well as their children's. And making it even more acceptable was that she had no doubts at all that Bob Baxter would have liked Matt Meredith and would have endorsed him as his boys' second father. Indeed, Matt had made the transition to a new relationship with Robbyn easier for her with his touching sensitivity. Matt wouldn't mention Bob's name very often to Robbyn or the boys. But when he did so, it was always in the proper context and it always sounded genuine and appropriate. Matt did not feel awkward at all about succeeding Bob Baxter in the role of husband and father because Robbyn and the boys made him feel comfortable. They rarely were comparative when it came to Matt and Bob, so Matt never felt that he had to measure up to a ghost. Matt was perfectly content to be himself. And because Matt had never met Bob, it made the situation rather seamless for him without self-comparison.

Of course, Bob's name would come up on holidays and the like. For instance, on Halloween, Billy made the comment that his dad hated chocolate after Matt had jokingly commented that he was going to eat one of Billy's Snickers bars.

Matt immediately said the right thing, defusing what could have evolved into a sad, nostalgic moment for Billy.

"Man, your dad must have been more disciplined than me," Matt said lightly. "I'm not proud of my sweet tooth."

"That's OK," Billy said with a smile. "I've got a sweet tooth, too."

Robbyn confessed that she didn't have a sweet tooth, but she flashed plenty of sweet teeth in her warm smile as she watched Billy and Matt split a Snickers bar.

After the boys had gone to bed on Halloween night, Robbyn and Matt sat in her kitchen, drinking hot tea with lemon. Matt didn't drink hot tea on a regular basis until he met Robbyn. Now he loved sharing that with her.

"I feel fortunate to have met two wonderful men in my life in you and Bob," she suddenly blurted out.

Her comment, out of the blue, startled and touched Matt profoundly. He looked at her beautiful face lit up with the glow of love, and it left him breathless.

Matt, who had been sitting across the kitchen table from her, arose and walked around the table. He put an arm around her, leaned down and gave her a gentle, loving light kiss on her forehead.

"You have no idea how much I love you and how much I love the thought of being married to you," Matt said, caressing her brunette ponytail. "I'm sorry I gave you pause to doubt me early on, what with Tiffany and all."

"Don't be silly," Robbyn said. "At the time, I still was dealing with being a widow. And I almost misread you. I thought you were this sex-crazed stud around town. I didn't realize you were just a cuddly homebody."

"So, I'm not a stud?" Matt asked, laughing.

"Only with me," Robbyn said, kissing him. "That's the way I like it."

"I always did like to play one-on-one," Matt joked.

"So, you're saying our lovemaking reminds you of playground basketball?" Robbyn asked, feigning insult as she widened her eyes to mimic pronounced shock.

"Nah," responded Matt, mischief replacing tears in his eyes. "Playground basketball is shirts and skins. With us, it's all skins. Which is good. I like you with your shirt off."

"I love you with your shirt off," Robbyn cooed. "And I know you love my boobs! But as ample as they are, I know that Tiffany's are bigger."

Matt's response was so sudden and so reassuring that it in itself permanently sealed their relationship for eternity.

He spontaneously and quickly unbuttoned her blouse and tenderly cupped his hands gently on her breasts.

"I could haven't made you more perfect if I had sculpted you myself," he said passionately. "The first time I saw you during baseball practice you turned me on. Big time. And you haven't stopped turning me on ever since."

"I love you, I love you," she exclaimed in a voice two octaves higher than normal.

"I love you, too," he said, each syllable dipped in a creamy broth of romance and passion.

With the boys sound asleep, they quickly and mutually descended to Robbyn's finished basement and made the most romantic love a couple can make on a 15-year-old sofa with soda stains.

After a series of orgasms had rocketed her through an epic journey of cascading and unceasing pleasure, Robbyn simply draped herself atop of Matt on the sofa, spent with exhaustion and tingled with an inner satisfaction known only to lovers. Matt, exhausted himself but basking in the post-coital glow, gently inhaled the sweet smell of Robbyn's flesh, finding the mix of her perfume and perspiration to be utterly intoxicating.

After a period of blessed solitude in each other's arms, Matt softly whispered into Robbyn's ear: "I'm beginning to seriously doubt that you are human. You simply HAVE to be divine."

She gave him a kiss that was so pregnant with fervor and passion that it sent his spirit, not to mention his penis, soaring to new heights. Shocking even themselves, who both thought they had parked in the terminals of exhaustion for the evening, they made love again. And somehow found the reserve of physical energy to reach even greater heights of pleasure.

After delicious climaxes had left them both limp in body and soul, they giggled at what they had wrought together, rejoiced in the sheer heat of their love, and wound up convulsed by silly, joyous laughter.

"You're gonna kill me!" Matt said with a huge smile.

"Kill *you*?" she shot back. "I'm getting too old for this. Hell, you're gonna make me bowlegged. What will that look like on our wedding day?"

"It makes me look like a real stud who's getting plenty of action," Matt said, sandwiching the words in between chuckles.

"Pig!" she said, playfully flattening his nose with two fingers.

"Well, I'd say this trick was a real treat on Halloween," Matt said.

"I'll pardon your pun, dear sir," Robbyn responded, her smile suddenly turning somber before adding, "because you have made this the most memorable Halloween of my life. I want you to hold me and never, ever let go."

They held each other until 5 in the morning. They would have laid there together forever. But two things prompted them out of their reverie. One was a fear of getting discovered by the boys. Two was because Matt's back had become stiffer than his penis had been earlier.

"I need to get home and get some sleep, darling," Matt said as he kissed Robbyn goodbye. "You've tuckered me out."

"Ditto," she said fondly. "By the way, once again I could tell that you really do like my boobs."

"Like your boobs?" he asked, his smile growing gigantic. "I can't get enough of them!"

"Well, I like your chest, too," Robbyn said, running her fingers across his pecs.

"Tit for tat," Matt said wickedly.

"Time to go," Robbyn said. "We sound like a couple of love-starved teens."

"Well, we're definitely not teens and we're definitely not love starved," Matt said as he left for home.

As Matt drove home, he kept replaying the wonder of that special night in his mind, a night filled with so many spectacular sexual and romantic moments that its very memory was a huge meadow to wander through. He still marveled over how Robbyn could be so simultaneously wholesome and sexy.

The night had left Robbyn numb on every sensual level. As she stared at the ceiling while lying in bed, her eyes were shiny and vacant, like two rain-streaked windows in an abandoned building. But her heart, mind and soul hardly felt abandoned. She knew and finally admitted to herself that Matt Meredith made her feel like no other man, including Bob Baxter, had ever made her feel.

Chapter Twenty Five

By the time Halloween had arrived in Tiffany Underhill's life, she had managed to put romantic thoughts of Braxton and Matt in her tinted rear-view mirror. All the publicity from "Drug Town" and the ensuing shooting in the streets of "Drug Town" had done wonders for her career. Anxious to show her diversity as an actress, she already had signed on to star in a romantic comedy, hoping to showcase her range. And her personal life was busy as well. After failing to find true love with Matt, she had decided to just have fun and date anyone who pleased her particular fancy that evening. In a few short months she slept with several guys, the latest being a European playboy/businessman who loved to dabble in polo and cocaine. Tiffany hadn't as yet caught the polo bug from him, but she had developed a taste for an occasional line of coke. She justified her indulgence by saying it was infrequent and it was innocent, just enough to take the edge off the pressures of her exploding career. With the premiere of "Drug Town" strategically located in Braxton, she and the studio were making grand plans to maximize the hype. The studio was going to announce on premiere night that it was making a $100,000 donation to the Braxton Emergency Shelter. As a publicity stunt/photo op, the studio was going to have Tiffany and her leading man, Bronk Cassidy, serve dinner to Shelter residents prior to the movie screening at the recently renovated Fairgrounds Square Mall cinema complex. And on the afternoon of the screening, Tiffany was going to hold a press conference on the very spot where her rental car had broken down prior to the shooting incident involving her, Matt and the drug dealers.

"I know that press conference is going to embarrass Matt," Tiffany had remarked to the studio PR chief. "But nobody is going to put a gun to his head to make him attend it."

The sarcasm in her voice was ample, conveying that her appreciation for him having saved her life had waned considerably, somehow lost in the deep void in her heart.

"Very nice, very nice, Tiffany," the PR chief replied with an equal dose of sarcasm.

Tiffany had grown contempt for Matt in recent months because, as her series of shallow relationships had graphically reinforced, she realized what she had truly lost in losing him to Robbyn. And because of her feelings toward Matt, she had lost any fondness at all for the city of Braxton that had jump-started her career as a leading lady. If it hadn't been for the grand opportunity of a publicity spike in Braxton, she would have wished that the premiere be held in Hollywood. She was not looking forward to seeing Matt or the town again. But since she had to go, she was going to make the most of it. And to prove to Matt that she didn't need him, she had persuaded her latest fling, Jean Paul Loiselle, a French winery owner, to accompany her to Braxton.

"This Braxton, does it have any four-star hotels there?" he asked Tiffany over champagne at breakfast.

"Yeah, right," Tiffany laughed. "But they do have several Econolodges."

"Super," Jean Paul said, rolling his eyes. "At least we're leaving for Paris the next morning. You will simply love Paris at Thanksgiving."

"I didn't think they celebrated Thanksgiving in France," Tiffany said, looking confused.

"We don't, my lovely," countered Jean Paul. "I was just playing with you."

"Well, this is no time to be funny," she said. "I'm bored. Let's shop on Rodeo Drive. You haven't spent any money on me for some time now."

"Yes, what has it been?" asked Jean Paul, again rolling his eyes. "Twenty hours or so. Perhaps you already have forgotten that lovely diamond necklace I bought you yesterday to wear to the premiere?"

"I haven't forgotten, my dear," Tiffany said. "But that necklace is as much for you as for me, isn't it? You want me to look hot on your arm that night, no?"

"Yes," Jean Paul smiled. "But I'd also like you to look hot with nothing but the necklace on this morning in bed."

"Forget about it," Tiffany snapped. "I'm not in the mood."

"You seldom are these days, darling," Jean Paul smiled. "Sometimes I wonder why you need a boyfriend."

Tiffany's frown suddenly morphed into a smile.

"To buy me things and to look good on my arm in *People* magazine photos and on Facebook and Instagram," she said.

"Sad, but you are only half kidding," he said with a sigh.

"Half kidding?" she fired back.

"You can be cruel. Why do I put up with you?" he asked.

"Nobody's making you," she snapped.

The autumn days in Braxton slipped by as quickly as the leaves slipped from the trees. The "Drug Town" movie premiere extravaganza had come to town, towing along a number of national media correspondents in its wake. Matt already had begged off from writing anything in the *Bugle* about the day and night's events. He felt his role should strictly be that of an honored but hopefully low-profile guest at the screening. His managing editor, Ned March, agreed to have his entertainment columnist and a feature writer cover the festivities. Matt definitely was determined to avoid the movie studio's and Tiffany's dog-and-pony shows. They involved the press conference at Buttonwood and Elm streets to recount the shooting incident with drug dealers that had terrorized the film's leading lady, and the photo-op dinner serving by Tiffany and leading man Bronk Cassidy at the Braxton Emergency Shelter. Representatives from the movie studio had sent Matt invitations to both events, but he had declined. Tiffany wanted Matt at both events, especially the press conference. It wasn't that she wanted to see him personally, knowing that it would be awkward. But she felt that his presence would help hype the movie and herself. However, she was too proud and stubborn to call Matt personally and request his presence. She had one of the studio's PR assistants call Matt.

Matt's response to the PR person's call was cordial but blunt: "Tell Miss Underhill to call me personally if she wants me there. She has my number."

No call was forthcoming, which wasn't surprising considering Tiffany's response when informed of Matt's reply.

"Well, I'm not gonna kiss his ass to come," she snapped. "If the jerk doesn't want to be a part of such a big story, well, he isn't much of a journalist."

Actually, Matt wished he could avoid the premiere screening at the Fairgrounds Square Mall cinema complex. But he knew it would look conspicuous if he skipped it. And he knew it would be good primary research for the book he was writing about his experience with Tiffany, the filming of "Drug Town," the Shelter scandal and the shooting incident.

To his surprise, Robbyn was excited about attending the screening. "It's going to be exciting, all the celebrity hoopla and all," she gushed.

"I don't consider Tiffany and Bronk to be celebrities," Matt said sarcastically. "I know Tiffany all too well, and Bronk puked in my car, forcing me to eventually sell it because the damn odor wouldn't go away. I should have had him pay for my new car."

"But we'll get to walk on the red carpet," Robbyn said cheerfully.

"Big deal," Matt snapped, adding sarcastically: "A red carpet outside a mall. Man, I'm sure those tabloid TV reporters will find the Fairgrounds Square complex to be every bit as elegant as the Kodak Theatre in Hollywood."

"That's where they have the Academy Awards, right?" Robbyn asked.

"The one and the same," Matt said. "Don't be looking for Tiffany to pick up any Oscars that night. Unless she's banging some guy who wins one that night."

"Remind me never to get on your bad side," Robbyn said.

"I could have been meaner," Matt said. "I could have said that she was having sex with Harvey Weinstein."

"Tiffany has too gorgeous of a body to waste it on a disgraced movie mogul like Weinstein," Robbyn said. "Or on Matt Lauer or Charlie Rose."

"Your body is as good as hers," Matt said.

"Yeah, right," Robbyn responded with a laugh. "You "don't have to flatter me by lying to me."

"You have a great body and you're better in bed," Matt said.

"Tell me you have expunged all memory of what Tiffany and all other women you slept with were like in bed or I'll wipe that silly grin off your face," Robbyn said, poking him in the ribs.

"Ouch, that hurt!" Matt said. "Enough said."

It was a good thing for Matt that he didn't attend Tiffany's press conference at Buttonwood and Elm streets in the badlands of Braxton. First, there were no bad guys in the neighborhood. Too many cameras and tape recorders from local, national and Hollywood media outlets, not to mention a number of police cruisers and officers for security, tend to make drug dealers crawl back into the crevices from which they came. Second, Tiffany's recounting of the shooting incident significantly embellished her role as heroine and diminished Matt's role as hero. In fact, a peeved Tiffany didn't even refer to Matt by name, choosing to call him simply "that reporter from the *Bugle*."

After the photo op and carnival for sound bites had abated, Jean Paul Loiselle remarked to Tiffany: "You are so brave, my dear. I am in awe."

"As long as I look hot in the photos, on social media and on TV, that's all I care about," snapped Tiffany. "You know, I'm glad that Meredith wasn't here. That lunkhead would have stolen valuable face time from me."

"Well, aren't we in a foul mood on your big day?" Jean Paul said.

"This is work, not fun," Tiffany responded as they climbed into a limo that would whisk them to the Braxton Emergency Shelter. "Besides, look around this damn town. It sucks. And now I have to make happy and feed some fucking soup to a bunch of homeless people. I hope they don't smell too badly."

Jean Paul had noticed that Tiffany's mood had grown increasingly sullen as the premiere day neared. And now that they were in Braxton for the premiere, her attitude had become unbearable.

"You know, you're not much fun these days," he said to her. "I hope once this event is out of the way, we can relax and enjoy ourselves in Paris."

"Well, we'll see," she said while trying to apply more mascara as the limo turned a corner.

"Just say I'm not going to be with someone who's always in a foul mood," Jean Paul said.

"Don't give me any shit today," Tiffany said, glaring at him with such intensity it appeared to an increasingly annoyed Jean Paul that her freshly applied mascara had grown daggers. "I'm under enough stress as it is."

"OK, my dear," Jean Paul said. "I'm, how you say, sensitive to your situation today. But today does not mean tomorrow."

"I'll worry about that tomorrow," she said, flashing him a quick smile and patting his thigh to placate him. "We're here at the Shelter. It's show time!"

"Yes, lights, camera and action," Jean Paul said wearily. "I could use a relaxing glass of Merlot right now."

"I could use some coke," Tiffany said, pushing up her breasts in her low-cut dress. "But that can wait until after the screening. After all, this is 'Drug Town' and this is my party night!"

"I'm sure it's going to be some night," Jean Paul said as he ushered Tiffany from the limo and into the applause of her throng of fans gathered outside the Braxton Emergency Shelter to pay her homage.

Tiffany's smile almost blinded her adoring fans, who screamed her name and wildly waved their arms at her.

Tiffany's smile didn't last long. It vanished immediately upon her seeing Jimbo Cummings and Millie Paxton standing next to Shelter executive director Bob Tolliver on the front steps of the Shelter. Her first instinct was to bolt and run back into the shelter of the limo. Realizing that would be embarrassing, her second instinct was to mutter "that fucking bastard" under her breath.

"What the hell is wrong?" a startled Jean Paul whispered to her. "Act happy. Smile!"

"That big lug over there is the former mayor who's been a real asshole to me," Tiffany said quietly but angrily to Jean Paul.

"Well, just be polite, smile and shake his hand," he said softly and reassuringly. "Then ignore the asshole. You'll never see him again. Don't blow a wonderful publicity scene."

Tiffany immediately regained her composure. Squeezing Jean Paul's arm with one hand and waving with the other, she stuck the smile back on her face and kept it there. Yes, the smile remained frozen on her face as she warmly greeted fans, Shelter board members, Bob Tolliver and Millie Paxton. She made sure all the television and still cameras caught her radiant smile. It was only when Jimbo Cummings shook her hand that her smile instantly was replaced by a cold, hard stare. Her look didn't startle Jimbo. On the contrary, he rather enjoyed it. He hated Tiffany for obvious reasons, and his malice for the woman who had humiliated him and cost him his career had spiked in recent months. This increase in venom had grown dramatically as the realization that he was finished in his town had become too vivid. And he had found himself to be the butt of many jokes by people who held him in disdain. He had lost the respect of even some of his cronies. Needless to say, the business and community leaders who had never embraced him but had tolerated him when he had a power base had now abandoned him in droves. Adding insult to injury, his personal finances were in shambles. He now needed to rely on Millie Paxton for money. She didn't begrudge him the money, but their relationship had evolved in light of his disgrace. She now had become the dominant personality in the relationship and he had resigned himself to taking a more docile role in their interaction. Now he was biting his tongue because he was utterly afraid to bite the hand that fed him. The only thing that gave some structure and sanity to Jimbo's recent existence was his anticipation of Tiffany's return to town. He had begged Millie to intercede with Bob Tolliver and Shelter officials to allow him to attend the celebrity food serving by Tiffany and Bronk Cassidy. Tolliver had very reluctantly agreed, only out of respect for Millie Paxton, the Shelter's prime benefactor.

As Tiffany and Jimbo shook hands and he basked in the pleasure of her obvious discomfort, he leaned over to sarcastically whisper in her ear: "Glad to see you again, my darling."

"Screw you," Tiffany whispered into his ear. "I'm glad you're finished. Stay away from me or I'll spill hot soup on your lap. Then we'll see what a big boy you are."

Jimbo's response was to tighten the grip on his handshake until Tiffany grimaced in discomfort. Not wanting to make a scene, he then relaxed his grip and turned his attention to Jean Paul and then to Bronk Cassidy. Tiffany stood there in a momentary daze, startled out of it seconds later when Millie Paxton and Bob Tolliver began gushing over her appearance at the Shelter and thanking her for the movie studio's generous contribution.

While they did so, she couldn't help but shoot a wary glance at Jimbo, who fired back a look that froze her soul.

It was a look of pure, unadulterated hate. And it curdled Tiffany's insides into a sour, sickening lump. She felt sick to her stomach. A cold sweat gripped her as a sense of dread put a hammerlock on her senses. In a panic, she wondered how she would be able to serve soup and sandwiches to Shelter residents without vomiting. But Tiffany always had been a trooper, so she stuck the smile back on her face and hoped her fear of Jimbo and her nauseous belly wouldn't betray her in front of all the media. She pulled it off by managing to never stray far from Jean Paul and Bronk during the entire serving process. They stood side by side as they dispensed soup and sandwiches to a number of residents. Somehow Tiffany found the inner resolve not to barf by swallowing nervously and frequently as she served food and made small talk with people.

Jean Paul noticed how uptight she was, saying, "For God's sake, relax."

"I can't," she said while pouring soup into a bowl held by a man who looked as if he hadn't showered in a month. "Jimbo, the ex-mayor, is making me nervous. I think he wants to harm me. I think I'm going to be sick to my stomach."

"You're with me," Jean Paul said. "Don't worry. You'll be fine. I won't let him get near you. Relax, and smile for the cameras!"

Jean Paul patted her gently on her shoulder. His reassurance gave her a small sense of relief. She privately cursed herself for being so mean to him lately. He was beginning to bore her and she planned on dumping him after they returned from Paris. But he wasn't a bad guy, she had to admit, a guy who had been good to her.

After they were done serving, Tiffany and Bronk gave a series of interviews to a posse of media types -- local and national, news and entertainment, print and electronic. Studio executives joined in the media circus, hyping the movie while taking credit for their $100,000 donation to the Shelter. While the media interviews were taking place, some of the guests and residents who had finished eating began to leave. Millie Paxton and Jimbo Cummings, however, were in no rush to leave. Millie truly loved the Shelter and was basking in the wonderful publicity the Shelter was receiving. She and Bob Tolliver also were interviewed extensively, taking advantage of the opportunity to extol all the wonderful works the Shelter provided to the community. Jimbo was treated like a leper by the media. They either ignored him or picked at the rotting scales of his fall from grace. Which means the few who asked him about the scandal received a sullen "No comment" from him. Millie was surprised that Jimbo had attended the event, thinking he would prefer not to swim in the media fishbowl. He, of course, would have. But he had another motive for being there: To slip a small dose of zinc chloride in Tiffany's soup. Not enough to kill her. Just enough to cause her to vomit after experiencing severe abdominal cramps. He wanted her to suffer, and he wanted to embarrass her on her big night. After researching zinc chloride on the Internet, he figured he knew just the right amount to put in her soup to cause her to get violently sick just about the time she was hitting the red carpet at the premiere showing of "Drug Town" at the Fairgrounds Square cinema complex. But now he was getting worried. The media interviews were taking longer than he had anticipated. And while Bronk and Jean Paul had partaken of some soup and sandwiches while talking to the press, Tiffany had not yet touched the bowl of soup that Jimbo had had Millie personally deliver to her -- the bowl of soup that had some zinc chloride swimming in it.

"Please ask Tiffany to eat her soup, it will make a great photo," Jimbo said quietly to Millie.

Millie was taken aback, rightfully wondering why Jimbo would care about a photo op for Tiffany.

"Why do you care if she looks good?" asked Millie, who also held no love for Tiffany but had been gracious to her nonetheless out of respect for the Shelter's grand occasion.

"I don't care about her, silly," Jimbo said lightly and convincingly. "I just think it would be a great shot for the Shelter."

So, Millie proceeded to walk up behind the seated Tiffany and whisper Jimbo's suggestion into her ear. Of course, she didn't mention that it had been Jimbo's suggestion.

"My stomach is a little queasy," Tiffany protested.

"An upset stomach? It must be your nerves, dear," Millie said. "Take it from me. A little, warm soup would settle your stomach. I used to feed soup to my children when their tummies were upset over anxieties at school."

Millie gave Tiffany a warm, grandmotherly smile and added: "And it would make a marvelous photo. We could have it framed and mounted here at the Shelter. After all, it's not every day we get a movie star to serve and eat soup here. We'll heat up your bowl in the microwave."

Tiffany succumbed to Millie's pitch, mostly because her ego had been flattered by Braxton's grand dame of civic causes.

Tiffany took a few spoons of the soup, then grimaced slightly.

"This soup tastes a little metallic," she complained to Millie.

"My soup tasted fine; it's probably just your upset stomach leaving a bad taste in your mouth," replied Millie, who had no clue that Jimbo had poured a small dose of zinc chloride into Tiffany's bowl. "I'm sure the soup will settle your tummy."

"I hope so," Tiffany said, a look of concern etched on her face. "I sure don't want to be sick tonight."

"Oh, heavens no," Millie said. "That would be terrible. Perhaps you should lie down and rest for a bit before the movie premiere at the mall."

"No, no time for that," Tiffany said, sounding more distressed. "Let me pose for a shot or two eating this soup, then I'm out of here."

Then she motioned to one of the studio PR assistants to assemble the remaining media, who took numerous shots of her eating her soup.

As they were leaving the Shelter, shaking hands with Shelter board members and officials, Tiffany whispered to Jean Paul: "I think I might be sick. My stomach hurts. My damn soup sucked. How was yours?"

Jean Paul patted her affectionately on the shoulder as he said: "That's a shame, darling. Perhaps one of the studio people can run an errand and get you something to settle your stomach. It's probably just nerves. Because my soup tasted OK. Not four-star restaurant quality, mind you. But not bad."

Tiffany heeded Jean Paul's advice and asked one of the studio PR staffers to have someone pick up some Tums at a drug store and bring it to the Fairgrounds Square cinema complex for her.

"If I toss my cookies in front of everybody at the damn premiere, I'll die of embarrassment," Tiffany said to Jean Paul as they climbed into the limo, which would take them to the theater.

"Actually, it probably would hype all the coverage," Jean Paul said, trying to lighten her mood.

"Fuck you!" Tiffany said, punctuating it with a loud burp.

"How ladylike," Jean Paul teased her. "At least you didn't splash me with your resounding belch."

But Jean Paul's attempt at humor fell on deaf ears.

"I feel awful, so try to be a little compassionate," Tiffany said, annoyed. "I may be sick right here in the limo. Grab one of those ice buckets just in case."

"My Lord, you are feeling badly, aren't you?" Jean Paul said as he rolled down a window and dumped the ice from the pail that had been chilling a bottle of champagne.

Tiffany was feeling acute abdominal cramps and faint. She also had this metallic taste in her mouth.

"I've got this rotten taste in my mouth," Tiffany said. "I don't want to have bad breath when I'm talking to people on the red carpet."

Jean Paul offered her a breath mint.

Tiffany put it her mouth but opted against chewing it because she was fearful that it would make her vomit.

"I'd rather gross people out with my breath than puke on their shoes," she said, her words bathed in misery.

"Perhaps we should call a doctor," said Jean Paul, who was getting alarmed but didn't want to convey his anxiety to Tiffany.

"A good idea," mumbled Tiffany.

Jean Paul instructed their limo driver to ask his dispatcher if he somehow could arrange to have a physician sent to the movie theater.

"Usually the odds are slim and none on something that like that happening, pal," the limo driver told Jean Paul. "You know doctors. But since she's a movie star, who knows? It's worth a shot."

The dispatcher called his family doctor's answering service. And when Tiffany Underhill's name was mentioned to the physician on call, he immediately volunteered to meet her limo at the Fairgrounds Square Mall.

Meanwhile, Robbyn and Matt were posing for family photos with the boys, who were making fun of Matt in his rented tux but who were genuinely impressed with how beautiful Robbyn looked in her elegantly simple black-and-white evening gown. Of course, so was Matt.

"Doesn't your mother look beautiful?" Matt asked the boys.

"Thank you," cooed Robbyn.

"Mom always looks pretty," Timmy said.

"The best-looking mom in the whole wide world," added Billy.

"Present company excluded," chuckled Cindy Loeper, who was snapping pictures.

"Well, I think Cindy looks pretty spectacular," Matt said, playfully sticking his tongue out at her.

"You look mighty good for a coach," Cindy chucked.

"But you look kind of goofy in that bow tie," Timmy said to Matt. "Do you have to wear a bow tie with a tux?"

"It came with the rental," Matt said, shrugging his shoulders. "So, I'm wearing it."

"Are you guys going to sit with Tiffany?" Billy asked.

"I imagine our seats will be near hers, but I'm not sure," Matt said. "If we do, that will be OK, right Robbyn?"

"Hey, what are friends for?" Robbyn said "But it will be OK. Of course, why do you have to look so handsome?"

"Tiffany isn't that friendly with you guys anymore, huh?" Timmy asked. "She always seemed nice to me."

"Tiffany is nice," Robbyn said. "But she now is a big Hollywood star, and she doesn't have time to be hanging out with us. Tonight's kind of an exception."

"I bet you she's really going to look pretty tonight," Billy said, giggling.

"She's going to look gorgeous," Timmy said.

"I'm sure she'll look fine," Matt said rather carefully.

"Never mind, boys," Robbyn said in a light-hearted but scolding tone. "It's time to go. Please behave for Cindy."

"Well, we'll look for you on the red carpet on television," Cindy said. "Just don't trip."

"Thanks for the encouragement," Robbyn said as she kissed the boys goodbye.

"It's show time!" Matt said, adjusting his bow tie. "I believe that is our limo waiting for us outside."

"Cool! I can't believe the studio sent a limo over for you guys," Timmy said as he raced out the front door to check out the stretch limo.

"Just like in the movies," Billy breathlessly added as he ran after his older brother.

"This is the movies, silly," Timmy fired back.

Robbyn and Matt felt a bit self-conscious as they walked toward the limo as a number of Robbyn's neighbors waved and wished them a good time.

"I could get used to being a celebrity," Matt said to Robbyn as they sat inside the spacious limo.

"Well, you should have stuck with Tiffany, at least until she dumped you for one of her European playboys," Robbyn said impishly.

"I think I picked the right girl, the one who would never let me get a big head," Matt said.

"Depends on which head you're talking about," Robbyn said devilishly.

Matt kissed her gently on the lips, but Robbyn squirmed away.

"My lipstick!" she cried in mock horror. "Don't mess up my makeup. You don't want me looking like some pathetic creature on the red carpet, now do you?"

"Even if you puked all over yourself on the red carpet, you're much too pretty to look pathetic," Matt said.

"Ever the wise guy," Robbyn replied. "But please don't jinx me. I'm nervous enough. My butterflies have butterflies."

"Relax," Matt said. "All we have to do is show up and look good. This is Tiffany's big night. We're just members of the supporting cast."

"Yeah, I wonder how she's doing right now," Robbyn said. "Her ego probably is out of control as we speak."

"She's so self-centered right now that she probably doesn't realize there's anybody else in the world. Her boyfriend, Jean Paul Whatever, probably had to pry her away from the mirror so they could hop in the limo to get to the mall theater," Matt said, chuckling.

"Nah, she wouldn't dare be late for this," Robbyn said. "I wonder how low cut her gown is."

"Oh, I'd say down to about her navel," Matt laughed.

"Well, you'd better just make eye contact with her," Robbyn said, pushing up her own ample breasts.

When Robbyn and Matt's limo arrived at the Fairgrounds Square Mall cinema complex, they couldn't believe how mobbed the place was. It looked as if half the population of Miller County had shown up for the premiere. As Matt and Robbyn were ushered out of the limo and onto the red carpet, there were plenty of cheers and applause from the crowd, many of them calling out their names.

"Jeez, you'd think we were in the movie," Matt said.

"Well, your shooting incident downtown with Tiffany made us all celebrities I guess," Robbyn said.

"I guess," said Matt as they peered into an endless array of cameras. "Being a reporter, being on the other side of the story feels damn awkward."

"Get used to it," Robbyn said.

"Don't know if I can," he said softly.

Several media representatives approached them on the red carpet, asking a series of lame and redundant questions about their relationship, about Matt's relationship with Tiffany and about the movie.

"We haven't seen the movie yet," Matt said.

"You didn't get an advanced screening?" a reporter asked.

"We're not Hollywood people, just private citizens of Braxton," Robbyn interjected. "We are pleased for Tiffany's success with the movie."

The crowd then exploded in a big gulp of noise, its cheers and shouts cascading upon two sudden arrivals, Bronk Cassidy and his date, a sultry, razor-thin brunette with piles of curls and wearing a lightning blue designer gown cut from as much material as a handkerchief.

"What an ugly dress," Matt said to Robbyn.

"It's a good thing it's skimpy or else that horrid blue would cause retina damage," Robbyn replied.

"Her fashion designer must be blind," Matt said.

"No kidding," Robbyn observed, giggling. "My eyes! My eyes!"

Then an even louder wall of noise erupted as the crowd caught sight of Tiffany and Jean Paul exiting their limo, with her displaying two miles of leg as she climbed out.

Standing just 30 yards away from them on the red carpet, Matt was surprised at how lousy Tiffany looked. He noticed that she lacked color in her face and seemed to be somewhat slumped in her bearing. And her erect carriage was something that Tiffany prided herself on. Plus, she wasn't smiling. She certainly didn't look anything like he expected her to on her grand night. He suspected that she would look spectacular, and that hardly was the case.

"Her gown is beautiful, a breathtaking beige, if beige can be breathtaking," Robbyn said of Tiffany. "And it is certainly low cut. You could play a football game inside her cleavage."

"Yeah, but even though she's finally smiling, her face doesn't look good," Matt said.

"Matthew, you *did* make eye contact after all," a surprised Robbyn said. "I'm impressed."

"I think she's sick or something," Matt said.

"Yeah, you may be right," Robbyn said.

Robbyn and Matt took a number of steps back toward the beginning of the red carpet to catch a closer glimpse. As they did so, they noticed that an assistant was handing Tiffany a glass of water and what appeared to be a roll of Tums.

"How about that! Our princess has a bad case of nerves on her big night. She has an upset tummy," Matt said.

"Oh, well, I'm sure she'll get over it. The crowd here loves her," Robbyn said.

Indeed, as Tiffany swallowed a couple of Tums, the energy and exuberance of the crowd buoyed her spirits.

"I think I'm going to puke, but until I do, this crowd is mine," Tiffany managed to say through a forced smile to Jean Paul.

"Just suck it up for a few moments until we get inside the theater," Jean Paul said. "You can slip into the ladies' room and do your business."

"Yeah, it's not like I haven't seen the movie or anything," Tiffany said, feeling even queasier now that she had some Tums in her system. "I have this damn metal taste in my mouth. And my cramps are so damn bad, I must be getting the mother of all periods."

"Just what we need, so much for lovemaking in Paris," Jean Paul said, trying to make her laugh and take her mind off her stomach.

Tiffany ignored him. She was too busy trying to keep her stomach contents from bursting through her throat. Her sense of panic was engulfing her.

Bronk Cassidy noticed Tiffany's distress and, accompanied by his date, walked over to comfort her.

"What's up, Tiff?" he asked. "You don't look so hot."

Tiffany never answered him. On the brink of fainting because her pulse had been weakened by the zinc chloride in her system, she suddenly lost all control. A geyser of vomit erupted from her throat, splashing all over Bronk Cassidy and all over herself. A stream of puke gushed down her cleavage. Making matters worse, she lost control of her bowels and a violent attack of diarrhea loudly and blatantly soiled the backside of her dress and began oozing down her legs. Overwhelmed with nausea and embarrassment, she collapsed into a heap of her own vomit and fecal matter. If there had been any more revolting and utterly embarrassing red-carpet appearances by a leading lady in the annals of Hollywood, it had gone unrecorded. And this hardly went unrecorded. As Bronk Cassidy recovered from his initial shock and his bellowing of the words "Fuck, she got me back for puking on her!" to kneel by Tiffany's side along with a befuddled and appalled Jean Paul, the large media contingent swarmed like locusts towards Tiffany -- cameras, tape recorders, microphones and cell phones in a full, reportorial frenzy. Matt and Robbyn raced to Tiffany's side as well. As Matt knelt beside her as the crowd stood in shocked silence, he heard the unmistakable cackling of a nearby Jimbo Cummings. He could see that Tiffany was unconscious, so he was quite relieved to find out that the doctor the limo service had dispatched for Tiffany had arrived on the scene. As Jean Paul, Bronk, Matt and some studio personnel stepped aside to make room for the doctor, Matt scanned the crowd to find

Jimbo. The mammoth politician wasn't hard to spot. Matt saw him standing less than five yards away, obviously enjoying Tiffany's discomfort. He had a huge grin on his face, the only person in the crowd who wasn't looking on with stunned concern. Matt at first thought that Jimbo was just getting a kick out of Tiffany's embarrassing collapse out of some sick revenge. But Matt's reporter's instinct stuck on the sense of revenge. For some reason, Matt suddenly seized upon the notion that perhaps Jimbo Cummings had poisoned Tiffany, perhaps taking advantage of her at the Shelter ceremony. Matt hadn't even been at the Shelter ceremony, so he had no way of knowing that Jimbo had been there. But Matt decided to play his hunch, because he feared Tiffany's well-being, if not life, hung in the balance. And if he embarrassed himself or pissed off Jimbo, he didn't care.

He suddenly sprinted toward Jimbo, who, his smile turning into a grimace as he saw Matt approaching, tried to run from him. It was a gross mismatch. Matt caught him and tackled him.

Jimbo's cry of pain reverberated throughout the crowd and was picked up by the media and cellphone videos. Matt took down the jumbo Jimbo with an adroit shoulder tackle to the former mayor's massive upper legs, dropping his ex-honor like a pile of rotting potatoes onto the macadam of the mall parking lot.

"You broke my hip, you broke my hip, you bastard!" Jimbo cried out in anger and in pain.

"You poisoned Tiffany, didn't you, you creep?" Matt bellowed at Jimbo as police and mall security pulled Matt off him.

"What the fuck are ya talking about?" Jimbo shouted, sitting up with the aid of several police officers.

"You're under arrest, Meredith," one of the cops barked.

A molten flash of anger almost melted Matt's forehead. But not his tongue.

"Screw you, Sam," Matt barked. "This damn asshole poisoned Tiffany Underhill!"

"Is that true, Jimbo?" asked Sam Kozlowski, the veteran cop.

Matt turned toward Jimbo again, twisted his right arm behind him, and hissed as the anger inside him reached a degree hot enough to curdle blood cells: "Look, you gave her something. Tell me what the hell it was so the doctor here can treat her properly. If you don't tell me right now, I'll break off your damn arm and then snap off the other one!"

Matt gave a jerk so violent that Jimbo's cry of pain could be heard in the dungeons of hell.

"OK, OK, I put a dose of zinc chloride in her soup at the Shelter dinner," Jimbo said angrily, tears of pain streaming down his flushed face. "But it was a little dose. The bitch deserved to be embarrassed."

Matt then rose and threaded his way through the throng where the physician knelt, attending to the still unconscious Tiffany.

"She was slipped a dose of zinc chloride, doc," Matt yelled. "The ex-mayor said he put it her soup at the Shelter dinner. He said it was a small dose."

"Thanks, Matt," said the doctor, recognizing Matt. "I'll give her an injection of atropine and alert the ambulance crew that we will have to flush her stomach. You may have just saved this young lady's life."

"Thank you, thank you, sir," Jean Paul said to Matt, patting him on the shoulder. "You're Matt Meredith, right?"

"And you're the new boyfriend, right?" asked Matt.

Before Jean Paul could introduce himself, Bronk Cassidy, cleaned up somewhat with the help of studio and mall personnel, said to Matt: "I thought you were a jerk. But you've been making a habit of saving Tiffany's butt. Thanks so much!"

"Well, she's not saved yet," said Matt, peering down at the prone Tiffany.

"I think she's beginning to stir a bit," said Robbyn, who had joined Matt by his side.

"Yes, she's going to be fine," said the doctor.

The ambulance siren roared toward them.

"Are you going to the hospital, Matt?" asked Jean Paul.

"That's your job and the studio's," Matt said. "Wish her good luck for me."

He grabbed Robbyn by the arm and said: "Let's get over to the ex-mayor. I want to make sure they arrest him. As for the premiere, I'm in no mood for movies."

Robbyn and Matt rushed over to Jimbo, who was being handcuffed and shoved into a police cruiser.

"What a terrible man!" Robbyn said. "How on earth did you ever suspect him of poisoning her?"

"I've seen poison victims before, and her violent reaction tipped me off," Matt said. "As for Jimbo, it was just a hunch because I could hear him cackling. I figured if anybody poisoned her, it would be him. Or maybe her new boyfriend who got sick of her."

"That's not funny," Robbyn said.

"I know, I know," said Matt, looking back to the ambulance where the crew was loading Tiffany. Jean Paul also climbed in with Tiffany's studio PR assistant.

"I guess they'll cancel the premiere," Robbyn said.

"They'll just postpone this and reschedule it with a lot of fanfare," Matt said. "The media will eat this up. Speaking of the media, here they come."

As the media contingent breathlessly interviewed Matt on why he had fingered the mayor as the culprit and added another chapter to the sensational off-camera saga of "Drug Town" in Braxton, one of the policemen pulled Robbyn aside and told her the police would be in touch with Matt in the morning for further details after they spoke to Shelter officials as well as to Jimbo and Millie Paxton, among others.

"I'm sure Matt will be most cooperative, he's a standup guy," Robbyn said to the cop.

"Matt's a good man, and he's an action hero again," said the cop. "Maybe they should put him in the movies."

"I think he's found his calling as a columnist," Robbyn said.

Matt finished up his round of media interviews by telling the reporters they all were fortunate that he had spoken to them and not reserved his comments for a *Braxton Bugle* exclusive.

Word came that the studio had postponed the premiere indefinitely. And then Matt's cell phone rang. It was Ned March.

"I know you begged off covering the event," March said. "But you are a newspaper man. And your heroics made this a big story. The features writer and entertainment columnist I had there wouldn't know a news story if it bit them in the ass. So, I want you to come into the office and help those clueless clowns and the police reporter bang out a great lead story for Page One. And if you're real ambitious, you can bang out an exclusive column we'll also run out front."

"You're a prick," Matt laughed. "You don't ask for much on my night off."

"Well, you're a newspaper man," Ned repeated. "You're supposed to report the news, not create it. But since you have this habit of creating it, you have to report it as well. By the way, nice job. I heard you may have saved Tiffany's life."

"Well, the medics would have figured it out eventually," Matt said.

"But you saved her ass by saving valuable time," Ned said. "They say they pumped her stomach and she's now feeling a bit better. She's out of danger. By the way, you'd make a wonderful detective, figuring out that Jimbo had poisoned her."

"Columnists and journalists are detectives," Matt said. "Did you forget Journalism 101? But I have no time for idle chit-chat. Robbyn and I are going to pay Tiffany a quick visit at the hospital, then I'm gonna haul my tired ass into the office."

"We're going to the hospital and then you're going to work?" asked Robbyn.

"We have to check up on Tiffany," Matt said. "And Ned drafted me to help write the Page One story and do a column."

"You're the man, and I'm proud of you," Robbyn said, kissing him. "And don't forget: You're my man."

"How I could I forget?" Matt said, smiling broadly. "After all, you are breathtaking."

When Robbyn and Matt arrived at the hospital, Tiffany was in a private room, accompanied by Jean Paul and two studio staffers. She was sitting up and relieved that her intense abdominal cramps had passed. But she was still utterly mortified about what had transpired at the "Drug Town" premiere. Or non-premiere, as things had turned out. When Tiffany saw Matt and Robbyn walk in her room, a sudden beam of a smile flashed across her lips and a vibrant spark of appreciation lit up her eyes.

"Matthew, Matthew, once again you saved my life," Tiffany said enthusiastically despite her lack of energy. "How can I ever repay you?"

Matt, holding Robbyn's hand in his left hand, grabbed Tiffany's hand with his right hand and bent over to kiss Tiffany on the forehead.

"You don't have to repay me," he said warmly. "I'm just glad you're going to be fine."

"The ER doctor said she is going to be fine," Jean Paul said. "I just felt so sorry for her, for her pain."

"The abdominal cramps really sucked," Tiffany said softly. "But the real pain is emotional ... I don't think I can ever show my face in public again. My career is ruined. I puked and shit in my gown in public and on television.

I'll be the laughing stock of every tabloid magazine, of every TV talk show, of every newspaper and all over YouTube. I'm sure it's already viral. I'm so pissed at Jimbo, but right now I'm glad to just be alive."

"The medical people told us that if you hadn't tipped them off to the zinc chloride in her system, she could have been in real trouble," Jean Paul said.

"I'm so glad you're going to be fine," Robbyn said.

Robbyn gave Tiffany such a genuinely warm smile that the actress couldn't resist blushing.

A visibly touched Tiffany reached out her hand to Robbyn and said: "I know it's been awkward for all three of us. But I want to be friends from now on. Matt's a great guy, but he's your guy. And now I have a great guy in Jean Paul. I thought he was self-centered and shallow ... until tonight. He's been a doll tonight and I now realize how much he cares for me."

"Me? Self-centered?" Jean Paul said in mock horror. "I thought *you* were the self-centered one."

"Me?" laughed Tiffany. "Well, maybe I was. But no longer. The last person I wanted to be tonight was me. I'm so embarrassed."

"I understand your embarrassment," Matt said. "But no need to be. The media will be very understanding. You were poisoned by a very sick man. You will be bigger than ever after this. People will sympathize with you. Trust me. I know how the media works. This is a great story, and you will be bigger at the box office than ever. 'Drug Town' now will have hype going through the roof. You'll be on talk shows all over the country."

"But this time Matt's not going with you on your media tour," Robbyn laughed. "He has a wedding to help plan, around Christmas time."

Matt and Robbyn both could sense that the smile radiating from Tiffany was genuine. She sincerely was happy for the both of them.

"Congratulations," she said. "Perhaps we could postpone the premiere of 'Drug Town' to your wedding night and make it part of the reception."

"I was beginning to like you again," Robbyn teased her.

"I think we'll hold the premiere in Hollywood," Tiffany said.

"Sounds good to me," Matt laughed. "Too much news happens here in Braxton. I have to run to work and help out with our coverage and write a column about how I tackled Jimbo. You know, I skinned both my knees and my right shoulder hurts. And my right arm still isn't 100 percent."

"Sorry," Tiffany said, her face turning somber.

"Hey, no big deal," Matt said. "I was so, so pissed at Jimbo for making you suffer through that ordeal. Thank God you are all right. And please take care of yourself. Jean Paul, take care of her or I'll tackle you."

"I've seen your tackling style," Jean Paul. "I don't know much about American football, but you look like you could play for the, what are they, the Philadelphia Eagles?"

"His ballplaying is restricted to coaching my boys in baseball," laughed Robbyn.

Matt leaned over, and Tiffany kissed him gently on the cheek.

"You'll always be my action hero," Tiffany said. "There always will be a place in my heart for you. Again, from the bottom of my heart, thank you!"

"Please don't get swept away by all the temptations of Hollywood and stardom," Matt whispered in her ear. "You're a good person. I care very much for you. Stay in touch."

"I will," Tiffany said, tearing up.

Robbyn hugged Tiffany goodbye, simply saying: "Be good to yourself and I'll look for you in the movies."

"No puking or diarrhea scenes, though," Tiffany said.

"Something a tad more romantic," Robbyn said, giggling.

Jean Paul accompanied Matt and Tiffany into the hall.

"She'll be fine, thanks to you, sir," Jean Paul said to Matt. "You are quite a guy."

"Hey, I didn't do anything spectacular, just trying to help out," Matt said with shrug. "But I've got to get to work."

"I know," Jean Paul said. "I'll pick up a copy of your newspaper tomorrow. What's it called?"

"The *Braxton Bugle*," Matt said, smiling. "We're the best paper in town because we're the only paper in town."

"Monopolies aren't necessarily a bad thing, no," said Jean Paul.

"Don't tell that to our business editor," Matt said, chuckling.

As Matt and Robbyn began to walk down the hall, they were surprised to hear footsteps behind them.

It was Tiffany.

"What are you doing out of bed?" Matt, Jean Paul and Robbyn practically asked in unison.

"Giving my savior a goodbye hug!" Tiffany exclaimed, who proceeded to do just that.

"I'll never forget you," Matt said to Tiffany, whose eyes were glistening.

"Nor I," Tiffany said. "But I want you to be happy with this lady."

Tiffany turned to Robbyn and gave her a warm hug as well.

"You'd better take care of this lug," Tiffany said. "Remember, he's a good guy to have around. If somebody is shooting at you or poisoning you, he's invaluable."

"He's not bad at taking out the trash and mowing the lawn, either," Robbyn said.

The three of them embraced.

And there wasn't a shred of awkwardness.

"You know, the studio almost decided to shoot 'Drug Town' entirely in Hollywood and not go on location here," Tiffany said. "How different life would have been for all three of us if that had happened."

"There would have been a lot less drama in our lives," Matt said. "Now, this time, I am out of here! I have a deadline staring me in the face big time."

Matt kissed Tiffany goodbye on the cheek and grabbed Robbyn by the hand, saying, "We gotta run."

And run they did. They practically sprinted to Matt's car. Matt almost broke the land speed record dropping Robbyn off at her house. But before he sped off to the office, he took her in his arms in the driveway while his car's engine idled.

"I just wanted you to know, dear lady, that I spent a lifetime looking for the love of my life," he said. "I essentially had given up hope. I should have had more faith. Because now I firmly and utterly believe I've found my eternal soulmate in you. Thank God I decided to coach the Cubs. I saw you and made a pitch for love."

Robbyn embraced him hard enough to feel his ribs.

"You know for a writer, that was a corny line," she said, laughing through her tears. "But I loved every syllable of it. Now, go before you get fired!"

Matt kissed her so deeply that Robbyn felt as if he had sucked her soul from her and made it one with his.

Matt raced to the office and shored up all the holes in the two news stories the features writer and entertainment columnist had put together. Then he wrote a poignant column -- one that lowercased his personal role in the premiere poisoning and focused on how Tiffany's star shone brightly in spite of Jimbo's dastardly deed.

The media frenzy in the wake of the "Drug Town" premiere poisoning of Tiffany was amazing in its scope. The print and television tabloids were comprehensive and brutally thorough in their coverage. Video clips of Tiffany vomiting and soiling herself went viral on social media, with the networks showing a little more restraint than the graphic videos screened on syndicated and cable shows. Video and blistering blogs on multiple sites were quite stark in embarrassing Tiffany. Such coverage undoubtedly would have totally humiliated Tiffany were it not for the reams and reams of overwhelmingly sympathetic multimedia coverage she received. The common theme was that of a crusading, public-minded, valiant actress who had dared to bring down a corrupt mayor and had paid an epic price in degradation. The studio encouraged Tiffany to be available for all media interviews and, like the true trooper she was, she made the rounds ranging from the TV tabloids to the network morning and late-night talk shows to the cable prime time spincasts. By the time the media had finished with the story, Tiffany was a first-name sensation throughout the world. Granted, she had been the butt of some cruel jokes, but for the most part she now was respected as a civic activist and budding superstar. Helping matters, of course, was that "Drug Town," which had its rescheduled premiere in Hollywood and was rushed into release, was a smash. It opened as the No. 1 film in the nation, a spot it would hold through the Christmas holidays -- a box office bonanza that had been generously fueled by all the media gas concerning Tiffany and Jimbo … and Matt.

Yes, try as he might, Matt could not avoid being dunked into the media fishbowl. He made it a point not to go traveling on the media circuit with Tiffany, especially because it would have triggered some residual resentment in Robbyn. But the media outlets kept plugging into Braxton and Matt wound up on all sorts of TV shows and in all sorts of publications that didn't fly the flag of the *Braxton Bugle*. Speaking of the *Braxton Bugle*, Matt, at the prodding of his editors and publisher, wound up writing a series of follow-up columns on Tiffany; on Jimbo Cummings' judicial proceedings; and on the smash success of "Drug Town."

With all that going on, plus working on his own book, house hunting with Robbyn (they found their five-bedroom Sorbonne Township dream home, complete with a big yard and pool, for $625,000), and trying to get ready for the Christmas-week nuptials, it suddenly was Christmas Eve and everything was stirring in Robbyn's house. Robbyn and Matt had planned on a quiet Christmas Eve with the boys while they finalized details for their wedding in two days. But their friends kept stopping by to share in their holiday and wedding excitement.

First, Robert and Betty Thaxter stopped in. Robert not only was Robbyn's boss at the advertising agency he owned, he was a deacon at St. Ignatius and would be helping the monsignor say their wedding Mass.

"I think I'm even happier than you two are," Betty Thaxter gushed as she tip-toed around wrapped Christmas presents stacked here and everywhere in the living room.

"Me, too," said Robert Thaxter, who actually was wearing a green sweater with red reindeer prancing across his chest. "You will be the most beautiful bride I ever saw, Robbyn."

"What about me, dear?" Betty Thaxter asked in mock horror.

"I should say besides you, dear," Robert said, grinning.

"You always were quick on your feet, Bob," said Matt, who had been hoping to be alone with Robbyn and the boys on their first Christmas Eve together. "Care for a drink?"

"No alcohol," Robert Thaxter replied. "Not with midnight Mass tonight."

"Egg nog straight-up for two?" asked Robbyn.

"That would be lovely," Betty replied.

As the four of them sat drinking egg nog in the living room while Timmy and Billy watched a holiday college football bowl game in the family room, another group of visitors arrived: Cindy Loeper, her husband Bill, the orthopedic surgeon, and their son Derek.

"We were just driving home after doing some last-minute shopping and we decided to see how the two lovebirds were doing," Cindy gushed as Derek raced into the family room to join the Baxter boys.

After introducing the Loepers to the Thaxters, Matt had to confess to Cindy and Robbyn that he had never met Dr. Bill Loeper.

"He's always putting some poor soul back together so he doesn't get out much," Cindy joked.

Bill Loeper was an amiable if somewhat sheepish guy who didn't mix well socially. But he made it a point to commend Matt for his role in pinching Jimbo for the poisoning of Tiffany.

"You undoubtedly saved that actress considerable complications," Bill Loeper said as he sipped his egg nog.

"Well, just trying to be helpful, Doc," Matt said. "By the way, so you're an orthopedic surgeon, huh?"

"Yes, I am," Bill replied.

"Well, my back's been killing me in the morning ever since I tackled Jimbo," Matt said. "I have to do a lot of stretching just to get loose. And I have had a little pain going down my left leg at times."

"Could be a lumbar disc problem," Bill Loeper observed. "You should make an appointment and we'll take some images and examine you."

"And if my medical insurance doesn't cover it, we'll make Jimbo pick up the expenses," Matt joked.

"Oh, Matt, that's funny," giggled Robbyn.

"Jimbo already is a patient of Bill's," Cindy chimed in. "He needs a hip replacement. He blames it on Matt's tackle. I'm surprised that Jimbo hasn't sued Matt."

"Will you be doing the hip replacement on Jimbo in prison?" Matt asked, only semi-joking.

"Well, probably not," Bill said. "But I'm sure his judicial proceedings will take some time."

The doorbell rang. When Robbyn answered the door, she almost swallowed her egg nog glass when she saw who it was. Standing before Robbyn's very eyes were Millie Paxton and Tiffany Underhill. Millie and Tiffany both knew the sight of them together would shock whoever answered the door, so their smiles were wide enough to park your car on.

"Uh, Tiffany? Er, Mrs. Paxton?" asked Robbyn, stumbling through their names as if someone had slipped bowling balls into her mouth.

"Surprise, surprise!" Tiffany chirped.

"Merry Christmas, dear," Millie said, adding, "Please call me Millie."

Robbyn stood there transfixed for a moment or two, then recovered and invited them in for a drink.

"Uh, is Jimbo with you, Mrs. Paxton, I mean Millie?" Robbyn asked as she ushered them into the living room.

"Heavens no, I've dumped that bastard," she laughed as she loudly made that announcement to a totally startled Matt as well as the Thaxters and the Loepers.

Matt, of course, received a double dose of shock when nanoseconds later he saw Tiffany trail Robbyn into the living room.

"Tiffany? Mrs. Paxton?" is all Matt could muster from his mouth.

"Call me Millie and pour me a Scotch," Millie said with a twinkle in her eyes. "Tiffany and I are celebrating Christmas as well as the end of bad relationships, aren't we young lady?"

"Indeed we are," Tiffany said, smiling mischievously. "Hi, Matt!"

"You and Jean Paul broke up?" Matt asked, asking the obvious.

"I got bored with him, he was such a playboy and self-centered," Tiffany said. "How about a gin and tonic?"

"You declined our wedding invitation," Robbyn said.

"I did because I thought I would be in France with Jean Paul for the holidays," Tiffany explained. "But I'm not.

Hopefully you can squeeze me onto the wedding invitation list. I'm in town anyway because Millie graciously invited me to spend Christmas with her."

"I felt so sorry for the poor dear when I found out that Jimbo, that louse, had poisoned her; I had to make amends," Millie said. "So, I extended a holiday invitation."

Matt and Robbyn then recovered enough of their poise to introduce Millie and Tiffany to the Thaxters and the Loepers.

"I must say Millie that we are glad you jettisoned Jimbo," Robert Thaxter said gently. "You two never were a good match, in my opinion."

"Absolutely," chimed in Betty Thaxter. "You are so refined, and he's so, well, uncouth."

"Well, they say love is blind and I must have been as blind as a bat," laughed Millie. "So glad Bob punched him."

Cindy Loeper then rushed up to Tiffany and practically knelt before her in reverence.

"You remember me, Tiffany, don't you?" she asked breathlessly. "I'm Cindy Loeper. We met at dinner during one of those baseball tournament weekends."

"Absolutely," said Tiffany, whose feigned enthusiasm masked her vague recollection of meeting Cindy. "And this handsome gentleman must be your husband."

Tiffany went up to Bill Loeper, whose face had turned redder than the blood gushing from a burst artery, took his hand, one that never (thankfully) shook like that during surgery, and kissed it.

After fighting off the impulse to have a stroke and a coronary, Bill Loeper managed to spit out the word "Charmed" before recessing back into the shadows.

"Please sit down everyone," Matt said. "Fortunately, we have plenty of chairs in here. Robbyn, could you help me fix some drinks? Anybody need an egg nog refill or anything else?"

When Robbyn and Matt went to the kitchen to prepare Millie's Scotch and Tiffany's gin and tonic, Matt quickly whispered to Robbyn: "Do you believe this? Is this some sort of damn Christmas Eve fantasy?"

"Or nightmare?" Robbyn whispered back. "Millie and Tiffany spending the holidays together? And Tiffany horning her way into our wedding. I think the bitch came back for you. Why the hell else would she come back to Braxton right before our wedding?"

"Don't jump to a wild conclusion," Matt cautioned her, despite having privately jumped to that very same conclusion. "We'd better make their drinks and get back out there."

"I don't have time for all this company," complained Robbyn. "I can't believe they all just showed up unannounced on Christmas Eve. Don't they know we're getting married in two days? And that tomorrow's Christmas? I'll be up all night and look like shit on our wedding day."

"Calm down," Matt said, kissing her gently on the forehead. "You've never looked like shit a day in your life."

They quickly made drinks for Millie and Tiffany and poured themselves beers.

"Actually, I could use a shot of hard liquor," Matt said. "This is unreal."

When Matt and Robbyn returned to the living room with the drinks, Millie proceeded to make a toast.

"Here's to Matt and Robbyn," she said sweetly and dramatically. "May they have many years of happiness together. They're good people and have been great friends of the Shelter. Personally, I would like to apologize to both of them for the actions of my former boyfriend."

"No need for apologies from you," Matt said. "You were guiltless."

"Well, I was guilty by association, and guilty of poor judgment in relationships," Millie said.

"Well, thankfully you've seen the light," Matt said.

"Why don't you accompany Tiffany to our wedding?" Robbyn asked. "I assume you don't have a date for the wedding, Tiffany."

"That is so," Tiffany said, smiling. "I've got the hottest film in the theaters, but I don't have a man. Actually, I'm sick of men. Millie would be delightful company."

"Likewise," said Millie. For the next two hours the Thaxters, the Loepers, Millie and Tiffany drank, chatted and laughed with Matt and Robbyn.

When they all had finally left, a weary Robbyn said to Matt: "Do you believe I'm the one who invited her to our wedding?"

"What choice did you have?" Matt asked. "Besides, I think Tiffany is over me. I think she sincerely wanted to come to the wedding. And I believe Millie's invitation to have Tiffany spend a quaint Christmas with her was genuine."

"Well, enough about them," Robbyn said, sighing. "We've got some more presents to wrap and some loose ends to tie up for the wedding."

"Jeez, I was going to go home and catch some Z's," Matt said playfully.

"Do that and you'll be in traction on your wedding day," Robbyn said giggling.

"Before we get to work, let's sit with the boys for a few minutes," Matt said, turning serious. "With all the unexpected company, we've sort of neglected them on our first Christmas Eve all together."

"It's so easy to love you," Robbyn cooed.

They walked, holding hands, into the family room and shared a delightful Christmas Eve with the boys. As they all laughed and talked, Robbyn couldn't help but soak it all in, thanking God that He had ushered this wonderful man into their lives. For the first time, she admitted to herself that she was as happy now as she had been with Bob Baxter. And she could admit it without feeling guilty about it. Which was a godsend of a relief unto itself.

After a wonderful Christmas Day spent with Timmy and Billy as well as with assorted extended family members of Matt's and Robbyn's, the happy couple managed to tie up a few loose ends for the wedding.

"Well, I guess I should go home, for the last time to sleep alone," Matt said, laughing. "After all, it's considered bad form for the groom to sleep with the bride on the eve of their wedding."

"Not to mention sleeping in the same house as the bride's two boys," Robbyn said, giggling. "I need to sleep tonight anyway. I don't want bags under my eyes tomorrow. Besides, you'll get all the sex you want next week. I'm just crossing my fingers that my period doesn't arrive early. As you know, I'm not the most regular girl when it comes to menstrual cycles."

"If your period comes early next week, I'm going to be one horny bridegroom," Matt said, feigning horror. "So, keep your legs crossed."

"How are we going to make love if my legs are crossed?" Robbyn asked, smiling. "You're not saving the kinky sex until after the wedding, are you?"

"Me? Kinky?" asked Matt. "Hell, no. I'm a Little League coach, for God's sake."

"Well, then, Coach, take your balls and go home," Robbyn laughed, "pun intended. I'll see you in church. Give me a nice platonic kiss, you big hunk, and then hit the road."

Instead, Matt gave her a rousing, passionate kiss that made her nipples so hard they almost left impressions on his red-and-green Christmas sweater.

"Wow, I can't wait for the honeymoon," she laughed.

"A week in the Bahamas, there won't be any time for sex," Matt joked. "We'll be doing too much swimming, snorkeling, body surfing and drinking."

"Sounds like a game plan, Coach," Robbyn said, her face and eyes crinkling with delight. "See ya!"

He kissed her gently on the lips, gave her a bear hug, and went home, singing Christmas carols to himself on the drive to his house.

When Matt walked in his house, he decided, since it was just 10 o'clock, to sit and relax for a bit, sipping egg nog and listening to Christmas carols. He was a traditionalist when it came to the holidays and simply loved carols, egg nog and all the trappings. He had gone to great lengths to decorate the inside and outside of his home as well as Robbyn's. As he sat there, enjoying the solitude and savoring the dawn of his new life, a jolt of shock shot down his spinal column when his doorbell rang about 30 minutes later.

"Who could that be?" he asked himself as he scrambled to the front door.

He dreaded opening the door, assuming that somebody at his front door this late on Christmas Night meant that somebody was in trouble.

When he opened that front door, the shock of seeing the person in his doorway put all his nerve endings on full alert.

"Tiffany! What are you doing here?" he asked. "Uh, where's Millie? You alone?"

"Millie's asleep and I'm bored," she said. "You know, it's cold out here. Could you please invite me in? Hell, I'm not going to bite you -- or rape you."

She then brushed past him into the foyer, giggles accompanying her. Matt watched her fling off her striking black leather coat and toss it onto a chair. Wearing tight jeans, a white V-neck sweater that accentuated her breasts, and spiked black boots, Tiffany hardly resembled Mrs. Claus.

"Aren't you going to offer me some wine?" she asked, coyly. "And relax. I'm not here to hit on you. Just hang out for a bit and then go back to Millie's house. The old lady is a dear, but at her age, she isn't much fun after 10."

"OK, have a glass of wine, but then you're out of here," Matt said, feeling uncomfortable about entertaining her alone on the night before his wedding. "I have to get my beauty sleep for tomorrow."

"You? Beauty sleep? You're gorgeous all the time and you know it. Good looking men always look good, even when they look like shit. Women don't have that luxury."

"I'm not sure I follow that," Matt said, beginning to relax a bit. "Let me get you some wine."

"Won't you join me in a glass?" she asked, stretching her arms over head.

Matt, who couldn't help but notice Tiffany's breasts straining against the constraints of her tight sweater, said, "Well, I'm drinking non-alcohol egg nog."

"How cute," Tiffany said, putting her arms back down by her sides. "But egg nog is fattening. And bad for your arteries. You don't want to have clogged arteries on your honeymoon, do you? After all, having sex 24-7 puts a mighty strain on a man's heart. And you're not getting any younger."

"Aren't you in a playful mood?" Matt observed, experiencing a heightened sense of anxiety about her presence and her intentions. "I'll pour both of us a glass of Merlot. After all, red wine is good for the heart."

As he went to fetch the bottle and the glasses, he heard Tiffany call out into the kitchen: "Merlot is good. My heart could use a bit of repair these days, not to mention nights."

Those words stabbed Matt in the heart as if they were daggers. It was obvious that Tiffany, devoid of a relationship at the moment, had come trolling for a pre-nuptial fling. And he wanted no part of it, but he didn't want to be totally rude and simply toss her out.

As for her part, Tiffany wasn't totally sure of her own intentions. She was intrigued by the danger of making love to Matt on the eve of his wedding, and she certainly had been horny since she had dumped Jean Paul. And down deep she knew that Matt, more than any man, met most of her basic needs. And she was truly grateful that he had helped save her life on two occasions. But these emotions and feelings were tempered by a true regard for Robbyn and the wonderful life she seemed to share with Matt and her kids. Part of Tiffany didn't want to be selfish and spoil the equation for them. But part of Tiffany, as was her wont, was extremely selfish. Consequently, she sat there sitting in a paradox of passion and confusion as Matt returned with the wine and glasses.

As they drank first one glass and then a second, they made small talk about the movie and their past as well as about Robbyn and the boys. Tiffany seemed to be getting tipsier than she should have been on two glasses, leading Matt to suspect that she must have been drinking somewhat before her arrival at his house. Her inhibitions grown lax with her increasing level of intoxication, her selfish and sexy side got the best of her. Startling Matt with her quickness, she suddenly sprang from her seat and jumped on his lap, nearly knocking his half-full glass of Merlot flying.

"What the hell!" Matt snapped. "Not this! Not now! Not ever!"

"You know you want me!" Tiffany said, looking tousled and eminently doable. "Don't deny it. So, we fool around a bit tonight. So what? I'm not gonna tell Robbyn. Are you?"

She then gave him a deep kiss, but he pushed her off him and onto the floor, where she landed in one embarrassed and angry heap.

Once again, her self-esteem with men -- despite her beauty, her body and her Hollywood stardom -- had suffered a significant setback. Enraged, she grabbed the nearest object she could find to vent her anger. She snatched up a baseball autographed by Philadelphia Phillies Hall of Famer Mike Schmidt that Matt kept on his coffee table as a conversation piece. Matt didn't notice her grabbing it until it was too late. She fired the baseball and it struck him right smack on his eye, leaving an instant round welt around his eye and the foundation for what likely would be one epic shiner by the time his morning nuptials commenced.

"Damn, that hurts!" Matt hissed in anger, embarrassed by getting caught off guard by Tiffany and fearful what his eye would look like the next day and wondering just how the hell he would explain it to Robbyn. "What the hell did you do that for? What did you expect me to do? Screw your brains out in my living room on the night before my wedding? Come on. Get the hell out of here! And don't dare show up at my wedding! You hear me?"

Matt was screaming so loud he was afraid the neighbors might hear him. He still was playing Christmas carols while he and Tiffany talked. And as he dashed to look in the mirror above his living room sofa to survey the damage to his eye, he couldn't help but notice the irony of "Silent Night" playing in the background.

"Jesus Christ, Tiffany, look at my damn eye!" he yelled. "I'm gonna look terrible tomorrow. What the hell do I tell everybody? Especially Robbyn?"

Tiffany recoiled in horror and shame as she got up and gingerly approached him. The look of his angry eye made her nauseous.

"I'm, I'm, jeez, I am so, so sorry," she said as she convulsed into tears. "I don't know what got into me. I guess I still want you, yearn for you, and I got carried away. You shouldn't have given me a second glass of wine."

"No shit!" Matt snapped. "I shouldn't have let you in here!"

"You know, I admire you for being so faithful to Robbyn," Tiffany said. "And now I know for sure that you're over me. I have closure."

"Screw your closure," Matt yelled. "It's always about you, isn't it? You have closure and I'm blind in one eye. My wedding pictures will be a real treasure. Do you have any idea how much wedding photos and a video cost? Of course, how could you? You've never been married because you're too damn selfish. Even though you're hot and you're a star, you're alone because nobody can live with you. You don't have room for anybody else in your heart. You only have room for you in your heart!"

Matt's piercing words hit the bull's-eye in Tiffany's psyche. She knew each and every word he had just shouted in anger were on the mark. She slumped to her knees, crying profusely. At first Matt thought she was acting and just being dramatic to elicit sympathy. But soon he sensed that her sorrow was profound. He bent down to console her, and she looked up at him with her face awash in bitter tears.

"God, I'm sorry," he said, his anger melting in the face of her pathetic appearance.

"No, I'm the one who's sorry," she said. "You're right. I am a selfish bitch. But for once, let me do something nice. Let me get you some ice. Your eye is scary. It must be killing you."

"It's throbbing," Matt said wincing as Tiffany arose from her knees, kissing him gently on his forehead, and retreated to the kitchen to get ice.

"Do you still keep your plastic baggies in the pantry?" she asked calmly, as if nothing had happened.

"Yes," Matt said, sitting down on the sofa.

He, too, felt sick in his stomach. What and how much he would tell Robbyn about all of this kept spinning in his mind and heart until it made him nauseous.

"Do you want me to drive you the hospital?" Tiffany asked, her voice now coated with sweetness and light. "You should have your eye looked at. Can you see all right with it?"

"Things are a little blurry," Matt said. "But I'll be OK. I've been hit in the eye before with a baseball. But I know it will look like hell tomorrow. Thanks to you."

"I'd better go," Tiffany said, going over to get her coat.

"You'd better," he agreed.

She put on her coat and expected him to escort her to the door. She wanted to give him one final hug, for she already had decided that she never, ever wanted to see him again. But Matt intentionally ignored her. He sat on the sofa, applying the bag of ice to his ballooning eye. He heard the front door open and close. He was glad to have her out of his life, hopefully for good. He wondered if she would show up at the wedding but felt that she likely wouldn't. He blamed himself more than her for what had happened. He felt guilty because even though he had absolutely no intention of allowing matters to get out of hand, he was intrigued and flattered by the extent of her flirtations with him. He still felt a vibe of sexual energy when he was near her, but having felt that, he was absolutely convinced that his heart and body belonged solely to Robbyn. But how would he tell her what happened? The only thing he could think of at the moment was to tell her that he bumped into a dresser drawer while leaning over to get his underwear out for tomorrow. What a lame lie, he thought, especially for a man who wrote for a living. And he hated the thought of having to lie to her on their wedding day. But what alternative did he have? Tell her the truth? What would she make of that? More importantly, how would she deal with that? She might even cancel the wedding, saying that this had been the last straw and that she could never be secure, be comfortable that he would be faithful to her. As he sat there, morose and hurting, he could hear her saying those very words to him. How could he just stand there in the sanctuary of the church tomorrow, watching his bride come down the aisle and then noticing in alarm that his right eye looked like it had smacked into a Mack truck? What would Timmy and Billy say? They'd ask a million questions. He went into the kitchen for fresh regiments of ice. He figured he had better stay up all night icing his eye. Of course, his other eye would look terrible, too, from a night without sleep.

Meanwhile, Tiffany's departure from Matt's house hadn't gone unnoticed. The Thaxters, who lived nearby, had been driving by Matt's house on their way home from visiting their son and his family on Christmas. They clearly had seen Tiffany walk from Matt's front porch and get into her rental car parked in his driveway. Betty Thaxter had rubber-necked so violently that she had almost ruptured an upper disc in her back.

"Bob, that's, that's Tiffany Underhill coming from Matt's house!" she sputtered in shock and indignation.

"What?" Bob Thaxter asked, slowing down.

He, too, had caught a glimpse of the actress getting into her car.

"I wonder if Robbyn is at Matt's house or was he entertaining Tiffany alone," Betty said.

"I don't want to know," Bob Thaxter said. "And neither do you. It's none of our business. We saw nothing. If Matt is screwing around with Tiffany on the night before his wedding, so be it. Robbyn's a big girl. It's not our place to be her spies."

"Nonsense, the girl is like a daughter to us," Betty said as they proceeded to drive home. "Doesn't she deserve to know if some hanky-panky was going on? After all, Matt and Tiffany do have a history together. And didn't you think it was strange that Tiffany suddenly showed up in town right before the wedding? I tell you, that girl is up to no good. She's out to wreck this marriage even before it happens."

"You're jumping to conclusions," Bob said, pulling into his driveway.

He didn't tell his wife that he was jumping to the very same conclusions.

"Of course, it could have been totally innocent," he continued. "Robbyn may even had been there."

"On the night before the wedding? Unlikely," sniffed Betty. "And with two boys at home? Who are you kidding? Matt and Tiffany were alone."

"I thought Tiffany said she was staying with Millie?" Bob asked as they got out of the SUV after parking it in the garage. "Maybe Millie was in Tiffany's car. That's it. Both of them were there, visiting Matt."

"How can you be so naive?" Betty asked him as they sat down in their kitchen. "Millie was not there. There was nobody else in the car."

"How could you tell? It was dark," said Bob.

"Not that dark, because Matt has his driveway lit because he has a basketball backboard on it," Betty said, furrowing her brow. "You know that. He shoots baskets at night in his driveway. I could plainly see that nobody else was in the car. I made it a point to look."

"OK, OK, so suppose Matt and Tiffany were there alone fooling around?" he said. "What are we gonna do? Ask Matt? He'll just tell us what we want to hear. Would he admit that he was screwing around with Tiffany? Of course not."

"We could tell Robbyn, tip her off and let her confront Matt," Betty said, pouring herself some ice tea.

"Doesn't she deserve to know?"

"Yes, I know," Bob said, pouring himself a Bourbon and water. "I know."

"You rarely drink at home," Betty said, "unless we have guests."

"Well, I am tonight," Bob said, rather emphatically.

"I may join you," Betty said, managing a false smile. "This ice tea, considering the circumstances, just isn't cutting it."

"So, what the hell are we gonna do?" Bob asked, perplexed and frazzled.

"If Robbyn were your daughter, would you call her?" Betty asked.

"Yes, yes I would," relented Bob.

"Then call Robbyn and simply tell what we saw and let her deal with it," Betty said forcefully. "It's the right and proper thing to do."

"And what if it was perfectly innocent? But Robbyn blows up and cancels the wedding," Bob said forcefully as well. "Do you want that on our hands? And why do I have to call her? Isn't this something better handled by another woman?"

"Don't be silly," Betty said. "You know her better than I do. You work with her."

"That's different," Bob said. "Oh, well, it's past midnight. I'd better call her before it's already too late. I just wished we hadn't seen Tiffany leave."

"But we did," said Betty. "And now we have to do what's right."

"Boy, this turned out to be some Christmas," Bob said, delaying the inevitable. "I have to go to the bathroom."

"Don't waste time, Bob," Betty commanded. "You're used to taking charge. Call her. But be gentle. Don't alarm her. Just give her a head's up."

"OK, I don't need to be coached," Bob complained. "I deal with crisis situations all the time in a calm, professional manner. I know what to say and how to say it."

He paused and grinned.

"I think," he said, shrugging his shoulders.

Betty arose from the table and walked over to where Bob was sitting. She patted him on the back fondly, leaned over and kissed him.

"You're a wonderful, loving, upright man and I'm proud to be your wife," she said warmly. "Thank you. Someday Robbyn will thank you for making this call."

"Or hate us forever," he said, shaking his head.

He picked up the phone and nervously punched in Robbyn's number.

"She's probably fast asleep, dreaming of her wedding later this morning," Bob said to Betty as Robbyn's phone rang. "I just hope this call doesn't wake up her kids."

But Robbyn picked up on the second ring, startling Bob Thaxter. Robbyn was so quick to pick up because she hadn't yet fallen asleep. Her mind racing with anticipation and excitement, she had found it impossible to fall asleep after going to bed shortly before midnight. But instead of tossing and turning, she had been relishing the opportunity to just reflect upon the good fortune that had come into her life in the presence of Matt Meredith. Of course, such happy thoughts were jolted in alarm when her phone rang at 12:25 a.m. on the morning of her impending nuptials. As she put the receiver to her ear, she almost was afraid to hear who it was and what he or she was calling about. She blinked her eyes and braced for the bad news, for the thunderbolt that would shatter her fairy tale of happiness. Consequently, when she heard the soothing, mellow voice of Bob Thaxter on the line, she relaxed for an instant ... then immediately grew concerned that something terrible must have happened to Betty Thaxter, or heaven forbid, to Matt.

"Bob, Bob, what's wrong?" she said, the alarm and anxiety riding tandem in her throat. She sat up in bed as a cold chill gripped her.

"Uh, nothing, nothing terrible has happened or anything like that," Bob Thaxter said, trying to be reassuring but not liking the tenor and timbre of his own voice.

"Well, you didn't call me at 12:30 in the morning to congratulate me on my wedding later today or give me a post-honeymoon copywriting assignment," Robbyn said, forcing a quick, nervous giggle.

"Well, obviously not," Bob said.

"Well, please get to it," Robbyn said, her impatience and dread overpowering her usual polite demeanor.

"All right," Bob said. "I apologize for the late hour, but Betty and I just ended a debate on whether we should share something with you that we both saw tonight."

"What?" demanded Robbyn, the volume in her voice surprising even her.

"Remember, Betty and I consider you to be almost like a daughter, and we felt obligated to tell you, well, something that we think you should be aware of," Bob said almost too casually in an effort to minimize his words. "Something you should know before your wedding ceremony."

"Well, for God's sake, WHAT?" Robbyn snapped.

Even Betty Thaxter had grown impatient with her husband and snapped as well.

"Please tell her NOW before she thinks it's something even worse," Betty said loud enough for Robbyn to hear in the background.

"Betty and I saw Tiffany leaving Matt's house alone late tonight as we drove home from our son's house," Bob said simply, cutting to the chase. "Now, it probably was perfectly innocent and all that. And we debated about telling you. But we felt you should know in time to decide what, if anything, you had to do or say to him in light of this. Again, it probably was no big deal. Robbyn? ROBBYN!?"

Robbyn had slumped back down on her pillow. She suddenly was a forlorn figure, frozen prone in heartache and despair and lost love. She finally had overcome any doubts and suspicions concerning Matt's fidelity, especially when it came to Tiffany. Now, in the context of all that had transpired in the past between Matt and Tiffany, all that came flooding back into her heart like a cruel tidal wave, drowning any desire she had to marry Matt and to share her and her boys' future with him.

"Say something, Robbyn!" Bob Thaxter barked into the phone. "Are you all right? Please don't be upset and please don't jump to conclusions. Just call Matt and ask for an explanation. We didn't mean to alarm you. If we did, please forgive us."

Betty Thaxter grabbed the phone from her husband and quickly added: "You poor dear. I know this is difficult. But we know Matt like a son, and we don't think anything untoward happened tonight. Still, we felt you had to know."

Finally, after a seeming eternity of silence, Robbyn, her voice cracking, said mournfully to Betty: "As devastating as this phone call was, you've saved me from making the biggest mistake of my life."

Betty could hear Robbyn sobbing.

"Now, Robbyn, don't rush into anything hasty," Betty said loudly. "Please call him and confront him with it. But don't just unilaterally walk away from the wedding."

"I'm, I'm just tired ... tired of the uncertainty," Robbyn said softly, her voice sagging under the enormous weight of a broken heart. "Maybe it was perfectly innocent; maybe it wasn't. Still, what respectable man entertains a former girlfriend alone in his home on the night before his wedding? And even if there is a rational explanation, there still will be doubt in my mind and heart. Can I ever trust him, especially with her?"

"Of course you can if you love him and he loves you," Betty said in a quick attempt to salvage matters.

After a pregnant pause, Robbyn said: "It's over. I can't trust him. When I thought I could, I was in denial."

With that, she hung up.

"I think the wedding is off and she simply won't confront him," Betty said to Bob.

Betty and Bob Thaxter wore sick expressions, their anguish etched into their faces. They looked like two people who had just done something to ruin two lives.

"We should have kept our mouths shut!" Bob shouted, slamming his hand so hard on the kitchen table that it made him wince and spilled Betty's glass of ice tea.

Betty, startled by her husband's rare burst of temper, stood transfixed watching the ice tea pool on her kitchen floor.

"Maybe we should call Matt," Bob said.

"I think we've meddled enough," Betty said.

"Look, we were the catalyst in trying to get to the bottom of this," Bob said. "I think we just called the wrong person. Let's tell Matt what we saw and what Robbyn's reaction was when we tipped her off. If he's innocent, he'll fight for her. If he's guilty of an indiscretion, his pitch to win her back won't be sincere and Robbyn will be smart enough to see through that. She'll know in her heart if he's telling the truth."

"Her heart has been through hell a few times," Betty said solemnly. "Now, it's broken again, and I don't think she's even interested in mending it."

Betty was correct in her assumption. Robbyn was devastated. She was simply sick at heart, sick of the whole thing. In her despair, she wanted to let it all slip away. She was going to try to get a little sleep, then get up and call the pastor to cancel the wedding and ask him to call Matt. She then would call the Shamrock and cancel the reception in their banquet room. She didn't care what the Shamrock would charge them for the last-minute cancellation. She knew canceling the wedding would make her the object of speculation and possible humiliation, but she didn't care. Wedding gifts could be returned, arrangements adjusted. She kept beating herself mentally, wondering why she hadn't been just content to enjoy life with her boys and enjoy her memories of Bob Baxter.

"Why did you have to die, Bob?" she cried out.

The sound of her own voice startled her. She clasped her right hand over her mouth, praying that her outburst hadn't awakened Timmy or Billy. After a few moments had passed, she was grateful that they hadn't stirred. So she remained in bed, alone with her thoughts, some of which cried out to at least call Matt and ask for an explanation. After all, she knew that Tiffany could be aggressive. It could be, Robbyn rationalized, that Tiffany just showed up on her own initiative and had been cast out by a Matt who had remained faithful to her. But such thoughts were overwhelmed by thoughts that Matt was a rogue and that he and Tiffany always would have a sexual attraction that would stick in Robbyn's craw for eternity.

Matt couldn't sleep either. His throbbing right eye, his commitment to icing it all night to minimize the swelling, and his anguish over what his explanation to Robbyn should be conspired to sentence him to a sleepless night. He still was in his living room, his carols and egg nog distant memories, when his phone rang, shattering his somber silence. When he said hello, he was sure it was Tiffany on the line, pleading forgiveness.

"Matt, did I wake you?" said the voice belonging to Bob Thaxter.

"Bob? Bob Thaxter? What the hell are you calling me for at this hour?" Matt asked. "What's wrong?"

"Well, maybe nothing; maybe everything," Bob said, trying but failing not to sound too dramatic.

As Bob told Matt what he and Betty had seen and what Robbyn's reaction to their phone call had been, Matt's spirits sagged so low that had they been tangible commodities they would have ebbed from his body and pooled beneath the sofa he was slumped on.

"I'm sorry we got involved," Bob said for about the 10th time, "but we thought Robbyn needed to know. You're not angry with us, are you?"

"Hell, yes!" snapped Matt finally. "What do you expect me to be? Tiffany showed up uninvited at my house. After a couple of glasses of wine, she puts a move on me. I resist. She gets pissed and fires my Mike Schmidt-autographed baseball from point-blank range. Nails me in my right eye. I'm getting a beaut of a black eye on my wedding day. And two of my best friends see Tiffany leave my house and assume that I'm screwing around on Robbyn. So they call her and now she's going to cancel the wedding and ruin both our lives. How could you two think so little of me?"

"You're right, we both underestimated you ... but we know that you and Tiffany used to have a relationship," Bob said sheepishly.

"Everybody in this fucking town thinks I'm some sort of a hound, a real pig," Matt yelled at Bob. "If there were two people who should have known that reputations and perceptions aren't always reality, it should have been you and Betty."

"OK, OK, I believe you. We're terribly sorry, aren't we, Betty?" Bob said lamely.

Betty nodded yes.

"Betty is sorry, too," Bob said.

"Well, big deal," Matt said sarcastically. "After all, it's a little late to un-ring the bell."

"Not necessarily," Bob said, warming to a sudden idea. "You have perfect physical evidence to convince Robbyn that you're telling the truth: your black eye. Get the hell over to her house and tell her the truth! And show her your damn eye. And next time don't let a sexy actress you had a relationship with into your home. What were you thinking?"

"I don't know, but I'm going over to Robbyn's house now," Matt said. "Of course, she may not open the damn door."

"Do you want me to call her?" Bob asked.

"I think you've made enough calls tonight," Matt said, forcing a laugh.

Then a moment of inspiration struck his addled mind.

"Actually, make one other phone call," Matt said. "You call Millie Paxton's house and ask for Tiffany. Tell Tiffany you're picking her up and that you and Betty are bringing her over to Robbyn's house. Tiffany feels bad about what she did. Well, now it's time for her to pay the piper. She can back me up. Between you, Betty, Tiffany and my damn black eye, Robbyn's gotta believe us."

"Done!" yelped Bob. "And if Tiffany doesn't want to come, we'll kidnap her!"

"We're doing WHAT?" said Betty in astonishment when her husband told her what he and Matt were intending to do. "No, we're not! It's crazy!"

"Crazy or not, we owe it to Matt, and to Robbyn," Bob said. "We started this mess and we're going to help clean it up."

"Tiffany and Matt started this mess, not us," Betty corrected him.

"Actually, I believe Matt and it was solely Tiffany who started this mess," Bob said. "Of course, Matt was crazy to let her in for a drink."

"What?" asked Betty.

Bob quickly synopsized for Betty what Matt had told him about his visit from Tiffany.

"Now, I've gotta call Millie," Bob said. "Thank God I know her a little or I'd be embarrassed as hell."

"I'm still embarrassed as hell," Betty said. "We're both swearing a lot tonight."

"God will forgive us," Bob said, looking up Millie's number. "Hopefully she answers her phone in the middle of the night."

Millie did and seemed perplexed and confused over why Bob and Betty Thaxter had to pick up Tiffany and take her to Robbyn's house for a visit at this ungodly hour of the night. Bob tried to explain matters without going into too many details, but the lady, befuddled by her age and by her drowsiness, didn't quite grasp matters.

Finally, Bob simply said: "Millie, I'll explain later. Just wake up Tiffany and tell her that Betty and I will be picking her up in 10 minutes. And she had better be ready at the front door or I'll lean on my horn so loudly that every cop in the county will be at your house!"

"OK," Millie said, rubbing the sleep from her eyes. "I will wake up Tiffany and tell her you're picking her up."

When Millie walked into Tiffany's bedroom, she found the hottest actress in America sitting up in her bed, looking forlorn and lonely.

"What's wrong, my dear?" Millie asked more out of compassion than curiosity. "Miss your boyfriend?"

"I wish it were that simple," Tiffany said softly. "I feel terrible. I did a stupid thing tonight. I went to Matt Meredith's house just to chat, and well, as you know, he and I had a thing going for a while."

"I don't think I want to hear this," Millie said, sitting down on the bed.

"Nothing happened," Tiffany said. "Matt's a good guy. I tried to, well, seduce him. He resisted. I got angry. I hit him in the eye with a baseball and now he has an ugly black eye and some explaining to do to Robbyn."

"Mercy, mercy," Millie said. "So that's why Robert Thaxter, whom you met on Christmas Eve at Robbyn's, called and said he's picking you up any minute and taking you to Robbyn's house."

Tiffany felt her knees buckle. And she was in bed.

"What?" she asked, her ears popping in disbelief.

"He's doing what? Well, suppose I don't want to go?"

"I think he's leaving you little choice in the matter, short of making an ugly scene," Millie said. "He sounded like it was urgent or else the wedding might be canceled. I'm not sure. I was half-asleep. But you'd better get dressed."

Tiffany sat there for a minute, trying to collect her thoughts. She assumed that Matt must have told Bob Thaxter what had happened and now they were on a crusade to save the wedding. At first, Tiffany balked at going along, feeling terribly awkward about having to face Robbyn, as well as Matt. But then she relented, realizing that she needed to atone for her indiscretion to ensure that Robbyn and Matt held their scheduled nuptials.

"Well, nobody can call me selfish this morning," Tiffany said, managing a wan smile. "I'll go."

"Do you want me to come along, for moral support?" Millie asked.

Tiffany was genuinely touched by Millie's offer.

"You know, I'd be honored," Tiffany said. "But this is such a terrible inconvenience for you in the middle of the night."

"Nonsense," Millie said. "I'm awake now. I won't be able to fall back asleep anyway."

Both women quickly got dressed and actually were at Millie's front door waiting for Bob and Betty Thaxter to pick them up. Betty was accompanying Bob because she assumed that Tiffany would be more comfortable if another woman accompanied her to Robbyn's house.

When Tiffany saw that both Thaxters were in the car, she wondered how many people would be attending her confession.

After Bob Thaxter had ushered Tiffany and Millie into his SUV, Betty turned around in her seat and said warmly to Tiffany and Millie: "I only came along for moral support. Matt told us what happened after we probably mistakenly called Robbyn and told her that we saw Tiffany leaving his house."

"Well, I know you were protecting her and trying to alert her to the possibility that Matt may have cheated on her with me," Tiffany said bluntly, "but I wish the hell you had asked me first. If I didn't respect Robbyn so much and care for Matt, I wouldn't be here."

"We know," Millie said, smiling and patting Tiffany on the leg. "This is all unfortunate, but we're here for you and Robbyn. And for Matt."

"Well, I certainly have plenty of moral support for my big confession to Robbyn that I did indeed hit on Matt and he spurned my advances," Tiffany said, shrugging. "But if my embarrassment saves their wedding, well, I guess it's the least I can do."

"Well said," said Betty.

"I admire you for doing this," said Bob. "I know it's awkward and all. But Matt and Robbyn are good people, and Matt needs you to vouch for him. By the way, no one here is judging you."

"It's no crime to love a man and not know when to let go," Millie said. "Believe me, I'm Exhibit A. Look how long I hung onto a jerk like Jimbo."

"Don't be too hard on yourself, Millie," said Betty in a soothing voice. "When you get to our age, good men are hard to find. Fortunately, I still have Bob."

"Well, thank you, dear," Bob said as he pulled in front of Robbyn's house moments after Matt had parked in her driveway.

When Matt got out of his car, he was stunned to see the entourage exiting the Thaxters' SUV. He expected just to see Tiffany and Bob, not Betty and Millie, too. The presence of the two older ladies made him feel even more uncomfortable in what had to be the most forebodingly awkward and eminently critical time of his life.

"Well, we've got quite the crowd here, don't we?" Matt said nervously.

"We all care, that's why we're here," Betty said.

"I know," said Matt, looking with dread over at Tiffany.

When Matt saw the pathetic look on Tiffany's face, it somewhat tempered his anger toward her for the black eye. When she rushed up to him to get a closer look at his eye in the darkness and caressed his left cheek as she begged his forgiveness, his hard feelings began to soften.

"It means a lot to me for you to be here to help convince Robbyn I've been faithful to her," he said. "I know this must be awkward for you."

"Your eye looks awful," Tiffany said.

Millie, Betty and Bob all drew near to check out the black-and-blue eye that was angry and scary looking.

"Oh, my," said Millie. "Your eye does look awful."

"Maybe you should postpone the wedding," Bob said, laughing softly.

"Oh, Robert!" scolded Betty.

"I said postpone, not cancel," Bob countered.

"Well, we had better ring Robbyn's doorbell before we're arrested for loitering in her driveway in the middle of the night," Matt said. "Not that I'm anxious to do this."

"Don't you think you're going to startle her and the boys by ringing her doorbell?" Betty asked.

"Perhaps you should call her with your cell phone," Millie said.

"But if she hears my voice, she might simply hang up," Matt said.

"The same goes for me," Tiffany said, trying not to smile.

"Well, I've already messed up one phone call to her tonight," Bob said.

"For heaven's sake, I'll make the call," Betty said. "Give me your cell from the SUV, Robert."

So as Matt, Tiffany, Millie and Bob huddled around Betty in the moonlit darkness of Robbyn's driveway, Betty called Robbyn's number as they held their collective breath in a state of pulsating anxiety.

Matt's stomach plunged down a mineshaft of nausea as his inner thoughts twisted in sickening knots over the frightening possibility of losing Robbyn forever.

Robbyn, whose fitful attempts to get some sleep had been fruitless, hesitantly picked up on the third ring. She expected it to be Matt, begging her forgiveness. And she already had programmed herself to hang up at the sound of his voice. She was through with his explanations. She was through with him. So, when she heard Betty Thaxter's voice on the line, she was caught off-guard and said "Hello" almost by reflex, if not by design. She was in no mood to talk to anybody.

"Robbyn, so sorry to bother you again at this ungodly hour," Betty said as sweetly as she could. "But I'm standing here in your driveway with four people who simply must talk to you!"

"In my driveway?" Robbyn asked.

She bolted out of her bed and rushed to the window in her bedroom to look at who was huddled with Betty in the middle of the night in her driveway.

"Yes, I'm here with Bob, Millie, and, uh ...."

Before Betty could bring herself to mention that Matt and Tiffany were with them as well, she heard Robbyn say in shock: "Oh my God! Matt and Tiffany are with you TOO!"

"Yes, Tiffany and Matt want to explain to you exactly what happened and more importantly, what DIDN'T happen,"

Betty said, her voice suddenly animated. "Robbyn, there is no need to cancel the wedding."

"Oh, yes there is," Robbyn said defiantly. "There's nothing more to say. Please tell everybody to just go home. And leave me alone. I need my privacy. This is a terrible day."

"I'm begging you," Betty said. "Please hear them out. This doesn't have to be a terrible day. It's your wedding day."

"No, it's not!" Robbyn shouted, hanging up.

"She hung up! She won't talk to us," Betty said in disbelief.

"Let me talk to her," Matt said. "I'll call her."

Betty handed Matt the phone and he promptly called Robbyn's number. Robbyn, meanwhile, sat crying on her bed, letting her phone ring until the voicemail message kicked in. Matt chose to hang up instead of leaving a message.

"Damn, she's not picking up," Matt snapped.

"Now what?" asked Tiffany.

"Well, I do have a key," Matt said. "Let's just go in. I should have done that first without us calling her."

"I don't think any of us are thinking rationally tonight," Bob said.

"I should say so," Tiffany said. "I sure wasn't. This is all my fault."

"Well, maybe she'll have me arrested, but I'm going in there and fight for the woman I love," Matt said.

"I can't believe I'm doing this, but I'm going with you," Tiffany added.

"We all are," Bob quickly said. "I feel like some sort of weirdo standing out here on the driveway."

"Not to mention the cold," Millie said. "I should have brought my fur coat."

"Amen," chirped Betty.

Matt walked up to the front door, inserted his key and walked in, followed by his comrades in matters of the heart.

"I just don't want to alarm her," Matt whispered to Tiffany. "The last thing I want is for her to start screaming at our intrusion and scare the hell of the boys."

"So, you're not just going to go up to her bedroom?" Tiffany asked.

"Call her again, and if she doesn't pick up, just tell here we're all in her living room and we're not leaving until she comes down and talks to us," said Bob, taking charge.

Which is exactly what Matt did.

Robbyn sat transfixed on her bed, listening to Matt leaving his message on her voicemail. She was sick of him, sick of the whole deal. But the tenacity that he and the Thaxters were showing on her behalf, not to mention Millie Paxton and yes, even, Tiffany -- well, it forced her to weigh her options. She figured she had two of them.

One option was to ignore them, try waiting them out and cancel the wedding.

The second option was to at least listen to what Matt and Tiffany had to say. Of course, just because the Thaxters and

Millie Paxton were swallowing their story was no reason for her to buy it.

She pondered what to do. She prayed what to do. She knew that the future direction of her life, not to mention that of her boys, was predicated on her decision.

Matt was growing impatient. So, he called her again and left a terse message:

"I didn't cheat on you tonight, just ask Tiffany!" he said, almost begging as he added: "Please listen to us. If you don't, you might regret it for the rest of your life. I know I will."

Robbyn broke down, almost choking as she yelped in exasperation: "Oh, God, why does life have to be so complicated at times?"

Her heart felt pulled in two opposite directions, and it literally ached. Her chest pains seemed to be ushering in an anxiety attack.

She hung up the phone and looked in the mirror. The Robbyn that stared back at her totally freaked her out. She looked like a traumatized woman whose emotions had been violently pummeled. Her fire-engine-red-rimmed eyes startled her, and her poor nose was even redder from crying. She took the deepest breath of her life and walked zombie-like out of her bedroom.

As she descended the stairs to the first floor, she surrendered to a feeling of resignation that Matt and Tiffany would tell her what she wanted to hear and that there was be no tangible evidence to lend credibility to their explanation.

Totally embarrassed by her appearance, Robbyn walked into the living room and nervously cleared her throat so loudly it sounded like a lawn mower starting. All five of her uninvited guests stood up and stared at her. Robbyn noticed Tiffany first and briefly was pleased to see that not even movie stars look that good early in the morning, especially without makeup. Then Robbyn caught sight of Matt's black and blue and somewhat purplish right eye and her stomach caught in her throat.

"Matt! My God, what happened to your eye? It looks awful!" she cried out, forgetting herself and running up to him for a sympathetic closer inspection.

Her genuine concern absolutely excited Matt, ushering into his heart a strong surge of hope that the nuptials could be salvaged because she must not hate him altogether.

But then Robbyn caught herself, remembering that she and Matt were not the couple they had been just hours earlier. She backed away from Matt, and quietly said hello to everybody in the room. Everybody but Tiffany, who did not miss the oversight and accurately perceived it as a slight. Meanwhile, that sudden rush of hope that had been freshly pumped into Matt's heart suddenly hardened inside a deep freezer of despair. Robbyn's mood change had been that abrupt, that striking. Matt sensed he and Tiffany had better be utterly convincing or the wedding was off.

"If you think my eye hurts, you should feel how much my heart hurts," Matt said, his sincerity obvious to everyone in the room but Robbyn. "The very thought of losing you forever is absolutely crushing me."

"Spare me the drama and your writer's verbiage," said Robbyn. "The bottom line is that you and Tiffany somehow always seem to be getting between you and me. For some reason, you haven't been able to definitely choose between her and me. And I won't live the rest of my life married to a guy whose heart, or part of it, belongs to somebody else. Especially someone as aggressive as she is."

Robbyn cocked her head and looked defiantly at Tiffany.

"Robbyn, again, this was all my fault," interjected Tiffany. "I showed up uninvited at his house. I put a move on him. He totally resisted me. I got angry and threw one of his baseballs at him and hit him in the eye. See for yourself. Look at his eye."

"I did," Robbyn said, "and it's ugly. But how do I trust you? Or, more importantly, him? He could have smacked his eye on a number of things. And even if you did throw a baseball at him, who's to know if you didn't do it after he fucked your ears off?"

A silence engulfed the living room. Millie and Betty both tried to look cool, considering Robbyn's choice of words. But it's difficult to look cool when you look like you just swallowed a couple of goldfish.

"Why would all of us be here if we didn't believe them?" asked Bob, trying to be a catalyst to get Robbyn to soften her stance.

"Indeed," said Millie. "It's past 3 in the morning. I think we all have some better place to be."

"Like asleep in our beds," said Betty. "But we love both you and Matt and we don't want you to make a mistake because of a misunderstanding."

"A misunderstanding rooted in an insecurity that you no longer have to feel," Matt said loudly.

"Damn it, he's so over me and so into you!" Tiffany said. "I can be a selfish bitch. And I was selfish trying to rekindle something with him. I'm sorry. But don't punish him because of me! And don't punish yourself!"

"Don't punish both of us!" Matt implored Robbyn, walking towards her. "Do you want me to beg you?"

He dropped to one knee in front of her.

"You're embarrassing me," Robbyn said, her heart, her mind and her soul spinning with sensory overload, afraid she would hyperventilate.

She leaned over, grabbed his hands and helped him stand up. She peered into his face, saw the sincerity in his eyes, and maybe most important of all, saw the impression the seams of the Mike Schmidt-autographed baseball had left around the corner of his right eye. More importantly, she also could see his love for her beaming from his damaged eye.

"OK, Coach, I've caught your pathetic pitch for love," she said, melting into his arms. "Actually, I guess Tiffany literally has made the pitch. I can see the seams of the ball ringing your eye. And your love for me in your eye!"

“So, you'll marry me today?" Matt asked expectantly.

She looked at his gargoyle eye and a radiant smile spewed fireworks.

“Handsome guy like you?” she said softly. “Yes, I will marry you today.”

He kissed her so deeply and lovingly that she knew, once and for all, that she was his for eternity.

Millie, Betty, Bob and even Tiffany began cheering and clapping.

Matt and Robbyn turned to them, beaming.

"What the heck is going on?" asked Timmy, who along with his brother, had come into the room unnoticed.

"Hey, where did you get the shiner?" asked Billy.

"Like I always tell the guys at practice, you should always keep your eye on the ball," Matt said, laughing.

"Amen," said Robbyn.

There weren’t many hours remaining until dawn on Matt and Robbyn’s resurrected wedding day, but they and the people whom had helped them re-cement their bond still had to get some sleep. But sleep would prove to be a wispy, fleeting endeavor for all of them, almost as impossible to catch as a butterfly dipping and soaring across a meadow. An excess of emotions, thoughts and memories made it difficult for them to sleep soundly even though all of them had taken up residence in the terminals of exhaustion.

Bob and Betty Thaxter were too excited -- and relieved -- that Matt and Robbyn were proceeding with their nuptials to fall into a deep sleep. They both initially were silent partners in bed, but they were much too amped up over their nocturnal adventures to avoid any pillow talk.

"It was agonizing there for a while, thinking we had messed up Matt and Robbyn's lives," Bob said, rolling over to cuddle his wife and risk poking out an eye on one of her curlers.

"I never, ever would have forgiven myself," Betty replied. "Thank God it all worked out."

"Well, I do believe God had something to do with it," Bob said, "but the clincher in convincing Robbyn were the seams of the baseball. Imagine that!"

"The course of lives and relationships hinge on so many things, some of them seemingly so trivial, and they have enormous consequences," Betty observed.

"Tell me about it," Bob laughed. "If your car hadn't broken down that day outside my office, I never would have even met you. I probably would have married a movie star instead."

Betty laughed, but also playfully smacked her husband on his thigh.

"Movie stars like Tiffany don't pop up in Braxton all that often," she said.

"Thank God," Bob said. "This town just wasn't built for people like her."

Later, before they both briefly drifted off to sleep, they individually reflected upon the wonderful marriage they had so thoroughly enjoyed. But in actuality they rarely thought individually anymore. They almost always were of like mind.

They were a couple in every sense of the word. Years of a great relationship truly had made melded two people into one.

Before Betty nodded off, a smile of contentment and peace crawled across her lips. The smile didn't go unnoticed. Bob saw it and said a fervent prayer, thanking God for his wife.

Millie Paxton also went to bed that morning with a sense of relief so strong it seemed to scrape fenders with her stomach acid. Relief that Tiffany had done the right thing and had gone to bat for Matt, although Millie had been appalled that Tiffany had tried to seduce Matt on the eve of his wedding. But the biggest chunk of relief that Millie felt was for eradicating the dastardly Jimbo Cummings from her life. She knew that if it hadn't been for the chain of events unleashed by Matt and Tiffany, she might have eventually made the biggest mistake of her life and married Jimbo. As she curled up like a baby under her huge comforter, Millie almost felt nauseous that she once had shared that very same bed with the beastly Jimbo. So, she focused her thoughts instead on how special Robbyn and Matt could be as a couple and marveled at how they had managed to survive such turbulence in reaching that destination.

"Of course, they aren't at the altar yet," Millie chuckled softly as she looked at the alarm clock flashing 6:07 a.m. in the darkness of her immense bedroom. "There's still a few hours left until the wedding."

She, too, fell asleep with a smile on her face.

Tiffany, meanwhile, was hardly smiling in her bed in the largest of Millie's three guest bedrooms. While Tiffany was not nearly as egocentric as many celebrities, she did have a more intense self-focus than your average librarian. So, she couldn't help herself for feeling glum and sorry for herself that Matt was marrying Robbyn and not her. But what really was keeping her wide awake was the realization that Matt truly loved Robbyn and that Matt was more comfortable sharing Robbyn's strong family values and raising a family in Braxton than he would have been sharing a high-profile life with her. Tiffany finally admitted to herself that Robbyn indeed was a better fit for Matt. That admission rattled her core, because she still loved Matt.

"Of course, I was outmanned," she rationalized aloud, "by Timmy and Billy. I never had a chance between the two boys and baseball."

Tiffany sighed deeply, almost whispering: "And Robbyn sure the hell doesn't look like your typical Braxton mother of two, damn it."

Tiffany rolled over, clutching a pillow in her arms and feeling terribly alone.

Robbyn, meanwhile, had a smile big enough to hang some wash on it. Euphoria was why she couldn't fall asleep. She felt completely at peace, realizing that any doubts she may had harbored concerning Matt's fidelity finally had been put to rest. Her closure on that thorny issue had made her love for him bloom ever more intensely in the brief time since she had gone back to bed in the early morning. Lying on her back and staring at the ceiling fan, she marveled at how fortunate she was to have found two good men like Bob Baxter and Matt Meredith.

"Thank you, Jesus," she prayed aloud, "for both of them. Take care of Bob up there with You and take care of Matt, the boys and me down here. Now please let me fall asleep so that I don't look like an absolute witch on my wedding day!"

Matt was in no mood for sleep. Even though he was lying in bed, he really didn't care if he fell asleep because his mind was so preoccupied with so many thoughts. He knew he would be eternally grateful for dodging the biggest bullet of his life by persuading Robbyn to marry him. He swore that he would never, ever do the slightest thing that might cause Robbyn to ever again doubt his fidelity. And while he felt indebted to Tiffany for joining them on the desperate plea visitation to Robbyn's house that morning, he still was quite angry with Tiffany for trying to seduce him and then for firing the baseball at him. His eye still throbbed a bit and he wondered how Robbyn would feel every time she looked at their wedding photos and saw his black eye.

"Every time she sees it, it's going to remind her of Tiffany," Matt said. "Fuck!"

His anger flaring, he needed to expel some energy to dissipate his hostility. He grabbed a tennis ball from atop his nightstand and started bouncing if off his bedroom ceiling, alternating catching it with his left and then his right hand.

While playing catch with himself for about 10 minutes, his anger gradually melted into a glow of satisfaction that warmed his inner core. He, more than ever, was completely convinced that Robbyn was the perfect mate for him. She had everything he had ever wanted in a woman – a good girl with a good heart, a good sense of humor, a good sense of family values, a good body and who was good company and a good lay. And he loved how she loved to read and write as much as he did. They shared a deep affinity for language and the written word and also were never at a loss for words in their conversations. Factor in his love for Timmy and Billy, and Matt could not even believe that he had Ping-Ponged back and forth between Robbyn and Tiffany.

"I didn't realize how fucking superficial I can be," he scolded himself as he put aside the tennis ball. "I think I just got wrapped up in all the glamor and mystique of being with a movie star. Which blinded me to what a superstar Robbyn truly is in every way."

Later that morning, Robbyn and Matt were married in a beautiful, poignant ceremony at St. Ignatius Roman Catholic Church, an upscale parish in Sorbonne Township.

Billy and Timmy, resplendent in their black tuxes and hair that actually remained combed in place during the ceremony, simply were adorable as the co-best men.

The focal point of the ceremony, however, was Robbyn in her simple but elegant wedding gown that exquisitely framed her lovely body. But Robbyn's real splendor that day was her face, which glowed with abundant happiness. The sight of her walking down the aisle literally took Matt's breath away. And the sight of Matt left Robbyn breathless as well. His tux showcased his athletic figure quite adroitly. But nobody noticed his tux. Everybody was looking at his ugly black eye.

After they exchanged vows, they kissed to a standing ovation from all their guests. Clapping along was wedding crasher Tiffany, who was glad she chose the waterproof mascara.

The reception at the Shamrock Braxton Ballroom in nearby Providence was a kaleidoscope of memorable moments and joyous celebration.

Of course, Matt's grotesque shiner triggered all sorts of conversation. Fueling additional speculation was Matt and Robbyn's coy response to all the queries from their guests.

They were humorously vague, saying simply that Matt had been hit by a pitch for love that he hadn't seen coming. Even when vigorously pressed for details by some of their guests, most notably Cindy Loeper, they wouldn't reveal any more details.

Of course, many of the guests thought it quite amusing that Tiffany caught the bouquet. But their comments about her were limited. After all, it was a day when nobody wanted to talk much about Tiffany. It was a day when Robbyn, flashing an aurora borealis of a smile, was the only leading lady in the room.

And her leading man was a guy with a prince of a black eye.

CPSIA information can be obtained
at www.ICGtesting.com
Printed in the USA
BVHW03s1331110818
524206BV00001B/6/P

9 781609 106669